VLAD DRAGWLYA
Son of the Dragon

TIMOTHY E. RODRIGUE

Published by Gate 6 Publications, LLC
23891 Partridge
Denham Springs, LA 70726, USA

First Gate 6 Publications Printing, October 2011
10 9 8 7 6 5 4 3 2 1

ISBN 978-0-615-44883-1

First Edition

PUBLISHER'S NOTE
This is a work of historical fiction. Names, characters, places, and incidents either are the product of the author's imagination or are used in historical context. The publisher does not have any control over and does not assume any responsibility for author or third-party websites or their content.

This book is dedicated to my family, especially my wife and son; to those who couldn't help themselves on August 29, 2005; and to the titans who piqued my interest in their own way about this subject: Florescu, McNally, Babinger, Stoker, Lugosi, Karloff, Chaney Sr., Chaney Jr., and Noel—The Magnificent One.

A Note from the Author

Growing up just outside of New Orleans there was always a sense of the afterlife in the air. Even though people died, it never seemed like their spirits left. In a place where everyone does their best to live life to the fullest, it's nearly impossible to convince the soul someplace better could exist, I suppose.

Engulfed in an atmosphere made up of Mardi Gras mixed with a gumbo of various religions most heavily seasoned with Catholicism and Voodoo, I was introduced to Universal's rogues gallery of monsters. Somehow, seeing Dracula, Frankenstein, the Phantom, the Wolfman, and the Creature led to reading about them. There always seemed to be more information about vampires though. Then came the reality. I learned about the monsters behind the monsters, the real-life people who either didn't fit the norms of society and those who created societies to suit their own needs and wonts.

Among the books I was reading that featured pictures of Bela Lugosi, Boris Karloff, and others was slipped in what I perceived to be cartoon drawings of a man who didn't look anything at all like Bela Lugosi. Here was a man, eating it seemed, surrounded by people suspended in midair on spikes while he did so. Honestly, I can't remember the first time I saw the name Vlad Țepeș, but I know it was probably long before any youth should have done so. Those "cartoon drawings" were actually frontispieces of Dracula pamphlets and manuscripts. What I was reading had gone from being fantasy to nonfiction, and it was fascinating to me.

I absorbed *In Search of Dracula* and *Dracula: His Life and Times*, both by Radu Florescu and Raymond T. McNally. They fanned my desire to write this book, and I am very much grateful to both of them for introducing me to the "Son of the Dragon," or "Devil" if you prefer.

The historical record concerning Prince Vlad III is far from complete. For the purposes of storytelling I have taken some liberties, but only when absolutely necessary. Throughout the manuscript, text from actual correspondences and recorded speeches was reproduced when available. My intent from the beginning of this journey has been to tell the true story of *The Impaler*, to delve into who he was as a man and as a madman. There is no twist at the end. There are no fangs to be found, no aversion to garlic or mirrors, and no stakes around to be pounded into the hearts of the undead. But, there is more than enough in the reality to make up for the absence of vampires. Of that, I assure you.

Just as Florescu and McNally before me, I have used the names of people and places in the way they are internationally best known—usually with the Christian name anglicized. That is not always possible or even prudent though. For those of you who wish to correctly pronounce unanglicized names that appear in the book, I have included a guide on my website to do so.

If you have any questions about the book, visit my Facebook page (Timothy E. Rodrigue), visit www.dragwlya.com, or feel free to e-mail me at Dragwlya@hotmail.com.

Timothy E. Rodrigue

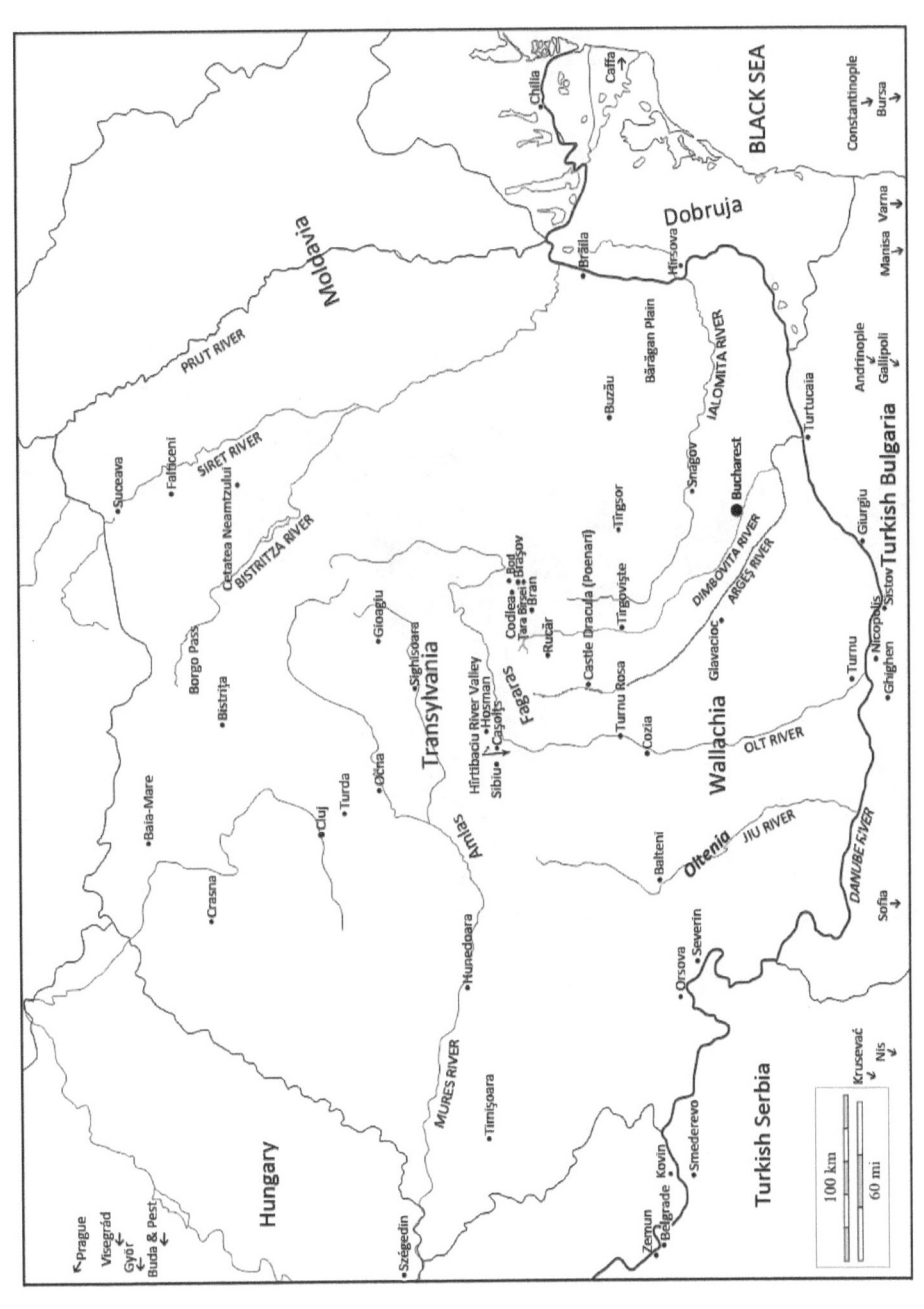

"From this arises an argument: whether it is better to be loved than feared. I reply that one should like to be both one and the other; but since it is difficult to join them together, it is much safer to be feared than to be loved when one of the two must be lacking."

The Prince, Published in 1532
Niccolò Machiavelli

INTRODUCTION
NUREMBERG
February 8, 1431

Four separate crusading forces had been sent throughout the 1420s by soon-to-be Holy Roman Emperor Sigismund to combat the Hussites, followers of Czech reformer Jan Hus who was burned at the stake for heresy in 1415. Each had suffered devastating defeats. Nearly a year had passed since Sigismund, the king of Hungary, Croatia, and now Bohemia, had convened a council to organize the latest attempt to battle the seemingly unbeatable Protestant forces. Fearing the ever expanding Ottoman Empire as well, the king was determined to initiate a crusade to rid Europe of Muslim intervention permanently.

High dignitaries and royalty from every corner of Europe had been called to meet this morning in the double chapel of the imperial fortress in Nuremberg for the induction of a new member, a Wallachian named Vlad, into the Order of the Dragon. The order existed primarily to secure political supremacy in Europe for the House of Luxemburg. Its numerous other objectives included protecting the German king and his family, defending the Holy Roman Empire, and crusading against the Ottoman Empire.

Vlad had served the king as a negotiator and diplomat for years. His intention of capturing his ancestral land was well known. The Romanian principality had come under the rule of his half-brother, Alexandru Aldea, whose open dealings with the Ottoman's Sultan Murad II did not sit well with Sigismund. Before nightfall, Vlad would receive the official staff of office and be crowned Wallachia's prince—a challenge to the legitimacy of Aldea's rule and a strong statement for the crusade against the Ottomans. Vlad faced the king as twenty-three inductees of the order looked on. Not a sound emitted from within the chapel until Sigismund spoke.

"Today we welcome into the order a man who has worked tirelessly for our causes. For years, I have sought his advice. Never has that advice failed me. In time he will become an even greater asset in the fight against the Ottoman Empire."

Vlad watched as the king motioned over a guard holding a medallion. Sigismund took hold of its chain, and Vlad gazed at the golden circle as it dangled. The medallion bore a two-winged dragon that hung on a double cross, its four paws outstretched. Its mouth was opened halfway, and the beast's cleft tail curled around its head.

Holding the medallion above Vlad's head, Sigismund recited the mottos of the order, which were engraved on the cross in Latin: *Oh how merciful is God* and *Just and Faithful*. After reading these words, the king placed the chain around Vlad's neck. Sigismund smiled when Vlad raised his head back up and then presented him to the others at the ceremony. For Vlad, the honor was more than the repayment he had expected for taking part in minor diplomatic assignments.

"Gentlemen, a feast is being prepared for this solemn occasion," Sigismund proclaimed. "I am certain you will find the food to your liking. I look forward to dining with you this afternoon." With these words, the ceremony ended, and everyone began leaving the chapel. Vlad turned to thank him.

"My lord, I will be eternally grateful for this."

"I hope so. Having you as an enemy would be most unfortunate."

"You have nothing to fear, my lord."

Sigismund's smile returned. "Good...Now, I want to introduce you to someone." The king motioned for a man standing to his right to approach.

He was roughly Vlad's age, of medium height, and had auburn hair that contrasted sharply with his deep brown eyes. Vlad took particular notice of the man's high forehead.

"Prince Vlad ... Ioan Hunedoara."

Vlad extended his hand, as did Ioan. "An honor to meet you, your highness."

"The pleasure is mine." Vlad had heard much about this simple court page, especially how impressed the king was with his courage and militaristic abilities.

Sigismund turned to Hunedoara. "Ioan, accompany Prince Vlad for the remainder of the day. Extend to him every courtesy."

"Of course, my lord."

"Good. Vlad, your induction will help bring about necessary changes. I hope you are ready for this evening."

Vlad's tone was unwavering. "I have been waiting for this evening for a long time, my lord. I assure you. I am ready."

"Good. I'll leave you two now." Sigismund exited the chapel, followed closely by his entourage.

"Is there anything you require at the moment?" Ioan asked.

"Merely your absence. Excuse me." Abruptly, Vlad walked off to meet with some of the other Dragonists still present.

Ioan watched as Vlad spoke with a small contingency of men.

He will be a hindrance to me.

Vlad caught the page's stare and had the exact same thought.

Vlad's coronation began at twilight in the fortress' throne room. Among the dignitaries present were Friedrich von Zollern of the House of Hohenzollern; Grand Master of the Teutonic Order Klaus von Redwitz; nobles from the kingdoms of Hungary, Bohemia, and the empire; and several boyars from Wallachia—rich landowners who had grown prosperous since Vlad's father had ruled.

"I ask now for your allegiance to me and to the Holy Roman Empire."

Vlad stared at Sigismund. His response was just as resolute.

"My natural lord and sovereign, at whose court we are assembled to accomplish very great things, I now swear my allegiance to you and to all that this empire holds to be the truth."

Sigismund motioned the guard holding the official staff of office.

"I invest you as duke of the Transylvanian districts of Amlaş and Făgăraş and present you the staff of office. In return for these honors, once on your throne, you must give protection and free exercise of religion to those of the Catholic faith, especially the Franciscan Minorities. Do you agree to comply?"

Although his country was rooted in the Orthodox faith, no other choice existed but to answer in the affirmative if Vlad ever expected to rule his ancestral land.

"I do."

Sigismund looked over the assembled crowd.

"Vlad is tasked with ridding the throne of his brother, Alexandru Aldea, and returning it to its rightful standing in the empire. I present Vlad II, prince of Wallachia."

Vlad faced those gathered.

"I am honored and will not rest until I rid the Dăneştis of my throne. My *half-brother*, and all rulers like him, must be deposed. The spread of the Ottoman Empire must be ended.

"Not everyone may survive to see Wallachia restored to its former glory, myself included. But this principality is worth everything to me, and I will do all that is necessary to assure its return to the empire...All hail Sigismund!"

Those assembled burst into cheers for both the king and the new prince. After a few seconds, Sigismund raised his hand for the crowd to once again become silent.

"Let the festivities commence!"

Throughout the night bonfires blazed, illuminating the sky as Nuremberg celebrated Vlad's crowning. Dancers, performers, and merchants livened the city streets. Crowds feasted in the public square. They all seemingly understood the full importance of the day's festivities. In reality they knew only a part of is true significance.

A mock tournament, one in which only the most skilled knights were allowed to participate, was organized for the king and his court near the Tiergarten Gate on the outskirts of town.

Eventually, Vlad's turn to compete came. He wore the green cape of the Order of the Dragon and his shield bore the emblem of his newly acquired throne—the Wallachian Eagle. Lance in hand, Vlad glanced toward his opponent as he was announced to the court. Facing him was a knight displaying the emblem of a raven.

Sigismund turned to Hunedoara.

"Who do you think will win?"

Hunedoara answered without turning to face the king.

"It would be foolish not to pick Vlad in a fight … especially a fair one."

Vlad's lance slammed into the knight's chest, knocking him from his horse. Almost instantaneously, the knight stumbled to his feet and unsheathed his sword as the crowd erupted. Throwing down his lance, Vlad rounded and drew his sword. He charged toward the knight and delivered a strike that forced the knight to drop the sword from his stinging hands and concede defeat. Again the crowd burst into cheers. Vlad dismounted and acknowledged a now standing Sigismund. Compelled by the king's actions, Hunedoara stood and feigned appreciation with mild applause.

From the stands, a golden buckle was thrown to the newly crowned prince that landed at his feet. Vlad bent over and picked up the gleaming trinket.

A suitable trophy.

"Impressive!" Sigismund yelled his appraisal to Hunedoara as much as he did to Vlad. "An effortless victory!"

The page did not respond verbally. He simply nodded and kept hidden his disdain for the victorious prince.

He will be a nuisance.

CHAPTER I
DRAGWLYA'S BIRTH
SIGHIŞOARA
December 15, 1431

Months after his official coronation, politics were interfering with Vlad's dream to rule Wallachia. Sigismund had decided leaving Alexandru Aldea in control of the principality served his interests. Aldea was an alley of the prince of Moldavia, Alexandru the Good, an enemy of Ladislas II of Poland—bitter rival of Sigismund.

To appease Vlad, Sigismund named him military governor of Transylvania and charged him with guarding Wallachia's border while monitoring Aldea. As of late, Aldea was allowing Turkish armies passage to Transylvania through the principality.

During the spring, Vlad decided to use the recently rebuilt fortress at Sighişoara as his headquarters because of its central strategic location. Its walls spanned three thousand feet around the city and were reinforced to hold against any Turkish artillery. This, combined with its massive donjons, made Sighişoara seemingly impregnable. Convinced he was secure, Vlad had his wife and son join him.

Peering out of the window at the end of the corridor, Vlad listened to the noises coming from the room behind him. Shafts of orange and red light fought the black of night to gain control of the sky while the waxing crescent moon did its best to avoid being overtaken by the dawn.

Cneajna's screams intensified. It would not be long before Vlad's first child by his second wife arrived. His son from his previous marriage, Mircea, was now almost three and, much to Cneajna's dismay, had already gone on a crusade with him. She argued such close proximity to a battlefield was no place for a child. Smirking, Vlad wondered how many times he would hear similar protests.

With the thought passing, Vlad heard one final yell and the crying of an infant. Instantly he rushed toward the room where Cneajna had been for over eighteen hours. A midwife attending to her met him, delaying his entrance. She wore a smile as she spoke.

"Congratulations, my lord…You now have *two* healthy sons."

Vlad looked past her at a second midwife now bathing his newborn son. He could see Cneajna struggling to free her body completely of the labor process and fixed his stare again on the midwife blocking him.

"Is she alright?"

"They are both fine." The midwife glanced back, received a nod of approval, and continued. "You may see them now."

Placing the infant into its mother's arms, the second midwife addressed Vlad. "We shall leave you alone for a few moments."

Vlad slowly crept over to his wife's side and gazed down at mother and child. The newborn offered only sporadic cries as his body adjusted to having so much freedom of movement.

"Isn't he the most beautiful thing you have ever seen?" Cneajna asked as she met Vlad's eyes with her own.

"Almost." A knowing glance let Cneajna know he placed her beauty above all. "He is strong…as are you." Vlad leaned over and kissed her on the forehead.

Vlad cautiously lowered himself down next to his wife and stared with wonder at his son.

"Here…hold him." As she lifted the baby from her bosom, Vlad reached for the newborn. The child willingly accepted the new position and settled silently. Vlad looked at Cneajna and smiled proudly.

"What should we name him?" she asked.

"Do you have anything particular in mind?"

"Alexandru."

Vlad's face contorted with disgust before he answered. "What sort of name is that for my son?"

"It was my father's name."

"Yes…and it is also the name of my enemy."

"How about Sigismund? Perhaps it would win you more of his favor."

"I doubt that." Vlad turned back to the infant, who had shown his disapproval by urinating through his swaddling clothes and all over him. "It would appear the name does not satisfy him."

"What do you mean?" Vlad raised the child. Cneajna, who now understood, began to laugh. "Sigismund does not suit him. He has inherited your manners and should be named after you."

Vlad pondered the thought for a moment as he looked about for something dry to wrap around his infant son. Once he had done so, he turned and gave the child back to Cneajna. She had all but fallen asleep. The only sign of life she showed was the hardly visible rising and falling of her chest. No woman he had ever met compared.

The eldest daughter of Alexandru the Good, Cneajna was the sister of Prince Iliaş and Prince Bogdan II. Vlad and Cneajna were married six years ago, following his return from a diplomatic mission for Sigismund. Their union formed an alliance with the principality of Moldavia, a move by Vlad to further his chances for Wallachia's throne.

"Mommy, mommy, mommy!"

Vlad turned and discerned Mircea's silhouette emerging from the darkness, running toward him as fast as he could. Mircea tried, with little success, to stop and crashed into his father with enough force to knock only himself down. Vlad laughed quietly for a second at the sight of Mircea collecting himself on the floor and then became serious.

"Were you running with your eyes closed?"

The boy stood up slowly and brushed himself off. "Sorry, father." Mircea tried desperately to peek around his father, who was now blocking his view. "Can I see mommy?"

"Not now. She's resting."

"Can I see it?"

"It—your brother is resting also. You can see him later."

Excitement overcame the boy. "A brother! What's his name?"

"His name is Vlad." The new father could not hide his pride, but Mircea looked puzzled.

"But that's your name."

"It is."

"So how will you know people are shouting for you and not him?"

Vlad smiled. "I'll know."

"Oh," Mircea replied still confused as he attempted to peer around his father and felt his clothes. "You know you're wet."

Vlad spun him around and gave him a light slap on his rear. "Go on. I'll send for you later."

The boy ran off and disappeared into the darkness. Folding his arms, Vlad smiled and turned to see Cneajna smiling back. He dropped his arms to his side slowly and shook his head. "He woke you."

"It's all right. It won't take much for me to fall asleep again."

"Eighteen hours of labor…"

"You should get some rest, too."

Vlad looked out at the rising sun. "I couldn't sleep… even if I wanted to."

A knowing look of concern crossed Cneajna's face.

"Before long you will be on the throne. Have faith in yourself… Sigismund does."

"Hmphf. If that were true, I would be on the throne already… Get some rest."

"Only if you promise not to worry so much."

Vlad walked toward the door, but Cneajna stopped him by calling his name. He turned around to answer. "I promise." Leaving without another word, he closed the door behind him.

Cneajna looked at the door for a moment before finally closing her eyes with a sigh. *It's a promise I know he can't keep.*

CHAPTER II
NOCTURNAL ACTIVITIES
SIGHIŞOARA
December 18, 1431

Approaching four years old, the extremities of little Vlad's maturity and capabilities were tested daily through various physical and mental challenges; withstanding the cold, snowy days of Romania and the illnesses they produced among them.

Vlad and his brother were cared for by Cneajna, numerous matrons, and the exiled boyars of his father's court. They were always the center of attention. How to dress, basic manners, and that they would someday hold exalted positions in life were lessons Vlad and Mircea were not allowed to forget. The ladies of the court also taught them Romanian, the children's native language and that of command in the army. Their tutor was an elderly, highly educated boyar who often found young Vlad intriguing.

Vlad and Mircea learned various foreign languages from the boyar, including Latin, the language used in diplomatic correspondence, and were taught political science. This included the theory of divine right of sovereigns.

"You were *chosen* by God to be the sons of a prince. That means it is *God's* will for you to one day rule…Do you understand?"

Vlad looked at the old scholar with countless questions. Even at this age he displayed a tremendous amount of reasoning and intelligence. "There are two of us…How will God decide who is to become prince?"

Amazed at the child's insight, the tutor responded. "When the time comes, you will receive guidance to answer such questions from both Him and those around you. But trust yourself above all."

Hardly satisfied, Vlad attempted to inquire further but was silenced by his tutor before he could ask another question.

"Remember, it is better to be feared than loved." This lesson, continuously taught to the young princes, was the foundation upon which their entire education would be constructed. Vlad began to ask another question and was interrupted, this time, by Cneajna.

"The day has ended for you two."

Vlad began to ask his question once more, but the boyar shook his head chuckling. "Tomorrow, my prince…tomorrow."

Mircea tugged at his brother as their mother led them to their chamber. Watching them leave, the boyar wondered just how many questions were crammed inside the child's head.

Ending tutoring sessions for sleep always frustrated little Vlad, but every so often he was compensated. Hearing rattling chains, the young prince instantly sat up and sprung to the window.

Occasionally, a hanging would take place late in the evening. Vlad rested his chin in his hands and stared. With meager light from an almost new moon, he stood transfixed as a prisoner was led from the jail in the Councilmen's Square to the Jewelers' Donjon. Vlad had managed to sneak in and watch once but since that time had always been discovered when trying to hide out in advance and kept away. Though he could only view the prisoners being led to their deaths now, this little taste of the executions excited and delighted the boy.

Mircea sighed audibly. "Get back in bed."

Vlad did not bother to answer or look at him. He continued to stare out of the window longingly, well after the prisoner had disappeared into the donjon. Mircea's numerous pleas failed to gain his brother's attention and, like always, the elder brother finally gave up and fell asleep.

The prince's body became rigid as two guards carried the prisoner's corpse out of the donjon. It was easy to see the man's neck had been broken. Death had been instantaneous, painless. This criminal did not die from strangulation as others he had seen. It made him wonder why all criminals were not made to feel pain when they were executed. It was, after all, their punishment. They *should* experience torment before dying. But what sentence would be enough to ensure that? Consumed by his thoughts, Vlad failed to notice the door to the chamber being opened.

"Why are you out of bed?"

Slightly startled, Vlad turned to see his mother standing behind him. After glimpsing out the window quickly, he reluctantly crawled back into bed and pulled the covers up to his chest.

Cneajna peeked out of the window and immediately closed her eyes at the sight of the corpse being carried away. Making her way over to the bed, she leaned down and kissed her son on the forehead. "Stay in bed, and go to sleep."

The little prince nodded as his mother tucked him in with strong feelings of discomfort and concern.

It is as though he enjoys watching the hangings.

Sigismund had been crowned emperor two years ago, and Hussite uprisings in Bohemia consumed his attention through most of October of this year. Focusing on the rebellions made him almost oblivious to the inroads the Turkish had made through Wallachia. Additionally, his favor remained with Alexandru Aldea. Only recently had the Wallachian prince's ties to the Turkish managed to infuriate Sigismund.

Vlad had been instructed to purchase the weaponry he required and to begin gathering an army for a campaign to oust Aldea. The invading force would be composed of exiled boyars, Romanians from Amlaş and Făgăraş, and any mercenaries he could afford. Granted the right to mint his own coins by the emperor, Vlad's abundant treasury made purchasing them and weapons easier. In his audience room, Vlad contemplated how to solidify his power in Transylvania. He would immediately form an alliance with the neighboring German cities of Braşov and Sibiu, thus gaining military support. At the moment he was drafting a letter to the head of Braşov's city council.

> Know ye that my Master the Emperor has entrusted me with the protection of this region, and pray do not without my consent make peace with my enemies in Wallachia. I pray that like good brethren and friends you will follow me and give me your assistance.

Since his return to Romania, Vlad had commonly become known as Dracul, literally "the dragon" in his native tongue. Dracul could be interpreted as "the devil" as well, and Vlad's enemies eagerly attached satanic connotations to the term originally attributed to him as an endearment. The peasants of the land called him Dracul because he had chosen the emblem for his shield; the boyars used the term because Vlad was a Draconist. He looked up from his correspondence, knowing he was no longer alone.

"How long have you been there?"

"I've only been watching you for a moment." Cneajna's voice sounded uneasy, worrisome.

Vlad stood and approached her. "What's wrong?"

Cneajna sighed. "Vlad is … such an impressionable child. I caught him watching a prisoner being carried away from the gallows."

"He doesn't fall asleep easily. Besides, he must learn there are those who deserve punishment and what that ultimately means." As he spoke, Vlad remembered one particular instance when his son was a mere infant and Cneajna could not get him to sleep.

With his son crying nearly uncontrollably, Vlad spoke softly to him, reassuring him. To his relief, little Vlad ceased screaming. Immediately, Vlad realized it was not him but his brilliant medallion that had soothed the child. Vlad saw in his son's eyes a look he knew well—desire and determination. The child reached as far as his arms would allow, attempting to grab the golden medallion as it shone brightly around his father's neck.

Vlad smiled at the boy. "Not yet, my son. Your turn will come in time. This is mine to play with for now."

"What are you thinking about?" Cneajna had to repeat his name before Vlad heard her.

"I was remembering when he was a baby...trying to get him to sleep."

"Hmmm...I remember many of those nights...This fascination of his—"

"I will speak to him...okay?" He took her by the shoulders, watching her eyes. "You look tired."

Cneajna nodded before answering. "I am...I pray our next child will not be so restless."

Vlad's eyes widened with excitement. "Our *next* child?"

With a smile and three quick nods, Cneajna confirmed Vlad's suspicion, and he immediately embraced her.

"Have you thought of any names yet?"

"Maria if it is a girl. Radu if it is a boy." Cneajna's suggestions were firm.

"*Radu?*" Cneajna nodded as Vlad shook his head and sighed. "Better than Alexandru at least."

She pulled away slightly to look into his eyes. "Come to bed with me tonight."

"I will be there soon, I promise."

Vlad let Cneajna go and watched her leave. He returned to his seat and continued preparations for the campaign, finding himself distracted by the thought of his unborn child. Already he had dismissed Cneajna's concern for their son.

CHAPTER III
THRONE OF THE DRAGON
OUTSIDE OF TÎRGOVIȘTE
December 14, 1436

Vlad Dracul's campaign for the throne once held by his father had begun two years ago. Progressing south, along the Danube, Vlad's army fought off several Turkish leaders. Numerous battles and two winters had taken their toll. Upon hearing that Alexandru Aldea lie on his deathbed, however, the Wallachian decided to make one final charge before year's end.

Vlad's use of cannons as a mobile weapon had proved invaluable and would do so again during this skirmish. He had gained tremendous ground since the end of November, and it appeared that after seven years of waiting, Vlad would finally make his dream reality.

Fires blazed into the frigid night as Vlad regarded the soldiers gathered before him, some of whom had been with him since the beginning. He watched as firelight danced on faces he knew well and on others he did not know at all.

"My friends…The past five years have been the longest of my life. Although many have given their lives for this cause, the final goal has yet to be reached…Tomorrow, it will be achieved.

"Throughout these long years, I have asked much of you. Tomorrow, I ask for much more. Your will and determination have kept us in the fight. Tomorrow, either we succeed or else Wallachia, and ultimately all of Europe, will be conquered by the Ottoman Empire.

"Those who do not survive to share in the victory have my word…you will be remembered. Tomorrow, Wallachia will be restored to the former glory it knew under the leadership of my family!"

Vlad could see an array of feelings in the faces of his men. Hope and fear abounded, but the consensus seemed to be the need for an ultimate resolution. Their eyes showed unending hunger, but he was unsure if it was desire or simply malnourishment.

"God will be with you. Tomorrow night, we *will* celebrate our triumph and revel in the glory of our victory!"

The men began to cheer and chant the name of Dracul, who raised a fist into the air. Imagining himself finally becoming the sole prince of Wallachia made him smile. He turned to make his way to his tent once the chanting began to diminish and was stopped just before entering by one of his captains.

"Gather the others," Vlad instructed the captain. "We will review the plan again."

"Of course. I am confident your brother's armies will be easily defeated, my lord."

Vlad's stare burned through the man. He hated any inference that Alexandru Aldea was a member of this family. It was embarrassing enough that Aldea was his half-brother. For this captain to refer to Aldea as a full-fledged brother of his was an insult and a grave mistake. Abruptly, Vlad's mannerism changed from intense to enraged. He grabbed the captain by the collar and drove him to his knees with a quick jerk downward, tightening his grip around the helpless man's neck as he towered over him.

"Do not refer to that bastard as my brother ever again … understand?"

The captain tried to muster enough oxygen to answer, but could only wheeze and give a slight nod while his face turned red then purple.

Throwing the man down forcefully, Vlad muttered something unintelligible in disgust. As the captain clutched his throat and coughed, Vlad turned and entered his tent. Staring at the silhouette of the man who had just taken him to the brink of death, the captain wondered how long it would be before he were allowed to stand in his presence again.

December 15, 1436

Vlad exited his tent and took notice of the recent snow flurry blanketing the ground. Looking to the horizon, he could see forbidding clouds and could hear the rumbling thunder of an approaching storm.

Perfect.

A silence hung over the camp that did not sit well with Vlad as he watched his men preparing for the last charge. Stretching his arms above his head, Vlad listened to the oncoming tempest. He could hear a few of his commanders ordering the men in preparation for mobilization and was able to discern the captain he nearly strangled to death last night. Though he was somewhat impressed with the man, the urge to kill him for his unintentional insult remained.

Aldea's castle stood out from the rest of the landscape to the south but appeared to become one with the sky as Vlad stared. Slowly, his attention turned toward his army once more. The time to begin the charge was quickly approaching.

Vlad mounted his horse, eager to attack. Preceded by his cannons, every inch Vlad advanced his army pumped more adrenaline through his veins. The castle dominated the skyline now, appearing to sprawl upwards endlessly because of its massive towers. Without warning, cannon fire from the castle echoed the natural thunder already filling the air. This proved to be the signal for Aldea's force outside the castle walls to begin its charge. Finally, the battle had begun.

Vlad's primary objective was to disable the castle cannons as quickly as possible. The only way to accomplish this would be by getting inside. Aldea's forces were fighting hand-to-hand with his own as he looked at the commander riding next to him.

"The moment their infantry ranks are broken, advance the juggernaut!" Vlad shouted.

The commander was about to answer when he noticed one of Aldea's soldiers racing toward them on horseback. Quickly, the commander drew his sword and rushed past his leader. With one swing he flipped the soldier backwards off his horse. Vlad watched as the commander then raced off.

There was little time to think about what had happened as another one of Aldea's soldiers approached. Vlad unsheathed his sword and charged. After a solid blow, the soldier remained mounted, forcing Vlad to cock his arm and swing again. This time, the soldier fell. A clap of thunder immediately followed blinding light and opened the sky for the rain to fall.

As the battle raged on, Vlad ordered a small contingent to prepare a battering ram to bust down the castle doors. Hearing his men cheer, he followed the outstretched arm of one of them. His men had broken through and cleared a path for the anticipated juggernaut. They had been led by the commander who had abruptly charged off earlier.

Surveying the battlefield, Vlad could see that his army, once outnumbered three-to-one, had the momentum. The opposing forces were nearly even. Compelled by his men now forcing the doors of the castle open, Vlad rushed to join them.

Aldea's cannons had stopped firing. The only thunder remaining came from Vlad's artillery and the sky. Looking up, Vlad smiled and sheltered his eyes from the rain. As the final blows were being delivered to the castle doors, the sun burst through the clouds, seemingly transforming the wet stone of the castle into silver.

Realizing they were beaten once Vlad entered the castle, most of Aldea's remaining soldiers began swearing allegiance to their new leader. Throughout the castle, Vlad's contingent fought Aldea's personal guard, which proved to be no match for the attacker's determined force. With every step, they drew closer to Aldea and the moment Vlad had waited for so long to arrive.

Aldea's wife and her handmaidens met Vlad as he approached his enemy's chamber. Tears blurred the vision of the dethroned princess as she passed him.

"What should we do with them, sire?"

Dracul turned toward the soldier who had posed the question. No one had called him sire before.

"Let them go. Lead them out of here, and make sure no harm comes to them."

More conscious of his manner, Vlad turned back to the chamber, aware his men knew he would sit on the throne. He grabbed the handle of the door and pushed it open. A few soldiers tried to follow, but he refused them with a simple stare before he closed and bolted the door.

Aldea's lifeless body lie before him.

Except for Vlad's subtle breathing, not a sound could be heard in the room. He paused only a moment before the furious pounding of his heart forced him to move across the room. Involuntarily holding his breath, he looked down at the quarry that for so long had eluded him.

Satisfaction and disappointment existed all in that one moment. Vlad was now prince, but Aldea's life had ended mercifully and unlike the manner Vlad had envisioned countless times. He stood there motionless and stared at the white sheet covering his nemesis. It was a fulfilling yet frustrating. The full implication overrode the latter emotion quickly.

Wallachia now belonged to him.

Glaring at the form of the man who had haunted his dreams for years, Vlad wished he could have run him through with the blade of his sword. Shaking his head, he suddenly laughed quietly and continued to do so until removing the cover from Aldea's face. Vlad's laughter ceased as he contemplated how easily it could be him lying there. Once he stopped dwelling on the thought, his laughter again filled the room as he stared at his dead adversary's face once more before walking toward the bolted door.

Upon exiting, Vlad ordered his guards to dispose of Aldea's body. Unaccompanied, he then proceeded outside and was met by the commander who had led the contingent through Aldea's defenses.

"Congratulations on a well earned victory, sire," the commander said with a slight bow.

"I commend you."

"I was only doing my duty."

The prince and commander ventured farther out to the cheers of Vlad's army. As he smiled, Vlad raised his arms in triumph before quieting his men so he could be heard.

"Alexandru Aldea is no more!" Again the men cheered. "Tonight there will be a feast held in *your* honor!"

Vlad's army cheered as the commander began to shout, "Long live Vlad Dracul, prince of Wallachia!"

Taking the commander's declaration as their cue, the men began chanting the name "Dracul."

CHAPTER IV
LEARNING TO SWIM
TÎRGOVIŞTE
April 19, 1437

News of Sigismund's imminent death was widespread. The Holy Roman Empire, however, was not alone on the cusp of vast change.

Left unchecked, Sultan Murad II's momentum and territories were growing rapidly. He had conquered Serbia and Bulgaria. Plans for the final attack against the significantly diminished Byzantine strongholds were underway, and the Ottoman's proximity to Dracul forced the Wallachian to sign an alliance with them. This betrayal of his oath, this new political sensibility, was Dracul's only means to protect his interests.

Dracul contemplated the consequences of his action in solitude. The plundering of his cities and the stealing of his people's children for service in the Janissary Corps did not sit well with him. But simple peasants could not possibly comprehend that the alliance was the only means of saving Wallachia from total dominance. While he pondered the situation, Cneajna entered with Radu following her.

Cneajna, Mircea, Vlad, and Radu joined Dracul at Tîrgovişte in February. Since then, life became different for everyone. This was especially true for the sons of the prince. Education and apprenticeship for knighthood dominated Mircea and Vlad's lives daily. The core of their studies remained the same as before, but the lessons were substantially advanced. This included the much harsher conditions under which their physical training took place. Presently, Mircea and Vlad were being taught how to swim.

Dracul looked up. Seeing Radu produced the frightening image of his own sons being led away in chains to serve the sultan. Dracul shuddered visibly.

"What's wrong?" Cneajna was unaccustomed to seeing him react to anything in such a manner.

"Nothing...I'm fine." His answer failed to convince even himself.

"Are you certain?"

"Yes." Quickly he moved the focus of conversation to Radu. "And what are you doing here?"

"He wanted to see his father."

Dracul picked him up, compelled to imagine him as a minion of the sultan. "Really?"

The child looked up with deep blue eyes. "I want to go swimming like Vlad and Mircea."

Dracul chuckled, "Not yet, my son...You should not be in such a rush to grow up. It is not as much fun as you imagine."

With no understanding of what his father could possibly mean, Radu retorted, "Swimming is always fun."

Mircea and Vlad paddled until they reached the center of the small lake, some fifty yards away from shore. With them rode their mentor, a knight instructed to train them by Dracul.

"Place the oars inside of the boat." The children complied. "For me, there are two ways back to land. For you, only one…Up!"

Careful not to flip over the small craft, the two boys rose slowly. Vlad watched the waves lapping against the boat. The water was too cold for a pleasurable swim, but this was not meant to be fun.

Their mentor's voice was deep and firm. "I will watch you from the shore. I will *not* get wet, so neither of you had better drown. Now go."

Fear swept over Vlad as he looked into the clear lake. To him the water appeared dark and murky, beyond purification because of the knight's words. Mircea took one last look at his brother, then at their mentor. He smiled at the knight and faced the shore.

"Go!" screamed the knight as he rocked the boat from side to side.

Vlad fell overboard first and yelled as he plunged into the water. Every inch of his body stung from the cold, and he was paralyzed from the shock momentarily. Vlad struggled and fought his way back to the lake's surface. Looking up, he could see Mircea diving in beside him. Almost instantaneously, the knight grabbed the oars and paddled back to shore.

Mircea popped his head out of the water and watched as his brother thrashed wildly. He then caught sight of the knight rowing away. After staring at their mentor for a few seconds, he glanced back toward his brother, still splashing desperately. Mircea shook his head. He had grasped the concept by their second outing. Vlad, now for the fourth time, appeared to be on the verge of drowning. Mircea swam to his brother and attempted to relax him.

"Stop moving around so much! Kick your feet!"

Hearing Mircea's voice helped Vlad regain his composure. Eventually the younger of the brothers lasted a few seconds at a time before he found himself underwater again. Mircea was helping him constantly. Now, on shore, the knight watched the two boys approaching slowly. Internally, he smiled approvingly of the elder brother. Externally, he showed no sign of satisfaction. Mircea served as a crutch for Vlad as the two emerged from the water.

"You must stop relying on your brother." Vlad's entire body shook from the cold and fear. "He will not always be there to rescue you." The knight turned his back on them and walked off, signaling the end of the lesson.

Mircea motioned toward the boat with his head as he spoke to Vlad. "Come on…I can't carry it alone."

BRUSA
July 14, 1437

Once Sigismund's death was declared publicly, Europe's leaders aligned themselves according to their own best interests. For Dracul, the decision led him and three hundred boyars to the city of Brusa to meet with Sultan Murad II. Though the sultan had made the atmosphere festive, this was still a day of submission. Dracul was forced to pay a tribute of ten thousand ducats as Murad spent most of the morning and afternoon seeking his advice on how to conquer the last strongholds of Byzantine.

"How well acquainted are you with Ioan Hunedoara?"

Dracul's nostrils flared. Hunedoara, now viceroy and governor general of Transylvania, had sworn loyalty to the Hapsburg Archduke of Austria, Albert II. Albert had married Sigismund's daughter, Elizabeth, and was crowned king of Hungary. He had chosen to concentrate his efforts on the danger posed by the Turkish inroads that threatened his capitals of Buda and Vienna.

"I know him well."

"My spies report he has been given the task of defending the southern portion of the kingdom. I will not allow the Hungarians to proceed with any designs they may have to control the land."

"What do you suggest?"

"There is only one free Serbian fortress left outside of Belgrade."

"Smederevo." A look of astonishment and realization overcame Dracul as he said the word. "Are you actually contemplating-"

"My plan has already been set in motion."

Dracul was astonished by the thought that the sultan would be attacking his own father-in-law, George Branković.

"Go and enjoy yourself. There will be more than enough time to discuss plans later."

As Dracul walked off, Mehmed Neşri, the governor of Bulgaria, approached the sultan. He bowed and Murad bade him to sit by his side. Staring at the sultan's latest acquisition, Neşri spoke.

"I do not trust him, my liege."

"His allegiance will be made clear soon enough...Should that create any difficulties, he will be handled properly."

"He is already a problem."

The look on Murad's face suggested there was nothing he wasn't prepared for. "If he poses any threat, he will be easily contained."

As the sultan abruptly stood and walked away, Neşri's eyes shot from his master to

Dracul.

I shall show you, my liege…

SERBEŞ
March 15, 1438

More than two weeks ago, Murad began the first of numerous raids into Transylvania. In an effort to keep favor with the sultan, Dracul accepted his invitation to accompany him. Already countless cities had been pillaged and thousands killed. Many were outraged with Dracul initially, but most feelings of betrayal quickly transformed into gratefulness. Those being conquered now believed they stood a better chance of leniency if they could surrender to a fellow countryman.

By request of the city's mayor the sultan, along with Mehmed Neşri, Dracul, and others, now met with the council of Serbeş outside of the city gates. The mayor was a short, portly man, whose black moustache was thicker than Dracul's. His voice was sincere as he pleaded with the Turks.

"We will surrender to Prince Vlad under the condition you do not take our people away as slaves. We will give you anything else you desire."

Neşri snarled at the mayor. "You are in no position to dictate the terms of your surrender!"

Sensing the situation would soon deteriorate, and pitying the desperate mayor, Dracul interjected. His opportunity to remain a dutiful Draconist now presented itself.

"My liege, this man wants only what is best for his people." There was a slight hint of sarcasm in Dracul's voice, far too minute for anyone to detect.

Neşri leaned over to the sultan and whispered. "You see. His is protecting them. He has no wish to serve you."

After a few seconds, Murad spoke. "We shall take half of your treasury and anything a contingent of one hundred can carry…We will take none of your people."

Though thankful his people were out of immediate danger, the loss of so much money distressed the mayor. "Thank you, sire. Our city is grateful to you."

Neşri's contempt was evident as he glared at Dracul, who knowingly smirked back at him. His hatred for the infidel only intensified.

"Does this arrangement satisfy you, Prince Vlad?"

Though preoccupied with Neşri, Dracul answered immediately. "The arrangements are very generous; a most favorable decision, my liege."

Neşri continued to stare at Dracul.

"Good." The sultan turned to address one of his other soldiers nearby. "Proceed." With that simple command, the soldier rode off to gather the men needed for the incursion.

Dracul accepted Murad's offer to return home shortly after the conclusion of the expedition. By month's end, the Turkish treasury overflowed and more than seventy thousand Transylvanians were taken prisoner to serve and suffer as slaves of the Ottoman Empire.

CHAPTER V
SMEDEREVO FALLS
SMEDEREVO
August 27, 1439

Pope Eugenius IV successfully restored order to the Roman Catholic Church. At a council held in Florence, the pontificate labored to reunite the Roman Catholic and Eastern Orthodox churches and did so on the fourth of July. Realizing how essential this reunion would be for any possible crusade in the defense of Constantinople, Emperor John VIII of the Byzantine Empire made certain to attend.

The council inspired Dracul to change his mind about siding with Murad. He asked the sultan for forgiveness when he decided not to accompany the Turkish on their attack of Smederevo, citing problems within his own principality. Another reason for his decision was the growing popularity of Ioan Hunedoara.

Since being made governor general of Transylvania, Hunedoara had become known as the *White Knight* of the Wallachians because of his astute abilities as a political and military leader. Dracul hated the man but knew it was in his best interest to remain in his good favor.

With the gates forced open, the Turkish army poured into Smederevo. George Branković watched helplessly as his men were slaughtered. He had lost sight of his sons, Gregor and Stepan. His focus now centered on the preservation of his own life. In anticipation of the battle, Branković had prepared a small contingent of ten men for his family's escape. It appeared he would be the only one using the route. Hurriedly, he retreated to the hidden entrance of a secret passage in the chamber serving as his war room and thanked God it was still accessible.

As the Turkish closed in, Branković entered his headquarters to find only four members of his contingent present. He gulped down air to regain his breath and spoke.

"Where…are the others?"

"There are no others, sir."

"What?"

"Killed almost instantly upon the Turks' entrance into the fortress."

Though disheartened by the loss of his men, Branković quickly convinced himself it was for the best. The smaller his party, the easier success of escape would be. Even so, the absence of Stepan and Gregor distressed him greatly.

"Fine. Let's waste no more time."

The soldiers revealed a secret passage in the floor by lifting the stone panel that covered it. Branković ordered each of the soldiers to take one of the torches in the room and then instructed two of the men to enter the passage. He followed the first two and ordered the others to reseal the entrance.

Shortly after the entrance was again covered, two Turkish soldiers stormed into the room. They were followed by others who held both Gregor and Stepan captive. Neither had been injured significantly, but Stepan had sustained an arrow wound to his right arm. The Turkish soldiers threw Branković's sons down and then moved away from the door. Murad's entrance elicited silence, save the heavy breathing of Gregor and Stepan. Both had resisted capture until being thrown on the floor.

The sultan looked at Gregor as he shouted. "Where is he?"

Gregor looked up at him. "Who?"

"You know *exactly* who. Where is your father?"

"I don't know." Gregor was hit by one of the sultan's men. Stepan retaliated in defense of his brother, only to find himself knocked back to the floor.

"Next time they will not be so lenient. Now…where is your father?"

Blood ran from Stepan's split chin as he looked up at the sultan. "Go to Hell!" He was hit instantly and with more ferocity than he had experienced in his lifetime.

"I'll find him," Murad said. "When I do, all of you will suffer immensely." He turned and walked out of the room before Gregor and Stepan said anything they would have to be killed for immediately.

Complying with the sultan's order, the soldiers dragged Branković's sons away. Once outside, Gregor and Stepan saw the massacre they had escaped and were compelled to wonder if their father had been successful in fleeing. Gregor glanced at Stepan.

"Were he not our brother-in-law, I am certain we would be dead now."

Holding together his throbbing chin, Stepan remained silent. Sarcastically, he commented to himself. *Yeah…good thing.*

For almost four hundred meters, the light of the torches had guided them. Nearing the end of the tunnel, the despot continuously peered over his shoulder past the two soldiers behind him. He prayed he would not see the sultan's men and hoped, by some miracle, he would find Gregor and Stepan.

"I am afraid they did not make it sir," said one of the soldiers.

Branković's head spun back around, away from the soldier. "They are alive…I know they are. Murad is ruthless, but he is still my son-in-law. Most likely, they have been captured.

One of the soldiers in front of Branković glanced at him. "Sir, I can see the exit now."

Abruptly, the tunnel stopped at what appeared to be a dead end. The four soldiers each grounded their torches and began clearing loose rocks from around the boulder blocking the exit. Sunlight flooded the once darkened tunnel and blinded them all as the stones gave way. The men staggered into the open, blinking and rubbing their eyes in an attempt to adjust to the light. Once they could see clearly, the soldiers made a perimeter check to ensure the Turkish were nowhere to be found before allowing Branković to exit. After securing the area, one of the soldiers called out to Branković.

"Sir, it is safe."

For a moment, the sun impaired Branković's sight, causing him to raise his hand to cover his eyes. "Conceal the exit."

While resealing the escape route, one of the men questioned Branković.

"What do we do next sir?"

Branković simply answered, "To Hungary."

CHAPTER VI
DRACUL'S GAMBLE
TÎRGOVIŞTE
January 22, 1441

Journeying to Hungary took Branković and his men the whole of September and the first week of October. Upon his arrival, the Serbian despot reported to Albert all that had transpired, concluding with his escape. The king sympathized and knew immediate action must be taken against the Turkish. Albert began gathering his army and summoning troops to Vienna. The crusade, however, never began.

On October 27th, Albert was struck down by dysentery as the small army he gathered stood by helplessly. Replacing him would prove daunting. In dying without an heir, Albert placed the kingdom in a bitter power struggle, one nearly culminating in civil war. The succession of the throne now lie with Albert's widow, Elizabeth.

Consumed by the desire to rule, Elizabeth announced her pregnancy with Albert's child. Although she indeed was pregnant, many suspected the pregnancy to be the result of an affair. The timing of the announcement had been too convenient for anyone to accept it blindly.

Elizabeth would accomplish her scheme with the help of her mother, Emperor Sigismund's widow. She was supplied with the counts of Cilli as allies and even turned newly elected Holy Roman Emperor Fredrick III sympathetic toward her cause. Elizabeth was determined to preserve the legality of the infant's succession by having her lady-in-waiting steal the crown of St. Stephen from the fortress of Visegrád. Once born, the child was crowned Ladislas V. Furthering her chances, Elizabeth named the Holy Roman Emperor the child's guardian and appointed Enea Silvio de Piccolomini as the child's tutor. Many understood if Elizabeth were allowed to continue her self-indulgence, Hungary would grow weak. Ioan Hunedoara was among them. He, and a majority of Hungary's nobility, made the young Polish king, Ladislas III, their candidate for the Hungarian throne.

Realizing she lacked the necessary support to suppress Hunedoara and the nobles, Elizabeth succumbed to them under the condition that if the Polish king were to die without any heirs, her son would gain the throne. This caveat was agreed to with no intention of it ever being honored. With the matter settled, Ladislas III sent Hunedoara to entice Dracul to renew the crusade against the Turks.

Dracul sat with Mircea beside him as the governor general of Transylvania spoke.

"You swore an oath to Emperor Sigismund that you would defend Christianity. His death does not absolve you of the commitment you made."

"Sigismund made me wait *years* before allowing me a chance to gain my throne—a promise he made to me when I was inducted into the order. Why should *I* not wait before fulfilling my oath?"

Hunedoara grew more frustrated with each ridiculous response uttered. "You do not have that option! You agreed to the terms; no one forced you! It was *your* choice; you were not obligated!"

Dracul slammed his fist on the table in front of him, kicked his chair back, and stood. "Not obligated? This was my *father's* throne, *my* family's throne! I had every obligation! Sigismund wasn't obligated to support Aldea…This is my home, governor, take care how you address me in it."

Dracul's chest heaved as he considered having Hunedoara killed and with good reason. Hunedoara had been assuring the son of Dan II, Basarab III Laiotă, that Wallachia's throne would soon be his. At present, Laiotă held the distinction of being the only man Dracul hated more than Hunedoara. It would not take much for Hunedoara to surpass him though.

"So then, you choose to side with the Turkish?"

"I choose to side with no one. I am a neutral party, an innocent bystander in this whole affair. Return and tell you king I refuse his demands…If he wishes to order someone, tell him to put Laiotă on my throne…as you continue insisting you will."

Knowing Dracul had been made aware of his dealings with Laiotă, Hunedoara made no attempt to deny it. "I only told Basarab Laiotă the inevitable."

"And what is that?"

"That if your treachery continues, he will become prince. And it probably won't even be the empire that finally destroys you."

"Leave now…before you are unable to."

Hunedoara turned and walked away from Dracul without another word. Upon reaching the door he looked back. "You are making a grave mistake."

"Goodbye…governor general."

Seconds passed before Mircea addressed his father.

"*Are* you going to remain neutral?"

Dracul looked at Mircea, so different from the small child he remembered running down that darkened corridor the night Vlad was born. "For the time being. If at all possible, I will not provide the Turkish a reason to be upset…You doubt my reasoning?"

"I trust you father. But what will the Turkish say when you do not fight for them either?"

"The Turkish are easier to manipulate than you think. By next year they will control the Danube. I am in no immediate danger as long as they are successful."

"And if they are not successful?"

Dracul smiled. "Then it won't matter. If the Turkish fail, I will simply reaffirm my vows with the empire. Ridding myself of Hunedoara is a priority though…one that must be accomplished soon."

ADRINOPLE
March 15, 1442

Dracul's assertion had been correct. The Turkish now controlled the Danube and most of the key fortresses along it. In keeping with his policy of neutrality, Dracul had allowed Şihabeddin, the Turkish Bey of Rumelis, to enter Wallachia, giving the Ottomans easy access to Transylvania. When asked why he would not fight for the sultan, however, Dracul simply answered that many domestic problems required his immediate attention.

When the Turkish campaign finally ended, thousands had been killed. Many of the survivors were mortally wounded, destined to die slowly through the torment of infection. The victory had been a glorious one for Ladislas III. Many beys were killed, and the remnants of the army had retreated home.

Seeing the devastation his force had suffered, Murad's suspicion that Dracul was not totally fulfilling his obligation was aroused. Others, particularly Mehmed Neşri, helped heighten those suspicions.

"Neither Ioan Hunedoara nor George Branković is loyal to you. Nor should you believe that Vlad Dracul is a true friend…He is fickle."

"Vlad Dracul is an excellent warrior, Neşri. I do not want to destroy such a tremendous asset."

"What use is an excellent warrior if he sits idly by while his ally is slaughtered? He is not true to our cause, my liege. Dracul only wants what is best for himself."

Murad looked at Neşri with a smile. "Don't we all? He would be an unwise and unfit ruler if he did not look out for his own best interests. It is our duty to make him realize what those interests should be…and what is best for his welfare. Once spring has arrived, I will invite both he and George Branković here. Then we shall see their true allegiance."

"And if they do not come?"

Murad's smile disappeared. "Then the world will be shown why they should have."

Neşri smiled. "Finally you will see what I have tried to tell you all along."

"I hope you are wrong. We need Dracul to defeat Hunedoara."

"Hunedoara is a simple puppet, my liege."

"No. Hunedoara is a worthy adversary and must be reckoned with. He grows powerful too quickly. Once I defeat him, the rest of the empire will fall into place. Once he is gone, all of Europe will belong to Allah."

Despite Murad's words, Neşri refused to believe the simple governor general to be the key to all of Europe. Hunedoara's existence, while bothersome, surely would not decide the fate of this or any other empire.

CHAPTER VII
HOSTAGE
GALLIPOLI
May 20, 1442

Dracul accepted Murad's invitation and agreed to meet with him at Gallipoli. He left Mircea, now thirteen, in command of Wallachia during his absence and brought Vlad and Radu along with him. Cneajna objected, but Dracul insisted their education would be enhanced by the journey.

As the party neared the city, a Turkish contingent waited in plain view. Dracul glanced and smiled at his sons as they rode beside him. Vlad, now ten, had excelled in every aspect of his education, especially horsemanship. Radu, now seven, was not quite as advanced in his learning as his brothers but always managed to achieve the required task. Though his face failed to convey it, uncertainty, doubt, and unrest crept into Dracul's consciousness. The presence of Mehmed Neşri concerned him.

What is he doing here? Dracul turned to the commander on his left. "I have a bad feeling about this."

"Do you wish to turn back, sire?"

"No. Running would only confirm any suspicions they harbor. Besides, we would not get far."

Vlad had been listening to the conversation. He sensed his father's apprehension but, instead of becoming fearful, was intrigued. Radu, in stark contrast, was terrified, trembling with fright.

Finally the two contingents were mere meters apart, and Dracul acted as though Neşri's presence pleased him. "Good morning, governor. This certainly is a surprise."

Dracul's pleasantries were immediately dismissed by Neşri. "I am here only to reveal to you the true reason you have been asked to be here."

"What do you mean?" By this time, Dracul's men had been surrounded. Neşri's lips twisted into a wicked smile as the prince looked around.

"You are accused of treason and other crimes against the sultan. Seize him!"

Two guards moved toward Dracul with chains as Neşri had ordered.

"What about my men?"

"They will be set free...Ignorance can be corrected."

Dracul looked at his two sons. "And what about them?"

Neşri glanced at the prince's two sons. "They will be taken care of. As long as you do not try anything foolish, they will be allowed to live." Neşri looked at two more of his men and then glanced at the children. "Chain them as well."

Vlad became angry as Neşri's men approached. He dismounted and prepared to attack the soldiers. Radu simply sat still and watched in fear as his brother fought to escape. After being thrown to the ground, his father called to him.

"Vlad stop! You are only making matters worse!"

Vlad looked up at his father as he caught his breath. "Surrender?"

Dracul looked at his son with understanding. "I am not telling you to give up, only to be sensible. Use your head for something other than a target...Do as you are told."

The boy was bound and picked up off of the ground by the Turkish soldiers.

"You are mistaken in your belief that there will be another day to fight."

Dracul turned to face Neşri.

Radu had begun to cry even before being pulled off of his horse, and Dracul could only watch as his sons were dragged off through the Turkish contingent.

"Where are you taking them?"

"I already told you. They will be well taken care of. You should be more concerned about yourself." The governor looked at one of his men. "No more talk."

With that, the soldiers led Dracul toward Gallipoli as the prince's men watched helplessly. Shocked at the event they had just witnessed, the men simply stood still until the last of the Turkish soldiers disappeared from view.

ADRINOPLE
June 17, 1443

Following a short stay in Gallipoli, Murad had Dracul transported to his capital of Andrinople. For nearly a year, the Wallachian languished without knowing what had become of Vlad and Radu. Dracul's numerous pleas for an audience with the sultan had gone unanswered and unfulfilled. For weeks, he did his best to simply retain his sanity, knowing that at any minute he would be brought before Murad. When that did not happen, however, apathy began to consume his spirit. Finally, he gave up all hope of ever being set free and returning home.

After months of doing what he could to remain sharp mentally, Dracul arrived at the conclusion he had been forgotten. The guards paid him no attention, other than to supply him his meals when they remembered to, and they certainly did not hold him in high regard as a political prisoner.

Dracul had resigned himself to the fact that he was going to die someday in this rank enclosure. That was the reason why he hardly stirred when his cell door was unlocked.

The image of two guards approaching him came into focus. One of the two unlocked his chains and ordered him to get up. He apparently did so too slowly, and the two men each grabbed a shoulder to throw him to his feet. They led Dracul through the palace to Murad's throne room; he could see the sultan, seated and surrounded by numerous beys.

"Good morning, Vlad Dracul. I trust you have slept well."

Dracul looked at him and answered dryly. "Excellently, my liege."

The sultan stood and began walking toward him methodically. "Do you long for your freedom?"

"Am I a prisoner, my liege?" Dracul's response was sarcastic.

Murad laughed before resuming the conversation. "You were not the only one I invited to meet me. I also asked my father-in-law to join me. He was wise enough not to come...Why weren't you?"

"I did nothing wrong, my liege. I had no reason to be afraid."

Murad stared at him with dissatisfaction. "You left my army to be devastated by the Hungarians!"

Seeing the sudden change of approach, Dragwlya decided it best not to argue the point. "My liege, if I have offended you by my actions, then I am sorry. My only duty is to serve you."

Murad continued to stare at him and nodded his head. "Good...That's *very* good." As he walked back to his throne, Murad spoke. "I have a proposition for you. You are allowed to go free under certain conditions. First, you will pay me an annual tribute of ten thousand gold ducats...Second, you will swear on both your holy book and the Koran never again to engage in any treacherous activity...Third, as your new act of fidelity, you will send me a contingent of five hundred Wallachian boys who will serve in my Janissary Corps. Do you agree to all of these terms?"

This last condition of Murad's was meant to infuriate Dracul, yet it would be the sultan who would be startled. Dracul did not answer immediately, but gave the impression he was deep in thought, contemplating the sultan's ultimatum.

"My liege, your terms are reasonable, but I do not feel they adequately reflect my loyalty."

Astonished and curious, Murad replied. "What do you propose, Vlad Dracul?"

Dracul stared into the eyes of the sultan and answered unwaveringly. "My liege, as proof of my devotion, I wish to leave my sons, whom you currently hold captive, in your custody."

Murad's face failed to convey his disbelief. "You are willingly giving me your sons?"

"Yes, my liege. Provided they are still alive of course."

"They are alive and well. They have been moved to Tokat." Relief overcame Dracul as the sultan continued to speak. "If you remain loyal, no harm will come to them."

"I shall, my liege."

"Should you cross me again, they will suffer immensely. I guarantee it."

"I understand, my liege."

Murad looked at Dracul and smiled. "I hope so...for your sons' sake."

Dracul looked at the faces of the beys present in the room. None appeared happy about his release. Murad picked up a Bible and a Koran and walked over to Dracul.

"Place your right hand here," he said lifting up the Koran. "Do you swear to remain loyal to me?"

Dracul's attention and stare were focused fully on the sultan now. "I do, my liege."

Murad lowered the Koran and held up the Bible. "Now, place your hand here." Dracul placed his hand on the Bible. "Do you swear to remain loyal to me?"

"I do, my liege."

"Good." Murad slowly lowered the Bible. "You will be given provisions and an escort home."

"Thank you, my liege. I will make certain the safe return of your men through my land."

"See that you do. Do not underestimate me again, Vlad Dracul. Your next stay will not be nearly as lengthy. Guards, bring him to his escorts."

CHAPTER VIII
THE VARNA DEBACLE
NICOPOLIS
September 3, 1444

Hunedoara's victories over the Ottomans throughout 1442 in Transylvania gave Pope Eugenius IV enough hope to declare the crusade to liberate the people of the Balkan Peninsula during the spring of last year. The crusade was designed also to solidify the union agreed upon at Florence in 1439 between the eastern and western churches and to reassert the prestige of the papacy. This last measure would destroy the numerous antipopes and crush the movement for constitutional government of the Roman Curia.

Papal Legate Cardinal Giuliano Cesarini had been the one to actually bring together the forces involved. He received great assistance from the papal legate in Venice, Cardinal Gondolfieri, and from Enea Silvio de Piccolomini, Prince Ladislas Posthumus' tutor. Under Hunedoara's leadership the Christian army, numbering around twenty-five thousand and consisting of Poles, Romanians, Serbs, Germans, and Austrians, left Belgrade in the fall. Because of his need to continue solidifying his power after a year-long absence from the throne, Dracul sent only a small contingent under Mircea's leadership to join the Christian force.

The army fought impressively, winning at Nis and Sofia. It appeared the entire Balkan Peninsula would eventually be liberated; that the moment had arrived for the Turks to finally be run out of Europe. Winter brought hard snows with it, however, and made the passes in the Balkan Mountains of Bulgaria impossible to cross. Consequently, Hunedoara was forced to order the Christian army to retreat to Belgrade.

At year's end, a treaty was proclaimed at Szégedin by the Polish king and at Andrinople by Murad. The truce allowed for the return of some captured forts to the Serbs and the Hungarians and set free all hostages, including Vlad, Radu, and the sons of George Branković. To this point, none of them had been released. The Christians signed the treaty and swore to it on the Koran and Bible. Their agreement extended a five-year truce with Murad, one he much needed in order to confront enemies in Asia.

Cesarini implored the Polish king in autumn to start a new crusade against the Turks. The Pope absolved the Christians of their treaty with Murad on the grounds the sultan was an infidel and had the papal legate put Hunedoara in command of the empire's army. Although Cesarini's hope to rid Europe of the Turks strongly guided him, his desire to destroy the Turks altogether drove him. He was planning to involve the crusading army in a combined effort with the Venetian fleet, whose task would be to deny the sultan's army entry to Europe by way of the Bosphorus.

It had been dubbed the Varna Campaign and, as the Christians set out for battle, an appeal had been made to Dracul for help. Unlike the crusade of 1443, where the Christians penetrated into Balkan territory, this time they were to advance along the Danube. Dracul was now meeting with Hunedoara and others at Nicopolis to discuss his participation in the fighting and the plan of attack.

Dracul approached the Christian camp on the bank of the Danube and surveyed the tents set up to house the troops. There were far fewer than he had expected to see.

"Thank you for coming personally, sire," said Cesarini. "The contingent you sent to fight in last year's crusade was of great service. Your son's leadership was exemplary. Please, come inside."

Dracul, Mircea, and the few men he had with him led the way into the leaders' conference tent. As Dracul passed Hunedoara, the two exchanged glances. Mircea also stared at Hunedoara. He despised the man more than Dracul did.

The council opened, and Dracul surveyed the gathered commanders of the Christian army. Hunedoara glanced at Dracul and spoke.

"Prince Vlad, you have been asked here to participate in the crusade. We have-"

Dracul interrupted him without hesitation. "Is that what you are calling this?"

A look of confusion fixed on the faces of those present.

"What do you mean?" asked King Ladislas.

Dracul looked at the king. "How many men do you have encamped, sire?"

"Fifteen thousand," responded the king.

"Fifteen thousand?" Dracul said with a laugh shaking his head. *An inconvenience.*

Hunedoara's agitation with Dracul blossomed quickly. "Why do you find that so amusing?"

Fire blazed in Dracul's eyes as the smile dropped from his face. "The sultan goes on *hunting expeditions* with more troops than you are proposing to bring into this battle." He turned his attention toward the Polish king. "Sire, I strongly urge you to turn back and abort whatever plans you may have. Your men will be killed if you don't." He addressed the commanders next. "Most of you will be as well."

The comments infuriated Hunedoara. "Your assertions are baseless! You have no knowledge of our strategy! Already the Venetian fleet is at the Bosphorus to prevent the Turkish from landing in Europe!"

Dracul sat calmly, shaking his head once more. "The Venetian fleet? You situation is even more dire than I thought."

Hunedoara slammed his fist on the table before him. "I-"

This time Cesarini cut off Hunedoara. "Ioan, please … Prince Vlad, why are you so certain we are doomed to fail? You have seen the results from our efforts last year. Why so much doubt?"

"The Venetian fleet is poor at best. They will not prevent the Turkish from landing.

Murad has already lost to you once. He will not let it happen again."

"Ridiculous!" cried Hunedoara. The governor general dropped all pretense of respect for the prince as he addressed the council. "Dracul's allegiance is obviously still to Murad! He should never have been allowed to be here!"

"Murad is currently holding two of my sons hostage at Andrinople! I have already endangered their lives by just being here among the spies he has hidden in your camp, Hunedoara! Forgive me if I do not share your optimism in a crusade destined for failure!"

"Is that the real reason for your resistance, or does the thought of not fulfilling your oath to the Turkish keep you from fighting?" Hunedoara's tone was accusatory.

"My oath is not what troubles me. My conscious does. I will not knowingly send fifteen thousand victims to their deaths. To prove to you I support this cause, I will commit a contingent of four thousand cavalrymen under Mircea's leadership."

Mircea quelled his concern. After hearing what Dracul had just told the council, however, he had every reason to be apprehensive. Dracul continued to look at Cesarini.

"Surely this proves to you how much I wish to rid Europe of the Turks," said Dracul.

"I do not doubt your loyalty, Prince Vlad," said the king. "We only wish to have as much cooperation as possible."

"I understand, sire. My concern for everyone's safety is all I wished to voice."

"I understand."

Hunedoara could not believe the sincerity with which Dracul was able to make up feeble excuses and found it harder to accept the king and others were so receptive to them.

"Your offer is appreciated," said the king. "We shall be eating shortly, so if no one has anything further..."

Mircea stood up, "Sire. As a representative of my father and Wallachia, I will defend this cause whole-heartedly."

The king smiled. "Thank you, Mircea. Your services are considered invaluable. Anyone else?...No? Then we are adjourned."

Dracul rose and walked out with Mircea. Hunedoara caught up to them.

"You may deceive the king and Cesarini, Dracul, but you don't fool me."

"Perhaps you are just too foolish to comprehend reason," Mircea quipped.

Hunedoara glared at him and snarled, "Be careful who you tangle with, *boy*."

Dracul stepped in front of Mircea. "Are you threatening my son, Hunedoara?"

Hunedoara stared into Dracul's eyes. "Yes, and not idly. Once I uncover the scheme you have devised, I will make it known, and you will be exposed for what you are."

Dracul stared back at Hunedoara. "Attempt to hurt my son, and you will suffer immensely."

Hunedoara's eyes unlocked and flickered away from those of Dracul. The latter stopped Mircea from saying anything with a touch of his son's arm as the former strode away.

"He must be disposed of immediately," Mircea said quietly.

Dracul continued to watch Hunedoara. "I agree. But what do you suggest? He is the *White Knight* of the peasants. Killing him would only incur the people's wrath against us. First, we must show everyone his true intentions."

"Which are?"

"I don't know, but I intend to reveal Hunedoara for what he really is."

"And what is that exactly?"

"I have yet to decide."

VARNA
September 29, 1444

The Christians had set up camp on one of the hills overlooking the Black Sea and the seaport of Varna. As the sun began to rise, King Ladislas and the other commanders spied on the Turkish forces encamped on the outskirts of the city.

Resisting the urge to make Hunedoara appear inept proved impossible. "You should have listened to my father," Mircea stated boldly—a reference to the Venetian fleet's failure to stop the Turkish from landing. The effort, and the fleet, had been a disastrous loss.

"Shut up you little-"

"Enough!" shouted Cesarini.

"We have no time for pointless bickering," Ladislas intoned. His eyes were again affixed to the Ottoman forces. "We are outnumbered at least three-to-one."

"Our only chance is to fight them in the valley," said Mircea.

Hunedoara begrudgingly concurred. Doing so nauseated him. "I must agree with the boy."

"All right," Ladislas agreed. "Have your men prepare while we finalize our plans."

In awe, Cesarini continued to survey Murad's massive army. "May God be with us all."

The Turkish forces easily overpowered the Christians. Ladislas fought to turn the tide alongside his men, witnessing their slaughter from the frontline. A sharp cry came from his horse and, as the charger reared, Ladislas realized it had been hit by a spear. The animal bucked, throwing the young king. With a dull thud, he slammed to the ground but rose with sword in hand as the battle raged around him.

Instantaneously surrounded and with no chance his men would be able to get close enough to assist him, Ladislas began swinging his sword wildly. He turned and was struck on the head. Dazed slightly, Ladislas felt the warmth of blood running down his face. Again he took the offensive and raised his sword above his head. His sword came down and clanged against that of a Turkish soldier. With a block and then a thrust requiring little energy to execute, the soldier threw the king backwards. As the young king struggled to regain his balance, there came a punishing blow from behind.

Ladislas dropped his sword and raised his hands to grasp the blade sticking through his abdomen. The Turkish soldier withdrew his sword as the king gasped for air. Set free of the blade, Ladislas fell to his knees and then backwards, clasping his stomach and trying futilely to hold in what blood remained.

A ring of Turkish soldiers formed around Ladislas. Looking up, he could see the blade of one of the soldiers raised, ready to strike across his neck. Just as he cried out in horror, Ladislas' legs popped up into the air. The blade did not go all the way through, and as the soldier attempted to pull it from the king's throat, he was prevented from doing so by another.

Raising his foot above the blade, the second soldier muttered something unintelligible. Ladislas gagged on his own blood as his body grew numb. The foot of the soldier landing squarely on the blade would be the last image his mind would process. Two of the soldiers grabbed the slain king's body while another took his severed head. Proceeding to a nearby hill, they placed the head on display for all to see.

Almost immediately, Hunedoara gathered some of the Wallachian troops to retrieve Ladislas' remains. Nearby, Mircea watched as the Christian soldiers abandoned the fight. Cesarini had disappeared some time ago, and Mircea wondered how long ago the papal legate had fled. He would have to do likewise before long. No matter how hard they tried, or what they tried, Hunedoara and the Wallachians failed to get near the fallen king's body. The governor general stared at the spike in despair, knowing his own fate if he continued to disregard opportunities to escape. Fortunately, the Wallachians knew the hills and passages of the region well. In short order, Hunedoara rode away with a hastily composed contingent, wondering if Mircea had fared any better, hoping he hadn't.

After nearly an hour of riding, the lead troops slowed in the middle of a mountain pass. One of them retreated back toward Hunedoara. The pallor of the man's face unnerved him.

"What is it?"

"I-" The soldier was visibly distraught and Hunedoara simply rode past him and through the parted soldiers before him.

What now?

The sight was ghastly, second only to the suspended, lifeless face of Ladislas that had stared at him from the hill. There, on the ground in the road, was the naked, blood covered body of Cesarini. The crusade was now a complete failure. With minimal instruction, Hunedoara had the papal legate buried.

Dracul was right.

CHAPTER IX
ARRESTED
DOBRUJA
October 17, 1444

Mircea returned to Tîrgovişte shortly after the massacre at Varna. His account of the events enraged Dracul, who ordered that Hunedoara be arrested the moment he set foot in Wallachia. The troops who had been the only reason for Hunedoara's escape became guards tasked with delivering the peasants' *White Knight* to Dracul. A council of war had then been called and convened in Dobruja.

Hunedoara stood before the council, bound in chains. His rage grew with every word spoken by Dracul and became infinite as Mircea condemned him as well.

"It is unforgivable!" exclaimed Mircea. "This man is the solitary cause for the deaths of more than fifteen thousand men!"

"I cannot be held accountable for the tragedy that occurred at Varna! The Venetian fleet was supposed to stop the Turkish from landing! I cannot be blamed for *their* failure!"

"Yes, you can, and should be," Dracul retorted. "Members of the council, I personally warned the governor general the fleet would fail in its attempt to stop the Turkish. My advice was ignored. He had complete disregard for the welfare and safety of *your* men."

"Because of his overconfidence," interjected Mircea, "no backup plan was ever discussed. There was no possibility of retreat and, because of this *blatant* negligence, men died needlessly, a *papal legate* was beaten to death, and King Ladislas' *head* was displayed on the field of battle!"

The chairman of the council cast a stern glance at Hunedoara. "Why was no secondary plan made?"

Hunedoara sighed heavily. "Our agreement for the plan drawn was unanimous."

"Members of the council, it is safe to evaluate the governor general's judgment as poor," said Dracul. "He must be held personally responsible for this travesty."

Mircea interjected. "I ask Ioan Hunedoara be found guilty of his crimes, including murder."

Hunedoara looked at Mircea, longing to drive a sword through his heart. "I am guilty of nothing!"

Mircea shook his head in disgust and looked back at the chairman. "If there is any justice, he will be executed immediately."

"You insignificant-"

"Enough!" screamed the chairman. "Guards, detain the governor general until the council has reached its verdict."

As two guards approached and flanked him, Hunedoara stared at Mircea. Though he said nothing, his glare conveyed his intent for revenge.

"The council will reconvene once we have reviewed this matter fully. Until that time, we are adjourned."

Dracul turned to Mircea as the councilmen dispersed. "Don't be overconfident. I doubt this council will share your desire to see him executed."

"There can be no sentence but execution for Hunedoara," Mircea retorted.

The council took two days to reach its decision, and Mircea tried to persuade individual members to side against Hunedoara whenever the opportunity presented itself. Now, as the young man stood beside his father, he smiled, certain he would soon hear Hunedoara's conviction and death sentence.

Hunedoara was led in by two guards. The sight of the man in chains made Mircea smile.

"Ioan Hunedoara, you are accused by both Vlad Dracul and his son, Mircea, of numerous crimes; among them, the deaths of more than fifteen thousand men. The decision of this council is unanimous. Of these crimes, you are found guilty."

Mircea's smile returned, broader.

Dracul saw his son's reaction. "The verdict is not the sentence."

"In this council's judgment, the only suitable punishment is death."

Mircea merely smiled at his father without a word as the chairman continued. "However..."

This single word twisted Mircea's stomach in knots. Simultaneously, hope had the same effect on Hunedoara.

"...because of your gallant and noble efforts in the past, it has been decided you will be spared this fate."

Relief filled Hunedoara as Mircea became furious.

"What? You find him *guilty*, but because of his past actions his present ones are disregarded?!"

"Mircea," said Dracul. "Silence."

The chairman tried to calm him down. "We understand your feelings Mircea, but-"

"Obviously you do not understand!"

Sternly the chairman continued. "We have rendered our verdict, and it is final. We ask that you pursue this matter no further."

"How can you let someone get away with murder on such a grand scale?" asked Mircea.

"That is enough, Mircea!" said Dracul.

Abruptly, Mircea turned to face him. "Father-"

"*Enough!*"

Mircea looked over only to find Hunedoara wearing an unrestrained grin.

"Dracul, this council asks that you ensure the safety of the governor general's journey through Transylvania when the time comes."

Pausing to first look at his son, Dracul answered much to Mircea's anguish. "I will comply with the council's wishes."

"Good," said the chairman. "This matter is now completed. Guards, release the governor general at once. We will reconvene this afternoon."

Propelled by anger, Mircea rounded to face his father. "How could you possibly agree to such terms?"

"I warned you that this was going to happen. Like Hunedoara, you chose not to listen."

Remaining silent, Hunedoara eavesdropped until Mircea broke away from his father long enough to take notice of him.

"Regardless of the council's decision, this matter is not concluded!"

"For once, boy, you are correct," Hunedoara answered, still smirking.

"You will pay for what you have done!"

"That is enough, Mircea!" said Dracul.

"Afraid your son will not be able to finish what he starts?"

Dracul turned from his son and stared at Hunedoara with every ounce of loathing in his body. "I have no wish to see you die quickly, Hunedoara. Leave now...before *I* carry out the sentence you should have received."

Hunedoara smiled and exited as Dracul physically restrained Mircea.

"Hunedoara will receive his punishment in time," Dracul whispered. "I will make certain of that."

ANDRINOPLE
October 18, 1444

Because of their father's treachery, Vlad and Radu's terms of imprisonment had become harsher since their transfer to Murad's court. They had been taken to Bursa and Manisa along with the other hostages and the court as a reminder to their parents of their situation. Not all of the parents were worried; not many cared and not all were intelligent enough to take Murad's threats seriously.

Three years ago, when Vlad and Radu initially arrived at Andrinople, two of the other hostages were punished for trying to conspire with their family. Gregor and Stepan were communicating with their father, George Branković, regarding plans of escape. Upon the discovery of their correspondence, the sultan had the two princes blinded with red-hot irons. This occurred despite the tears and pleas of their sister, Maria, Murad's wife. Gregor and Stepan were released after the campaign of 1443, because their father had been the only European leader loyal to the treaty of that campaign.

Another hostage at the court was George Castriota, a nobleman from Kruja. Being in his early twenties, the younger hostages looked up to him as a sort of uncle. The captives were tutored daily by scholars with the best knowledge of cultivated traditions of Ottoman education. Not all of the pupils were hostages though. A student one year younger than Vlad also studied under the tutelage of these same men—Mehmed, Murad's second son. The students were to learn the Koran, Aristotelian logic, and applied and theoretical mathematics. Vlad assimilated the Turkish language quickly, speaking it as though it were his native tongue.

One notable scholar at the court was Ahmed Gürani, a Kurdish philosopher. His six foot four, muscular body was made all the more imposing by his thick, long black beard. Gürani had been granted the use of the whip on every student, and none defied him, save one.

Gürani jerked his whip back after lashing Vlad for a third time. Still the child refused to yield. With a fourth crack, the boy finally fell to his knees. His back seemed paralyzed yet on fire as the scholar scolded him and watched him struggle to get to his feet.

"Never have I seen such a child!...You are a scourge! Your father undoubtedly *wanted* you taken captive, just so he would be rid of you!"

The comment elicited Vlad's stare immediately as he blocked out the pain.

Gürani smirked and then became lost for a few seconds in thought. "Your father's name...Dracul. It means dragon in your native tongue, does it not?"

"Yes."

"And yet it also means *devil*," Gürani said with a smile. "How appropriate. Since you are in fact the *son* of the devil, I think it would only be fitting that you should be named as such. Therefore, from now on I shall call you...*Dragwlya*." Laughing, he turned away from the boy and began to leave. "Lesson over."

"Will you never learn?"

Vlad Dragwlya looked up to see Radu, staring down at him. "I will not serve the Turkish as you do, coward. You're a disgrace."

Radu looked around at all of the other pupils watching. The hatred the brothers shared for one another was obvious and stemmed from their polar opposite personalities. Dragwlya always behaved intolerably enough to be beaten, whereas Radu always remained obedient.

"Stop it, you two!" said Castriota. "How do you expect to survive without working together?"

"He is a hindrance to my survival," said Dragwlya motioning with his head toward Radu. Radu began to charge but was held back by Mehmed. "Let him go!" commanded Dragwlya while flipping over to sit up. "Something so small is hardly a threat."

Radu tried continuously to escape Mehmed's grasp with no success. Dragwlya's comment rang true. He was small. The younger brother of Dragwlya, however, was the most handsome of Dracul's children. Radu's good looks drew the attention of the women at the sultan's court and aroused interest from others.

Mehmed willingly held Radu back as he addressed him. "Calm yourself."

Dragwlya felt ill as the sultan's son all but embraced his brother. "Have a good grip on him, Mehmed?"

Mehmed glanced over Radu's shoulder and responded. "You would be wise to follow your brother's lead."

"Not if that is an indication of the treatment I would receive."

"Stop, all of you!" exclaimed Castriota. "Vlad, just go before you cause any more problems. Mehmed, take Radu out of here."

"It will be his pleasure," sneered Dragwlya.

Castriota rushed over to Dragwlya and grabbed him by the shoulders. "We have enough to put up with already without your constant fighting! Try and *act* like a human being for once!"

Dragwlya wrestled the man's hands off of his shoulders. "Don't ever touch me again."

Castriota stepped back and allowed the boy to leave without any further incident. The eldest of the hostages hung his head as he watched Dragwlya walk away. *I would have given him up, too.*

CHAPTER X
RADU AND THE TREE
GIURGIU
June 6, 1445

With May drawing to a close, the papal Burgundian fleet began sailing up the Danube River, intent on avenging the Varna debacle and finding the bodies of both King Ladislas and Cardinal Cesarini. Under the leadership of Walerand de Wavrin, the fleet sailed with the assistance of Mircea and Dracul. Hunedoara, one of the driving forces behind the campaign, joined the expedition as well, hoping for a chance at atonement. Although they failed to agree upon much, Dracul and Hunedoara managed to suppress their strong hatred for each other, compromising for victory's sake. Mircea, however, had to be held in check constantly by his father as he tried to intimidate Hunedoara.

Ultimately, the compromise appeared to pay off. The fleet had attacked the Turkish forces of Turtucaia with success and would soon begin the battle for Giurgiu. Mircea would lead Dracul's forces with a plan similar to the one he had used to capture Petretz during the campaign of 1443. In that battle, Mircea used cannon fire to destroy one of the city walls, leaving a gap to lead his troops through. His forces attacked the Turkish, killing all but about fifty of the sultan's men. Those who survived were thrown to their deaths from the castle roof into the murky moat below.

Turkish cannons began firing upon the approaching combined forces, prompting de Wavrin to give the order for Mircea's men to begin their assault on the city walls. Dracul rode alongside Mircea as the Wallachians' artillery pounded the stone barrier before them. Aboard one of the vessels, Hunedoara was away from immediate danger and, thankfully, away from Mircea and Dracul.

After time, defeat became a certainty. Ammunition had run low, and all the men had left was their faith in their god. Eventually, that failed as well. Mircea's plan had worked, and the Turkish remaining for the battle's end now fled for their lives. Once the fleet landed, the men rushed onto the banks of the Danube to storm the city. The battle ended before de Wavrin's men entered the gates. Already Mircea had conquered the Turkish bey in command and had taken prisoner all who had survived.

Mircea and Dracul stood at the city gates, ready to greet de Wavrin and their nemesis. As they approached, Mircea could see the tremendous smile upon Hunedoara's face. He turned to his father and whispered, "Look at him...As if *he* contributed to this." Dracul gave no reply.

"Well done, both of you!" shouted de Wavrin. "Mircea, your strategy was excellent; its execution flawless."

"Thank you, sir."

"Yes, very well done," added Hunedoara dryly.

Mircea looked at the man, wishing he could strike.

De Wavrin could sense the friction and tried to separate them as quickly as possible. "Governor Hunedoara, would you go and make a report of the condition of the city?"

Hunedoara continued to stare at Mircea as he walked past him and Dracul. "Certainly, sir." *I cannot allow either of them to live any longer.*

ANDRINOPLE
November 17, 1446

Although it was nearly midnight, Murad's palace had at least two residents still stirring.

Radu continued searching for places to hide, but Mehmed found him no matter where he ran. Crouching behind a pillar, Radu's chest heaved as he tried regaining his breath. All the while he prayed he had finally lost his lustful pursuer. Then he heard his name.

Now eleven years old, Radu was by far the most handsome creature Mehmed had ever laid eyes on. Radu sighed in distress as the sultan's son called out to him and ventured to peek from his hiding spot only to see a very drunk Mehmed stumbling around. All of his inhibitions were gone, enabling him to ramble on about what he intended to do to Radu. Mehmed's desires were the same whether he was intoxicated or not. Alcohol only amplified them.

Radu did his best to remain motionless. Fear overtook him as his entire body shook, and he began praying once more that he would not be found. With tears streaming down his cheeks, the words of his prayers began to choke him. His throat closed around his windpipe, and he tried to consume more air by sporadically breathing through his nose. Radu fought as best he could, but inevitably his crying cut off his oxygen, and the combination of elements forced him to cough.

Mehmed immediately traced the sound to the pillar. He rushed over to it just as Radu attempted to escape and elicited a shriek from the boy. The sultan's son stood, smiling at him. Radu remained still, sobbing. Seeing the boy cry, Mehmed made a sorrowful looking face.

"What's wrong? You know I would never hurt you."

Radu tried to flee, but even in his drunken state Mehmed managed to block him.

"Please, let me go!" Radu cried. Mehmed only moved closer to him. Once he reached the boy, he embraced him.

"Am I upsetting you?"

Radu did not answer, continuing to sob instead.

Mehmed began working one of his hands down the boy's heaving chest. As he reached Radu's stomach, he whispered to him, "You can go...to my room." He then reached down to the boy's crotch.

Radu cried more, but it was now a cry of rage. He managed enough will to throw Mehmed off of him, and the sultan's son fell to the floor. Instantly he sat up, his eyes and mouth wide with surprise. Radu began to rush past him, but Mehmed was able to trip the boy enough to cause him to fall.

Struggling to get to his feet, Radu could feel Mehmed clutching his legs tightly. Looking back, he could see him smiling. Mehmed rose to his feet and pulled Radu closer. With a forceful kick, however, Radu freed himself of Mehmed's grasp for a second time.

Infuriated, Mehmed began charging. As he did so, Radu drew his sword. The weapon merely hung from his hand harmlessly. But Mehmed failed to stop, and the blade penetrated his side. He looked up from the wound at Radu, who looked equally as shocked. Backing off of the blade slowly, Mehmed held his hands over the wound. Following a quick glance at the gash, Mehmed's voice emitted slowly and drawn out.

"Owww."

Again his gaze met that of Radu and he laughed. Radu watched as Mehmed's eyes rolled up into the back of his head. Every muscle of his body locked when the sultan's son fell to the floor. His heart pounding, Radu fought through the tears and kept repeating the same words over and over.

"I didn't mean to...I didn't mean to."

Holding up the blade, he stared as Mehmed's blood gradually trickled toward the hilt. Hearing Mehmed groan caused him to look down. Panic-stricken and hyperventilating, Radu dropped the sword and ran. He nearly cleared the doorway before the metal finished clanging on the floor. He searched throughout the palace for a suitable hiding place. None existed. Through his tears, he found an exit outside, stared up into the high reaching branches of a tree, and began to climb after taking a quick look back toward the palace.

Radu grasped branch after branch, finally settling on one more than fifteen feet above ground. Breathless, he leaned against its bark and stared at the crescent moon, wondering how long it would be before he were found and executed. It did not happen before he quietly cried himself to sleep.

As the first rays of light penetrated the blanket of leaves and hit his eyelids, Radu woke groggily. Initially, he thought it might have all been some horrible nightmare. Feeling the abrasiveness of the tree bark and opening his eyes assured him otherwise.

Radu scanned the ground, certain there would be a horde of men trying to find him. He found the gardens vacant. Glancing toward the palace, he expected an entourage of the sultan's men to exit at any moment with swords drawn. An eternity passed before he decided to climb down. Halfway he lost his grip and, with a yell, crashed to the ground. After sitting up and rubbing his head, Radu heard chatter and saw the guards he anticipated earlier emerging from the palace. He attempted to scamper away to no avail. The guards caught him easily. Just as he had the night before, Radu kept repeating the same thing over and over.

"I didn't mean to."

The guards were all but dragging Radu as they entered Murad's throne room. His sobbing continued, and once he saw the sultan it escalated to all out bawling. Seeing the boy's state, the sultan tried to calm him.

"What's wrong, child?"

Radu looked and saw Mehmed standing next to his father. "Please, my liege, I didn't mean to." He then looked directly at Mehmed.

"Radu," said Murad. "My son has something he wishes to tell you."

Unwillingly, Mehmed spoke. "I am...sorry, Radu. I apologize for my behavior last night. My actions were demeaning to you and Allah, and it will never happen again."

Radu was amazed and, once Murad ordered Mehmed away, he concluded he would not be executed. Relief overcame him as he watched the sultan's son disappear and heard the sultan order him returned to join the other hostages. The guards nodded and led Radu down a corridor opposite the one Mehmed had traveled. As he entered the room, the eyes of all the others fixed on him, including those of Dragwlya, who sprung to his feet and rushed over to him.

"Did you really try to kill Mehmed last night?" Dragwlya's voice resonated with genuine pride.

The boy looked up into Dragwlya's eyes. "I...I didn't mean to. He...just wouldn't leave me alone, and when I tried to stop him...he just kept coming. I didn't even know it had happened until the blade stuck him."

Dragwlya's pride was replaced by disgust. "I see...We also heard you tried to escape. Is there any truth to that?"

"I...I was afraid. I ran out into the gardens and I...I..."

"You what?"

"I climbed a tree." The boy's head fell.

Dragwlya stared and sighed. "You are a disgrace to our family's name...Pathetic."

With all of his hatred, Radu screamed and lunged, but Dragwlya deftly dodged the attack and held out his leg for Radu to trip over. From the floor, Radu glared as anger continued to build within him. As he rose to his feet, Dragwlya began mocking him. Unsheathing an imaginary sword, he implored his brother to charge, laughing almost uncontrollably as Radu did so.

Once again Dragwlya moved out of the boy's way. He added to Radu's momentum by pushing him on the back. The younger of the two smashed into the wall and fell to the floor. He remained there and began sobbing. Dragwlya uttered only a single word.

"Weakling."

Castriota needed to see no more. He grabbed Dragwlya from behind by the shoulders before the boy knew what had happened and threw him against the wall. Dragwlya turned around and could see Castriota coming to grab him again.

Though he tried to fight his older opponent off, Dragwlya did so with no success. Castriota pinned his arms behind him and drove Dragwlya to his knees. "Doesn't feel as good when you're on the receiving end does it?" Dragwlya continued to struggle, trying to get free, but Castriota's grip was viselike. The older hostage looked over to Radu. "Come here," he commanded. Radu slowly got to his feet, rubbing his face where his cheek had met the wall. He walked toward Castriota.

The inclination to strike Dragwlya tempted Radu as he watched him trying to escape like a wild animal caught in a trap. Castriota urged the boy to act upon his impulses. "Do it! He deserves it!"

The boy studied his brother and then those around the room. "No. Let him go."

"What?"

"Let him go. Hitting him would only make me more like him…I don't want to be like him."

Castriota complied with Radu's wishes and let him go. Dragwlya spun, breathing heavily, and glared into the man's soul.

"I warned you not to touch me again." Dragwlya rounded to face Radu. His shoulders dropped, forced down with an exhale of frustration as he walked away and whispered just loudly enough for Radu to hear.

"Weakling."

CHAPTER XI
DEATHS IN THE FAMILY
TÎRGOVIŞTE
November 6, 1447

After being informed by Murad the lives of his sons had been spared, Dracul was offered renewed negotiations. Under the terms of the new treaty, he was obligated to expel more than four thousand Bulgarian refugees who had fled to Romania during the campaign of 1443, and ordered to abandon the fortress at Giurgiu and the other townships captured the prior year. By agreeing to the terms, Dracul provided Hunedoara the opportunity to set in motion the plan for his death and that of Mircea.

Hunedoara portrayed Dracul as treacherous and as the sultan's servant. Simultaneously, he attempted to find an ally to place on Wallachia's throne, eventually narrowing his choice to Vladislav Dăneşti. Already they had reached Tîrgovişte, intent on killing both Dracul and Mircea.

Light snow flurries fell as the sun began to sink below the horizon. Dracul stared at the flakes landing silently on the slow currents of the Dîmboviţa, a tranquil scene disturbed when Mircea flew into the room shouting.

"Father!"

Dracul turned with a jerk as his son rushed over to him.

"Hunedoara and Vladislav are here with a contingent!" Mircea explained as he caught his breath.

Dracul acknowledged him with a puzzled look. "What?"

"They are preparing to attack!"

Dracul recovered instantly. "I should have killed him before. Now I have even more reason to. Have the city gates closed."

"Yes, father." Mircea rushed out of the room and bumped Cneajna as he did. She stumbled backwards but managed to stay on her feet. Mircea apologized and continued his dash for the gates.

Dracul went over to her. "Are you all right?"

"I'm fine. What's the matter?"

"Hunedoara is here to remove me from the throne."

"What?" Cneajna gasped.

"Mircea is having the gates closed now. They won't get in...I have to ready the men." Watching Dracul rush off, Cneajna did not share his confidence.

Moments later, Dracul convened with his commanders. While briefing the men, one of his troops barged into the room. Dracul stopped in mid-sentence as he turned to look at the man. Concern overcame him as he took in the man's tattered uniform and witnessed his labored breathing. "What's happened?"

"Sire, we have been betrayed by the boyars. They have attacked the men stationed at the gates."

"What?" Dracul's concern was audible. "The gates," he uttered. "Where is Mircea?"

"The peasants have joined the boyars, sire. I believe they have captured him."

Dracul's face reddened with anger, fear, and frustration. "Find my son!"

"Yes, my lord."

"Now!"

As the man flew out of the room, Dracul turned and looked around at his commanders. "What are you still doing here? Get out there!"

The commanders answered in unison. "Yes, sire."

Dracul raced to the nearest window overlooking the gates of the city and tried desperately to pinpoint Mircea. All he saw was chaos. Beyond the gates, he could see the contingent coming for him.

Bastard.

Mircea slowly opened his eyes, the pain in his head bordering on unbearable. He could see torches all around him, but his vision was blurry. Lifting his head, he saw the trees reaching upward, seeming to embrace the early night sky. The pain hit harder. Lowering his head again, Mircea realized he was surrounded by some of the city's citizens and boyars.

A shadowy figure walked over to him and spoke. "Welcome back to the land of the living. Your stay will not be long."

"Where am I?"

The figure's face came into view, one Mircea recognized as a boyar. "You are at your funeral," he said pointing to something next to Mircea. With the words of the boyar striking fear into him, Mircea glanced hurriedly to see the shallow pit the boyar's finger was indicating.

Mircea tried to get up, but a tortuous searing sensation throughout his body was the only result. He looked down to see open fractures on both of his legs. Escape was impossible. The boyar motioned, and two other men came toward Mircea.

"Before you kill me and put me into that pit, tell me who gave the order for my assassination."

"You already know, but you are mistaken about one thing."

Mircea's response came in the form of an inquisitive stare.

"You will not be killed before being thrown in. You are to be buried alive."

"My father will kill you all!"

"Hold your tongue, Mircea. It would be wise to hold your breath as well." The boyar motioned again to the others as he laughed.

The two other men moved forward with the citizens cheering them on. One grabbed Mircea by the arms, the other by his feet. He screamed in agony from the intense pain that shot through him as his body was thrust up off the ground.

Holding Mircea next to the pit, they began swinging him back and forth and finally let go. Mircea screamed as he flew through the air and crashed into the side of the wall opposite of the one from which he had been thrown. His body rolled and, when he reached the bottom, he landed face down.

Spitting the dirt from out of his mouth, Mircea let out a meek moan. Tears of fear and pain flowed freely down his cheeks. He lay there helplessly, then in horror because of what he felt next. Dirt pounded his back, covering him like a damp, unwanted blanket. Eventually, the loose earth reached his head. He yelled, but no sound came out of his mouth. Within seconds, he was completely surrounded by darkness, unable to move. As he began to slip away into unconsciousness, Mircea's last thoughts focused entirely on Hunedoara and vengeance.

Dracul anxiously awaited news of Mircea's whereabouts. Hunedoara would soon enter the city, but Dracul became hopeful as one of his men entered the room. His hope was quickly extinguished.

"Sire, you must leave now."

"Have you found my son?"

The soldier looked at him, betraying none of the despair that filled him. "No, sire." Dracul sighed. "My lord, I fear that unless he has fled the city, you son is dead."

"You are right … He has left the city. I will contact him later…somehow."

"Of course, sire." The soldier briefly felt something he never expected to for his prince—pity.

Dracul and the soldier met with a small escape party assembled earlier. They traveled south toward the Danube, hoping to find refuge with the Turkish. All the while, Dracul hoped Mircea had in fact fled. Cneajna looked at him. Guilt and anger consumed every fiber of his being.

"It wasn't your fault. You couldn't have known-"

Dracul looked at her sorrowfully. "I should have known … I should have known better."

Dracul's party had nearly reached Snagov and could hear a rider approaching them relentlessly from behind. Soldiers quickly encircled Dracul and Cneajna for protection, until the approaching horseman was stopped and identified as Cazan, a loyal boyar and Dracul's former chancellor.

"Do you know where Mircea is?"

Cazan looked Dracul in the eyes as he answered. "I'm sorry, my lord. Mircea is dead."

Dracul stared at him in disbelief. "You are certain?" He asked, knowing full well that Cazan would not relate such news if he were the slightest bit uncertain.

"My lord, Mircea was taken by some of the boyars and citizens of the city and brought out into the forest. They beat him extensively, breaking both of his legs… He was then buried alive."

Cneajna had heard everything and instantly began to wail in disbelief, grieving the loss of the child she had raised as her own. Motioning to one of his men, Dracul had her taken away to avoid hearing any more. He stood motionless, absorbing what Cazan had just told him. After a moment, Dracul reached down to his side and took off the sheath holding the Toledo blade given to him in Nuremberg by Emperor Sigismund. He held it out for Cazan and, with apprehension, the boyar took the sword from him. Next, Dracul lowered his head, reached up, and removed the medallion from around his neck to give to Cazan as well.

"My lord, what are you doing?"

"Cazan, you are to give these to Vlad. Ride to Andrinople. Tell him everything that has transpired."

"It will be done, my lord."

"Leave immediately."

"Yes, my lord." Without another word, Cazan rode off the same way he had come.

Dracul watched the faithful boyar disappear into the darkness and then ordered his men back to their positions. Again they started for the Danube.

Cneajna had seen the transaction between Dracul and Cazan and considered the danger she and her husband were facing. She knew their chances of survival were small now that Dracul had entrusted another man with the duty of delivering two of his most prized possessions to his heir.

With the hour approaching midnight, Dracul inquired as to their location.

"My lord, we are nearing Bucharest."

They were approaching a small village surrounded by marshland. "What village is this?"

"Bălteni, my lord."

"We will stop for a few moments for the horses to drink."

"My lord, do you really wish to stop?" asked one of Dracul's soldiers.

"No, but the horses must have water."

They arrived at the edge of the marshland and tied up their horses, allowing the animals to drink. As the men sat, resting from the ride, Dracul decided to relieve himself.

Seeing him move away from the party, one of his men approached. "My lord, would you like someone to accompany you?"

Dracul answered him, "No, captain."

"As protection, sire."

"Sit and rest."

"Yes, my lord." The captain felt uneasy watching Dracul walk off into the marshes. Still, he did as instructed and returned to where the others were.

Dracul avoided the water as best as he could and settled on a spot. He looked around, fearing what might be hiding out there, shrouded by darkness. The hooting of an owl caused him to jump, and his heart seemed to penetrate his chest with every beat. Dracul cursed the creature, then himself for being so paranoid. Smiling as he reached into his britches, Dracul quietly mocked the owl's cry. His taunts ended abruptly though when he heard something else. More than the sound, however, there was a feeling something was watching him.

Dracul strained his eyes, trying desperately to fix his vision on whatever was out there. Now he could sense it was not something but *things*. He searched through the trees, attempting to see what the slight splashes now surrounding him were being caused by. The answer came soon enough. Something was running toward him. Dracul unsheathed his sword and focused on the shape as it emerged. It was someone, not something—one of Vladislav's men.

The soldier brandished a dagger in his right hand, and his movements were accompanied by the splashing of others. Dracul glanced around swiftly and, not surprisingly, found that some of his six or so attackers were boyars. He swung his blade as the first soldier lunged and made contact. Vladislav's soldier fell to his knees and watched aghast as his hand sailed through the air, still clutching the dagger. Dracul smirked at the sight of his victim holding his bleeding nub and turned to face another opponent.

The second assailant, yet another soldier, was more intelligent than the first in that he was armed with a sword instead of a dagger. Dracul sensed it would not be long before the group ambushed him simultaneously. Another soldier joined in the fight, and Dracul now constantly rotated back and forth to defend himself. As predicted, one of the boyars soon entered the fray, armed with a dagger. Dracul saw him out the corner of his eye and turned to face him. Overcome with fear, the boyar attempted to stop in his tracks but instead slipped and fell. Dracul smiled and rounded to continue fighting.

The soldier, whose hand Dracul had amputated, had used some rope intended for Dracul's neck as a tourniquet to slow his blood loss. Though weakened, he drew a second dagger and stared at Dracul. The Wallachian had disposed of one soldier and was about to be engaged by a boyar with the fortitude to actually face him. Staggering, the injured soldier headed back toward the melee.

Seeing the boyar before him raise his sword above his head, Dracul quickly raised his own weapon to block the blow. The wounded soldier, sensing Dracul's vulnerable position, realized his chance. Just as the boyar's blade clashed against Dracul's, the soldier with the severed hand charged.

Dracul winced as the small cold blade penetrated his body. He maintained his block, even as the amputee twisted the dagger farther into his flesh and called for everyone left to join in the killing. Dracul cried for help, an agonized scream that penetrated the marshes. Certain they had accomplished their task, the assassins removed their blood soaked blades and let Dracul's corpse collapse. Racing away from their victim, the soldiers and boyars glanced back to witness help arriving too late.

The escape party reached their fallen leader and could see the assassins slipping away into the darkness, their identities hidden. One arrogant assailant, however, began shouting.

"Death to the Devil!"

Everyone recognized the voice as that of a boyar, confirming the Wallachian had been murdered by his own countrymen.

Surrounding their fallen leader, Dracul's men stared, filled with a sense of failure. The soldier who had offered Dracul protection, and had been denied, bent down to raise Dracul's upper body out of the shallow water. As he lifted him up, Cneajna reached the small circle of men. She knew intuitively he had not survived the attack, and there was no hesitation as she pushed her way through.

Cneajna took a deep breath and then opened her eyes. The initial sight nearly broke her. She stared as the soldier held Dracul's head and torso out of the water, now a blackish-red color. She looked at her dead husband's face and exhaled violently. Her stomach grew queasy as she became lightheaded.

Seeing her state, the soldier holding Dracul ordered one of the others to escort her away. He then ordered the men to help him get the body out of the marsh. They lifted Dracul and somberly carried him away, each glancing at his face and at one another.

The sight repulsed them. No one had bothered to close Dracul's eyes. Each soldier had the sickening feeling of being glared at personally and of being asked why they had not stopped this from happening.

CHAPTER XII
NEXT IN LINE
ADRINOPLE
November 11, 1447

Those who had accompanied Dracul on his ill-fated journey had taken his body to the village of Dealul, where he was buried in a small chapel. Cazan, upon learning of Dracul's death, immediately left for Andrinople and reached his destination in five days. After meeting with the sultan, he was allowed to converse with Vlad privately.

Cazan had been led to a small room by one of the sultan's men, where he now sat silently. He was accompanied only by the Toledo blade, Dracul's medallion, and his thoughts. He had not enlightened Murad fully on the events responsible for his visit, just what was necessary to see Dracul's son.

The boyar rose as Vlad entered the room and found himself staring in amazement. Cazan felt he was seeing what Dracul must have looked like at sixteen. Before him stood a young man with flowing black hair past his shoulders, wearing the same upper lip-covering mustache as Dracul. The expression on Vlad's face teetered between determination and spite. His eyes held fire in them but were brutally cold.

Vlad's attention focused immediately on the Toledo blade. Once he passed through the room's doorway, the Turkish guard that had escorted him left and closed the door.

"Please, sit down," said Cazan motioning to a chair in front of Vlad.

The young prince slowly moved forward; his gaze transfixed on the sheathed blade. After Vlad sat, Cazan lowered himself into his own seat and continued to stare at the features of Vlad's face.

"I doubt you recall, but my name is–"

"Cazan…You served as my father's chancellor."

The boyar was taken aback at Vlad's recollection of him. "Yes."

Peering closer at the blade, Vlad realized his father's medallion rested alongside it. He looked up at Cazan with an inquisitive stare.

He knows, thought Cazan. "My visit is not a joyous one, I am afraid."

"My father is dead."

"Yes." The boyar's gaze never wavered. "I am truly sorry."

"How did it happen?"

From the moment he began his journey, Cazan tried to decide how he would tell Vlad not only about Dracul's assassination but that of Mircea as well. Even now he remained uncertain of what words would come out of his mouth. "Your father was killed by a small band of boyars and Vladislav's soldiers in the marshes of Bălteni. He has been buried in Dealul."

"How did you retrieve his blade and medallion?"

"I met with your father outside of Snagov five nights ago. He asked me to bring these to you, knowing his life may be in danger."

A horrible realization swept over Vlad. "Why didn't he ask you to give these to Mircea?"

"That very night, I informed your father of Mircea's death."

Knowing the response in advance failed to soften the blow. "How did he die?"

Cazan took a deep breath and lifted his head slightly before reluctantly divulging the gruesome details. "Your brother was captured by some of the boyars and peasants of Tîrgovişte. They beat him, tortured him, broke both of his legs, and buried him alive."

Vlad's face was emotionless, but each word Cazan spoke enriched his desire for revenge.

"I will avenge the deaths of my father and brother. Vladislav's death will be by my own hands." Vlad's intentions were displayed clearly by his eyes. His words were unnecessary.

"Prince Vlad, I present you the Toledo blade given to your father by Emperor Sigismund and his medallion, investing you as a member of the Order of the Dragon."

Cazan's sentence was nearly interrupted by the guard who had led him to the room.

"I suppose this means our meeting is adjourned," said Cazan.

"It does," responded Vlad.

Cazan rose. Vlad did likewise, picking up the blade and medallion before falling in behind him. The boyar turned and faced the young man as he neared the doorway. "Your father was a great crusader and a very wise man. Learn from the mistakes he made. There were not many, but they were costly."

"I do not make mistakes. I force others to."

Vengeance was tangible in the room as Vlad's words resonated. Cazan turned around and once again headed for the doorway. Vlad attempted to follow but was instructed by the guard to sit back down.

Sitting alone, Vlad held up his newly acquired medallion. Rays of light danced on it as he slowly rotated it in the air. Vlad stared at the dragon and silently reaffirmed his vow to his father and brother.

You will be avenged.

CHAPTER XIII
SHORT REIGN
TÎRGOVIŞTE
December 23, 1448

Murad officially informed Vlad of the assassinations of his father and brother at the end of last year, prompting a series of unsuccessful escape attempts. Even after being caught and punished each time, Vlad persisted. Growing tiresome of this continuous battle, the sultan decided to end it by making him an officer at court and his candidate for Wallachia's throne last summer. Vlad now awaited his opportunity to strike at Vladislav II.

Castriota, whom Murad called Iskander, a reference to Alexander the Great, had been given the title of bey by the sultan. This proved insufficient to keep him from deserting. During Castriota's flight from Andrinople to Albania, those accompanying him heard the Turkish calling out his name as they pursued. "Iskander Bey" was heard, however, as "Skanderbeg." The name became Castriota's new identity for his new position, leader of the Albanian army. Skanderbeg had since aligned with Hunedoara.

In his attempt to establish an anti-Ottoman front along the Danube, Hunedoara entered deep into Turkish territory by way of Serbia and planned to have Skanderbeg's army join his own. By combining forces, Hunedoara, Skanderbeg, and Vladislav would penetrate farther into Turkish territory along the Danube. The plan failed to unfold as envisioned.

Hunedoara began mobilizing his troops and had Vladislav flank his left side, while Skanderbeg's men constituted the rear guard. They reached Kosovo Polje on October 14, 1448, but Turkish spies had relayed their movements the entire time. Murad's beys were informed of the army's exact location and, after extensive planning, the second battle of the Field of the Black Birds began three days later.

During the first two days of battle, the ranks of the Christian army were almost totally decimated. Its sole defense now rested on the remainder of the Albanian rear guard. For Hunedoara, it was Varna all over again. In desperation, he ordered Skanderbeg's contingent to advance in an attempt to save what remained of the Hungarian and Wallachian contingents.

The order was refused.

Skanderbeg retreated north, planning his escape so that its route would take him through George Branković's principality. It had been one of many looted by the Christian army as it had passed through the countryside. Upon setting foot on Branković's land, Skanderbeg was taken prisoner.

Hunedoara barely managed to escape. His men had abandoned him, and to many he seemed to simply have disappeared. Like Skanderbeg, Hunedoara headed north through Branković's principality. He too was arrested. Branković had him sent to Smederevo.

The defeat of the Christians signaled to Vlad he should begin his quest for the throne of Wallachia. He gained support from the Danubian pasha, Mustafa Hassan, who supplied him with a Turkish cavalry and a contingent of troops. Although the campaign was successful, Vlad realized his political survival depended greatly upon Murad's continued success.

To Vlad, the capturing of his throne had been almost entirely meaningless. No one of consequence had been killed in its attainment, and his father and brother had not been avenged. Already he had been asked by Vice-Governor of Transylvania Nicolae of Ocna to explain his sudden coup in person. Knowledge regarding the whereabouts of Hunedoara was requested as well. Vlad refused to appear and instead sent correspondence.

> Forgive me, but I am unable to meet with you. To do so would only arouse suspicions in the mind of the sultan who would have me killed at his earliest convenience. I have no official information pertaining to Governor Hunedoara, but believe him to have been killed in battle. If he should return to Transylvania, however, I will do my best to establish peace with him.

For three days and nights Murad had remained at Kosovo Polje, burying his dead. In doing so, he had allowed the remnants of the Christian army an uncontested retreat. Vladislav was among the survivors. The deposed prince gained the assistance of the prince of Moldavia, Petru II, and persuaded the remnants of the Hungarian army to join him in an attempt to retake his throne from Vlad Dracul's son. Since that time, Vladislav had crossed the Danube and had reached Tîrgoviște.

Snow covered the ground, reflecting the red hue of the early morning rays that shone in a cloudless sky. Vladislav was ready to order the attack.

Although only seventeen, Vlad understood that because of Murad's negligence, he would not control Wallachia after today. The young prince's men were outnumbered and overmatched. Vlad stared and surveyed from the safety of his castle. More than anything, he wished to rush out and kill Vladislav. Wisdom forced him to concede that any attempt to do so would be futile and fatal. Knowing revenge would have to wait, Vlad made plans to flee back to Murad's court.

"Are you ready, my lord?"

The prince remained quiet and continued to stare at the invaders. A moment passed before he simply shook his head to indicate to the guard he was not.

"Very well, my lord." The guard exited after answering.

Focused solely on the army before him, Vlad thought about the past two months.

Sleepless nights plagued with the need for revenge and the hours pondering the possibility of his assassination had become countless. With the impulse to stay and fight welling up inside him again, Vlad called for the guard once more and turned away from the window once the man made his presence known.

"We shall leave shortly."

After acknowledging the prince, the soldier waited for further instructions. Vlad turned to view the scene again. He could hear preparatory commands being shouted by Vladislav's commanders and then the battle began. Consumed mostly by disappointment, the prince watched as the enemy rushed toward his city and tried not to think of how long it would be before he ruled again. Disgusted, he watched his soldiers being overrun like children and decided to leave immediately. He turned slowly and walked past the Turkish guard without saying a word.

CHAPTER XIV
DRAGWLYA MEETS STEPHEN
SUCEAVA
December 30, 1449

During two months of captivity, Hunedoara negotiated a deal with George Branković. In exchange of his freedom and other concessions, his son, Matthias, would marry Elizabeth Cilli, Branković's daughter. Hunedoara's return had not been joyous. The peasant's *White Knight* had lost much prestige and power, and the titles of viceroy of Hungary and governor of Transylvania had been stripped by Ladislas and the Hungarian Diet. Having never been fully accepting of Hunedoara, the diet was glad to be rid of him.

Hunedoara did retain the titles of count of Bistrița, Severin, and Timișoara; still controlled vast estates in Transylvania; and remained supreme military commander on the eastern front. He also remained in command of an important army of mercenaries now gathered at his castle.

Upon reaching Andrinople, Vlad learned Radu had repeatedly fulfilled Mehmed's lustful desires. Radu was now both Mehmed's protégé and minion. Additionally, he had become a full-fledged officer in the sultan's court. Such circumstances made Vlad's decision to flee to Moldavia easy. The principality was ruled by his uncle, Bogdan II, and Vlad felt he would receive a positive reception. He traveled north, following the Siret River until finally reaching Suceava.

Vlad's trek was long and made alone. Throughout the journey he questioned not attempting to kill Vladislav. His reasons increasingly sounded like excuses and were intensified by an unsettling reality—he would have to wait for another opportunity to rule and had no idea when or how that chance would arise.

A guard stopped him as he reached the main entrance of Bogdan's castle shortly before noon.

"What do you want?"

"I am here to see my uncle." Vlad's response was solemn.

"And who would that be?" asked the guard sarcastically.

Vlad was growing more impatient by the moment, but because he was wearing no visible signs of royalty, the guard's adherence to his duty was justified. "Prince Bogdan."

"And who might you be, sir?"

An incredulous stare answered the guard's query first. "Prince Vlad III, son of Vlad the Great, sovereign and ruler of Ungro-Wallachia." Vlad's tone and menacing emerald eyes prompted the guard to act quickly.

"Forgive me, my lord. Come with me," the guard urged. Vlad was ushered in and brought to Bogdan's throne room.

Once the guard entered, Vlad sighed heavily, his patience exhausted. Seconds later, Vlad entered just as the guard was about to announce his arrival.

Seeing his uncle stirred within Vlad images of his father. They looked similar despite Bogdan's lack of a moustache and chestnut colored hair, were approximately the same age, and each demanded total respect. Bogdan rose from his throne and walked over to him. His smile was comforting.

"Vlad, what are you doing here?"

Bowing slightly, Vlad answered, "Good morning, uncle. I require asylum from the Turkish."

Bogdan stared at his nephew and saw both physical weariness and mental anguish. "I always have room for family."

Vlad managed a weak smile, "Thank you, uncle."

"I suggest you rest now. We can speak later. My guard will show you to your room."

Vlad thanked Bogdan once more for his hospitality as the prince motioned for the guard to escort his newly arrived guest to his quarters.

A younger man entered in time to catch a glimpse of Vlad being led away. "Who was that?"

Bogdan turned and saw his son, Stephen, standing there. He looked very much like Bogdan and had an even greater commanding presence. "Your cousin…Vlad."

"Vlad?" said Stephen in surprise. "I believed him to be in Andrinople. How did he-"

"I don't know. He looked too exhausted to carry on a conversation. I'll let him rest before asking him. Don't you have a lesson soon?"

Stephen sighed. "Don't I always?"

"Go on."

"Yes, father."

Unwillingly, Stephen exited through the same door he had entered. Bogdan smiled as he did so. His son's intelligence, at fifteen years of age, rivaled that of many of his tutors. Bogdan constantly procured monks and other scholars to teach his son new ideas and innovations. His greatest hope was that Stephen would someday be able to use what he learned to rule Moldavia wisely.

Vlad woke from much needed sleep later that afternoon. He stretched his arms above his head and heard voices in the corridor—his uncle's and a younger man whom he did not recognize. It felt as if he had not used his legs in years. His knees cracked as he stood, and stiffness in every muscle reminded him of the journey he had recently completed. Reaching the door, Vlad listened to the second voice again. Still unaware who it belonged to, he opened the door.

Seeing Vlad emerge from the room, Bogdan spoke. "Ah, good afternoon. I trust you slept well?"

"Very well. Thank you."

"Vlad, I would like you to meet your cousin, Stephen."

Stephen's face was charged with energy. He extended his hand. "Pleased to meet you."

Vlad reached to shake the young man's hand.

"Supper is almost prepared. I would like you to join us to discuss the events responsible for your being here…among other matters."

Once in the dining hall, Vlad explained what had led to his flight to Moldavia, including the gory details of both Dracul and Mircea's deaths and Radu's indoctrination.

"I could not stay any longer," said Vlad. "Mehmed is practically sultan and is unlike Murad in every way. Wallachia will never be under my control again if I leave the decision to the Turkish."

Bogdan had lost his appetite during Vlad's account of Mircea's assassination. Since then he had hung on his young nephew's every word. Stephen was equally shocked at the gruesome way his cousin had detailed his father and brother's deaths. Vlad simply continued to eat ravenously.

"And what of your mother?" asked Bogdan.

Dragwlya swallowed a mouthful of food before answering. "She has gone back to Sighişoara."

"Well," said Bogdan, "I have heard enough. You are welcome here for as long as you wish."

"Your generosity is appreciated."

Astonished at all his cousin had endured, Stephen found his own life comparatively uneventful.

"Stephen is tutored daily by the finest scholars. If you wish, you may join him in his lessons," said Bogdan. "It would give you a chance to continue your Romanian education where you left off."

"I would be foolish to decline such a gracious offer. Thank you."

From across the table, Stephen let out a sigh of relief. "At least I won't suffer alone."

"Ignorance is a man's worst enemy, Stephen. Ignorance makes slaves of men."

"Someone else who understands that besides me," Bogdan said.

"Maybe I shall someday acquire the knowledge to see things as you do, father."

"Knowledge is a raw material. Your father also possesses the wisdom to use it."

Bogdan was almost relieved at the course the conversation had taken. "I think having you here will do Stephen a world of good."

"I will be happy to help in any way possible, uncle." Knowing he may someday need Stephen's aide in regaining his throne, Vlad was willing to provide his assistance.

Like his cousin, Stephen knew he might someday need an ally as well.

Over the next few months, Vlad and Stephen's friendship grew, as did their passion for their respective thrones. Their competitiveness drove one another. Daily they pushed one another to the brink of what they were capable of physically and mentally. They forced one another to be smarter, stronger, faster, better. They learned together the evils polluting their world and quickly recognized the life of a prince could mean a lifetime struggle, depending upon how one maintained order and control.

CHAPTER XV
THE OATH
CRASNA
June 14, 1450

Smoke from the cannon fire had overpowered Crasna for three days. Supplies were running low and fear infected the men like the plague, threatening to break their spirits at any moment. Now, at the onset of dusk, all was quiet as Vlad and Stephen sat staring at Bogdan in the command tent.

The Moldavian prince had mobilized to counter the invading Polish force and had brought his son and nephew along. They may as well have been brothers. As Bogdan paced nervously, Vlad and Stephen continuously glanced at one another. Finally, one of them broke the silence.

"If I may offer a suggestion."

Bogdan stopped and turned. The prince's stare instantly met the dark emerald eyes of his nephew.

Vlad rose to his feet slowly and kept constant eye contact with Bogdan. "We are still outnumbered at least two-to-one. We must exploit our advantage. We know the landscape far better than the Polish. There has to be something about the land that they have yet to discover; something we can use to defeat them."

Stephen's stare was fixed upon his cousin. "We have been over the maps hundreds, thousands of times. There's nothing."

Vlad peered down at his younger cousin. "There has to be something."

"He's right, Vlad. There is nothing." Bogdan sounded resigned to defeat.

Vlad walked intently to a table where maps of the area were lying. Bogdan and Stephen looked on and shook their heads as the young man studied the parchment. Tracing a path with his finger, Vlad suddenly stopped and tapped the spot with an upbeat rhythm. A wry grin appeared.

"There is something."

Bogdan and Stephen exchanged glances of bewilderment as they moved toward the table. Bogdan stared at Vlad's finger then, not comprehending, looked at his nephew. "What?"

Stephen tried in vain to see what his cousin was showing them, but whatever it was remained completely oblivious to them both.

"I knew you wouldn't see it," said Vlad proudly. "It's too obvious."

Bogdan and Stephen scrutinized the map harder, still not comprehending.

"What's too obvious?" asked Bogdan.

Vlad exhaled a silent laugh as he faced the prince. "This is where the Polish have chosen to encamp, correct?" he asked tapping the map. "Why has it taken us so long to realize he is already virtually surrounded?"

Bogdan and Stephen peered closer at the map and finally realized what Vlad was talking about. Before them was a militaristic blunder of Varna-like proportions. They had encamped in an enclosure of hills. There were only two passages, one leading to Poland and the other to Moldavia. Bogdan drew back from the table enlightened and looked at Vlad, nodding his head in approval.

"If we had realized this sooner, this battle would be over," said Bogdan.

"We know now," said Vlad.

Bogdan nodded. "Ready the men."

While the Polish army rested, Moldavia's troops prepared for the surprise attack. Hours before dawn, Bogdan's soldiers began their march. They moved toward the encampment in three separate groups; one led by Bogdan, another led by Vlad and Stephen, and the third by one of Bogdan's captains. Scouting parties were sent earlier to quiet any Polish spies. Bogdan knew Ladislas would become suspicious once the spies stopped reporting. Timing meant everything if this attack was to succeed.

They were within half a mile when Bogdan decided to deploy. Silently, the contingents began moving toward their respective positions.

Lying in his bed, Casimir Jagiello, king of Poland, dreamt of his armies overtaking the Moldavians. Cannon fire rang in his head as his men shouted cries of charge, while the opposing force screamed in terror. The king stirred a little bit, marveling at how easily his enemy was being defeated.

Casimir's dream was interrupted when one of his men rushed into his tent, yelling frantically. Still somewhat in a haze, Casimir realized the sounds of battle were real. The dream was a waking nightmare.

"Your highness, the Moldavians are attacking!"

"How did they reach us without us knowing?" Still awaiting an answer as he raced out of his tent, Casimir hurriedly looked around at a camp that had erupted into utter chaos. He stared, mouth agape, in disbelief at the contingent of Bogdan's men being led through the passage opening toward Moldavia. Retreat was his first instinct, but the thought was quickly shattered once he turned and saw the passage to Poland had been cut off.

Rushing back into his tent, the king suddenly stopped, shocked by the exclamation he heard being shouted by his men. He looked out and confirmed for himself that a third contingent was moving in from the surrounding hills. Cursing his oversight, Casimir prepared himself for the attack. Frantically he dressed, armed himself, and ran out into the midst of the battle. His army, which once outnumbered the Moldavians three-to-one, now teetered on the edge of annihilation.

Vlad and Stephen continued to advance the blockade and attack from the passage facing Poland. They had made it around the hills undetected, making the trap flawless. As he rode into the enemy camp, Vlad swung his blade at anyone who dared approach him. There was a devilish grin on his face as he ran his victims through. It was a smile of exhilaration, of pleasure.

Bogdan's force continued to move in from the Moldavian side, and finally the Polish lost any hope of victory. Casimir stared at the spectacle, cursing himself for making such an idiotic mistake. He prayed he would one day be able to rectify it.

SUCEAVA
June 15, 1450

No one slept. The victory celebration had lasted well into the morning hours, and Vlad and Stephen observed the festivities from atop Bogdan's castle. They listened to the music as the wind whipped around them and watched people dancing to lively melodies being played.

"We fought well, cousin."

Stephen chuckled slightly. "If not for your scrutiny, we may not have been here to talk about it."

Vlad nodded his head slowly as he answered. "True. But a plan is nothing without proper execution. Not all of the success was my doing…I wish to make a pact with you, Stephen."

Stephen's response came with a hint of uneasiness. "What do you mean?"

The familiar wry grin had returned to Vlad's face once more, and his eyes commanded Stephen not to look away.

"Do you believe as relatives we should assist one another whenever possible?"

"I suppose." Stephen's tone asked what course this line of questioning was forging.

"Good. Then I offer that whichever one of us reaches his throne first shall help the other gain their throne. Agreed?" Vlad extended his right hand.

Stephen extended his hand. The wind began to gust around them, drowning out the music and revelers below, while flashes of lightning flickered in the distance. "Agreed."

"You will not regret this, Stephen." Unsure of how to answer, Stephen allowed the moment to pass without uttering a word. "We appear to be in the path of a storm," said Vlad moving his attention away from his cousin.

Stephen stood silently, oblivious to what Vlad had just said. His concentration was consumed by the oath he had just taken.

"The celebration might be forced to come to an end after all. What do you think?" Vlad turned and saw his cousin standing there with a blank stare. "Stephen?"

Suddenly back in the moment, Stephen spoke. "It seems as though it is going to rain."

Vlad smiled as he again looked down on the crowd. "Do not worry, Stephen. I will keep my word. I swear it."

"I do not doubt you. I only wonder which of us will be helping the other."

"Hopefully *neither* of us will. Perhaps we shall gain our thrones simultaneously."

"I doubt we will be so fortuitous."

Vlad could sense Stephen's anxiety. "I am sure the time will come soon for one of us to sit on the throne."

"If it is to be soon, then I hope it is you who will rule first."

Vlad gazed toward the horizon. The faces of his father and Mircea stared back at him from the heavens, asking when they would be avenged. Stephen had said something, but Vlad was not paying attention. He only answered the images he saw before him. "Soon...I promise."

"What?"

Vlad regained his composure and looked at Stephen before improvising an answer. "The storm. It will be here soon."

"Perhaps we should go inside now."

"You go on. I wish to be alone for awhile."

"I'll see you in the morning then." Without waiting for a response, Stephen turned away, allowing his cousin his desired solitude. While walking, he glanced back, wondering why Vlad's demeanor had changed so quickly. He also wondered what purpose there was in Vlad asking him to take such an oath. Stephen genuinely hoped he would never need to fulfill such an agreement. He was not ready to face the world without his father, and circumstances might change. Having Vlad on Wallachia's throne may not always be in his best interest.

CHAPTER XVI
MEHMED SECURES HIS THRONE
THE ISLAND IN THE TUNCA
February 3, 1451

Today marked a new beginning. The start of a new year would be celebrated through-out the Ottoman Empire with no one reveling more than Murad. At winter's onset, he had retired to the island in the Tunca River near Andrinople, as was his custom. It was his refuge. Here he would forget the past year's disappointments and find some sem-blance of peace from the rigors of ruling. Construction had even begun on a new palace to provide extra seclusion.

Though known to binge occasionally, no previous experience compared to this spectacle. With the new year's celebration providing an incentive, Murad's indulgence in alcohol was unparalleled.

"More…Now!"

Murad had not slept in more than seventy-two hours, a direct result of a chance encounter. While crossing into Andrinople from the island, he was approached by an almost hysterical dervish. At the time, Murad's only companions had been two of his intimates, Saruca Pasha and Ishak Pasha. Out of his respect for the dervishes, the sultan, against his intimates' protests, allowed the man to address him. He would soon com-mit himself to heed his intimates' advice more stringently in the future, what little of it remained.

The meeting lasted a scant fifteen minutes, but it was long enough to send Murad's thoughts reeling. Pleasantries lasted only seconds as the dervish quickly began fore-telling the futures of both Murad and the empire. The prophecies terrified the sultan enough that he immediately returned to the island and forgot his business in Andri-nople. During the brief exchange, the dervish informed Murad his death was imminent. The dervish was a pupil of Sheikh Buhari, who thirty years earlier predicted Murad's victory over Düzme Mustafa, a pretender to the throne. That lineage added immensely to the sultan's fear.

Since the meeting with the dervish, the thought of his own death never left Murad's mind. He continued to drink, hoping to quell the premonition. But the wine only inten-sified it and created the false hope that the next cup would bring with it relief.

One tremendous gulp emptied the chalice in Murad's hand. He waited for a few seconds, waited for the instant when his only thoughts would be in the moment and about the festivities that surrounded him. Concentrating on forgetting only made the memory of the dervish's words more vivid. The notion he would never forget angered Murad enough that his chalice flew across the room. All heard the mixture of the cup clanging against first the wall and then the floor coupled with Murad's scream, a cry of pain, of emotional distress.

Only Murad's intimates understood what he was screaming about when he began begging Allah for forgiveness and pleading for his life to be spared. His cries for mercy, however, quickly became shrieks of unbearable torture. Sweat seeped through his skin. Mehmed's once articulate words became garbled gibberish. His eyes rolled upward, and the world grew dark as he lost all bodily sensation. His face slammed hard onto the table before him. No one paid him much mind. Everyone had seen this happen before and, as always, the sultan's attendants rushed to his side to assist putting him to bed.

As they grabbed Murad, the servants realized something was different. The sultan had always responded to being carried out. He would complain he had no need for sleep and that he wished to continue drinking. His body had never felt so lifeless. They stopped and tried to rouse him.

Ishak Pasha searched to find Saruca Pasha once he learned Murad had not responded to any of the servants' inquiries. It took only a second for him to recall the words the dervish had delivered on the bridge, and he considered the ramifications Murad's death would have for him personally. He started after being tugged at from behind and found Saruca clutching his garb with an expression of shock and fear.

"Something's wrong," said Saruca.

"I know, come with me."

Quickly, Ishak led Saruca to the spot where the servants were holding the body of Murad. One of them looked up as the intimates arrived.

"We cannot wake him."

Ishak was quick to respond and act. "Nonsense!" Flinging aside the servant's concern, Ishak motioned for Saruca to help him lift Murad off of the floor. "Come, my liege. You have indulged enough this evening…The new year will have to continue without you for awhile…You," he said to the servant, "tell Halil Pasha he is to come to the sultan's chambers immediately."

Ishak and Saruca laid Murad's body on his bed and simply stared. Without saying a word, thousands of thoughts flew between them, each presenting a scenario worse than the one previous.

"Damn the dervishes," Saruca allowed the comment to pass under his breath.

"Hold your tongue, Saruca, lest they damn you."

Saruca offered a quick prayer to Allah. "What do you think Halil will do?"

"He will do what has always been done—keep the sultan's death a secret from the population until a successor has been named."

"Do you think that is possible?"

"Why not?"

"You saw the servants' faces…They know. And many will not be pleased with the thought of Mehmed becoming sultan once again, especially the Janissaries. His accession will be opposed."

The door to the room opened and closed just as quickly.

"Is he dead?" Halil Pasha entered like a whisper and spoke in a voice marginally above one.

Ishak regarded the sultan's grand vizier with certainty. "He is."

"Who else knows?"

"No one else knows," answered Ishak.

"We must inform Mehmed at once."

"Are you certain that is what you want, Halil?" asked Saruca.

Halil had been staring at Murad's body, knowing the duties that were his to carry out. Unlike Saruca, there was no question in his mind that the tasks must be performed. Despite the fact he would be endangering his own life, Halil would do that which Murad had entrusted him to do. "There is no choice. I must obey my master's orders."

Saruca nearly laughed. "You pushed for Mehmed to relinquish the throne and retire to Anatolia. Do you have any idea what will happen once Mehmed is enthroned again?"

"No...I don't." Halil took his eyes off of his fallen master's body to look at Saruca. "Do you know what will happen to the empire without a sultan to rule it?" Saruca flinched and moved his stare away from Halil's as the grand vizier continued. "I may die, but I will do so for Allah. Fearing what *may* happen is not an option...Mehmed will do what he sees fit...regardless of the advice he is given."

MANISA
February 9, 1451

Less than an hour after sunrise, Mehmed felt too much of the day had already been wasted. After breakfast, he decided to explore his surroundings on horseback. Just yesterday he had broken in the latest addition to his stable, an Arabian stallion. Much like himself, he found the beast headstrong, unwilling to comply. Unlike himself, the horse would not ultimately have its own way.

Mehmed approached the stables, ready to take on the day's next challenge. Murad had charged him with selecting a suitable site nearby for a palace to be built. It would serve as the vacation home for Mehmed's half-brother, currently only eight months old. To Mehmed the child was a rival, not a relative.

Since being relieved of the duties of sultan, mundane tasks such as this were all Mehmed had been given to do. He knew Grand Vizier Halil Pasha's insistence was to blame for his short reign.

He has instilled in my father the notion that I am unworthy.

Truthfully, Mehmed's gluttony for everything fine and expensive brought with it fear and loathing from many who felt the empire was plummeting into decadence. Those closest to Murad made certain he understood what would become of the Ottoman Empire should his son be allowed to continue on in such fashion. Murad ignored most of their counsel but not that of Halil.

What's this?

An odd scene was forming as Mehmed drew closer to his destination. Many of his servants and guards had gathered, along with someone he did not recognize—a messenger it appeared.

"Good morning, my liege." The messenger greeted Mehmed before he even dismounted. "I have traveled from Andrinople at the command of Halil Pasha to bring you this."

Hearing the grand vizier's name had brought feelings of ill-will to the forefront of Mehmed's mind. Those thoughts were heightened as the messenger produced a sealed parchment and handed it to him. Taking the correspondence from the man, Mehmed broke the seal and unfolded it. Halil's signature flashed in his eyes and Mehmed flushed with hatred. The feeling passed once he began to read.

Breathing heavily, Mehmed let his hand holding the letter fall. He saw everyone, including the messenger, eagerly awaiting what they presumed to be terrible news.

"The sultan is dead."

A few gasps were uttered, but most were muted by grief. The empire had prospered greatly under Murad, and his benevolence was unmatched. He had made war only when draw into it by other nations, for the protection of what belonged to him. Everyone understood Mehmed's ideology was far different.

Amidst absolute quiet, Mehmed remounted his stallion and peered over the crowd.

"Let those who love me, follow me."

Without another word, Mehmed turned the stallion around and raced off. He would travel north to Andrinople as Halil had requested. Every moment of his journey would be plagued with thoughts of revolution and treason. Solutions must be found immediately to combat those who would oppose him.

ADRINOPLE
February 15, 1451

Preparations were made secretly for Mehmed's arrival by the viziers. They had ridden out to greet him earlier in the afternoon as he approached the city and, hoping to avoid much notice, hurriedly ushered him into the palace. Few suspicions were aroused, but some wondered about the unexpected presence of Mehmed and the disappearance of his father. The populace had not seen Murad for twelve days.

Mehmed gave no thought to sleeping tonight. Remaining awake and waiting would be agonizing, but soon enough the ceremony enthroning him would take place. Then he would set in motion plans for the empire he had held in reserve while his father still lived. Closing his eyes, Mehmed released breath fueled by content. Everything would proceed as he desired. Nothing could deter the inevitable.

Violently the doors of Mehmed's chamber flung open. The eruption of sound forced him out of bed in one fluid motion as he reached for the nearest weapon. His hands found the handle of a sword and he grabbed it to guard himself from his attacker. Only a winded bey appeared though.

Ali Bey held his hands up in a defensive posture, trying desperately to regain enough air to explain why he had burst into the private chamber of the sultan unannounced.

"I beg you, forgive this most horrid intrusion, my liege!"

Mehmed's chest heaved as the man assured he meant no harm.

"What is the meaning of this? I should strike you down where you stand!"

Ali's posture remained defensive as the sultan's sword remained cocked and ready to fall upon him at the slightest hint of treachery. "My liege, it is imperative that you listen to me… A Janissary happened upon the body of your father and has escaped from the palace, intent on making his death known. By tomorrow all of Andrinople will know. You must remain here. I have posted guards outside your doors to protect you from any insurrection."

Mehmed's transition to power had run too smoothly thus far. This sudden complication did not surprise him.

Allah has always had mysterious ways of testing me. I would have expected no less.

"What is being done now?"

"A contingent has been dispatched in an attempt to track down the Janissary and return him to the palace, my liege." Ali Bey was certain the sultan would react with more concern. Mehmed's lack of emotion forced Ali Bey to reevaluate some of the feelings he harbored about Mehmed, but the sultan's mind was suddenly elsewhere. Something about this struck him as peculiar.

"Why you?"

Seeing the sultan lower his sword, Ali allowed his own hands to relax from the position they had instinctively taken. "My liege?"

"Why have *you* come to warn me? Surely you could have sent someone else as you made your way out to capture the Janissary."

Shame resonated in Ali's voice as he answered. "Forgive me, my liege, but it was I who had the final chance of confining the Janissary to the palace. I failed. That is why I felt I should be the one to inform you."

"I see."

The simple two-word answer frightened Ali. Mehmed's reputation for having a short temper was now being tested. How long would it be before the sultan allowed his true self to be revealed?

"Do all you can to arrest the Janissary and bring him back to the palace...You are free to go now."

Relief filled Ali as he stared at Mehmed. "Thank you for your leniency, my liege. I vow to never fail you in my duties again."

With a wave of his hand Mehmed dismissed the man once more and watched him leave. Somehow he would make the bey understand the importance of not disappointing him. For now, he let the matter rest. It was more important that the revelation of his father's death to the general population did not interfere with the future of his empire.

A sense of futility invaded Mehmed's mind once he realized there was no course of action for him to take to stop word from spreading. He would not rush out into the night after the Janissary and place his own life in danger. He couldn't. Once again, Mehmed knew he would have to do what he had done to reach this point. He would have to adapt.

ADRINOPLE
February 18, 1451

Further attempts by the viziers to convince Mehmed to wait proved pointless. They pleaded for him to be patient until his safety could be assured. He assured them absolute safety would never exist. Arrangements for the ceremony continued well into the morning hours.

Much of the populace remained uncertain as to whether the ceremony would actually occur. Those in Mehmed's household, those who truly knew him, understood that once he ordered something to take place it would take place. After thirteen days, efforts to keep Murad's death a secret had failed. After only three days, the entirety of Andrinople and much of the surrounding area knew.

Not caring about the concerns of the viziers or the possible dangers he faced, Mehmed allowed the idea of becoming sultan again to drive him. He would rule as he pleased, without worry of repercussions from his father. Mehmed would be free to do as he wished. Free to conquer the West.

Uncertainty due to unsettling fear best described the attitudes of the nobles and viziers gathered around the new sultan. None of them knew what their position would now be, or if they would have one for that matter. Some wondered if they would be executed for having a role in prematurely ending Mehmed's previous reign. None felt comfort of any kind as the sultan addressed them.

They are afraid... They should be. Unfortunately, I need most of them to ensure as little upheaval as possible. I demand their respect and obedience... nothing more. In time that respect will come through fear. For now, I am content just to have their attention.

"Why do my viziers stand aloof?"

The room had been in near silence before Mehmed's statement, and his voice nearly deafened everyone. They stared at him then at one another, trying to determine exactly what it was they should be doing. Mehmed's question had been directed to Sihabeddin Pasha, the former chief of eunuchs, who stood to his immediate right. It was to him that he gave his first order as sultan.

"Call them, and tell Halil to take his accustomed place. As for Ishak, let him as governor of Anatolia accompany my father's corpse to Bursa."

Within moments, a quiet processional began as the pillars of Murad's reign approached Mehmed. Halil led the others to their fate and now stood before their new master. Those present found what occurred next to be miraculous.

All remained silent as Mehmed extended his arm and offered his hand to Halil. With only slight hesitation the vizier knelt down. Taking the sultan's hand into his own, he gently kissed and released it.

They trust Halil's judgment... They will follow his lead.

"You are all to be confirmed in your previous positions. Your service and loyalty to my father were unmatched. I know you will serve me in the same manner."

After confirming his father's subjects, Mehmed called for his stepmother. This was their first meeting since his arrival. As she was beckoned to do so, she bowed and began to approach him. Seeing her only stirred hatred within Mehmed; hatred for her and for what she and Murad had created. After being married to Mehmed's father for twenty-six years, she gave birth to a rival.

Mehmed suddenly held up his hand, an indication for the woman to wait before coming any farther. Out of the corner of his eye, the sultan spotted Ali Bey and called for him.

With a bow, Ali spoke. "Yes, my liege?"

Mehmed's voice was a whisper. "Go to this woman's quarters and drown her son."

The order had been given without a hint of remorse, so much so that Ali needed a moment to process what he had been ordered to do. The expression on his face, however, never changed.

"My liege?" Ali's hushed tone voiced thousands of questions.

Mehmed threw the man a look of impatience and unquestionable authority. "Have you forgotten your vow so quickly?"

Guilt shone through Ali's eyes as he remembered his failure to stop the Janissary from escaping the palace. "I... have not forgotten, my liege. My duty will not go unfulfilled."

"It would be a shame if you were to fail me again... Go."

Bowing somberly, Ali swallowed the lump in his throat and began the journey to the quarters of Mehmed's half-brother, Ahmed. Once he had left, Mehmed again beckoned his stepmother to approach. She greeted him in proper fashion, acknowledged him as sultan, and almost immediately displayed grief over the loss of her husband. Mehmed offered her words of comfort as they exchanged memories of Murad. Their dialogue continued for nearly ten minutes before being interrupted by the frantic cries of a servant woman screaming for Mehmed's stepmother.

The sultan smiled as the woman turned with panic in her eyes. Mehmed glanced skyward.

I hope you are watching, father. This is the proper way to rule an empire.

Looking around his throne room and court, Mehmed eventually focused his stare on Radu. Dracul's son followed him virtually everywhere. No question existed as to why the Wallachian was kept so close. The smirk on the sultan's face grew larger, sinister. Radu tried desperately to look away but could not. His gaze was fixed on Mehmed's menacing grin.

"What is it? What's wrong?" Murad's widow shouted, knowing the matter must be serious for the servant to impose upon the audience in this manner.

The woman regained enough breath to say one word. "Ahmed."

Murad's widow read the expression on the woman's face and immediately ran toward her chamber. She raced to her son, growing increasingly worried. Upon entering his room, she searched but could not find the child. The other woman finally caught up to her as she turned to search elsewhere.

"Where is he?"

Breathlessly the woman answered, "In the baths."

Panic-stricken, Murad's widow ran again and found a crowd already there. She slowed as their faces confirmed what she already knew. Her stomach twisted as she passed through them, making it difficult to breathe. Then she saw him.

There, lying motionless on the floor, was Ahmed. Falling to her knees by his side, she screamed his name. She collapsed over him, and his cold, wet skin pressed against her as she cradled the boy in her arms. Slowly she began rocking back and forth, all the while talking to the child, insisting that he awaken and answer her. Tears streamed down her face as she stared at his pale body and wide-eyed expression. Her son had drowned. The marks on the back of his neck betrayed that he had been held down. Murdered.

The crowd parted for Mehmed. He immediately turned his attention to Ali Bey, now kneeling beside the grieving mother.

"What has happened?" Mehmed asked Ali.

"The boy has...drowned, my liege." Ali barely got the words out of his throat.

Mehmed glanced at the woman. "Someone take her away from here."

Ali moved closer and made the mistake of looking into the widow's eyes as he tried prying the boy away from her. The pain she felt swelled in him also, making him wish he too were dead. Lifting her off of the floor, he began leading her out of the room. He walked past the sultan and exchanged with him a long, knowing stare. Ali wanted to strike him with more force than he possessed. Fully aware of the consequences, he merely looked away in disgust; disgust meant more for himself than for the sultan.

Mehmed looked at the child and shook his head. "A sad accident. Another tragic death." Nearly all of the viziers had followed the sultan, including Ishak. "Ishak, you will carry my brother's body with you to Anatolia, along with my father's."

"Yes, my liege."

While a guard came forward to retrieve the small body, Mehmed spoke just loudly enough so everyone in the room could hear him. "May you already be with Allah... my brother." Mehmed shot his gaze around at the people still in the room. "I wish to be alone. Everyone leave."

Once he was the solitary soul in the baths, Mehmed silently addressed his father.

I did only what needed to be done. The child belongs with you. I am rightfully sultan and will not leave myself vulnerable to assassination by having another who carries your blood in his veins at my court. You created the child in life, care for him now in death.

OUTSIDE OF SUCEAVA
October 27, 1451

Mehmed's ascension to the throne brought with it the promise of peace, albeit at a price. Not everyone conceded as easily as he wished, and the Moldavian boyars were incensed that their prince was one such person.

Bogdan flatly refused to pay a tribute that would have included livestock, gold, and peasants to be given up as slaves, making him so unpopular with the nobility they planned his assassination. Another claimant to the throne, Aaron Petru, had been championed by them already. He served as leader of the rival faction and was Bogdan's brother.

Petru had been awaiting an opportunity to gain the throne since last year and, after much consideration, uneasily decided with the boyars that today was his time. Much preparation had gone into Bogdan's demise, and the greatest advantage the current prince's enemies possessed was the overwhelming amount of families wishing to simply appease Mehmed, regardless of the cost or suffering it brought the common people.

We should not be here.

For at least the thousandth time the thought passed through Vlad's head. He shared this feeling with his uncle every time the opportunity presented itself and was always casually dismissed. Bogdan felt his nephew was far too concerned, far too cautious about even the minutest details. Vlad saw his uncle as careless and unwilling to listen to reason.

After declining to partake in the festivities, Vlad watched alongside Stephen as Bogdan merrily danced with the other guests. A reception was now being held in celebration of a wedding that had taken place earlier for the son of one of the boyars. Knowing the boyars' pro-Turkish attitude, Bogdan had been somewhat wary of attending but felt the gesture of accepting the invitation should be made. Vlad and Stephen could not have disagreed more.

Together they watched the prince laugh and sing as the music carried him in circles far from them to the other side of the hall. The reception had lasted for nearly six hours now and most everyone had become intoxicated, including Bogdan. Their senses dulled, the guests hardly felt it when someone else bumped into them or when they themselves stumbled and interfered with the dancing of another guest.

Each time he passed before his son and nephew, Bogdan waved and tried emphatically to coax them into joining the jubilation. They always refused, preferring to keep a watchful eye on as many of those in attendance as possible. With a dismissing gesture, Bogdan again was whisked across the floor.

At the farthest point he could be away from Vlad and Stephen, Bogdan lost his place in the dance and appeared confused. He looked around, spinning slowly, trying to figure out what to do. Another one hundred and eighty degree turn put the prince face-to-face with his nephew and son.

Vlad knew something was wrong. He stared at his uncle and grabbed Stephen's arm, forcing his eyes to look in the same direction. Seemingly paralyzed they stood there, trying to move toward him, trying to understand what was happening. The look of gaiety had vanished from Bogdan's face completely, replaced by one of shock. Vlad saw his lips move.

"What did he say?" asked Vlad.

"I don't know." Stephen's reply bordered on frantic as he finally broke free of whatever force had held him back for this long and took his first step toward his father. Doing so, both he and his cousin watched Bogdan drop to his knees and then face first to the floor. They made a mad dash toward him, forcing those around Bogdan to stop their celebrating long enough to discover what had happened.

Gradually the onlookers grew until everyone was simply standing and staring as Stephen and Vlad flipped Bogdan back over to ascertain what had happened. Immediately Stephen began to question his father, trying to extract some answer from him that made sense. Propping up his father from the back, Stephen felt what he perceived to be sweat drenched clothing. He swore he could feel the perspiration running down his arm. Then the gasps and screams started.

"Father, what's wrong?"

Vlad was the first of the two to understand completely=. Bogdan's blood had begun to pool on the floor. Without any explanation, Vlad gently took his uncle by the shoulders and turned his body slowly. Now they both understood. Bogdan had been stabbed numerous times. Upon seeing the wounds, Vlad's eyes quickly darted from guest to guest, searching for the perpetrator. Everyone looked guilty. Bogdan's guards were now arriving at their fallen leader's side.

Resting Bogdan on his back once more, Vlad stared into his uncle's eyes, knowing that the injuries were fatal. The prince coughed up blood as Stephen looked to his cousin for a reassuring sign that could not be given. Looking back to his father, he could see him slipping away. Then, with one last rise and fall of his chest, he breathed no more.

The hall erupted into chaos as guests, fearing for their own safety, fled. Soon only the conspirators would remain, wanting to confirm for themselves Bogdan's death. Vlad could see tears forming in Stephen eyes and instantly began thinking of his own father and brother's assassinations. He knew Stephen's feelings and suffering all too well.

"Stephen, we must take your father and leave now."

Stephen failed to answer and continued to stare at his father in disbelief.

"Stephen, I understand what you are feeling, believe me. But you must regain your senses now."

Vlad's words had no effect. He sighed and looked down at his uncle. Grabbing his cousin by the shoulders, Vlad forced Stephen to see him. "You don't have time to mourn!" He shook him, snapping the young man out of his trance-like state.

"You're right. Petru will arrive soon with an army to continue his attempt at stealing my throne…We must be ready."

With a sigh almost of relief, Vlad motioned to some of the gathered guards to help carry the prince's body. Stephen felt queasy standing up and nearly vomited as he began to stare at everyone present in turn. Intensely, he searched for any hint as to the identity of his father's assassin.

Grabbing his cousin's arm gently, Vlad spoke. "Stephen. We have to-" He cut off his own sentence after seeing the expression of hatred and rage on Stephen's face. "Stephen?"

Wrenching his arm free from his cousin, Stephen addressed no one in particular. "I *will* find you and exact revenge! Your treachery will not go unpunished!" He turned to face Vlad. "Let's go."

The short journey home seemed to last a fortnight. Silently, the mourners carried the body into the castle's chapel and laid it in front of the altar. Vlad dismissed the guards once Bogdan's corpse had been put down and then spoke freely with Stephen.

"Stephen, we have major decisions to make immediately."

"I know," said Stephen thoughtfully. "I just–I just never prepared for this. I never thought-"

"Neither did I when it happened to me, but it did. We must decide how to defend ourselves and retaliate. We don't have the forces to compete with Petru. He has the support of all the boyars now…Their will is his will." Vlad thought for a moment. "We have to go to Transylvania."

"What? That's not an *option*…With Hunedoara in charge of all military operations on the eastern side of Transylvania, that's suicide!"

"We can make it through."

Stephen felt no confidence in the suggestion. "Where will we go then? Bistritz?"

"No. We'll take the Borgo Pass toward Sighişoara and from there go to Braşov. They have no interest in backing Vladislav. I am positive I could gain support there."

Stephen shook his head in disbelief. His father had been killed. Now, his cousin's plan to escape their own deaths included fleeing through territory controlled by the man who had masterminded the murders of Vlad's own father and brother. For a moment Stephen mentally searched for another viable option. There was none. "When do we leave?"

Vlad nodded his head, aware of just how much Stephen trusted him. "As soon as possible."

"As soon as I settle all the necessary arrangements for my father."

"Agreed." Vlad could see the fear and anxiety swallowing Stephen. "The time for your revenge will come, just as mine will. Right now you have to suppress your feelings and do what is best for your own survival."

Stephen answered by nodding his head.

"Go make the arrangements for your father."

CHAPTER XVII
SANCTUARY
NEAR BRAŞOV
March 8, 1452

Vlad and Stephen reached Braşov unscathed in January. For much of the month conditions appeared favorable for Vlad to begin a campaign for his throne, but changes in February drastically affected his fortune.

After learning Vlad was residing in Braşov, Hunedoara demanded the mayor and city council expel him from the country. Together, Vlad and Stephen fled once more. This time their paths led in separate directions, however, with Stephen returning to Moldavia.

At the beginning of February, an even more inferior candidate had replaced Petru. Stephen surmised the campaign for his throne would begin shortly. Vlad deliberated extensively about joining his cousin but finally decided to risk staying in Transylvania. His flight from Braşov would not lead him as far as Stephen's had.

Not until sundown did Vlad leave Braşov. Hoping to gain refuge at the estate of a certain boyar, he ventured south. With the moon reaching its zenith, Vlad's destination came into view.

The estate seemed to rival the Carpathians in height and was larger than Vlad expected. A sense of urgency compelling him, he hastened through the gate and proceeded to the main entrance. Now less than a foot away from the door, he raised his hand to grab the knocker and, grasping the cold iron, hurriedly knocked three times.

Nearly deafened by the sound that broke the stillness of the night, Vlad released the knocker and whirled around. It felt like someone were right over his shoulder, but nothing out of the ordinary appeared as he searched through the shadows. Behind him the door creaked open slightly. With a quick jerk, he turned and saw a woman regarding him severely.

Cautiously, the woman allowed the door to open farther until finally she was in full view. She looked to be in her mid-thirties, her short, thin body just tall enough that her head reached Vlad's nose. She was visibly intimidated, and her voice shook slightly as she spoke. "May I help you?"

Though within he felt the need to turn around once more and make certain no one had followed him, Vlad managed to keep from showing the woman how much his flight had affected him. "I am Prince Vlad III of Wallachia. Is your master at home?"

His statement surprised the woman. Princes did not normally make such evening excursions and, to her knowledge, Vladislav II was the reigning prince of Wallachia. "He is. Is he expecting you...sire?"

"No. But I must speak with him."

"Please come in." The woman called him sire as a courtesy, just in case he was the prince. Moving away from the door, she motioned for Vlad to enter.

No longer resisting the urge, Vlad stole one last glance behind before entering. By this time, his eyes were more adjusted to the interior of the estate than they were the outside. All he saw was darkness.

"Wait here please."

Vlad turned to see the woman walking down a corridor. When she finally disappeared, he began taking in his surroundings. Fine vases and extraordinary portraits hung on the walls, one in particular immediately captured his attention. He stared at it, examining every inch. The portrait was of a middle-aged man with almond-shaped, emerald-green eyes and a curled up mustache. Determination radiated off the canvas from him.

"He was a great man...and a good friend."

Vlad smiled as he heard the voice. He turned around and saw Cazan staring at the painting.

Cazan moved his glance to Vlad. "I thought you might come here."

"Then you know why I am here."

"Everyone knows." Cazan walked toward Vlad, stopping a few feet before him. "Hunedoara hated your father... He hated Mircea. He will not rest until the name Vlad Dracul is forgotten entirely and all who are of his blood have been exterminated."

Vlad looked at him smirking. "Plans often change. If nothing else, I am certain of that."

Cazan knew he was right and chuckled. Vlad laughed as well. "You may stay here if you wish."

"Humbly, I accept your offer. My imposition will not last long."

Cazan shook his head. "There is no imposition. Come, you must be hungry."

"I would prefer a bed to anything else right now."

"Very well then, my lord. Tomorrow we shall have breakfast and can talk then."

Gradually, the morning light crept up the side of Vlad's bed. When it reached his eyelids, Vlad immediately opened them. He lie in bed awake, feeling the warmth of the rays as they illuminated his room. Stretching and yawning, Vlad sat up and threw the covers off. He set his feet on the floor, rubbed his eyes, and stood to begin dressing.

Cazan sat at the dining hall table and ate breakfast, waiting for Vlad to join him. He looked out a large window that gave him a complete view of his garden behind the estate. Cazan smiled, remembering the way he and his wife would share one of the benches nestled among the shrubs so long ago. Twenty-three years had passed since he had lost her. Still she was in his thoughts every day. The way she looked, the way she spoke, the way she moved, every nuance remained fresh in his mind. Hearing Vlad's voice caused the memory to fade.

"Good morning, Cazan."

The boyar stood. "Good morning, sire. I trust you slept well."

"Very much so. I hardly wanted to get out of bed this morning." Vlad pulled out a chair across from Cazan and sat down. A few seconds passed before he spoke. "What do you want to ask me?"

Cazan lowered himself into his chair once more and laid down his utensils, which for some reason he had not thought to let go of when he rose to bid Vlad good morning. He did so now to keep himself from eating anymore before his guest was served.

"I realize how little time you have had to contemplate this, but what are your intentions? Or would you rather wait until you have eaten to discuss such matters?"

"I have been running for years. Your realization is correct. I have not been able to plan for my future as necessary. I have not lost my desire for my throne, Cazan. Before long you will witness how hungry I truly am."

ANDRINOPLE
March 15, 1452

Mehmed peered at the full moon as he traveled the streets incognito. Ventures such as this accompanied only by two intimates were frequent and allowed him time to think. Tonight, roaming aimlessly, he thought only of conquering Constantinople and Emperor Constantine XI Dragases.

As he walked, Mehmed became enthralled with the very idea of Constantinople being in his possession. He imagined ruling his empire from the great city and pictured himself at the altar of the Hagia Sophia, proclaiming the Moslem creed. Just as he finished reciting it to himself, a man approached him and proclaimed, "Long live."

The unwanted interloper had recognized the sultan and greeted him customarily. Mehmed cursed the man audibly. Undetected, the sultan pulled a hidden dagger from its sheath and stabbed the man four times in the abdomen before he continued on. Mehmed pondered the challenge of Constantinople, growing more frustrated until resolving to seek the advice of another. Swiftly he returned to his palace.

Halil Pasha yawned as he was led to the sultan's chambers. With him he carried a golden bowl and the question of why he had been dragged out of bed at such an absurd hour. He was instructed to enter and, looking back, watched as the guards left. His hand trembled slightly as he reached for the handle and, turning it, he let out a tremendous sigh.

Sitting on his bed, Mehmed remained fully dressed from his walk. Halil stared at him and could see the sultan was lost in thought. Cautiously, he approached. A few seconds passed before Mehmed looked up with a sudden jerk to find Halil standing before him. The sultan's attention was immediately drawn to the bowl. Almost instantly Halil laid the present at Mehmed's feet.

"What is that for?" asked Mehmed eyeing the vizier.

Halil looked at the bowl and then back at the sultan as he rose to full height. "Custom decrees that when a noble is summoned to his master at an unusual hour, he must not appear with empty hands."

Mehmed closed his eyes and shook his head. "I have no need of your gold. I only want your help in taking possession of Constantinople."

Halil closed his eyes and began praying to Allah. He knew this day would come. He knew Mehmed would attempt this and had even told Emperor Constantine of the young man's ambitions. Most European leaders believed that Mehmed would be easily manipulated. They were mistaken, and Halil knew it. He opened his eyes again and saw determination and desire in the eyes of the sultan.

"Allah has already subjected the greater part of the Greek territories to you, my master. Certainly he will grant you possession of the capital as well. Even now your servants vie with one another by sacrificing their wealth and very blood to realize that end."

Mehmed stood up and placed a hand on Halil's left shoulder. He gestured down. "I have tossed and turned for many nights in that bed...Riches, power...They will weaken you if you let them. I must not let my wealth soften me, my men, or you. I need your help. With your guidance we will fight bravely. Through the power of Allah and his prophet, by Allah's grace, we will take the city!"

"Do you wish to begin your conquest of the imperial city now, master?"

Mehmed looked at the vizier and laughed. "No. I am sorry to have brought you here so late in the evening. Go. I will call for you later."

"Thank you, master." Halil bowed and left the room. He glanced back at the sultan, who was now walking around his room, apparently rejuvenated.

The vizier closed the door behind him and leaned his back against it. *May Allah have mercy on those whom he conquers.*

CHAPTER XVIII
FAILED ASSASSINATION
CAZAN'S ESTATE
September 26, 1452

Against the advice of his host, Vlad returned to Braşov frequently to continue planning for a campaign. Eventually, his ventures proved costly. Upon learning that Vlad was still residing in the vicinity, Vladislav sent an official letter of protest to the mayor. Cazan learned of the correspondence.

The sun had just finished its climb over the horizon. Vlad sat in the dining hall, eating breakfast. He stared out into the garden, remembering the night he first arrived. Stabbing at a piece of sausage with his knife, Vlad's thoughts turned to Vladislav. Repeatedly he thrust the knife, ravaging the piece of meat, imagining it to be his adversary. Cazan entered as the prince struck down his breakfast.

"Your situation has become more problematic."

Realizing Cazan was talking to him, Vlad looked up from his plate inquisitively.

"Two days ago, the mayor of Braşov received a letter from Vladislav."

Vlad immediately stared down at the mutilated meat on his plate.

"He's demanding you be driven out of the country."

Vlad looked out into the garden again. "Hmpfh."

"I suggest you leave at nightfall, my lord."

Vlad immediately turned toward Cazan. "You believe I should go?"

"For your own safety, yes. Stay here long enough, and they will find you. If they find you, they will kill you." An awkward silence followed before Cazan continued. "I have made arrangements for you in Sibiu."

Vlad continued to sit, silently staring out of the window. As Cazan awaited a reply, Vlad contemplated his situation. Forcing a sigh, he nodded.

"I shall go."

Relief overcame Cazan. "Good. This is for the best."

Vlad shook his head negatively. "My father and brother should have been avenged by now."

Cazan put his hand on Vlad's shoulder and stared at him. "Leaving is the only course of action that guarantees you will someday have another chance."

HUNEDOARA CASTLE
October 7, 1452

A steady, heavy rain fell as Hunedoara's morning grew more dismal with each passing second. Before him stood a messenger from Sibiu. The boy, no more than fourteen, shivered as water dripped from his soaked clothes, forming a puddle around his feet. News of Vlad's short flight from Braşov to there outraged Hunedoara. He sat and scrutinized every inch of the letter the mayor of Sibiu had sent. After reading the correspondence for a fifth time, Hunedoara crumpled it up and threw it.

"Damn!"

The sound of Hunedoara slamming a fist down on his chair rivaled the thunder outside and more than startled the messenger. Hunedoara looked at the trembling boy.

"Get him dried off and fed." Hunedoara pondered this latest predicament as the boy was led away. Only after some thought did he finally give the appearance of satisfaction and rise from his chair. "Have a messenger prepare to ride."

OCNA
October 14, 1452

Reading the penned words of Hunedoara, Vice-Governor of Transylvania Nicolae of Ocna realized the ex-governor was not wasting any more time. Hunedoara was no longer trying merely to have Vlad expelled from Romania. His letter proved his intent to fully exterminate Dracul's family.

October 7, 1452

Nicolae,

Dracul's son has completely ignored all orders to exile himself. You are now charged with the task of ridding the country of him once and for all. He is staying in Sibiu. The authorities there have already been alerted to his presence, but have been unsuccessful in driving him out.

Vlad has been seen in the village of Gioagiu where some are trying to reestablish him on the throne. You will hire an assassin to plan an ambush in Gioagiu. If possible, they should kill the conspiring boyars as well.

Ioan Hunedoara

GIOAGIU
October 22, 1452

Vlad neared the village of Gioagiu to meet with some anti-Vladislav boyars as the sun set. By the time he reached the agreed upon meeting place, darkness had already descended. He knocked and the door was answered by the same servant who always opened it. She led him to the room they had been meeting in since Vlad first fled to Sibiu. He was welcomed by the boyars and others loyal to him.

"Good evening, sire," said one of the boyars.

Vlad felt undeserving of the title. "Good evening."

Everyone in the room rose to their feet as Vlad progressed toward the head of the table. After he pulled out his chair and sat down, the others followed suit. Vlad then examined the small council before him and was dismayed with his assessment.

I would be better off if they were helping Vladislav.

Suddenly, the doors of the room were flung open. Vlad stared at the wiry young man who had rushed into the room. He stopped a few feet in front of the table, his chest heaving.

"I assume," said Vlad, "you have an excellent explanation for your actions. For your sake, I hope I am right."

The young man answered as he struggled for air. "Sire...you have to leave...now! Assassins...Assassins have been...hired to kill you...tonight! It is a miracle you made it here alive."

"Assassins hired by whom?"

The young man's answer was timid. "Nicolae of Ocna and Ioan Hunedoara." He swore Vlad's emerald eyes turned blazing red at the mention of the second name.

"Get out," said Vlad.

The young man quickly left.

Vlad began mumbling softly to himself, envisioning the faces of Nicolae of Ocna and Hunedoara. His tone became a roar, cursing the vice-governor and the former governor of Transylvania. One of the boyars dared to make a suggestion.

"Sire, we should plan your escape immediately."

Vlad just looked at the man. "I am tired of running."

His comment made the boyars wonder if he might actually be contemplating resisting an ambush meant to assassinate him. Instantaneously, he put their minds at ease.

"This will be the *last* time."

Upon learning the assassins were approaching from the north, a plan was devised and implemented for an escape south toward Tîrgovişte. Vlad became convinced they had lost Hunedoara's men only after the party had reached Poenari. While his men set up camp, Vlad walked alone. He looked over the land and was struck by one particular bluff above the Argeş River.

On the left bank, ruins of a castle erected over a hundred years ago by one of the early Basarab princes remained. Vlad stared across the Argeş and realized how strategic a position the castle had occupied. Something else caught his eye. On the right bank, Vlad could see the foundation for a rather large structure had been laid, a castle to be constructed under his grandfather's reign. His father had considered completing the project. Obviously, he never had the chance.

I will complete what you began, grandfather.

CHAPTER XIX
THE BASILICA
THE VICINITY OF ANDRINOPLE
November 4, 1452

Mehmed's vision of a conquered Constantinople materialized more with each passing day. Earlier in the year, the sultan began his quest by trying to disprove the notion the Greco-Venetian fleet was superior to his own. He declared the Bosporus impassable to all nations who refused to pay an allotted fee, consequently provoking attacks. To continue the enforcement of this declaration, the sultan also ordered the building of a fortress on the European side of the strait.

The castle was constructed at the narrowest point of the Bosporus. Its placement virtually guaranteed the sultan the ability to destroy any ship trying to pass. For this reason the fortress, which had been erected in less than five months, became known as Cutthroat Castle. Sinking ships was not, however, to be the only means by which Mehmed would accomplish his objective.

Mehmed looked on in delight as the *Basilica*, his newest toy, was prepped for its initial test shot. It was an oversized cannon Mehmed commissioned specially for Constantinople. He had been fascinated by cannons ever since his father had told him how Vlad's brother and father successfully used the weapon at the sieges of Petretz and of Giurgiu in 1445. Now he watched as Urban, the weapon's calibrator, made final adjustments.

Urban was also the cannon's forger, a Braşovian whom the sultan had made a deal with to produce his awesome weapon. The forger's name had been made known to the sultan after his enemy, Emperor Constantine, rejected the price of Urban's cannon as unjustifiable. For Mehmed, no amount was too great if it meant conquering Constantinople.

Shortly after construction of Cutthroat Castle began, Mehmed sent for Urban and posed the question, "What is the largest cannon you can construct that would be capable of battering down the huge walls built by Emperor Heraclius?" The artisan's answer was now before him.

The *Basilica*, twenty-seven feet long with a forty-eight inch bore, was capable of firing projectiles weighing six hundred pounds propelled by one hundred and fifty pounds of gunpowder. More than seven hundred men and fifteen pair of oxen finally positioned the weapon.

"How much longer?"

Urban continued to motion to the men working the cannon as he answered. "Almost ready, my liege." He then yelled to the men. "Halt! Clear out the animals!"

Mehmed watched the exodus of men and beast moving away from the most powerful force ever devised. He watched Urban speak with the weapon's operators, men the forger had brought with him from Braşov. The sultan was unable to make sense of the instructions Urban gave. Abruptly, the team of firing experts left and headed toward the *Basilica*. Mehmed followed them with his eyes for a second and then focused on Urban, now approaching him.

"It won't be long now, my liege!" Urban could see anxiety had taken control of Mehmed. He had urged the operators to work quickly.

"Good. The sooner I know my arsenal, the sooner I can plan against my enemy."

By this time the operators had recruited a few of the cannon movers to load the *Basilica* and were now in the process of finishing the task. One of the operators looked back and waved his arm. Urban did the same. Lowering his arm, he faced the sultan. "We must find a suitable observation point."

Mehmed nodded and began backing away. Continuously, he looked over his shoulder as he and Urban made their way to a small ridge that would serve as a barrier against any falling debris capable of injuring them. Eagerly, they stood behind the natural bunker, awaiting the shot sure to be heard throughout the Islamic World signaling the end of Christianity.

"Ready, my liege?"

The answer came quickly as Mehmed, too excited to answer verbally, nodded. Urban, aware of Mehmed's lack of patience, raised his arm. Seeing him do so, the canon operator did the same in reply. Urban lowered his arm and faced the sultan once again.

"You should cover your ears, my liege."

Paying him no heed, Mehmed instead just stood expressionless, mesmerized by the weapon. He stared hard, squinting to see the experts fire the weapon. The sound of the gunpowder igniting was the most tremendous boom the world had ever known. Hundreds of men crouched and grabbed at their ears, trying desperately to block the noise. Urban stood still with his fingers protecting his eardrums as he watched the sultan do something very impulsive and incredibly idiotic.

Before Urban could stop him, Mehmed was standing on top of their protective bunker, following the projectile with his eyes as it sailed effortlessly through the sky. Gravity began to pull it back to earth as Urban continuously shouted at Mehmed to return to safety. The sultan, however, refused Urban's pleas, mostly because of his reverie with his newly acquired prize. Then the shockwave hit him. It slammed into the sultan, throwing him back forcibly enough that he fell off the rocks. By the time Urban reacted, Mehmed had collided with the ground but was already springing back to his feet.

Rubbing his head, Mehmed perched himself atop the bunker in time to see the immense object shot from the *Basilica* force its way into the earth. Hearing the sound of the crash, Mehmed allowed an overjoyed smile to cross his face as a fairly sizable mushroom shaped dust cloud appeared. Mehmed looked at Urban and nodded in approval.

"You have done well. You shall be rewarded handsomely."

Now approaching the impact crater, Mehmed watched as the dust cloud crawled toward Andrinople. He was genuinely awestruck and stopped at the crater's edge. At its center, the hole was no less than ten feet deep, funneling up to a diameter of approximately thirty feet. Mehmed failed to find words to express his feelings.

"Are you satisfied, my liege?"

The sultan's eyes were opened wide.

"Yes." Mehmed repeated the word four more times before finally breaking his gaze from the crater to look at Urban. "You have done me a great service, Urban. I am more than satisfied."

"You received only that which you have paid for, my liege."

"The price was well worth it."

For a moment, silence filled the air, enveloping the two of them just as the *Basilica's* cloud of dust had enveloped a small portion of Andrinople.

"There are a few limitations you should know about, my liege." Urban's voice was timid as he prepared to give the sultan important instructions about the cannon.

"What do you mean...limitations?" The smile disappeared from Mehmed's face, along with his budding satisfaction.

"My liege, because of the cannon's massive size, you will be limited in its use. First, you will always need the men and oxen you saw here today to move it. Second, because of the enormous amount of heat produced by firing the weapon, you must limit yourself to using the *Basilica* no more than seven times a day. Anymore than that and you would be risking a very powerful and deadly explosion."

Mehmed transfixed completely on the number Urban had uttered. "Only seven times per day?"

The words rang in Urban's ears louder than the firing of the *Basilica*. "My liege, this cannon will do more damage with seven shots than all the others you have will do combined in the same amount of time." Urban prayed Mehmed would agree.

Silently stroking his beard, Mehmed turned his attention back to the crater. He glanced upward as though he were awaiting some advice from Allah. Seeing Mehmed was in serious doubt, Urban quickly thought of something to say.

"The *Basilica* is meant for an initial attack."

Urban's words began to work their way into Mehmed's thoughts. Slowly, the sultan began to agree. He began nodding his head again. "Yes." Looking back at the *Basilica* he continued. "This weapon has been designed to strike first, sending my enemies into a frenzy. It is not meant for continuous assault. It should be used to weaken strategic points for the smaller cannons in my arsenal."

The sultan's explanation sounded logical to Urban. In fact, the forger wished he had thought of it himself. "Yes, my liege. Now you understand."

Mehmed continued to nod his head, simply repeating the word "yes" while picturing the walls of Constantinople crumbling under the assault of his army.

HUNEDOARA CASTLE
February 19, 1453

The past four months had brought dramatic changes. One, creating the most controversy, was the union of the Orthodox and Catholic churches. Though agreed to by the emperor, nearly everyone despised the marriage. No pious Orthodox Christian would seriously entertain the notion of attending a mass at the Cathedral of St. Sophia. Some of the union's effects were more impactful, particularly for Wallachia.

In January, it became apparent Hunedoara disapproved of Vladislav, especially his relationship with the Turkish. Urged by his boyar council, the prince completely turned his back on those who had helped him gain the throne and adopted a pro-Turkish stance. In an attempt to dissuade Vladislav, Hunedoara seized the duchies of Făgăraş and Amlaş, the latter he gave to the citizens of Sibiu. Făgăraş and its surrounding territories he kept for himself.

Hunedoara's ploy failed, and hostilities between he and Vladislav grew until the ex-governor decided to remove Vladislav from the throne. Unfortunately, he lacked the key element to carry out his plan—a candidate to replace the current Wallachian prince.

Deciding to come here had been torturous. Vlad had contemplated this scenario since the night on the Bluff of Poenari when he vowed to accomplish what his grandfather had abandoned. Only after seeing how deteriorated the relationship between Hunedoara and Vladislav had become did he finally choose to ask for the unthinkable— help from his family's murderer.

One would never have guessed it was early afternoon. Black clouds dominated the sky, strangling the sunlight. Vlad's doubt increased with each step. How could he possibly make peace with this man? Vlad's hatred for Hunedoara had never ceased growing. There would never be peace, merely a cease fire.

If he did manage to come to terms with the ex-governor, Vlad knew he would always have the feeling somewhere in his mind that an alliance betrayed his father and brother. Apprehension wormed its way into his head and he thought of turning back, heading away from Hunedoara's castle for the millionth time. And yet, he knew Hunedoara was his only real chance of regaining the throne.

Vlad's concentration was snapped by a flash of lightning that lit up the castle before him and a crash of thunder that somewhat startled him. He gasped, quickly glancing up at the same time, and viewed the home of Ioan Hunedoara. Lightning illuminated every last detail of the edifice. He stared and examined every inch of brick and mortar, until the last arch and line were committed to memory. In many ways it reminded him of a cathedral. Any holy resemblance, however, was overshadowed by the thought of the devil lurking within. Hesitantly, Vlad proceeded.

In the Knight's Room of his castle, Hunedoara sat quietly and listened as the council members each took their turn to comment on the two acceptable courses of action that could be taken. The motions were now repetitive, making Hunedoara impatient with the bickering group.

"Enough!" Hunedoara's voice quieted the others as he stood up. "I am tired of arguing this like children! Vladislav has conceded to the Turkish. We need to oust him before Mehmed begins occupying the area."

One of the seven council members was bold enough to argue his case against that strategy again, inciting a peer to challenge him. Again it appeared the room would erupt into a shouting match once more when a knock at the door forced everyone's stare to breakaway. The handle turned and, as the door slowly opened, one of Hunedoara's guards occupied the entrance. He was a man of great height and build, intimidating to most. Still, he crept into the room nervously and stood motionless after he had closed the door.

Hunedoara looked at the man, waiting for him to speak. Finally, he provoked the seemingly mute guard. "Yes, what is it?"

The guard tried to speak, but his parched throat did not allow him to do so. He swallowed what little saliva he could accumulate and began. "Sir, there is someone here who wishes to speak to you. He says it is quite urgent and that he must meet with you immediately."

Hunedoara could see the man getting more uncomfortable and tried to speak calmly. "Who is it?"

The guard answered reluctantly. "Vlad Dragwlya, sir."

Hunedoara asked the guard to repeat the name, certain he had imagined what he had heard.

"Vlad Dragwlya, sir," answered the guard once more.

Hunedoara remained quiet and tried to bring himself out of the state of shock he had entered seconds ago. Silently he echoed...*Dragwlya?*

Everyone's attention focused on the ex-governor. They all waited, staring at a man who appeared to be either deep in thought or at a complete loss. After what seemed like hours, the council members saw him begin to nod repeatedly. He stopped doing so only when he answered the guard.

"Send him in after a moment."

After nodding and answering, the guard executed an about face and left. Once the door had been closed, the council members began murmuring to each other. One of them finally questioned Hunedoara.

"What are you thinking, Hunedoara?"

No reply came, and another member spoke.

"You cannot be contemplating placing Dragwlya on the throne-"

The raised voices of all the members effectively cut off the rest of the man's sentence. Hunedoara allowed the debate to continue for only a few seconds more.

"Silence!"

With the voices quieting, one member raised his above the others for Hunedoara to hear.

"You cannot seriously be considering replacing Vladislav with Dracul's son! Especially after what you did to Dracul and Mircea."

"What other option is there? Besides, I know better than to just thrust Dragwlya on the throne. He will only gain Wallachia's reins after proper training. It will be as though I am on the throne myself." Hunedoara could see the skepticism surging through the council members' faces.

"You had better be right about this, Hunedoara," one exclaimed. "You can hardly afford *another* tragedy."

Hunedoara knew it was a reference to his losses at Varna and elsewhere. He restrained himself from lashing out. Quietly, he intoned, "I will keep him under the strictest supervision."

Just as Hunedoara finished his sentence, the door to the Knight's Room opened. As the hinges creaked, everyone's head turned to focus on the unexpected guest. Their first glimpse of Dragwlya made them think Dracul's ghost had entered the room. He and the guard came within a few feet of the table at which the council was sitting and stopped.

Dragwlya's face betrayed nothing as he studied the stares of contempt and utter disbelief of the council. Collectively, they wondered what had led Dragwlya to, of all places, the castle of his father and brother's murderer. Dragwlya now stared at the mastermind behind the assassinations.

"Good afternoon, *gentlemen*." Though his face did not show it, Dragwlya's tone made known his feelings. No response came. The stares of the council members were stone and reminded Dragwlya of gargoyles perched atop cathedral walls. "I hope I have not interrupted anything important."

Losing control, one of the council members strongly voiced his opinion of the entire situation. Rising, the man shouted at Hunedoara. "This is ludicrous, we will not stand for it, Hunedoara!" The other members simply nodded and began murmuring to one another in agreement.

"Finally you stand in my presence."

Dragwlya's words did not go ignored. Turning and looking at him coldly, the councilman immediately sat down to counteract the young man's arrogance. Dragwlya was not surprised by the man's rudeness. Hunedoara knew the situation was beyond volatile.

"Everybody out. Now." Hunedoara looked at Dragwlya. "Except you."

Dragwlya stared into Hunedoara's eyes. Internally, the desire to kill him grew continuously. He focused his gaze elsewhere before the feeling overwhelmed him.

The council members protested initially, but the look Hunedoara gave them caused them to quickly become silent and file out. Once they had exited and the door had closed, Hunedoara focused his stare on the young man before him. For a moment he second-guessed himself. Then he remembered he had Dracul and Mircea killed because they dared to second-guess him. "Give me any reason why I shouldn't have you executed immediately."

Being in the home of the murderer of his father and brother frightened Dragwlya. There were no guards to protect him, nothing or no one other than himself who could fend off any attack. Despite knowing how badly things could become, he remained calm. His answer was immediate.

"You need me."

"I have no need or use for you."

"Then you approve of the manner in which Vladislav is ruling my principality?"

"What do you mean...*your* principality?"

"If not for your meddling I would still be on my throne, and that idiot you replaced me with would not be allowing the Turkish the means to conquer all of Europe! Helping me regain my land is the least you could do. You *owe* me that much."

"I owe you nothing! You want something from me? You wish to have your *birthright* back? If that is why you have come here, then you will *earn* it." Hunedoara realized he had let his plan slip. It did not go unnoticed.

"What must I do that I have not done already?"

All façades had fallen. Dragwlya and Hunedoara were now negotiating.

"You understand how serious the situation regarding Constantinople has become. If you want my help, you will only get it by helping me save the city."

"And how am I to do that precisely?" Dragwlya feigned ignorance.

"You know how Mehmed's mind works. You have served in his army and know his tactics...Having a brother in the sultan's camp may also prove to be an asset."

Dragwlya began quietly laughing. "Radu? He is useless; little more than a minion whose primary function is to please the sultan by bending to his will and every desire."

"Do you wish to rule again or not?"

"What must I do?"

"My terms are non-negotiable. I will give you a military appointment, and you will serve in some capacity at my court. Additionally, I will set up residence for you. If I detect for even a second you are wavering in your loyalty, this ends. You will be arrested and executed. Do you accept my offer?"

"When do you wish to begin?"

"Immediately. From this moment you are loyal to me and to the cause of Emperor Constantine. Any misconduct on your part will incur dire consequences."

"Understood." Dragwlya's answer resounded with seriousness.

Neither man blinked. Internally, Hunedoara felt the weight of Dragwlya's dark emerald eyes. They pierced him, and he labored to not let it show.

Dragwlya began thinking of his father and Mircea, giving him greater will to intimidate their murderer. The idea of Hunedoara's death took control of his head in a variety of versions until he finally settled on one that forced him to reveal a smile.

Convinced the tension had finally been broken, Hunedoara blinked. "Go, and tell that guard to take you to a room. I will speak with you later this evening."

Dragwlya nodded. "Fine." He started to walk out of the room.

"You will address me as *sir*."

Peering back over his left shoulder, Dragwlya's glare was accompanied by sarcasm. "Yes...*sir*." He held the stare for a few seconds before resuming his exit. Opening the door, he departed and gently closed it.

Hunedoara sighed heavily with uncertainty.

God help me if I am wrong.

CHAPTER XX
THE BREAD IS THE LIFE
SIBIU
April 7, 1453

Dragwlya understood he was more prisoner than protector. Hunedoara had charged him with guarding his southern flank. That Dracul once held a similar position was not lost on Dragwlya, and he wondered how his father had suffered through such a mundane task. Already he had grown bored and resentful that his mentor refused him the opportunity to reclaim Wallachia immediately. Compelled by boredom, Dragwlya found ways to amuse himself.

"No, that will not do." Dragwlya's voice was monotone as he expressed his disapproval of the stakes being prepared for the impalement of two thieves. The criminals had stolen bread from a city council member's kitchen to feed their starving families. Their pales were too sharp and would cause almost instantaneous death. Death without pain was unacceptable. "Round the ends more."

Immediately, the men began doing as commanded, but Dragwlya overheard one whisper to the other, "All they did was take some bread."

Dragwlya covered the distance between himself and the man quickly. "You believe they do not deserve their punishment?"

Trembling uncontrollably, the man barely managed a reply. "No...my lord. Just that... perhaps...the punishment is too severe."

The peasants under Dragwlya's control had witnessed things they once believed unimaginable; acts so horrible, their worst nightmares paled hopelessly in comparison. They thought they understood what he was capable of and thought they knew how far he would go to display his code of ethics and justice. They were all mistaken. Until now, Dragwlya had controlled himself.

The worker chastised himself internally for being foolish enough to question Dragwlya out loud.

"Too severe?" Dragwlya asked quizzically. "How so?"

Stalling for a second, the peasant tried to invent a satisfactory answer, fully aware none existed. "My lord...it would have been different if the men had stolen something of value such as gold or-"

Dragwlya needed to hear nothing further and stopped him.

"Something of value? These wretches stole food out of a man's mouth! Food meant to nourish and sustain him! Food to give life! What value do you place on life? These two have attempted to *murder* another man by starving him! What other punishment do you feel suits their crime?"

Confounded and amazed by Dragwlya's reasoning, the man simply wore a look of ignorance. "Forgive me...my lord. I failed to see the situation in that manner."

Dragwlya took a step back. "What we hold to be the truth stems from how and what we see."

"Yes, my lord."

"Question my judgment again, and I will have you fashion a stake meant for yourself."

Effectively ending the conversation, Dragwlya left the two men to their work.

Thankful his life had been spared, the worker swallowed the lump in his throat. Seldom did Dragwlya walk away, and his doing so was becoming regarded as a miracle because of its infrequency.

CONSTANTINOPLE
April 20, 1453

Two days was long enough for the most casual of travelers to journey from Andrinople to Constantinople. For Mehmed, his army, and arsenal, the march lasted the whole of two months. They had set out at the beginning of February and had not arrived until the second of April. Mehmed's heavy artillery already rested in position as he ascended the hill of Maltepe, where camp was made facing the St. Romanus Gate. Mehmed was determined to enter the city there.

Surrounded by some twelve thousand Janissaries, Mehmed regarded the doomed city. To his right, the Anatolian army held from Maltepe to the Sea of Marmara. His left wing extended to the Golden Horn and was manned by the Rumelian army. At the end of Friday prayer on April 6th, the siege began.

Nearly two weeks passed before Mehmed admitted to himself that little progress had been made. Nightly, the city walls were repaired, even the destroyed tower of the St. Romanus Gate had been reconstructed overnight. He realized Constantinople would not fall by a land attack alone.

Three hours after today's attack had begun, Mehmed grew restless. Helplessly, he watched his fleet fall ship by ship to three freighters and a single royal vessel. The adage "strength lies in numbers" had been proven false. By conservative estimates, approximately ten thousand men had already been lost, and he had been advised many more casualties were likely. Sensing defeat, the Turkish sailors began to withdraw from the battle, determined not to die. Their cowardice enraged Mehmed.

"No." Mehmed spoke the word, not yet believing his eyes. Standing up, he repeated the word again and charged for the shore. Breathlessly, he shouted at the sailors. "No! Stand fast! Regroup and attack!" None heard what he was screaming, but Mehmed took their lack of obedience as defiance.

Everyone watched as the sultan waded into the water up to his waist, continuing to curse his men, continuing to utter orders for them to resume fighting that were ignored.

"If not for the intervention of the Janissaries, you would have been impaled already. I have lost more than ten thousand soldiers, six ships, and you allowed your subordinates to retreat!"

Mehmed stared at Admiral Baltaoğlu, the commander of his fleet, and wondered how he had made such an egregious error. Baltaoğlu's face showed his disgrace, but that failed to satisfy Mehmed. This had been the first real test of the siege, and Mehmed knew how badly the loss reflected on him. Confidence would build inside the city walls. It would be more difficult to overrun Constantinople now.

"Your rank is lost, as are your possessions. The Janissaries saved you; your possessions will go to them as payment for your life. Take him away... Flog him."

NEAR BEŞIKTAŞ
April 28, 1453

Although the Turkish had suffered an embarrassing defeat eight days ago, just one day later the course of the campaign shifted completely. For the first time since the siege began, a part of the wall that had collapsed had not been repaired overnight. The barrage of cannon fire finally appeared to be having some effect. Halil was the first to understand that if allowed to continue Mehmed would be successful in sacking the city. He accepted a bribe and promised the Greeks he would do his utmost to protect the city from falling.

With the midday hour looming, Mehmed's war council convened near Beşiktaş. Not everyone seemed as determined as the sultan to engage in all out war.

"So much more could be gained from them if we simply demand it." All regarded Halil Pasha as though he were speaking with his head on backwards. "Demand seventy thousand gold pieces from the emperor in yearly tribute... demand more. Demand the right to appoint police officials; demand the right to appoint them all. No more lives must be lost in order to gain the city. We can gain it through intimidation. There is no reason for more bloodshed."

Many were stunned by Halil's suggestion that they simply end the fight, especially when it was theirs to win. Most were quick to remind him of that, including Zaganos Pasha.

"You simply want a yearly tribute when we have their greatest city in our grasp? Losing Constantinople will mean the death of their spirit. They will know no other city can survive."

Sheikh Şemseddin concurred. "Our allowance of surrender without defeat will only prove their god has the power to grant reprieves and mercy. We cannot allow that."

Minus Halil, the council unanimously voiced its approval for continuing to fight. Halil tried as best he could to hide his disappointment at the thought of losing so many riches from the Greeks.

"It seems your opinion is not shared, Halil." Mehmed's voice instantly silenced the council. "I remind everyone of the problem still facing us—an attack by land alone will not succeed."

All present murmured their agreement.

"Every attempt to enter the harbor has been disastrous. For many nights I have struggled to find the answer. Each night I have arrived at the same conclusion. It is necessary for a portion of the fleet to be moved into the harbor by land. We will waste no more time. The land will be cleared of underbrush, covered with planking, and with railing as needed. The smaller ships will be moved first."

He's found the way, thought Halil. *Constantinople will be his before summer begins.*

CHAPTER XXI
CONSTANTINOPLE FALLS
CONSTANTINOPLE
May 24, 1453

Fearful, and with the fate of his empire in dire straits, Emperor Constantine XI led a solemn procession to the Cathedral of St. Sophia, hopeful for divine inspiration or intervention. Although he did not feel like it, the emperor was imposing, standing more than six and a half feet tall and wearing plated armor along with a steel helmet because of the imminent threat to his capital.

Behind him followed the great icon of the Blessed Virgin painted by St. Luke, its twenty bearers, and both the religious and cynical. These last two groups were composed of those wishing to receive the Almighty's blessings and those who would rather see the sultan's turban in Constantinople before the red hat of any Roman Catholic Cardinal.

Although it was only mid-afternoon, darkness fell upon the city. Stopping to look upward, Constantine saw the sun vanishing little by little, a sight that terrified his people. Solemnly, Constantine forced himself to march again, gradually quickening his pace as he neared the cathedral. He could hear proclamations by would-be prophets, insisting this was a sign of disastrous events to come. The emperor ignored them, or at least tried to, until the unthinkable occurred.

From behind, Constantine heard the snap of wood and cables. A loud boom resounded through the city streets and shook the ground underneath his feet. He spun, all the while hearing the shrieks and moans of his people and more messages being proclaimed by the street prophets. In horror he stared into the eyes of the Blessed Virgin, now lying on her side.

In reality the cables had put excess strain on the planks used to carry the statue, snapping them. For Constantinople, it was another omen. Some of the men carrying the icon had been crushed partially or wholly. Hearing the echo of their screams, Constantine wondered if God had indeed abandoned him.

The remaining bearers of the icon struggled to restore it upright as shocked onlookers gasped and prayed. Now the sun was being concealed further. Its rays were also being denied passage by thick, heavy black clouds that seemed low enough to grasp. Laboriously, the icon was raised as lightning flashed throughout the sky. Constantine did his best to rectify the chaotic chain of events. He stood confidently, defying the oncoming storm with only his voice in his arsenal. The thunder only rumbled louder in reply. Then the heavens broke.

Everything not under cover was soaked within ten seconds. Constantine watched the streets clear and with a heavy sigh slunk into the sanctuary of St. Sophia. He genuinely prayed the dome atop it would not collapse and crush him.

Torrential rains turned Constantinople's streets into miniature raging rivers. Turkish troops encamped outside watched as the city vanished from their view at times, shielded by an opaque veil of water. In sharp contrast, the Turkish encampment experienced only a slight drizzle.

Mehmed stood outside his tent, looking upon the city he planned to control by month's end. Hundreds of Turkish campfires blazed as the sultan mentally reviewed his plan of attack. Like Constantine, Mehmed also grew unsure of his campaign due to these untimely acts of nature. The eclipse, the rain, everything worried Mehmed. Constantly his seers were reassuring him to no avail.

Abruptly, the rain ceased. Turning his attention toward the sea, the sultan hardly believed what he saw. Slowly creeping toward the city was a thick, white blanket of fog. Once again Mehmed sought counsel from his seers and rightfully so. No one had ever seen fog in Constantinople in May.

Constantine stood on the steps of St. Sophia, stunned by the fog infiltrating the city. It was so thick he could barely see the cathedral merely a few meters behind him. He convinced himself this was another sign from above. God was concealing his exodus from the city.

Eyeing the mist swirling around him, Constantine observed it had a reddish hue. Others noticed this strange characteristic as well. Watching them, Constantine saw someone point upward to the dome on top of St. Sophia. Turning, he gazed up and saw something that defied explanation. The bottom of the dome was glowing red, casting a bloody tint on the fog below. He could hear various explanations for this phenomenon. Many attributed the light to the campfires of the Turkish. Others insisted it emitted from the campfires of Ioan Hunedoara, finally coming to save the beleaguered city. The latter was wishful thinking.

Although Hunedoara had previously sent a delegation to the city, the realization that Mehmed planned to make good on his word of conquering Constantinople compelled him to withdraw his ambassadors before the sultan isolated the city. Along with Dragwlya, he arrived at the conclusion it would be wiser to defend his own borders, rather than try to save a city certain to fall. He had concentrated his forces in Transylvania and on his southern flank around the fortress at Belgrade, still under Dragwlya's command.

The red glow was not the result of the Turkish campfires either, however, and the eerie light had also grasped the attention of all in Mehmed's camp.

"What is it?" Mehmed's voice showed him to be both panicked and frustrated. While posing the question to each of his seers, his voice trembled. They responded by not responding. Finally, the seers collectively arrived at a conclusion to present to the distraught sultan.

"My liege?" The seer approached Mehmed timidly as the sultan simply stared, mesmerized by the red glow that had slowly begun to rise to the top of the dome. Even with all of his caution, the seer still failed in not alarming the sultan.

"What do you want?"

The seer tried to make his reasoning for the red glow sound believable.

"My liege, we have concluded that this, divine light, is another sign from Allah, assuring you that the true religion—our religion—will finally prevail in enlightening this ancient city and all of Europe."

Putting on his best airs, the seer stood confidently and awaited a response.

Not entirely convinced, the sultan looked back toward the dome of St. Sophia, knowing his seers were only trying to assuage him. He nodded his head a few times in agreement and then sat down to continue staring at the light causing him so much grief. The seer did not even try to convince him further. He simply walked away with a heavy sigh and explained to the others what had been said.

With one last pulse, the light flickered out after a few moments of illumination. The dome looked ordinary again. Mehmed prayed his army would not be extinguished as easily. Earlier this morning, he had proclaimed a general offensive by land and sea would begin in five days. Seventy-two ships had been transported across land into the Golden Horn, and the sultan even had a bridge constructed of barrels, hooks, and planks from Galata just to the north of the city walls that would support five men across. The proclamation came only minutes after Isfendiyaroğlu Ismail Bey returned to camp after being sent to provide Constantine one last chance to surrender. Isfendiyaroğlu had also been sent to determine the extent of damage done to the city walls and to the morale of the Greeks.

There would be no surrender. Constantine made that perfectly clear by telling Isfendiyaroğlu he would give thanks to God if Mehmed, as had his predecessors, decided in favor of peace. In addition to this, Constantine made the observation that none of the sultan's ancestors who had attacked the city enjoyed a long life. The emperor agreed to pay tribute, but not to surrender the city.

May 28, 1453

Mehmed continued bombarding the fourteen miles of walls and towers encompassing Constantinople day and night. The city's defense consisted of twenty thousand poorly equipped men from numerous nations, one papal contingent, and several small groups sent from various states. This was the only assistance Constantine had received to help ward off the Turkish attack. A fleet of sixteen fighting ships also aided but was so inadequate for the task it made the Venetian fleet of the Varna disaster seem like an invincible armada. Even Greek fire had been ineffectual against the Turkish fleet.

Hearing nothing after being constantly shelled for so long was unsettling, but the tranquil morning gave people reason to believe the sultan might simply abandon this campaign, that the Turkish would leave. Their judgment was warped by hope. Because the siege had proceeded according to his plans, Mehmed decided to give his men a day of rest. The sultan felt the bombardment had damaged the walls sufficiently for the final assault.

Stale air lingered throughout the city as thickly as the fog that had engulfed the capital four nights ago. Sitting alone in anguish, Constantine tried to block out the sound of nothingness pounding in his ears. Atop Constantinople's walls, he surveyed the battle scars that marred his city. He could also see the Turkish encampment, which had grown as silent as the city but with one difference. Mehmed's camp was at peace, the peace that comes when one knows victory is imminent. Constantine finally decided he could no longer bear the tranquility. He ordered a nearby guard to retrieve a messenger. Both men returned within the span of a minute.

"Yes, sire?"

The emperor responded without hesitation. "Go to St. Sophia. Tell the clergy they are to continuously ring the cathedral bells until I order them to stop. Tell them also to celebrate mass."

"In Greek or Latin, sire?"

Constantine wanted this to all be over. He hoped he would not be forever remembered as the man who lost Constantinople to the Ottoman Empire. The thought forced him to realize the place he would hold in the Christian world for all eternity and wore out his patience. "Both."

The passage of time from the messenger leaving to the first toll seemed like hours. Finally, Constantine heard the first few resounding tones. Emotionless, the guards watched their disheartened emperor stare into the heart of his enemy's camp. No longer an imposing figure, he was dwarfed by an opponent he understood could not be overcome.

All past differences had been cast aside. At this moment, hundreds of people were flocking to St. Sophia for mass, communion, and confession. Italians, Greeks, Roman Catholics, and Eastern Orthodox Christians alike filed into the cathedral to pray as one. For a moment the union of the churches proclaimed and loathed by so many became a reality. Perched above St. Romanus' gate, Constantine listened as the people sang in unison and desperation for mercy.

May 29, 1453

Turkish campfires continued to blaze into the dead of night as Mehmed looked over his army. He had consulted his seers one last time before deciding to begin his final assault, a consultation caused by the low hanging waning moon. After he was assured this was yet another sign from Allah of the victory to come, Mehmed made his preparations.

With a signal from the Turkish encampment to the fleet, the barrage began with cannon fire at half past one in the morning. Mehmed's men began cheering as shots echoed through the night, waiting impatiently for their march on the city to begin.

Suffering through another sleepless night, Constantine hung his head in despair at the sound of the cannons, the Turkish cheers, and the blaring of a marching tune being played by the Janissary military band. The upbeat song was his funeral dirge. He took notice of the moon and laughed as he remembered one of his own prophets proclaiming there would be such a moon the day the city fell.

"Sire, the army awaits your command." The voice was that of a young man, actually more of a boy. Constantine turned to look at the youth.

"I will be there momentarily." He knew his tone conveyed his feelings.

Mehmed watched his men advancing toward the once thriving metropolis. His army was led by the European mercenaries, whom he had purchased for a fair price, followed by his personal bodyguards, their weapons already raised should any of the mercenaries try and run away from the fight. Next came the Janissary corps, trailed by the regular Turkish troops.

Cannon fire erupted continuously from both sides as the sultan's men marched toward the walls protecting the city. Constantine had gathered his thoughts somewhat and was now defending the city alongside his men positioned at the St. Romanus Gate.

Five hours had passed since the beginning of the assault, and the weakened walls of Constantinople were still standing, baffling Mehmed. Again he stared at the crippled barrier, wondering what mystic energy continued holding it up. Within the city walls, the citizens were relieved and overjoyed that the attack of the Turkish was failing. Their joy grew upon learning the sultan's generals were turning back.

Seeing his generals retreating, Mehmed became enraged and jumped on his steed. He began cursing them, ordering them back toward the city as he rode. Once they could finally understand him, the generals quickly turned around, charging at full speed to renew the attack. Mehmed saw his intentions were clearly understood. No one was leaving until Constantinople was under Turkish rule.

As the sun climbed higher into the sky, the sound of crumbling rock roared over the blaring of the cannon fire. It was accompanied by a crescendo of cheers from the Turkish as they breached the protective barrier built by Heraclius so many years ago.

Constantine stood ready at the Gate of St. Romanus as the first of his enemies burst through furiously. This particular Turk was at least seven feet tall and weighed well over three hundred pounds.

The giant roared in exhilaration and glory of his triumph, screaming his own name, "Hassan!"

Constantine watched the behemoth raise both fists high into the air and then saw arrows penetrating his body, beginning with his heart. It was a small victory, and any savoring of it ended seconds after Hassan hit the ground and others began rushing through the breach.

Giovanni Giustiniani-Longo, the mason largely responsible for holding the city's walls together for so long, prepared for the fight. On a few occasions Mehmed had tried bribing Giovanni, first into revealing the wall's weaknesses and then into not repairing them. He would have none of it. Knowing the breaches could no longer be serviced, Giovanni had positioned himself at the gate along with most of the emperor's men and readied himself for the fight. His service invigorated everyone.

Hand-to-hand combat ensued, and Giovanni was one of the first casualties. Not as adept at fighting as he was masonry, the blade of a Turkish soldier cut through Giovanni's arm. Had he not dodged when he did, it would have been severed. He retreated as a fellow Greek engaged the Turkish soldier, giving him time to assess his injury.

Seconds took lifetimes to pass, but Giovanni quickly came to understand what so many had thought for so long. There would be no stopping Mehmed from overrunning Constantinople. Giovanni instantly abandoned the fight. Would this have been any other man, no hesitation would have occurred before the traitor was slaughtered. No one around him could comprehend his cowardice, however, and their shock allowed him to escape. Only one soul managed to question him.

Hurriedly, Constantine rode to meet him and dismounted.

"My brother, fight bravely! Do not forsake us in our distress! The salvation of our city depends on you! Return to your post! Where are you going?"

Slowing so he could be heard, Giovanni stared at the emperor and coldly answered. "Where God himself will lead these Turks!"

The defection nearly caused Constantine to lose all heart.

More troops began spilling into the city once another section of the wall collapsed, crushing many defending the gate. Breaches abounded, and reports were coming from the rear guard that the Turkish had entered the city from the harbor side through a gate mistakenly left open the day before. It became too much for Constantine to bear.

With a battle cry, the emperor drew his sword and rushed toward the oncoming enemy. Engaging in hand-to-hand combat, he threw his robe over one of the Turks and stabbed the blinded man. He had drawn attention to himself in doing so and soon found himself completely surrounded. Convinced of the hopelessness of the situation, Constantine's men fled, leaving their emperor to fend for himself. His eyes searched wildly but found no allies.

"Is there no Christian here who will take my head?"

Constantine's request was heard only by the sultan's men. Raising his sword into the air, the emperor cursed and damned the Turkish before flinging himself at them. As the soldiers rushed him, he swung madly, hoping to leave the world still a crusader for the cause.

A blow to the face instantly crushed the emperor's skull, and a second soldier plunged his blade into Constantine's back to make his death certain. Blood flowed freely and, after a few more unnecessary thrusts, the Turkish allowed his corpse to fall. One final prophecy had come true—the last emperor of Constantinople bore the same name as the first.

Street by street, the city succumbed to the sultan's onslaught until eventually his army reached St. Sophia. There they found morning mass still being celebrated. Knowing now that their prayers had gone unanswered, the priests fled, escaping through a secret panel in the southern wall, chalices still in hand. To the Turkish, still quite a distance away, the priests had simply disappeared into thin air. Outside, Mehmed's army continued to ravage the city, killing anyone who dared oppose them. Those who gave up were mercifully taken prisoner. To assure those who surrendered and were captured did not escape, the Turkish stripped and bound them using their tattered garments.

For three days, the looting continued. More than four thousand were killed; more than fifty thousand taken prisoner. The proud Turkish army awaited the arrival of the *Conqueror*, the name by which Mehmed would now forever be remembered.

On that third morning, Mehmed began his journey into the fallen city. His approach was a joyous one, and all cheered him as he rode past, save the prisoners whom he managed to catch glimpses from. Shunning their hollow looks, Mehmed moved through the Gate of St. Romanus. His men followed as he made his way to St. Sophia, and a smile crossed his face once the procession drew close to the cathedral. The golden dome shone like a welcoming beacon.

Dismounting, Mehmed allowed the smile to slip away. Solemnly, he ascended the steps and entered through doors destroyed by his army. Once inside, Mehmed's gaze fixed quickly on one of his men who was repeatedly striking at the once polished marble floor with an ax. Debris flew wildly as the soldier failed to recognize the arrival of his own leader.

"You there!"

Seeing the *Conqueror* not more than a few meters away, the soldier bowed down.

"Why are you compelled to destroy the floor?"

Baffled by the sultan's question, the man looked up and answered with certainty in his voice. "For the faith, my liege."

Is this a fair representation of those who fight for me? Of those who fight for Islam? Barbarian! Mehmed drew his sword and swiftly struck the man in his side.

"Content yourselves with the loot and the prisoners. The buildings belong to me!" Sheathing his sword, Mehmed called to some of the courtiers accompanying him. "Remove him."

Two courtiers carried the injured man away, and Mehmed allowed his eyes to wander around the cathedral. Evidence of mass destruction and what would be considered sacrilege by the infidels greeted him everywhere he looked. The items used in their masses had either been shattered or stolen, the statues of their saints defiled or destroyed. Mehmed imagined his men taking advantage of their women on the altars. Most revealing of the acts that had occurred, a huge crucifix lay on the floor, a Janissary hat still atop it. The cross had been paraded around mockingly.

Everyone was quiet as Mehmed proceeded toward the main altar. He halted and simply stared at the desecrated center of worship. Eyeing the pulpit, he summoned one of the viziers to his side.

"Yes, my liege?"

Unable to look away, Mehmed spoke. "Go up there and recite the words of witness."

"Would you not care to speak the words yourself, my liege?"

In his mind Mehmed still felt this place belonged to the Christians. He would not dare set foot upon the place they considered most holy. "If I did, would I have just commanded you to do so?"

The question was answered appropriately, and the vizier made his way to the pulpit. Stretching his arms wide, yet visibly uncomfortable, the vizier did as he had been told and spoke the Muslim creed. "There is no God but Allah, and Mohammed is His Prophet."

Mere seconds of silence passed before Mehmed spoke. "Summon the faithful for afternoon prayer."

CHAPTER XXII
REFUGEE
TÎRGOVIŞTE
June 25, 1453

Hundreds passed through the city daily, simply trying to survive after escaping the sultan's wrath. Each day was a mirror image of the one preceding it in Vladislav's capital. Today would be different.

Vladislav had received details of the unraveling of Constantinople from the beginning. To ensure he had a vivid, first-hand account, he had assigned one of his boyars to Mehmed's court two years earlier. Additionally, he sent a few faithful followers to Constantinople. Vladislav expected none of them would ever return, but word arrived earlier this morning that one of the informants was close to the city—Samuil, a Romanian bishop who had managed to escape after the final assault. Wallachia's prince was thankful the bishop's life had been spared and overjoyed he would be receiving more information.

Samuil finally reached the palace at mid-afternoon. Tîrgovişte was alive with merchants gouging the refugees, selling necessities for outrageous prices. A true man of God, the bishop gave alms to those he could afford to and to those he could not. The path to Vladislav's castle was obstructed by thousands of unfortunates, adding to the destitute that had always occupied the streets as their home. He couldn't possibly look away and ignore them.

The bishop gained a following of a few hundred, all trying desperately to reach him in an effort to receive money before he entered the castle. Seeing he was being mobbed, one of Vladislav's commanders ordered a squad of his men to ward off the crowd. Except for the most desperate souls pleading to the bishop's kind heart, little resistance came from the crowd to leave Samuil alone. The small gleam of hope in their eyes flickered out once he disappeared into the castle.

By Vladislav's order, Samuil was immediately escorted to the throne room. He was relieved the crowds were unable to follow, but nothing could stop their pleas for help or their longing stares from chasing after him. Traversing the halls of Vladislav's home, Samuil recalled all he had seen while fleeing Constantinople. Images of torture were clear, and he could still hear the deafening screams and cries of women, children, and men alike waiting in vain for a savior. They screamed until finally being silenced forever by the blades and devices of the Turkish.

A set of doors burst open before him, and Samuil was suddenly brought back to the present. Vladislav's boyars, servants, and other members of the court began cheering for the bishop, who had returned by some miracle of God. Grateful, Samuil managed a very faint smile and waved weakly to the audience. Looking directly ahead the bishop could see Vladislav smiling, clapping, and knew the prince was waiting to hear what news he had to share. The longer Samuil stared at him, the more he was convinced Vladislav did not belong on the throne. It was an odd emotion, a feeling that everyone in Wallachia would soon be under Turkish rule were Vladislav allowed to remain in power.

The cheering continued even after Samuil reached the throne and was finally silenced by a gesture from Vladislav.

"Like all of you, I am overjoyed to see that Bishop Samuil has returned unscathed." Vladislav's statement was only true of Samuil's physical condition. Mentally, the bishop had been severely maimed. "I'm sure we would all like to hear a few words from him."

The audience began to cheer and clap again for Samuil, who was now trying to shun the prince's offer. He did so without success and reluctantly spoke.

"I wish this homecoming would have occurred under better circumstances." Taking a deep breath and sighing, Samuil continued. "I have seen sights beyond belief; things I dare not describe to you. I do know the sultan has no intention of settling for Constantinople alone… He will not rest until claiming all of Europe as his own." Bowing his head, Samuil slowly turned to face Vladislav. The bishop looked up into his eyes, allowing the prince a glimpse of the pain he harbored within. "My lord, may I please speak with you privately?"

Vladislav only nodded. Lifting his left arm, the prince gestured to a room adjacent to the throne.

The crowd had now begun whispering to one another and, as the bishop followed Vladislav, the whispers did not take long to escalate into shouting.

HUNEDOARA CASTLE
July 14, 1453

News of Constantinople's fall reached Romania initially in the middle of June via ambassadors who had just managed to escape. Now the imperial city's fall was being related by refugees from Emperor Constantine's defeated forces. For weeks, Hunedoara had listened to various accounts of the siege and had heard what Mehmed had done to the populace. Survivors related graphic accounts of how the sultan had impaled citizens and placed them in the vicinity for all to see; just one of many terror tactics used by Mehmed to break Constantinople's will.

Hunedoara knew Constantinople was only the first step in Mehmed's grand scheme to take total control of Europe. The thought frightening Hunedoara most was that the likely location for the sultan to move his forces to next would be Transylvania. With Vladislav firmly under the sultan's control, Wallachia would be the gateway. Hungary would then be next to fall if Mehmed were not stopped.

Already the principality and city leaders of Transylvania were appealing for aid from Hunedoara, Dragwlya, and Ladislas V, the inexperienced king of Hungary. Oswald Winzel, the mayor of Sibiu, had gone so far as to ask the mayor and city council of Vienna and the Holy Roman Emperor for help. Acquainted with Mehmed's motives, Hunedoara ignored the useless advice Winzel willingly gave him. Instead, he preferred the advice of his personal envoy and confidant—János Vitéz.

Hunedoara listened to Vitéz intently. Vitéz was of medium stature, a few inches shorter than Hunedoara, and far from intimidating. His lack of physical prowess was made up for mentally. Vitéz's abilities as a statesman were unsurpassed, and as a diplomat he had proven himself to be a great asset.

"He will not attack Transylvania. He has no need to invade land he already controls. Mehmed owns Wallachia like the Turkish merchants who rule the streets of its capital. Vladislav is a puppet. Moldavia is worse. Petru Aaron's strings are held even tighter. The sultan will march around Transylvania on his way to conquer Belgrade. That will be Mehmed's next prize."

Everyone present began mulling the ramifications of losing one of the most strategic locations on the Danube. Standing on a hill at the confluence of the Sava and Danube rivers, Belgrade presented an awesome sight. Its string of tripled walls, outer fortifications, towers, and battlements instilled in all approaching enemies a sense of futility.

Hunedoara understood the magnitude of such a Turkish conquest. If Belgrade were to fall, the Danube would become the personal waterway of the Turkish fleet. Buda and Vienna would both be vulnerable, setting up the inevitable fall of Hungary and eventually the Holy Roman Empire. Personally, Hungary's conquest would end any hopes he held for his sons, László and Matthias, to one day rule. He shook his head in agreement with Vitéz, knowing he could not allow such a catastrophe to happen.

CHAPTER XXIII
MEHMED'S PLAN
ANDRINOPLE
July 14, 1454

Shortly after the fall of Constantinople, Halil Pasha's treachery was exposed. Mehmed had long suspected as much due to the passive attitude of his grand vizier and immediately had him imprisoned. Forty days later, Halil was executed. His intimates were stripped of their privilege and property.

Now in possession of Constantinople, Mehmed was hungry for all of Europe. Though he wished to simply charge off and decimate the whole of Christianity, he knew victory required careful planning. Europe, however, was not the only thing occupying his mind; Radu was as well.

Dragwlya's younger brother grew more handsome daily, arousing Mehmed's sexual desires all the more. At the height of passion, the sultan would fill Radu's head with promises of Wallachia's throne and guarantees of other treasures. Radu, for his part, was beginning to relish the notion.

Thus far this day was following the set pattern of many previous ones at Mehmed's court. The morning progressed with Radu receiving idle passes from the sultan, finding himself thankful they all went unfulfilled. Fortunately, Mehmed had been holding council with the beys of his army and would be for the next few weeks. At the heart of their discussions would be Europe's conquest.

"Belgrade is our first objective. We will attack through Serbia and then march north." Mehmed radiated confidence, knowing victory awaited him. Constantinople was defeated, not easily, but it belonged to him now. If the defenders of Christianity were not willing to unite to prevent *its* downfall, why would they present a unified front anywhere else?

"My liege?"

Mehmed was staring into the future when he had been so rudely interrupted. "Yes?"

"What about Transylvania?"

"What *about* Transylvania?"

The bey now thought his mouth should have remained closed. "I-Perhaps our entrance into the continent should be made through Transylvania."

To the bey's relief, Mehmed's manner remained calm. "Why would I do such a thing?"

"To gain control of the land, my liege."

Mehmed laughed. "Transylvania is already under my control. I rule it through those who have given in fully to our cause out of fear. Fear is the strongest weapon I possess in my arsenal, more powerful than even the *Basilica*.

"Going through Transylvania would be a waste of time and supplies. We will go around the Danube and the Carpathians to reach our goal. Once Belgrade falls, all of Hungary will follow. Then we shall move on."

"When do you wish to initiate your plan, my liege?" asked another bey.

"Next winter." His response brought about looks of disbelief. "You do not approve of my timing?"

One was bold enough to answer. "We approve, my liege. We just wonder why you wish to wait so long to begin this campaign?"

"It will take time to gather the appropriate men and manufacture the artillery needed for this campaign. There will be no underestimating of any sort. Nothing will be taken for granted. Are there any other concerns?"

This time no one voiced the doubts they might be harboring.

"Good. Then we will eat and begin to discuss your individual assignments later."

CHAPTER XXIV
CAPISTRANO
GYÖR
July 11, 1455

Hunedoara's realization he had acquired an incredible asset in his new protégé grew daily. Now confident in the risk he had taken, Hunedoara displayed his recent endeavor to anyone interested. This included the Hungarian Diet and the man presiding over it, King Ladislas. Ladislas had recently been declared of age by his guardian, Emperor Fredrick III, and Dragwlya and Hunedoara had attended his coronation ceremony in Buda. Both had pledged their allegiance to the king, and the occasion lent itself for developments to occur.

During the festivities following the crowning, Hunedoara reconciled his differences with Count Ulrich Cilli. A powerful relative of Emperor Sigismund, the count now served in the capacity of dedicated mercenary to his successor, Fredrick III. A second development came in the form of Dragwlya accepting the responsibility to ensure the protection of the Transylvanian frontier from possible Turkish attack. He agreed to this at Hunedoara's urging and with the full consent of both Ladislas and the Transylvanian Diet. Dragwlya felt he had regained a portion of his family's holdings. His father had once served in the exact same capacity.

Various generals of the crusading army had been called to convene in Györ by Hunedoara for assignments and to outline strategies for the campaign. To pass the time between official meetings, many of the commanders listened to various speakers. Tonight, one of those espousing the necessity for crusade was an older Franciscan Monk, Giovanni da Capistrano.

Dragwlya, Hunedoara, and János Vitéz stood among a crowd of more than eight thousand. All listened intently to Capistrano's voice, trying desperately to grasp everything the man was saying. This intense effort stemmed mainly from the fact hardly anyone fully understood Capistrano's words because they were spoken in Latin.

No one would have imagined the Franciscan Monk to be in his seventies by his booming voice. Combined with his frail, stooped frame, Capistrano's face gave the impression of a vivacious corpse, its eyes pushed back into its skull. His worn expression had been a fixture for some time now, testament to the numerous crusades he had fought through with both words and actions. Steadily, the old monk's voice began to crescendo, gaining along with volume the support of the men. He culminated with a line penetrating deep into their hearts.

"God wills it that we chase the Turks out of Europe, and for whosoever follows me, I will obtain plenary indulgence for him and his family!"

The remark met with instant cheering by the common men of Győr. Though the actual words he had spoken were not comprehended, the emotion with which he had voiced them had the crowd practically begging to join the crusade against the invading army of Mehmed. While the crowd continued to sing Capistrano's praises, the present commanding generals remained silent, simply exchanging glances with one another. A smirk appeared on Dragwlya's face that Hunedoara noticed immediately.

"What do you find so amusing?"

"They are an angry mob of farmers. What good will pitchforks be against Turkish swords?"

"They only wish to protect what is theirs."

"Surely they won't be allowed to fight with us." Though minute, there existed in Dragwlya's tone a tinge of fear at the thought of having these simple peasants fighting alongside trained soldiers.

"No. I do not want the blood of these men on my hands."

… in addition to the twenty thousand at Varna and that of my father and brother, Dracula added silently.

"They can do as they wish...as long as they do not interfere with our plans."

"They will simply get themselves killed."

Dragwlya's thought caused Hunedoara to cringe slightly, but he made no remark regarding it. Along with the other generals, he retired early for the evening, foregoing the revelry.

HUNEDOARA CASTLE
January 13, 1456

Toward mid-December of last year, Mehmed assembled the bulk of his army near Andrinople. Ninety thousand men and sixty-five ships placed in the delta of the Danube all but assured Europe of the Ottoman Empire's suspected attack on Belgrade. Still, major preparations for the campaign began only after Hunedoara's men learned of the mass production of mortars and cannons by German and other gunsmiths in the central Serbian city of Kruševać.

While talking amongst themselves, the generals present for today's meeting eagerly awaited the arrival of Hunedoara. Dragwlya surveyed the assembled group. Among them was his cousin, Stephen, now sitting beside him.

"What do you suppose is keeping him?" asked Stephen.

"He likes making grand entrances. He will be here shortly." Just as Dragwlya finished his sentence, the room quickly erupted into applause.

Eventually, those present settled down once Hunedoara was standing before them. Taking his time, he stared intently into the eyes of the crowd, preparing to convey the importance of the task at hand.

"I will not downplay what must be done if our cause is to succeed. Mehmed will soon begin his campaign, not just for Belgrade, but for all of Europe. Our focus must lie on how best to preserve our homes, our families, the empire, and Christianity. This will be a war of attrition. Mehmed will not stop until he has fallen in combat.

"You are all aware Giovanni da Capistrano has assembled men to fight against the sultan's army. They will not march alongside you. I will not let untrained men face a force of highly skilled soldiers. If they wish to fight they may, but it will be of their own accord, separate from us. We cannot afford the distraction of saving individuals while trying to preserve an entire continent from Islamic enslavement."

The meeting progressed into the assignments of each general, and the nature of their duties spoke to how essential the individual would be for the plan to have any hope of success. Hunedoara also installed secondary plans should any of the groups be overrun, a sweeping defense that allowed another general easy access to help out an adjacent regiment. There remained only two assignments not yet covered, those of Dragwlya and Stephen. At this point though, it seemed a foregone conclusion what their respective tasks would be. Their statuses mirrored one another. Each had been robbed of his birthright, and both the thrones of Wallachia and Moldavia were now occupied by puppets of Mehmed.

"Stephen, at some point early in the campaign, you will march toward Moldavia. This is your opportunity to defeat Petru and reclaim the land once belonging to your father." Hunedoara then turned to his protégé. "Vlad." Hunedoara now stared sternly into the eyes of Dragwlya.

Hearing his name made his heart race. Finally, the training and waiting were over. Now he would be free to act of his own accord.

"You and your men shall remain in Sibiu to watch the Transylvanian passes."

Hiding best he could his frustration and disbelief, Dragwlya decided to confront Hunedoara privately. If this were not the proper time for him to fight for his throne, the time would never exist. Perhaps his mentor never intended on giving him the chance to win the principality. Hunedoara's next statement caused Dragwlya to put such thoughts to rest and made him thankful he had chosen not to question authority.

"You may begin your campaign for Wallachia whenever you believe it appropriate." Hunedoara then addressed the two of them at once. "Your invasions will hopefully compel the sultan to keep troops on the Danube. We need all the relief we can get on land at Belgrade. I hope you two realize how vital your success is."

Dragwlya was the first to respond.

"Vladislav's reign will not see the end of this year. I assure you."

"The same holds true for Petru," interjected Stephen. "Before summer's end, Moldavia shall be restored to its rightful place."

Hunedoara sensed how confident the two young men were in their abilities and knew the feelings to be justified. "Good. You obviously understand what part you are playing in the overall scheme of this crusade." Hunedoara changed his focus to the entire group. "Our adversary will try to overrun us and back us into any corner he can. We must remain cohesive if we are to be victorious.

"Mehmed has already taken away land we hold sacred. Now he advances to take away our lives; the lives of our families. The battle has been brought to us. We must now take the fight to them!"

At this statement, all began cheering and shouting loudly in defiance of the Turkish and their sultan. Hunedoara smiled, recognizing his ability to rally any group behind him for a cause.

Listening to the cheering, Dragwlya thought how foolish everyone was for their perpetual gullibility of Hunedoara's words. They chose to listen to his speeches instead of recounting his failures. Their overconfidence in him had always been a weakness. It seemingly would always be something their precious *White Knight* could rely on being in his favor. In mere months, Dragwlya would reclaim the throne of Wallachia. No one could tell him otherwise and survive the consequences. He would be free to rule at his discretion—far away from the controlling hand of Hunedoara, far away from the rest of Europe.

"Today," continued Hunedoara, "our effort to stop Mehmed from destroying that which we hold dear begins. Eventually, we will recapture what is rightfully ours and ultimately eliminate all evil from Europe. Constantinople will be ours once more!"

Once again the group assembled erupted, causing Hunedoara to smile at the frenzy. *They are his to command*, Dragwlya thought. *Obedient dogs.*

SERBIA
June 3, 1456

Hunedoara's combined land and sea forces reached Serbia in late May, closely followed by the eight thousand simple peasants led by Giovanni da Capistrano. Daily, the aged monk tried desperately to convince Hunedoara to allow his men to join the crusade. Daily, he was denied, and each battle fought found the men of Capistrano fighting alone.

Customarily, Hunedoara sent a diplomatic appeal into each city his forces approached and had yet to receive a response of any type. The failure of the Turkish to send a reply was taken as a refusal to negotiate. Thus far, Hunedoara's forces had captured the Serbian cities that had maintained a precarious autonomy under the rule of the Turkish, and with each victory the men gained more confidence. An important element for any army to possess, confidence was a necessity for a force of less than ten thousand, considering that the force of the sultan numbered more than twice that.

Hunedoara had lost few men to fighting at this point, but another enemy was slowly taking soldiers away from him, Capistrano, and Mehmed. This particular threat had accompanied the Turkish forces from Anatolia, becoming more of a factor as the campaign wore on. Its victims were the old, the young, the weak, the strong, anyone it willed itself upon.

Everywhere the Turkish set foot, the plague became an epidemic. It had begun spreading during the summer, and fighting the Turkish now meant risking infection by an unseen enemy that could not be killed; an enemy that threatened to make dying a living hell.

Hunedoara awoke to a distinct fragrance filling his nostrils—the sickening odor of burning flesh. He sat up and gagged. For the past few nights, he had ordered pyres be built and the bodies of the dead burned. The stench engulfed the encampment and lingered heavily. After dragging himself out of bed and preparing to face a new day, Hunedoara crept out of his tent. A gentle breeze was blowing but was tainted by the acrid smell. Looking at the ground, Hunedoara saw what appeared to be snow. This being June, however, he realized it was actually ashes from the pyres. He gagged again.

"Sir, are you all right?"

Opening his eyes, Hunedoara saw one of his commanders standing before him. Clearing his throat, he answered. "I am fine. How many?"

"Eight more last night, sir. Two from sustained wounds; the other six from plague. All the bodies were sent to the pyre, per your orders."

Hunedoara nodded. "How many more have contracted the illness?"

"We are certain of twenty, sir…We suspect fifteen more. I fear it is only a matter of time before the whole empire is overrun."

Hunedoara let out a heavy sigh of disgust. "Maybe Mehmed won't want Europe then...or maybe this was his plan all along."

"The plague…as a weapon, sir?"

"A few of his men will die but far fewer than in battle." Hunedoara began to cough.

Refusing to openly question Hunedoara's health, the commander kept his suspicion to himself. Despite the absence of his words, Hunedoara knew what the man was thinking.

"I am fine, commander. I just need to get away from this stench for awhile, that's all. Call together the other commanders…including Capistrano."

"Sir?" The commander could not contain his shock.

"They have been with us all along. They are loyal, trustworthy, and they have the desire to save what is theirs. We need such men." Again Hunedoara began to cough. "Go."

"Yes, sir." Walking away the commander could not help but wonder how much trouble Hunedoara thought they were in to permit Capistrano to join the campaign. He also wondered how long it would be before Hunedoara's body was one of those being dragged out and thrown onto the pyre.

Hunedoara felt himself working harder to fill his lungs with air, gasping for breath. He was well into his sixties. Maybe this was simply old age finally catching up with him. If so, then why was a man whose age surpassed his own by roughly ten years, a man who fought with the heart of a twenty-year-old, not affected in the same manner? Perhaps Capistrano possessed a fighting spirit that he did not have. The years had never affected Hunedoara before. Maybe the physical abuse he had submitted himself to was to blame.

Hunedoara knew better.

The thought scared him more than the prospect of old age's ailments. Old age was a natural part of life. This was something different; something no one could conquer without God's intervention.

Hunedoara shook his head with anger, but the side-to-side motion was replaced with a vertical one as he began coughing once more. In the upcoming months his body, mind, and spirit would be attacked, then ravaged. Saving Belgrade would be the final goal he must accomplish. It would be as much for himself as it would be for his sons.

Hunedoara had to prove one last time he deserved the title of *White Knight*, that Varna had been an anomaly. Everyone must be shown. He had to make certain he did not fail again.

CHAPTER XXV
THE CONQUEST BEGINS
BRAN
June 16, 1456

After doing everything Hunedoara had instructed him to do, Dragwlya would today complete the second to last step before regaining Wallachia's throne. Finally, he would embark on the journey to exact revenge on one of the men responsible for the assassinations of his father and Mircea.

There were still two hours before dawn. Time had almost become meaningless in Dragwlya's planning, and sleep deprivation revealed just how anxious he was to leave Bran. Wanting the hours to speed by simply made them plod all the more, causing Dragwlya to find ways to occupy himself. He accomplished this mostly through his favorite pastime—punishing criminals and thinking about the thousands of ways he could ultimately exterminate Vladislav. He filled his days and nights with other impulsive acts as well.

Sitting on the edge of his bed, Dragwlya peered over his shoulder at the woman whom he had had his way with earlier. Though charming, educated, and beautiful, she now only registered with him as would any other discarded piece of refuse. Closing his eyes, Dragwlya bent over. Placing his face into his hands, he blew out the stale air in his lungs loudly enough that the woman stirred. She was not the first he had taken into his bed, not the last whose name he would quickly forget. They all looked and acted the same, none more special than the other. None measured up to his expectations.

Anchoring his hands next to his sides, Dragwlya pushed himself off of the bed and raised his arms above his head to stretch. He felt a tingling throughout his body from the motion and, yawning, made his way over to the balcony outside of his bedchamber. He leaned on the railing and looked east, toward Wallachia. Every night, no matter how briefly, he tried to imagine what it felt like to be buried alive. This self-inflicted torture had occurred since the day Cazan detailed to him Mircea's grisly fate. The very thought made him claustrophobic, sometimes to the point he labored to breathe.

In his mind, Dragwlya felt he had an eternity to think about everything. Being alone, truly alone, gave him so much time. He longed for his lost family and for someone to share his life with. There was no one he wanted to turn to, no one he felt he could confide in. Often his thoughts turned to Radu and the wish that his younger brother had the same fighting spirit he possessed. Eventually, the reality of what his brother had become created resentment. He wished Radu had been the one to be buried alive.

It was nearly midday now. Hundreds of conversations filled the afternoon air as

Dragwlya surveyed the army he would soon lead into battle. Comprising his force were a few exiled boyars, Hungarians, and Romanian mercenaries. Dragwlya viewed them with mixed emotions.

While overjoyed that so many had agreed to join him, Dragwlya recognized them for what they were—an angry mob at best. He wondered if they would trust one another in the heat of battle, an issue certain to play an integral role in his recapturing the throne. Escaping from his thoughts momentarily, Dragwlya stared up at the Carpathians. The pass at Bran opened wide, simply awaiting Dragwlya and his men. Conversely, the mountains themselves were foreboding, waiting to crumble and bury them, effectively ending the campaign before it began. The stone giants were darker today than usual, he thought. Dragwlya could not help but picture them as the entrance to the underworld. It would be up to him to lead his men through and overcome the devil lurking deep within.

"Are you ready, sire?"

Dragwlya swiftly turned to see who had addressed him. The commander was more confident than he was. Convinced of the man's determination, Dragwlya immediately let a smile come to his face.

"Yes, it is time."

The commander nodded his head sharply as he answered. "Yes, sire."

Instantly the commander rode off, anxious to start the campaign. Dragwlya continued to smile as the man raced away. He had the look Dragwlya himself possessed and the spirit of a warrior ready to overcome impossible odds.

Dragwlya felt nervous upon hearing the call for the men to begin moving out. The hair on the back of his neck rose. He breathed in deeply and exhaled, trying hopelessly to calm himself. Indeed the time was here; time for Dragwlya's rule, for Vladislav's demise, for revenge.

OUTSIDE OF BELGRADE
July 13, 1456

Combined, the men of Hunedoara and Capistrano managed to take every Turkish controlled city impeding their march toward Belgrade. Only two formidable obstacles remained—the Turkish flotillas on the Danube and the massive land forces of Mehmed blocking the city. Victory upon victory formed an invincibility complex in many of the Christians. Even the knowledge of how badly outnumbered they would be upon reaching Belgrade could not compel anyone to give up the fight. The men understood losing meant losing everything.

A fleet two hundred strong, twenty-two large cannons, two hundred seventy-eight smaller cannons and an army more than one hundred thousand strong lay entrenched, prepared to take Belgrade and then all of Europe. Like freshly fallen snow, the white tents of the Turkish blanketed the ground, presenting an awesome, almost incomprehensible sight to the crusaders. Mehmed had approached the fortress with a siege mentality, effectively cutting off supplies to Belgrade. Hunedoara had decided the first course of action required was to break through the flotillas that occupied the Danube. Relief had to be provided to the fortress, and Hunedoara realized how much better his chances would be if he were able to fight this battle from behind the city's protective walls. The fleet accompanying the men had arrived earlier last week and even now was engaged in fighting. Mehmed's armada continued to hold their own and, like their land counterparts, turned the Christian force away with ease.

Constantly, they were being pushed back and losing ground. Fatigue and reality were finally taking their toll on the army of simple men and soldiers. Hunedoara had expected it. He knew their fortune must run out sometime. He only wished it had not taken so long to do so. Being beaten now, when they had come so far, would be more agonizing than had they been totally annihilated at the onset.

"We cannot win, sir."

It was the first time the campaign had been openly doubted by any of the men. Hunedoara looked at the man with a stern stare and, as his chest heaved, scolded him.

"I have not come all this way to simply surrender! We will fight until every last man has breathed his final breath or until we have won!" Perspiration beaded and rolled down his face. Trying unsuccessfully to contain himself, Hunedoara began coughing uncontrollably.

"Sir, you are suffering from plague. You are dying." The man stared deeply into the eyes of Hunedoara, saddened at how sickly he looked. Day after day he watched more of Hunedoara's greatness fade and wondered how much longer it would be before it ceased to be entirely.

Hunedoara stopped coughing. "I may be dying, but unlike you I am not decaying."

Hunedoara's statement alarmed him. "What?"

"You are losing heart...if you have not already lost it completely. My health may be failing me, but my spirit is strong. My mind is strong. My will is determined, and I refuse to die until we achieve what we have set out to do. If you wish to quit, quit. I am not giving up, and I will fight with everyone else who has the strength to stand with me."

The man understood Hunedoara's determination now served as the only thing keeping him from his deathbed. "Sir, I commend your bravery, but a line must be drawn somewhere."

"The line *has* been drawn...Which side of it are you on?"

"I will not desert you sir, and I will not be called a coward. I have sworn to give my life for the empire...I will uphold that oath."

"Be certain you can keep your promises before making them … Now leave me."

"Yes, sir."

With only slight hesitation, Hunedoara collapsed onto his bed once the man disappeared from view. The plague had taken a toll on his body greater than he had allowed to show. His head ached as if someone were inside of it, pounding on his skull with a juggernaut. He would not be able to withstand much more but realized his death provided the Christian force an opportunity to abandon the crusade. He could not allow that to happen. He would not be responsible for their defeat again.

Quietly, Giovanni da Capistrano entered the tent of his ally. He stared at Hunedoara on the bed, listening to the governor's heavy breathing, watching his chest rise and fall unevenly. Hunedoara's tent reeked of death. Without a sound Capistrano continued to observe Hunedoara lingering in torment. He shook his head, trying to imagine the horrible pain and frustration the plague caused such a man. Eventually, this great crusader would succumb to an enemy he stood no chance of defeating and would die an undeserving death. Capistrano let out a heavy sigh and shook his head.

Surprised by the sound, Hunedoara instantly sat up, sweat coursing over his body like a hundred salty rivulets. His eyes focused enough to decipher the outline of Capistrano from the rest of his surroundings. Attempting to control his breathing, Hunedoara welcomed the monk in Latin.

Hearing the labored words trickle out of Hunedoara's mouth, Capistrano stealthily moved toward the bed and sat next to his comrade. Hunedoara gazed at the man, wondering what thoughts ran through the monk's head. Capistrano obviously understood what was happening. Looking at Hunedoara with his sunken eyes, Capistrano spoke after a brief moment of silence.

"I am sorry this has happened to you, my friend. Such a brave defender of God should not have to suffer so horribly."

"It is the fate I deserve." Hunedoara coughed. The look of surprise on Capistrano's face did not shock Hunedoara. "No...It's true. I deserve this. They are all right...I was the reason twenty thousand men were killed at Varna. There is no one else is to blame."

"Not true. All who have fought for you have done so because of their devotion to the empire."

"And I betrayed their trust. My foolishness, my overconfidence, killed them. Yet, in spite of my inadequacies...I survived."

"You survived and overcame those so called inadequacies because of what you possess. You survived because of your abilities and your faith."

"I would like to believe you, but I know better. This condition of mine proves it. God has finally seen fit to punish me for my sins." Capistrano stared at the open sores on Hunedoara's face as the latter began to cough once more. The sound of congealed liquid being forced from his lungs emanated from Hunedoara's throat as he covered his mouth to keep the saliva from spraying the monk. "I never was the *White Knight* of the people. It was an undeserved tittle...completely inappropriate."

"No! You *are* the *White Knight* and must continue to embrace your title. Not for yourself but for those who have bestowed it upon you. Your time and service to the empire and God will not end until we have saved Belgrade. You are the only one capable of saving Christianity from Mehmed."

Solemnly, Hunedoara shook his head. "You don't understood...I don't want to die. I want to see my sons take the reins I have left them...I want to finish what I have started." Hunedoara struggled to clear his throat and began coughing once more. He smirked and laughed slightly. "I am in no condition to be on the battlefield."

Capistrano looked down at his feet and sighed heavily. "I was mistaken. I believed you to be a different man. I thought you were a leader who would never give in to self-ishness. I see now I was wrong, that you would allow Islam to reign. Varna was not your fault. But if you die now, if you chose not to lead this army any farther, the deaths of many more than twenty thousand and that of Christianity will lie squarely and solely on your shoulders. This choice *is* yours."

Without another word, Capistrano rose from Hunedoara's bed and began walking toward the tent's exit. Hunedoara followed the monk with his eyes, saying nothing. Already he was deep in thought, recalling all Capistrano had told him.

Was it his duty to lead the crusaders to the end, or should he now allow the responsibility to lie with someone else? He had always found himself making decisions that would bring about monumental consequences. This situation was not unique. He had never quit before. Why did he wish to now?

Choosing not to fight the inevitable any longer, Hunedoara knew he must accept his shortcomings and end the torment he had subjected himself to for so long because of Varna. Why was he questioning himself when all that remained to do now was fight?

Volleys resumed the following morning. As another galley sank, the men cried out to Allah in anguish and fear. Hunedoara's forces had been gaining ground and were close to gaining the advantage on the river. Thus far two galleys had been sunk, and nearly fifteen smaller vessels of the sultan's fleet had been commandeered.

Mehmed shook his head in disbelief, laughing quietly. He was watching from a safe distance, trying to comprehend the inconceivable. Theoretically, it appeared simple enough. His forces outnumbered those of the Christians' nearly two to one. So why were his supposedly superior flotillas being overrun, allowing the crusaders an easy avenue to reach Belgrade? The men on their ships fought as if protected by some unseen entity that would not allow defeat to occur.

"*What* is happening to my men?"

The disgust in Mehmed's voice was undeniable to his viziers.

"Why is it my fleet has failed and my forces cannot destroy an army made up of *farmers*?"

The viziers stood mute, afraid to say anything. They had kept a strange looking star secret from Mehmed, not knowing how he would react. All the while they hoped it was a good omen. Now they feared the sultan should have been told. Unanimously, they agreed to never tell Mehmed of its appearance. Still, there needed to be some explanation as to how such defeats could be the will of Allah.

"My liege…" Mehmed anxiously awaited an explanation from the vizier bold enough to speak. "In truth, we do not know what has happened. We do not feel Allah is upset with you."

"Then why does he allow my ships and my army to be destroyed?"

"We do not know, my liege."

The answer was unsatisfactory. "If this is not *our* god's will, then it must be *theirs*!" Rarely did Mehmed suggest the Christian God's existence. Now the viziers knew he was beginning to lose faith.

"There is no other god but Allah, my liege. You must believe this."

"The Christian forces are near to defeating my flotillas and will use the path to gain access to the fortress! Blind faith will not stop them. Get out of my sight!"

Bravely, the vizier had taken a chance and failed. The others by Mehmed's side would not make the same mistake. Each one remained motionless, silently watching the sultan display his frustration. Shaking his head, Mehmed continued to watch as a third galley was overtaken.

"I need answers. Meaningful, useful answers. If you cannot give them to me, I will find viziers who can. Either tell me how to stop this, or you will each answer to my sword!"

Each of the viziers quaked at Mehmed's ultimatum. With perspiration seeping through their skin, all looked toward the battlefield and then to one another for the answer that would calm Mehmed. Victory was the answer he sought, but no matter how much staring they did, they would not be able to tell him how to achieve it.

Mehmed waited for a few seconds, long enough to paralyze them. "Hmphf. You know nothing." With that he walked off; away from their ignorance, their uselessness.

"We must tell him of the star!"

"No! Absolutely not! Telling him now would only infuriate him and make our deaths a certainty."

"He is right. If we tell Mehmed of the star, who knows what fate would await us?"

"Then what should we do?"

Blankly, the viziers studied one another, each wondering what the others were thinking, none knowing what to think. Finding an answer was always difficult. Finding one they all agreed upon and one Mehmed approved of was nearly impossible.

Idiots… fools. Why do I ever listen to them? Mehmed had found a new place to view the battle alone. *By Allah…* In awe, the sultan watched one lone Christian fight his way through four Janissaries. *How did he do that?* Only after a few moments did he finally begin to understand.

Certainly, he had more men with better training and a more powerful arsenal. They did not, however, fight with the amount of determination the Christians did. This was the one component Mehmed knew his men lacked, the one the Christians held in reserve. Hunedoara's men fought to protect what still belonged to them, what they still could lose. For Mehmed's men the crusade had become a fight to see how much land and wealth they could obtain, not a fight of defending Islam or their homes.

In his solitude, Mehmed contemplated how he could restore the fighting spirit of his men. What did he have to say for them to regain drive? A great cheer distracted him, and he now saw the Christians were winning the battle on the Danube. They would reach Belgrade. Allowing his head to hang, Mehmed listened to Hunedoara's men as they praised their god and cursed his.

CHAPTER XXVI
WALLACHIA RETAKEN
NEAR TÎRGOVIŞTE
July 18, 1456

Nearly three hours ago the sun began spilling over the horizon. Even in darkness, however, everything had felt familiar to Dragwlya. The landscape, the air he breathed, the sounds, everything. Inhaling deeply, the smell brought back countless memories. Some he wished had lasted forever. Others he knew would never leave him and were the reasons for his return. Now on the battlefield, most of his thoughts revolved around the latter, around his father and Mircea.

Across the way from him stood the army of Vladislav, the man who possessed what he deserved and desired. Killing him was all that remained hindering the end of his quest, of winning back his birthright, and retrieving Wallachia.

Dragwlya had reached the principality last evening. In making the final preparations for today, he noticed something odd—the unusual star, the same star witnessed by Mehmed's viziers. Though such stars were generally feared, Dragwlya considered it a sign from his father and brother, a sign of his glory yet to come, a sign of his victory over Vladislav. His feelings were so strong that he did not bother consulting his seers regarding it. Dragwlya was now more confident than ever, more determined than ever, and ready to rule Wallachia again.

Dew covered the entire countryside, and the tiny droplets of water greatly reflected the sun's light. The morning air hung heavily with humidity, and not a cloud appeared in the sky. It was a certainty the July heat would affect the participants of the battle.

Dragwlya grew more eager with each passing moment and issued orders he knew were repetitive. At this point he didn't care. There would be no mistaking what his plans were or how he expected them to be carried out. Already his hand was at his waist, firmly griping the blade once belonging to his father. Dragwlya passed much of the previous night simply staring at the weapon. It commanded much respect when wielded properly. He was determined to show that his capabilities with the blade had reached their full potential. Tightening his hand around the blade's hilt, Dragwlya recalled the day Cazan had brought it to him, the day he learned what had happened.

Only yesterday Mircea was saving him from the murky waters of the lake where he had learned to swim. Only yesterday his father was alive, teaching him the intricacies of battle, the art of war. The events, so vivid in Dragwlya's memory, happened a lifetime ago. Countless, unknown memories had been stolen from him. As the image of Mircea being covered with dirt filled his mind, Dragwlya's rage immediately brought him back to the present.

"Are you certain you understand all I have told you?"

"Yes, sire."

"I hope you are ready for a fight then."

"I am ready for victory, sire."

He smiled at the man's response. "Go."

Dragwlya now knew the confidence his men had in him. He portrayed himself as more than capable, and that is how he was perceived. Above all else, he knew they feared him; they understood the consequences of failure. He mounted his steed, prepared for the battle to begin.

Atop his horse, Dragwlya looked the part of St. George set to slay the dragon. In every way, he was ready to conquer Vladislav and the doubts lingering in the minds of all who thought his candidacy for the throne outrageous and implausible. Today there would be no negotiations, only winners and losers.

With a silent nod from their leader, Dragwlya's infantry charged. They screamed battle cries for their leader and obscenities at their enemies as they rushed forward. Even with the deafening sound of their shouts, Dragwlya could still hear the order for Vladislav's army to charge being given.

Thunder rose up from the ground as the two forces sprinted, ready to clash. Dragwlya looked on at the countless blades rising into the air, the sun danced back and forth across the battlefield on them as they were cocked, waiting to be swung. Anxiously, he anticipated the clanging of the first two swords.

Metal met metal. Dozens were injured, maimed, or killed on the first pass. Those who survived now battled to stay alive. Dragwlya was enjoying every gory second of the spectacle. Transfixed, he watched the life leaving both he and Vladislav's men like red rain, reveling in the knowledge it was all for his glory. He could barely stand being out of the action.

Soon the heavy cavalry of both sides joined the melee. Throughout the fighting, Dragwlya retained sight of Vladislav's position. With a quick jerk on his reigns, he darted out onto the battlefield, aiming only for Vladislav. Nothing else concerned him. His throne was the ultimate goal, but his revenge would be the means by which he gained it.

Riding across the battlefield, Dragwlya combated those who dared try and stop him. Their acts were foolhardy and each one that faced him realized their mistake only after Dragwlya was striking a deathblow. He continued to keep his sights set on Vladislav. It would be a matter of seconds before the two of them finally met.

Like the candidate for his throne, Vladislav understood the stakes involved and the man he now approached. Dragwlya was a being of ambition and heart who would not stop until he possessed what he had set out to gain. Vladislav, however, was not willing to simply give up what he had earned. He had worked hard to obtain this position and was not going to just abdicate.

Presently, the two leaders found themselves on the brink of colliding. It was too late to turn around; doing so would only make a coward of such a man. It would make him an easier target also.

The Toledo blade dripped with blood from several of Vladislav's men, glistening crimson as Dragwlya held it up to face his nemesis. Vladislav now understood and could see Dragwlya's determination. Jumbled thoughts ran through his head rapidly, giving the scene the feeling of some ridiculous dream. But there was no time to awaken. His enemy's steed now charged at him recklessly from only a few meters away. It scared him that someone could have such a cavalier attitude toward life. What Vladislav did not comprehend was that Dragwlya did not allow the idea of dying a chance to exist.

Dragwlya felt his hostility build as he approached the murderer of his father and brother. Everything disappeared from his view except for Vladislav. All motion around him slowed to the point of stillness. The sounds of battle still exploded from every angle, but they were distant, coming from a different time and place far from here. For Dragwlya the implications of this moment were abundantly clear—kill Vladislav, and all will be righted. With one simple thrust of the sword, Wallachia would again be in the hands of the family it truly belonged to. Countless images flashed through his mind, images of his father and brother. Now he could hear Mircea calling out to him.

Take the fight to him! Take the fight to him, and take everything from him!

With the sound of his brother's voice echoing in his head, Dragwlya shouted Mircea's name and swung the Toledo blade with all his might to meet the sword of Vladislav. The resulting blow knocked both men from their stallions. Neither concerned themselves with minor injuries they may have suffered due to the fall and quickly rose to their feet, ready to strike. Quietly, Dragwlya and Vladislav stood, their chests heaving, each waiting for the other to make the first move. Like sharks coming upon prey, they began circling each other before moving in for the kill.

"I've waited a long time to watch you die." Dragwlya's voice was clearly heard by Vladislav, even with the backdrop of a battle raging on all around them.

"I've never given you a thought."

Dragwlya sensed the smile on Vladislav's face and allowed a small smirk to cross his own lips.

"Pity you were not present when I had your brother buried alive."

Dragwlya's smirk immediately disappeared.

"He begged for mercy the entire time."

Rage drove Dragwlya. Reaching up slowly, he raised his face shield. His piercing emerald green eyes cut deeper than any blade, simply bypassing Vladislav's armor and ripping through his body. Hesitantly, Vladislav raised his own face shield. He had anticipated being swung at immediately after his comment and had prepared himself for the onslaught. This was hardly what he expected, and now he had to contend with the haunting eyes of a man who wanted revenge and would not quit until he had it.

Without much success, Vladislav tried to show the display was having no affect on him. Dragwlya knew otherwise by the way his enemy failed to stare at him for very long. He had penetrated his adversary's soul and knew it. Vladislav's words were a good front, but his eyes betrayed him.

"You will wish you had never said that." The dry words left Dragwlya's mouth screaming for vengeance. He moved into an attack stance once more without bothering to lower his face shield.

Forcing the saliva down his throat, Vladislav hurriedly lowered his face shield and took a defensive position. Metal struck metal repeatedly as they fought a lone battle amongst thousands of combatants. Each blow empowered Dragwlya just as much as it sapped his opponent.

Vladislav could feel his pulse racing, his heart pounding, ready to burst. Sweat had saturated his clothing, hampering his movements. He had been on the defensive since the battle had begun, and blocking Dragwlya's constant strikes was all he could do to stay alive. Between parries he hoped the opportunity to take the offensive would present itself.

Again Dragwlya swung at Vladislav. Everything taught to him by his father, Mircea, countless knights, and tutors was now second nature. Dragwlya fought without thinking. He could feel the adrenaline flowing through him, allowing his emotions to wield the blade. All except this piece of filth before him was irrelevant. The only thing justifying Dragwlya's life was Vladislav's death.

With a bold swing Dragwlya came down hard, missing Vladislav's body horribly and stumbling to keep his balance. Vladislav finally had an opening. Replicating the attack his opponent had attempted, he managed to hit Dragwlya squarely enough to draw first blood. Though the blade had gone at least two inches into Dragwlya's shoulder, he refused to cry out. Instead, he compared his wound to the pain his father and brother had suffered.

Vladislav withdrew his sword, blinking in amazement at his apparent inability to hurt his enemy. He stared as blood oozed freely from Dragwlya, waiting for a groan, a gasp, any sign that he had been injured. No such sign came. Dragwlya simply stood, staring at him.

Why does he not put his face shield down? Vladislav knew the answer to his question already, and Dragwlya's reasoning behind his action was working. Enraged by the apparent lack of damage he had caused, Vladislav began swinging wildly.

Dragwlya would not let Vladislav strike him again, and each blow missed worse than the last. Vladislav could not believe the speed his enemy possessed. He was too fast, as though he knew exactly where the attack would be coming from next. Frustrated, Vladislav continued to wear himself down, trying desperately to hit his opponent. For brief seconds, they would stare at one another. When they did, Vladislav had to endure Dragwlya's smirk. His lack of concentration was evident.

"Lower your face shield and fight!"

Dragwlya chuckled, working his blade ever closer to Vladislav's body. His enemy had lost focus, and Dragwlya now sensed vengeance was close. With a wild, exaggerated swing, Vladislav missed his mark badly, nearly turning himself around. Willingly, Dragwlya applied the extra force required to make Vladislav reach that mark with a push. The quick spin caused Vladislav to lose his footing.

Falling to the ground, Vladislav flailed frantically, knowing his mistake would likely mean his death. Even though he was motionless for less than a second, it was all the time Dragwlya needed. Though Vladislav quickly tried to get back to his feet, Dragwlya immediately forced him to stay down on his stomach.

As Vladislav had begun to get up, Dragwlya placed the tip of the Toledo blade against his neck. Gasping for air, Vladislav's heart raced at the same pace his mind did while trying to guess what his enemy's next move would be. Dragwlya gradually pushed Vladislav back down to the ground, pressing his blade increasingly harder into the throat of his foe to flip him onto his back. Vladislav offered no resistance. Thousands of feelings overloaded him, the fear of his own death being the most prominent.

Vladislav lie flat now, staring up at Dragwlya. His enemy stood like a stone sentinel watching over him, obviously savoring the moment he had waited so long for. Dragwlya continued to smile down at the murderer of his father and brother, anticipating the moment when Vladislav's anxiety would overtake him.

"You've won! Kill me!"

Dragwlya spoke not a word but instead slowly shook his head from side to side, signifying he was not yet ready to extinguish Vladislav's life. An extension of Dragwlya's own arm, the Toledo blade smoothly worked its way up from the neck of Vladislav to the bottom of his face shield. Gleefully, Dragwlya methodically lifted the guard, exposing the white face of an obviously petrified man. Upon seeing Vladislav's expression of sheer terror, Dragwlya could not help but begin to laugh.

"I remember when it was I doing the laughing." Vladislav had already given up any hope of living. He would now try to provoke as quick and painless a death as possible. "It was when they told me of your father's lifeless corpse sinking into the marshes of Bălteni!"

Dragwlya stopped laughing.

"I remember my men telling me how they stabbed him, over and over!"

Dragwlya remained silent.

"But hearing of Mircea's death gave me even more pleasure!"

"Shut up." The phrase escaped from Dragwlya's mouth as little more than a whisper.

"I especially enjoyed listening to how he was first broken and beaten before being thrown into that pit and buried alive!"

"I said...Shut *up*!" As the last word boomed from Dragwlya's very soul, the Toledo blade pierced through the back of Vladislav's throat and into the earth beneath.

Damn.

Dragwlya realize his enemy had gotten exactly what he wanted and that he himself had been manipulated into doing something irrational because of his failure to control his anger. Vladislav had escaped without suffering appropriately.

Never again will I allow my emotions to interfere with the proper punishment for my enemies.

Even though Vladislav's death meant he had reclaimed Wallachia's throne, Dragwlya knew his revenge was only partial. Much more remained to be done for it to be complete.

BELGRADE
July 21, 1456

Against almost impossible odds, Hunedoara and Capistrano's men fought their way through a superior foe and created a passage that allowed them to provide much needed relief to Belgrade. For days the Turkish tried unsuccessfully to enter the city before Mehmed recalled his men in an effort to formulate a plan that guaranteed victory. After a cease fire lasting all day, the sultan ordered an all-out assault beginning shortly after sundown. He placed the Janissaries at the helm of the attack, where they continuously gained ground and ultimately reached the outer defenses of the city. Now they were maneuvering to breech the city walls.

Hunedoara looked on as the Janissaries grew closer, debating if this was finally the end. It couldn't be. He had promised himself he would not allow another atrocity. He would not die until assured all he had fought to preserve for his sons was secured. Hunedoara would not die a failure in the eyes of those who idolized him. He must not. Each day, however, brought new complications.

As time passed, notable characteristics of the crusader faded away. Physically he grew weaker, and though he tried his best to conceal the agony he suffered, his men could see it. Never did they doubt his resolve. Whenever given orders, his men executed them without question. Approaching Hunedoara, Capistrano knew his counterpart was in crippling pain. The days had become strenuous for him also and, over the past few days, the old monk had begun to develop the same symptoms he had witnessed Hunedoara suffer through. At his age, Capistrano's body would be ravaged much faster. His only wish was to see Mehmed defeated before being called to His glory.

"Do you think they will penetrate the walls?"

Hunedoara nodded affirmatively. "Given enough time." His voice was wavering, and he saw the look of pity on Capistrano's face. "Do not grieve for me yet...I have one last fight in me."

The words brought a slight smile to the old monk's face. Instantly, he began wondering if his look of pity was for Hunedoara or the hardships he would soon endure himself. "It is impossible to call for reinforcements. We've reached the fortress but are cut-off from all our resources. If only we could place the Turkish in the same predicament."

As expected, the Janissaries penetrated the city. Reaching the fortress, they encamped on either side of the moat protecting the crusaders. The citizens of Belgrade were moved to the sanctuary of the fortress, and those who had not volunteered to join the fight gathered together to pray for deliverance. Hunedoara and Capistrano looked on, side by side, at the invading army festering below.

Although Hunedoara had convinced himself God had kept him alive this long for no other purpose than to see the crusading force victorious, he had no idea how that victory would come about. Defeat appeared inevitable. Where was the small insight he needed to gain the advantage? Silently, he reflected on the events of the siege. Nothing presented itself as useful; nothing had happened that Hunedoara figured to be significant enough to focus on. Throughout the night the only chord that continued to be struck with him was something Capistrano had said earlier.

If only we could find some way to place the Turkish in the same predicament.

Yes... if only, thought Hunedoara. But how could the Turkish be cut off from reinforcements? No solution seemed to exist, and supplies would begin to run low once more.

"At this rate, our ammunition will be exhausted in three day's time, sir." Hunedoara listened intently to the report of one of his generals while continuing to eye the Janissaries below. The situation grew more hopeless as the hours dragged on. "Assuming the fighting continues that long."

"Everything is in short supply. Do we have a surplus of anything?" The question was rhetorical, and Hunedoara never expected an answer.

"Only sulfur, tar, and bacon, sir. Hardly anything useful to us now."

Capistrano did not turn to look at Hunedoara as he addressed him. Had he done so, the monk would have noticed the gleam, so long ago extinguished in his friend's eyes, had returned, restored by the inventory given to him by the general. "Already the Janissaries are making preparations to scale the walls. As you have previously pointed out, we do not have the manpower to stop them everywhere."

Hunedoara felt God had finally spoken to him and shown him a ray of the light that to this point had eluded him. He was certain the Lord had provided him with the answer to his prayers through the messenger now before him. Hunedoara addressed the general once again, now with undeniable strength.

"Order your men to gather as many blankets and as much wood as they can. Tell them to take the doors off of homes. Have the sulfur, tar, wood, and blankets all brought to the top of the fortress walls immediately…Go now."

The general managed to move only a few steps away before Hunedoara addressed him again. "General…bring the sides of bacon as well."

Not at all certain of his counterpart's intentions, or sanity, Capistrano ventured to ask what Hunedoara planned to do with the hodgepodge being brought to the battlefront. The leader of the Christian forces, knowing Capistrano's mind, laughed nearly uncontrollably in addressing the old monk.

"I still have my wits about me…I am simply enacting your idea of separating the Turkish from their reinforcements."

Within the hour, the general fulfilled the request made of him.

"We must act quickly." Hunedoara had explained his plan to Capistrano and would now let it be known to all. "Soak the blankets in sulfur. Tar as much of the wood as possible. Once that is completed, throw everything into the moat, including the sides of bacon. Anyone not assisting with these preparations should find anything that will catch fire and return with it immediately."

Full of questions, the Janissaries surrounding the fortress walls watched as various items were hurled down toward them, over their heads, and into the moat. Fumes from the sulfur and tar stung their senses. Reportedly, sides of bacon had even been flung into the water. Perhaps the infidels finally realized their defeat and were making certain anything that could be used or consumed would be destroyed.

Light illuminated the darkness, followed swiftly by intense heat. Peering up, the Janissaries saw fire beginning to rain down upon them. They watched burning missiles plunge into the moat behind them, in front of them, or next to them as they attempted to cross it. Fiercely, the flames spread, engulfing the debris floating in the water. The inferno was growing, consuming whatever it came into contact with instantly. No one swam fast enough to escape it unscathed. They swam and screamed until succumbing to the pain or until emerging from the moat scarred forever.

Capistrano could not help but recall the story in which God gave protection to the Israelites to cross the Red Sea from Pharaoh's chariots by conjuring up a pillar of fire. He shared the thought with Hunedoara, going so far as to refer to him as Moses. Willingly, Hunedoara accepted the reference. Like Moses, he realized he would never enter the Promised Land to which he was trying to lead his people. Also like Moses, the commander of the Christian forces wished to at least see the land of milk and honey before leaving the world.

Fear gripped the Janissaries caught between the fortress walls and the wall of fire behind them. At all costs they would enter the stronghold and eradicate their enemies.

They would kill for Islam, for their sultan, and now for their fallen brethren. Oddly, the Janissaries met with no resistance as they scaled the walls or as they reached the top and crossed over in small units. No one blocked their entry into the fortress; they could see no one present and soon reached the streets of the citadel.

Remaining in their groups, the Janissaries ventured into the heart of the fortress, waiting for the attack. It did not come, and as more men scrambled over the walls the cheering began. Obviously, the Christians had given up, abandoned their posts, and were now fleeing through another part of the fortress. Collectively, the soldiers concluded the looting of Belgrade could begin. Confident, eager, and carefree they strode through the streets, unaware that none of them would live to see another day.

From nowhere, from everywhere, Hunedoara's men instantly appeared and surrounded the individual units that had been allowed entry into Belgrade. Hunedoara had ordered his men into hiding until commanded to show themselves once again and overrun the invaders. The ruse worked.

Eventually, Janissaries stopped entering the fortress, and those inside would never receive reinforcements necessary to battle an overwhelming army. Before long, Hunedoara's crusaders were once again the only living souls inside the citadel. They threw the bodies of the slain into the burning moat. Cheering once again erupted from inside the fortress, this time from the crusaders.

Morning light began filtering in through black smoke, revealing a gross scene of carnage. Somberly, Mehmed listened to the reports of how many men were lost while staring at the fortress he so desperately desired. The fire in the moat had yet to burn out, and a haze from the smoldering objects in it continued to rise, cloaking Belgrade. Mehmed ordered his cannons to stop firing, marking a break in the fighting. Seizing one of the few opportunities given to them, the Christians used the time to transport more troops and supplies to the fortress.

He continuously finds ways to fend off my attacks. I wonder if Constantinople would have fallen had he been there. Mehmed began to pay less attention to the reports, concentrating more of his attention on Hunedoara. Though he hated him for his ingenuity, the sultan still held Hunedoara in high regard as a warrior, as a man. Were he a Turk, Hunedoara would certainly be a highly decorated bey, possibly even a vizier. No thought had ever been given to corrupting him. It would have been a futile venture.

July 23, 1456

"By God they will rot right where they are!"

Another arrow pierced the air and struck between the ribs of an already dead Janissary. The Turkish line had moved forward to retrieve their fallen and, although ordered not to by Hunedoara, a few of the crusader units had left the sanctuary of the fortress through demolished ramparts and had taken up positions across from their enemy. Their taunts were only verbal initially, but after having their insults returned some of the more temperamental Christians began firing arrows into Turkish corpses. Increasingly, the arrows were nearing those simply attempting to carry away the dead.

With growing frustration, members of the Turkish provincial cavalry mounted, intent upon dispersing the harassing force. Their attempts were unsuccessful, and some sustained injuries during the informal skirmish. While the number of cavalry shrunk, the number of Christians began to grow. More of the crusaders ventured outside of the fortifications, finding a place among their brethren. Word of what was occurring eventually reached the Christian leaders. Capistrano arrived first.

The old monk made his way outside of the walls and began ordering the men to fall back. He noticed most of those he was shouting orders to were the common men who had volunteered to join in the fighting. Every step he took brought him closer to the fighting, away from the safety of the fortress. As loudly as he shouted, he knew his orders were falling upon deaf ears. Additionally, his presence had attracted an additional two thousand crusaders. If allowed to continue, the entire Christian force would exit the citadel. It was then that the thought struck him.

The Turkish were not ready for a fight. Capistrano knew this from witnessing the small units of crusaders forcing back the cavalry and Janissaries. This was the moment they had waited so long for. It must be. He could see readiness in the eyes of his men. They were prepared to die for their lands, their families. Although he knew it was not his place to lead them into battle, Capistrano knew it was not his place to deny them what they desired.

"Arm yourselves!" The monk drew his own sword and proceeded to charge into the fray, leading the men who had gathered. "The Lord who made the beginning, will take care of the finish!"

As one surging wave, the crusaders moved swiftly toward the enemy line, causing panic. Unsure of how to defend against such an unorthodox attack, the cavalry and Janissaries sat stunned, paralyzed by their own uncertainty. Fear soon gave way to flight, and Mehmed's men began abandoning their positions, not caring about their sultan's assured rage. Their primary instinct of survival superseded everything else.

Shortly after Capistrano had begun the charge, Hunedoara emerged from the fortress.

My God... He's gone mad.

It was the first thought to cross Hunedoara's mind, until he saw Mehmed's men were fleeing. Not wanting to relinquish the momentum the men had gained, Hunedoara ordered an all-out charge. This would be the last stand for Belgrade.

The sultan's personal bodyguard of five thousand Janissaries had been ordered to halt the retreat and to recapture the camp. They were ignored by the common soldiers, in whose minds the Christian God had finally saw fit to retaliate for the loss of Constantinople. Mehmed cursed his men's cowardice, becoming incensed at his disgrace. He armed himself, determined to take Belgrade alone if necessary.

Continuing toward the fortress, Mehmed cut down soldier after soldier. It did not matter to him that those he was killing were mostly Janissaries. Christian and Turk alike fell beneath his sword, but they were all the same. Everyone was against him. Stopping for a brief second before killing his next opponent, Mehmed glanced around and was compelled to admit the battle had been lost. It was a scene so shocking that the sultan failed to notice being struck on the shoulder.

Mehmed recovered, blocked a flurry of swings from a young Christian soldier and, wasting no time, countered by separating the man's head from the rest of his body. As the decapitated corpse crumpled to its knees, Mehmed absorbed the scene in disbelief.

Behind him, the bulk of his army was retreating, led or followed by a vast portion of his commanders. Though disgusted by the spectacle, he had the wherewithal to realize he would soon be standing alone. He prepared himself for the inevitability of his death but prayed Allah still thought him worthy of a happy afterlife before vigorously entering the melee once more.

Mehmed disposed of victim after victim. Perhaps he would not die today. Perhaps Allah had seen fit to bestow upon him the power to rid Belgrade of the Christians nearly single-handedly. Mehmed's confidence grew with every Christian life he took. He raised his sword, ready to slay yet another when, inexplicably, a burning pain shot through his thigh. An arrow had penetrated his leg.

Taking his opportunity, the crusader readied himself to make the decisive death-blow against Mehmed. As he swung though, an unexpected shove from behind sent him lunging toward his intended target. Unintentionally, his blade twisted and, instead of cutting into his opponent, the Christian hit the sultan in the head with its side. Mehmed was rendered unconscious and immediately collapsed.

Regaining his balance, the soldier thanked God he had not been injured, that the hit from behind had not been an arrow or sword. He also thanked God for a second, easier opportunity to rid the world of the Turkish leader. Setting his sights on the neck of the sultan, he swiftly raised his sword and brought it down as hard as he could.

Just as the blade was about to cut into Mehmed, the crusader found himself ripped from the ground, thrown back with such strength he thought himself to be flying. A Janissary had purposely rammed into him, knocking him away from his intended target. The two men crashed with a thud and, as suddenly as he had appeared, the sultan's bodyguard withdrew into the fray.

He hadn't noticed at first, but it was now painfully obvious to the Christian that the Janissary had led his attack with his sword. Feeling began to fade from his arms and legs as blood poured from the puncture in his abdomen. In a matter of seconds he lost the ability to hold himself up and, unwillingly, his upper body crashed back to the ground. He would not rise again.

SOFIA
July 26, 1456

Using nightfall to cloak their shame, the defeated Turkish forces hastily began their retreat from Belgrade. Mehmed remained unconscious as his army limped along for three days with one hundred and forty wagons in tow, carting the wounded to Sofia in Bulgaria. Most of the generals who survived secretly hoped that Mehmed would never wake, fearful of what he would do.

In all, the blood of approximately twenty-four thousand of Mehmed's best men had turned the battlefield and Blue Danube dark red. The defeat was disastrous, embarrassing. Mehmed's superior force had been outfought by farmers; his army had deserted him, leaving the battlefield without his command.

Under the care of his physician and grand vizier, Mahmud Pasha, the sultan's life was saved. During the dead of night he woke for the first time since receiving the blow to his head.

"I have had the most frightful dreams."

Mahmud breathed a sigh of relief upon hearing the voice of Mehmed, groggy as it was. Before he could utter a word, the sultan continued.

"Nightmares really…" Blinking the sleep from his eyes, Mehmed turned toward his grand vizier and found a face that exemplified sorrow and apprehension. "What is it? What's wrong with you?" Unexpectedly, the first surge of pain reverberated throughout the sultan's body. He winced, wondering what had caused it. It seemed to be concentrated in two areas, his leg and his head.

Reaching down, Mehmed felt the bandage on his thigh. His hands traced over the cloth until he grazed where the arrow had entered into his leg. Sucking in air through clenched teeth, Mehmed's eyes closed as his hands and fingers gripped the flesh surrounding the wound. His head throbbed; not only from being struck, but from the resulting concussion. Mehmed knew his nightmare was very much real. Opening his eyes once more, Mehmed stared at Mahmud with horrid enlightenment.

"No." He began to gently shake his head in disbelief as he uttered the single word. "It cannot be true."

The caution in Mahmud's voice could not be mistaken. "My liege…we retreated from the battlefield three days ago and are now at Sofia."

"No…It's impossible." Denial and delirium were in the sultan's voice. "It *must* be a dream."

"My liege…over twenty thousand are dead. Those who survived did so barely. We escaped only with our lives."

Mahmud's comment intrigued Mehmed. "You mean, not only have I lost Belgrade, but in retreating my army left everything behind?"

"Yes, my liege. Orders were given for the men to take only that which they could carry. All heavy armaments were abandoned."

Mehmed visually searched the room, trying desperately to find his sword. This disgrace was too much. "I have been bested by a mob of peasants and have armed them with more than two hundred cannons." That he had survived was dishonorable. Suicide was the only option. He hoped someday his people would eventually come to remember him for his conquest of Constantinople, not this failure. In a far corner, Mehmed spied the weapon that would end his suffering. "Summon my viziers."

"Yes, my liege." Mahmud answered and left to seek out the viziers, leaving the sultan alone.

Not caring about the pain, Mehmed swung his legs over the edge of his bed to stand. His feet planted firmly on the floor, the sultan pushed himself off of the bed and, uttering a brief cry of agony, fell back upon it. Breathing in and out heavily, he felt distressed, knowing he would never succeed in reaching the sword. His redemption would have to wait.

Dejected, Mehmed glanced to his bedside and spotted the instruments and elixirs of his physician. Not knowing for what he was looking, the sultan began rummaging through the mixtures. Allah had not forsaken him. In his hand he held the answer to his suffering, to his salvation. Holding the bottle up, Mehmed regarded its label, *Arsenic*, clearly.

The sultan closed his eyes and prayed for Allah to grant his sons wisdom so that they might someday rule more wisely than he had. Begging forgiveness for his failures, Mehmed's trembling hand uncorked the vial. Slowly he lifted certain death to his lips.

"My liege…No!"

Before Mehmed could save himself, the physician bounded across the room and knocked the vial from his hand.

Opening his eyes, the sultan stared at the man in disgust. His demeanor quickly became one of sadness, however, and with tears in his eyes Mehmed collapsed fully on the bed. Allah *had* forsaken him and would not let him die so easily. Sobbing, the sultan realized he would be forced to rectify his shortcomings in this world before being allowed to proceed to the next.

CHAPTER XXVII
DEATH OF THE WHITE KNIGHT
ZEMUN, SERBIA
August 11, 1456

Festivities had been continuous since the Christians had been saved from the Turkish. No one could enter Belgrade, or the whole of Serbia for that matter, without feeling relief. Even with the joyous celebrations, however, no one dared ignore for a moment the lasting reminder left behind by the Turkish of their incursion. The miracle delivering the Christians from Mehmed's forces was marred by the plague now ravaging much of southeastern Europe, including Hungary, Croatia, and Slovenia.

Fear of the plague had kept many from following in the crusade to save Belgrade from the Turkish. The dreaded epidemic was now claiming one of the few brave enough to confront it in the attempt to save his possessions for his sons, to save Christianity for those too afraid to die as martyrs.

László remained silent and simply stared at his father. Surely he could have retained all his possessions without dying. What had he proved? Those truly loyal may mourn, but once official condolences were given all would agree how foolish Ioan Hunedoara had been.

Hunedoara recognized his son's expression. He remembered having seen it before, remembered asking László what he was thinking. László's answer became a question he continually posed to himself.

What is to be gained from my dying?

Hunedoara had lost the power of speech days ago and would die without being able to tell his sons how he felt, of the hopes he had for their future. His hearing was gone, too. All that remained was failing vision and a glassy eyed expression. The *White Knight* was an empty husk of the man he had once been.

Over the past few hours, Hunedoara's coughing had intensified. The amount of blood he spat up increased steadily. László knew the end was approaching. He no longer knew how conscious his father was of his environment or if he had awareness of it at all. For all he knew, his father had not heard or understood a word that had been spoken for days. It was a feeling he never experienced for his father before and one he imagined had never been felt for the great Ioan Hunedoara—sympathy.

Though they had administered the last rites some time ago, the priests who had come to the side of Ioan Hunedoara remained, praying for one more miracle that would go unanswered. Throughout Hunedoara's life, God had either granted him success or at least the opportunity to rebound from defeat. This sickness was not God's doing, but it was His will.

For a moment, László thought his father was about to speak. Hunedoara's mouth slowly opened, seemingly to form a few words, possibly to tell his sons goodbye. The thought passed quickly. László had seen this before. He realized his father was not going to speak; not one syllable would leave his lips. László flinched and shielded his eyes.

Hunedoara coughed and gagged violently. His body convulsed as he vomited blood and pieces of his own stomach. László had suffered through the gurgling sounds his father now made enough already and immediately covered his ears in an attempt to block them out. Covering his ears only allowed his imagination to amplify the nauseating sound though, making it echo inside of his head. László shook with his eyes closed tightly and, hearing his father dying, began to weep. Although he had not done so since his childhood, he cried hysterically. After some time, the subtle touch of a hand on his shoulder calmed him. Through teary eyes, he gazed at the priest standing next to him. Instantly, the priest's head fell.

László knew. His hands fell to his sides, uncovering his ears, and revealed silence. His father had not coughed for more than a minute now, but László would continue to hear the hacking long after it had ceased. Slowly, he turned around.

Repulsive failed to describe the sight. László's eyes slammed closed and he gasped for air with the image of his father lying motionless, covered in his own blood, burned into his memory. He turned once more to leave. His slow march evolved into a sprint for the corridor, the distance to which inexplicably grew with each step taken. The contents of his stomach raced toward his mouth.

Reaching the corridor, László braced himself. Placing his hands upon the wall to his left, he vomited. Tears streamed down his face once more as he shook his head in vain to purge his mind of the sight he had just witnessed. He spun around against the cold stone of the corridor wall and, avoiding the contents of his stomach as he did so, sunk to the floor with his arms folded across his chest. The putrid smell of his vomit failed to faze him as he fell deeper into his own thoughts. The army at Belgrade was now his to command. His father's next fight would be at Armageddon.

Certain someone would be approaching soon, László readied himself to assume command. Hunedoara had successfully kept the Turkish from taking Belgrade. László's mission would be to rid the earth of them entirely, to restore Christianity's dominance and Constantinople as one of its strongholds.

To no avail, László spat out the horrible taste in his mouth. He would have to tolerate it until finding water to wash the rancid tang away. Moving to his left to avoid the mess he had made moments earlier, he put his hands on the floor and pushed himself up. As he reached his feet, he was met by two priests and two of his father's generals. For a moment, only silence and empty stares were exchanged. One of the generals eventually ventured to offer condolences.

"I am sorry, sir. Your father will be missed."

László nodded. As the others voiced their sorrow, he lifted a hand to signal for them to be quiet.

"I appreciate your sympathies. I ask that as you served my father you now serve me. I take full command of the southern army and will continue the crusade he began."

Silence dominated again. The two generals in László's presence saluted him in a display of their unquestionable loyalty. One then offered the promise the new governor wanted.

"As I served him, I now serve you."

László extended his hand to everyone in turn somberly.

"Prepare a funeral pyre for my father."

The order was directed to the priests, who nodded and left to comply. Many pyres had been set ablaze since the onset of the plague. This one would burn brightly in both the night sky and in the minds of those present forever.

TÎRGOVIŞTE
September 6, 1456

Night consumed the Wallachian countryside, enveloping it in a sense of urgency. Dragwlya listened as a crisp breeze rustled the trees. He sat alone in his chambers, staring at a blank piece of parchment. Necessity dictated he maintain good terms with those who had supported his quest, even those who had not done so of their own accord. One such group, the German Saxon cities, had been instructed to provide aid by Ladislas V. Nevertheless, Dragwlya had established acquaintances among them and may need their help in the future. With mostly contempt, Dragwlya picked up his quill, dipped it, and pressed the tip to the parchment in a laborious effort to write.

Noble Saxons,

As I have before, let me once again humbly thank you for your efforts in helping me realize my life's destiny. Your graciousness and unending generosity during the campaign to gain my throne knew endless bounds.

In August, Dragwlya had been officially elected prince by a small boyar council, complying with the fundamental laws of the land, and was anointed by the metropolitan in Biserica Domnească, the cathedral of Tîrgovişte. Amid the celebration, he bestowed upon himself the title "Prince Vlad, son of Vlad the Great, sovereign and ruler of Ungro-Wallachia and of the duchies of Amlaş and Făgăraş." The two duchies had been given to him by Ladislas V in return for his allegiance.

Writing the letter nauseated Dragwlya. He forced himself to compose it, knowing he would betray the Saxons if the occasion ever called for it. He continued to allow the quill to flow until he decided he had written enough.

> We have succeeded in restoring glory to Wallachia, and in winning a battle
> for the righteous. I have no fear of our relationship failing, and will always think
> of you as honest men, brothers, friends, and sincere neighbors. I request your
> presence at your earliest convenience in order to solidify a commercial treaty.

Vlad III, by the Grace of God Prince of Ungro-Wallachia, Duke of Făgăraș and Amlaș

Replacing the quill, Dragwlya massaged his closed eyes with his thumb and index finger. His priority was to create an alliance with those he knew would be useful and subservient. Already he had mentally drafted a commercial treaty to be ratified.

Should the Turks attack, Dragwlya would help defend the Transylvanian Saxons. He would renew his loyalty to Ladislas V and would allow the merchants to continue to practice their business as before. If necessary, Dragwlya would receive political asylum. As for the remaining terms, Dragwlya regarded treaties as he did dry, brittle sticks. They were easily broken.

September 14, 1456

The Turkish emissaries were waiting and would have to be appeased.

Dragwlya knew this would happen. Not even a month into his reign, Mehmed's suspicions were aroused. The prince wondered if he had been too anxious. *Time is seldom a luxury one has when attempting to fulfill one's dreams.*

In addition to establishing correspondence with the mayors of Brașov and Sibiu, Dragwlya had also written László, now governor of Belgrade and commander-in-chief of the Transylvanian territory. Hearing a name other than that of Ioan Hunedoara before those titles was disappointing to him. Dragwlya had wanted desperately to kill the man he knew to be truly responsible for the deaths of his father and brother. That Hunedoara had escaped his rightful fate sickened him. Death by plague was pleasant in comparison to what Dragwlya had envisioned and left him unsatisfied. Dragwlya knew a part of himself would never be fulfilled and, guiltily, that a part of himself had been lost in Hunedoara's death.

Certainly, Dragwlya did not consider Hunedoara a father figure, but the man had trained him and given him the chance he required to be prince. Without him, attainment of his throne would not have been likely. Though it tortured him to no end, on some level Dragwlya felt indebted to the murderer of his own father and brother. Regardless of what had happened to Hunedoara, Dragwlya's agenda would not change.

He was ready to honor commitments made long before beginning the campaign for his throne. He had a promise to keep to Stephen and would be sure to do so.

Stephen *was* family and, like Dragwlya, the victim of his father's wrongful and untimely murder. Just as Dracul's assassination took the throne away from his son, Bogdan's death had done so to Stephen. Dragwlya knew how anxious his cousin was to get back his birthright, but any action on his part would be designed to serve his own needs as well.

Since his coronation, Dragwlya had met repeatedly with a few dissident boyars of Moldavia. They had been inciting a revolution against Petru Aaron, Moldavia's prince, for some time. Dragwlya hoped Petru would soon be overthrown and exiled or killed. Either scenario ensured an easier path for Stephen to his throne and would help secure Dragwlya's northern border. These actions were perceived as allegiance to Christianity and caused alarm in Andrinople. Dragwlya's open scheming to remove the pro-Turkish Aaron from the Moldavian throne was the impetus for Mehmed to send his emissaries.

Breakfast had recently ended when Dragwlya received word of the emissaries' arrival. The mere thought of them made the food in his stomach churn. The prospect of meeting with them gave him a headache. He would stall as long as possible before granting them an audience. For a moment, he considered a nap to allow his meal to settle, but the idea of disposing of the Turkish and promptly sending them on their way provided him the incentive to stand and make his way to the throne room.

Staring through the doorway and seeing the already present emissaries nauseated Dragwlya more. He felt agitation and displeasure but managed to cloak them with a look of total bewilderment, as if questioning why they had any reason to be at his court. Once the prince had settled into his seat, formal greetings and salutations were made. Meaningless conversation gave way quickly as the head emissary pushed for reasons regarding Dragwlya's recent actions.

"Prince Vlad, the sultan wishes to know why you are partaking in such treachery. Is it your desire to make an enemy of the Ottoman Empire?"

It is a wonder they ever managed to establish *an empire.*

"You have my assurances. My dedication to the sultan is unmatched. These accusations are baseless; a feeble attempt to undermine the sultan's trust in me and drive me from my principality...How can I show Sultan Mehmed I am loyal to him alone?"

The emissary's answer was concise. "Sultan Mehmed demands you pay a yearly tribute of two thousand gold ducats and grant him the right of free passage for the Turkish army through Wallachia. You are instructed to travel to Constantinople and recognize these terms officially."

Fourteen years earlier when he had been a mere boy, Dragwlya witnessed his father's loyalty questioned. In good faith, Vlad Dracul had traveled to Andrinople to assure the sultan his allegiance lie solely with the Turkish. It was on that same journey

Dragwlya and his brother, Radu, were offered up as the symbol of Dracul's devotion. Dragwlya had no sons to give as his father had, and he refused to be placed in a cell once again.

"You must understand, I have just gained my throne. It is impossible for me to leave for a trip such as the one you suggest. Undoubtedly the sultan must agree such a journey would be a foolish gesture, considering the circumstances. It is vital I remain here to pursue the goals of your master, but I will comply with every other demand placed upon me."

Baffled, the emissaries stared at each other, each deciding individually how to hold a conference in front of the man they wanted to confer about. Becoming impatient with their lack of action, Dragwlya decided to prompt the emissaries.

"Surely you agree with my reasoning? Imagine if Tîrgovişte or all of Wallachia were to fall to our enemies while I was away. What would have to be done then? Is it worth risking the lives of the Turkish army over a simple visit? The decision is yours, of course ... I am only keeping the best interests of your master in mind."

Finally, the entourage came to an agreement and answered. "Sire, we believe your reason for not wanting to travel holds merit, but we do request you give us a tentative date as to when you *may* be able to pay homage to the sultan personally."

They are intent on having me go to Constantinople. Mehmed is waiting for me to hand myself over to him. "Tell the sultan I will be pleased to see him once my affairs are settled here; once I am firmly established. Now, in accordance with your arrival, my servants have prepared breakfast. Stay and take advantage of my hospitality for as long as you wish."

Frustrated with their failure to solicit a firm date from Dragwlya, the emissaries blankly stared at each another again. They were quite hungry and tired from the journey and agreed to be Dragwlya's guests. Perhaps if they remained long enough they might be able to extract a precise date from the prince as to when his visit to Constantinople would occur. Otherwise they would be forced to face the sultan without a real commitment. Uncertainty, they knew, was unacceptable to Mehmed.

"We thank you for your generosity, Prince Vlad."

Dragwlya smiled. "Excellent. Now, please adjourn to the banquet hall, you must be famished."

Led by one of Dragwlya's guards, the emissaries spoke freely once they were certain Dragwlya could no longer hear them.

"Mehmed will not approve."

"What else can we do? We cannot take him to Constantinople by force. Besides, you've heard the stories; what they say about him. He is just as possessed as Mehmed is."

Dragwlya knew no good could come from his torturing and killing the emissaries, though he had managed to find several reasons why they deserved it. Any such action would only incite Mehmed further, and Dragwlya had no desire to see Janissaries occupying Wallachia. He would have to tolerate the emissaries' presence for only a short time longer. God willing, they would be gone before nightfall.

CONSTANTINOPLE
September 30, 1456

The emissaries' stay in Tîrgovişte ended much sooner than even Dragwlya had anticipated. After eating, the party sent by Mehmed immediately resupplied and began the trek back to Constantinople. Though it had taken them three weeks to reach Tîrgovişte, only two weeks were necessary to arrive back in Constantinople. Once they were home, the most difficult part of their journey still remained.

Mehmed sat with Radu resting by his side. In the past few days, the sultan's lust for the younger brother of the prince of Wallachia had reached infinite heights. As his protégé slept, Mehmed ran his fingers through Radu's curly blonde locks. No one else in his court had blonde hair; everyone else was so plain, so identical. Variety was Mehmed's aphrodisiac, and Radu was indeed a unique treat.

The sultan waited patiently. In approximately one week, the newly crowned prince of Wallachia would walk into his palace, invited under the guise he was there to pay tribute and homage. Dragwlya would then be detained until Mehmed saw fit to place him back in Wallachia, if ever.

Keeping Dragwlya prisoner would provide Mehmed relief. He could prevent the prince from causing further harm and it would serve as a measure of revenge to Radu for all the suffering he had been forced to endure at his brother's hands. Mehmed thought the act might show Radu how much he cared for him. While lost in thought, the party Mehmed was not expecting back for a week arrived.

Mehmed did not realize they had entered. He sat quietly, still stroking the head of Radu until finally one of his viziers approached.

"My liege?" The words elicited no response. "My liege?" On his second attempt, the vizier received an answer.

Startled, Mehmed sat upright. The jolt woke Radu and retrieved the sultan from his reverie. "What is it?"

The sultan's gaze focused on the men now before him and instantly he recognized the emissaries. Their appearance intrigued and confused him.

"You have returned much sooner than expected...Where is Prince Vlad?"

Upon hearing his brother's name, Radu immediately stopped rubbing his eyes and became a bit queasy. Reacting much the same way, the emissaries stiffened with apprehension and fear. Swallowing the accumulated saliva in his mouth, the lead emissary prepared to answer. His palms became increasingly sweaty, and a bead of perspiration slid down the side of his face.

"My liege..." The emissary swallowed once more. "Prince Vlad is not here."

Visually taken aback, Mehmed responded. "When *will* he be arriving?"

"My liege, the prince has agreed to all of your terms. He will pay the annual tribute of two thousand gold ducats and will grant free passage through Wallachia should you desire access to Transylvania."

Mehmed's patience had worn out.

"*When?*"

The single word boomed, echoing in the halls of the palace. Even Radu was fearful of what Mehmed might do should the emissary fail once more to answer the question.

"My liege, Prince Vlad has asked us to inform you that now is not the most appropriate time for him to make the journey here. He feels leaving would endanger the safety of his throne; that it could fall into the hands of one of your enemies. Once he is firmly established as prince he will pay homage to you in person. In his stead, he has sent ambassadors to affirm his loyalty."

Mehmed simply shook his head in disapproval as his hand rose to cradle his forehead. He was monotone as he mouthed his disappointment. "I ask you to accomplish one simple task."

"My liege, I am sorr-"

Mehmed's hand left his forehead, palm toward the man as he spoke. "Leave me... before I settle upon a suitable punishment."

Before he could look up, Mehmed heard the sound of three men fleeing the throne room in a sprint. He chuckled to himself quietly, realizing he may have finally found someone whose level of cunning rivaled his own. Once again shaking his head, Mehmed peered over at Radu.

"Your brother is still quite stubborn." *He could cause distractions I cannot afford.* "I may be forced to deal with him personally. If so, he will not be causing problems for anyone ever again."

A smile streaked across Radu's face.

"That would make you happy?"

"Yes, my liege."

"Do you want his throne?"

Radu had never seriously considered ruling Wallachia. The possibility scared and enticed him all at once. Though ecstatic with the thought of ruling his homeland, he wondered how Vlad would react to his weakling of a brother being placed upon the throne. The thought of Vlad escaping from captivity or returning from exile to retake the throne terrified him. If Vlad dethroned him, Radu knew he would do so by killing him. With all these thoughts swirling in his head, Radu answered Mehmed with uncertainty.

"I would."

Mehmed could sense Radu's uncertainty and began to laugh quietly once more. "You don't seem confident. When the time is right, you will rule. I swear it."

Of all the foes Mehmed would have to deal with from now on, he was sure Vlad was the one, the only one, with whom he would have any difficulty. If forced to, he would replace Vlad with a candidate that assured stability. Because of Belgrade, he needed security to the north elsewhere if he would ever succeed in gaining inroads into Europe. It humored him to think that Wallachia, an insignificant speck, would play such an important role in the conquest of an entire continent.

CHAPTER XXVIII
DRAGWLYA'S QUERY
TÎRGOVIŞTE
October 27, 1456

Less than three months had passed since Dragwlya had recaptured his throne. As he prepared for his imminent purging of Wallachia, the plague relentlessly continued its rampage across Europe. Like the Black Death, Dragwlya would not discriminate between who suffered and who survived, but the boyars and nobility would most certainly be first on his list of endangered souls.

Dragwlya's first priority would be to rid the principality of potential usurpers. Their deaths would also eliminate many who had been involved in the murders of his father and Mircea. To accomplish this eradication, he would rely on the small force that had helped him secure the throne. Several families had been outspoken in their opposition to him. He did not have the luxury of waiting long before silencing them, especially the Taxaba family.

Dragwlya's army had foiled a revolt organized by Albu Taxaba's son earlier this month. For their treachery, the prince ordered the entire family impaled. Only the youngest of Albu's sons had managed to escape. Any group still wishing to see the prince overthrown knew revolution without outside assistance would be impossible, but the potential for them to cause harm was still far too great. Void of apprehension, Dragwlya decided to gain assurance further revolts would not occur.

In the great hall of Dragwlya's palace more than five hundred boyars and members of the upper nobility had gathered. Certainly, somewhere in this cesspool swam one or more of the accomplices to the deaths of Dracul and Mircea. They simply needed to be fished out.

While awaiting the arrival of the prince, the names of the boyars and nobility were recorded on parchment by members of the royal guard who now stood on either side of Dragwlya. Numerous attendees had asked why the action was taking place, but the only reply given was, "My lord has told me to do so." Those assembled would soon regretfully gain the knowledge they so desperately sought.

Dragwlya looked over the crowd, absorbing the tone of their questioning voices, relishing their ignorance. Sadistically, he smiled and leaned back. Today would mark the beginning of changes yet to come and would make certain the nobility's minds were ingrained with the knowledge of who Wallachia's true ruler was. No longer would they look to Heaven for guidance; they would know God's will through their prince. Dragwlya's gaze moved to the guards to his left and right. All gave him a nod of approval, signaling they were ready.

"You are no doubt wondering why I have summoned you." All talking ceased shortly after Dragwlya's voice was heard. "I simply require your answer to a solitary question." Murmuring began and steadily grew to a low rumble. "Your silence is necessary."

Once more the talking subsided, leaving only uncertainty in its wake. Everyone present knew Dragwlya had ambushed and slaughtered the Taxabas. They knew what he was capable of and willing to do to secure his throne. Many began to feel they had been gravely mistaken in ignoring their intuition to remain at their estates, and a consensual longing to be anywhere except Tîrgovişte took hold of the crowd.

"How many princes have you, my loyal subjects, known?" The question was directed to no one in particular, but each realized the query was to be answered individually. Dragwlya's emerald eyes descended to his left and rested upon a man who had held his estate for some time.

Being the first to speak in such a large group usually makes a man nervous; being the first to do so in this particular gathering was terrifying. Years raced through the boyar's mind, as did prince upon prince whom he had witnessed crowned, exiled, or killed. He strained to swallow the lump developing in his throat, preparing to give his answer with parched lips.

"Since your grandfather, my liege, there have been no less than twenty princes... I have survived them all."

The word "twenty" caused one of the guards to scribble a notation. Dragwlya listened to the noise but refused to look in the direction from which it had come. His mind remaining focused. His eyes shifted and came to rest upon a younger boyar. Dragwlya spoke not a word; the question still remained.

"I have witnessed fifteen, my lord."

Again a quill scribbled furiously, arousing the curiosity of those present. Muttering filtered through the crowd as each attendee looked to those around him with a blank stare, only to receive the same dumbfounded look in reply.

"Silence!" The echo of Dragwlya's voice was deafening. "Do not interrupt me again!"

Dragwlya's statement stifled everyone. They could barely breathe now, and the thought of uttering a single syllable was inconceivable. Not knowing Dragwlya's intentions caused absolute turmoil in the hearts of those already perspiring from guilt. Regaining his composure, Dragwlya focused his stare on the next man.

"How many?" This was the way the question was posed to those remaining. For nearly an hour, the only other sounds were shaky voices from those answering and the scratching of the guards' quills.

Silently, each of the nobles wondered how fearful he should be but reassured himself he had done nothing to incur the prince's wrath. Some tried desperately to recall what they could have done to possibly upset him, while thinking of ways to buy back his favor. Those who answered eight or less were now being escorted out of the great hall.

"Have they all answered?"

Dragwlya's question was directed to the guards on either side of him. Each man remaining in the hall could feel his heart beating. In near unison, Dragwlya watched the heads of the guards nod, assuring him they were ready to carry out any further commands. Purposefully, the prince rose from his throne and addressed his audience.

"How do you explain the fact that you have had so many princes in your land?" A need for vengeance saturated the question, which no one dared to answer. Nervously, the boyars looked at one another, fearing the worst. "The guilt is entirely due to your shameful intrigues!"

The crescendo of his voice filled the great hall with soldiers. Their presence was finally too much for some.

"I demand to know your intentions!" exclaimed one boyar. Similar statements filled Dragwlya's ears as the previous silence of the boyars and nobility gave way to shouting.

"You demand?" Once again, Dragwlya's booming voice silenced them. "Mercifully, I grant you the *privilege* of knowing my intentions … Each of you is guilty of the murders of Prince Vlad II and his son, Mircea. You will be punished accordingly! A stake has been fashioned for each of you!"

Dumbfounded, no one moved. Surely Dragwlya's sentence would not be carried out. The thought would continue to run through the mind of every nobleman and boyar even as they were being raised up on stakes in the courtyard, forced to stare at the infinite sky or the ground.

Those foolish enough to attempt an escape only succeeded in delaying the inevitable and caused themselves more pain. Defenseless boyars and nobles lost limbs fighting armed guards warned to confine them under penalty of suffering the same fate. Dragwlya's growing number of ornaments adorning his courtyard delighted him.

The prince could manage to think of only one thing listening to their screams. It did not occur to him to remember his father or Mircea. They had not crossed his mind since he had entered the courtyard. Dragwlya only pondered the inadequacy of his vantage point.

BRAŞOV
November 5, 1456

Braşov provided the sole surviving member of the Taxaba family sanctuary. The city was one of a remaining few where the possibility to meet in opposition of Dragwlya existed. Several boyars, all opponents of the new prince, had gathered there for that exact purpose.

Numerous conferences took place to decide the most efficient way to place the powers of the central government in the hands of the upper nobility once again. Those who were most ignorant called for revolution, an act most recognized as foolish. They lacked the men, the will, and felt good money should not have to be spent from their own purses to buy back what was rightfully theirs. Wisdom prevailed and sought a more economic route.

Everyone stared at Taxaba pityingly, like the orphan he now was.

"Many families have been murdered, aside from my own. We must reestablish ourselves as the true rulers of Wallachia."

Several conversations raced around the room as those present questioned the notion. The mayor of Braşov interrupted them.

"Taxaba is right. We must find a man willing to let us rule, even if he is unaware of it—a member of the Dăneşti clan perhaps."

"Why a Dăneşti?" The inquiry flew across the room from an indistinguishable source.

"By pitting the Drăculeşti and Dăneşti against one another, we force them to kill each other off. Seeing the ruling families battle weakens the people's faith in the monarchy, making it easier for us to secure the throne."

Once again the room filled with loud dialogues. Each individual held on tightly to his own theory and would not let go of it. Taxaba lowered his head into his palms, shaking his head in disbelief. *Dragwlya will remain prince forever.*

"Gentlemen, please!" Again the voice of the mayor quieted the room. "I am confident this is the plan our emphasis should be placed on. Together we can make it work."

Cries of agreement arose and, as the motion was backed, more became convinced by the mayor's words. For most, if their own plan was not put into effect, this one seemed to provide enough logic to try. Making plans, however, was easy. They wanted what they could not have—assurances that all involved would execute their given tasks.

BELGRADE
November 17, 1456

"He is within the limits of the city, sir."

Indecision engulfed László Hunedoara as he continued to scan the countryside, attempting to gain visual conformation of King Ladislas' entourage. He had invited Ladislas to Belgrade for an official visit, all the while wondering if now were the time to forcibly take the Hungarian crown.

King of Hungary was a title he wanted desperately. László's intentions of ruling were known to everyone, including Ladislas, and still he had managed to persuade the king to make the journey to give thanks for the deliverance from the Turkish.

Slipping deeper in thought, László pondered his dilemma. The decision should have been made months ago, not merely moments before the opportunity presented itself. But László had struggled with the choices, forcing himself into a position that would possibly affect the entire continent.

Some of his father's last words rang in his ears now.

Defend, my friends, Christendom and Hungary from all enemies… Do not quarrel among yourselves. If you should waste your energies in altercations, you will seal your own fate as well as dig the grave of our country.

Had Hunedoara intended for his own sons to abide by this and not seek greater power? Lost in thought, the governor did not hear the guard speaking to him until being questioned a second time.

"Sir?" This time the man placed his hand on the governor's shoulder in an effort to gain his attention.

"What?" László's shocked voice scared the guard enough that he stepped back a pace. Regaining his composure he spoke once more.

"Sir, what do you wish us to do?"

Ladislas reassured himself of the importance this journey held for Hungary's morale, that as king he must demonstrate the country's unity amongst its leaders. A full supporter of the monarch, Count Ulrich Cilli accompanied him, constantly making Ladislas aware of his personal reservations. Ladislas attempted to convince him the meeting was necessary for Hungary's security. With the fortress now dominating the skyline and growing larger, Cilli's doubts overtook him.

"Sire, your intentions are honorable, but Hunedoara intends to take your crown…It is as though you are willingly conceding it to him."

"Hunedoara will not attempt such a thing so soon after his father's death." Even as the words passed over his lips Ladislas doubted them. "He will not kill me without cause."

"No…with cause. *His* cause."

Ladislas sighed heavily. "Hunedoara is an honorable man."

"Honor often gives way to ulterior motives, sire." As the words left his mouth, Cilli spied Hunedoara's men emerging from the fortress. "Our escort."

Ladislas' gaze moved toward the gates of the city where some fifty men were now awaiting his arrival as the sun's noon rays struck the landscape head-on. No shadows would be present for actions meant to be shrouded or concealed by darkness. Everything was visible. This is exactly what Ladislas had hoped for—no surprises. Nothing could sneak up on him and pounce unexpectedly.

As Ladislas and Cilli proceeded, those accompanying them steadily began to fall back. They would remain within striking distance, but the king wished to show good faith, not fear and apprehension. This display of trust had been heavily debated by the count to no avail, and he mentally made note of yet another in a series of mistakes the young king was committing.

Nearing the drawbridge of the fortress, Ladislas and Cilli were greeted by a line of cavalry on either side of them in addition to a wall of fifty infantry before them. With each step deeper into the walls of men the visitors could feel and hear the ranks closing in behind them. The steeds of both men suddenly bolted as they were struck on the hides and crossed the drawbridge.

While trying desperately to control his horse, Cilli looked back in fear and caught a glimpse of the entourage, now useless, futilely racing toward the rising drawbridge. With his initial shock passing, Ladislas took hold of his horse and asserted what little control he now had. Fiercely, he grabbed at the reins, pulling back to stop the animal's charge, and watched with anxiety as Cilli's steed continued deeper into the fortress. Ladislas' pulse raced as the count's stallion reared up and Cilli was thrown. Cautiously, Ladislas began making his way over to the count but was surrounded instantly by László's men. The looks on their faces warned him that moving would likely result in his death. There was now no doubt. László intended to take away the throne. Ladislas peered again at Cilli's motionless body.

My pride is to blame for this.

Cilli pushed his upper body up off of the ground and gingerly moved his head around. No serious injury had been done; there would merely be some soreness here and there. More than pain, fear of what would happen washed over the count. Seeing Ladislas encircled nearly drove him to rash action.

Sensing Cilli's terror, Ladislas attempted to ride over to calm him, a gesture not well received by the guards who pulled him off of his horse and restrained him. Their abuse enraged Cilli, compelling him to charge. Ladislas cried out to stop him, but the effort proved futile.

Several guards rushed over and tackled Cilli, forcing him to the ground. They began beating him as he struggled to free himself and reach the king. He continued to yell as the guards detained him until, for seemingly no reason, his screaming ceased. The king stared into the huddled mass and watched Cilli pull something from his belt.

"Cilli don't!"

The cry came too late. Ladislas could see one of the guards grabbing in disbelief at the handle of the dagger now piercing his stomach. Infuriated, the guards began savagely beating the count. Continuous blows landed anywhere and everywhere until Cilli was so pummeled he no longer had the ability to scream out in pain. Ribs cracked, his head was driven into the ground repeatedly, and blood began to pool as Cilli approached unconsciousness. He knew he must be in pain, but with each passing second the ability to feel it faded. Finally, darkness dominated his sight and the pain no longer existed. Cilli had stopped fighting back, but the bludgeoning continued until a loud crack caused everyone to remain still.

The mob backed away from the count's limp body, save one soldier. Only now did he allow Cilli's head to slide from his blood-stained hands to the ground. He stared at Ladislas with a grin on his full red lips. Though the others had taken pleasure in beating the count, this one took satisfaction in the accomplishment of the mission given to him by László Hunedoara.

Ladislas knew Cilli's death had been no accident. Terror and hate swept over him simultaneously. The cruelty of this act required immediate retaliation, but the situation called for tact and a level head. Regardless of the consequences, Hunedoara would be held accountable.

The king of Hungary stood before László Hunedoara, barely resisting the urge to strike. Cilli's death was a premeditated assassination, planned by a man holding a grudge his father had once harbored. Ladislas convinced himself Cilli's assassination was in some manner retaliation on László's part, revenge for all the times the count had dared oppose his father. Cilli's murder was the most recent evidence of the feud between two families seemingly at war since the beginning of time. Ladislas now felt a similar feud brewing between the Hunedoaras and his own family. Any expectations of peace had vanished, as had Ladislas' hopes of leaving Belgrade alive.

Ladislas' eyes were wild. His stare and inner desire were all that did not maintain an air of complete calmness.

"Governor Hunedoara, do you intend to have me killed as well?" Ladislas' voice had the tone of a composed diplomat. László's reaction, by comparison, felt as forced as it was.

"The count's death was a terrible accident, your highness. He killed one of my guards. By all accounts it seems to have been an act of self-defense I would say."

"Others would not say." Ladislas allowed his tone to slip slightly.

László hesitated momentarily before continuing. "Everything will be done to atone for Count Cilli's untimely death."

"And how will you atone for mine?"

László blew a quick breath out of his nose as he closed his eyes and slowly shook his head. "I have no intention of killing you, sire, just as I had no such intention toward Count Cilli." The statement harbored a sliver of truth. László would not kill the king presently.

"Nevertheless, Cilli is dead, and you will be held responsible."

"I will make amends with the Cilli family, your highness. Those responsible for this tragedy will be properly reprimanded."

I promise you will. "You invited me for an official visit, which I made in good faith. I have come as promised. Since my arrival, I have been cut-off from my bodyguard, and a dear friend of mine has been murdered. As you might imagine, I am not anticipating the rest of my stay here to be pleasant...Have someone show me to my quarters, and admit my men."

"As you wish, sire."

Hunedoara motioned and a guard approached the king to escort him to his chamber.

You will pay dearly, Hunedoara. "I shall take my tour of the city this evening."

"Yes, sire." Hunedoara watched as the king was escorted away. *And I shall have all that I want.*

Word of Count Cilli's death spread throughout the empire quicker than the plague. No formal declaration had been made on the part of the Cilli family or the Hapsburgs against Hunedoara. Still, it seemed a time would come when the leaders of Eastern Europe would have to decide with whom to side.

CHAPTER XXIX
MEHMED'S EPIPHANY & THE EXTRA DUCAT
BUDA
January 8, 1457

Christmas passed in typical fashion, allowing the new year to begin quietly for most. For two individuals, however, the holidays brought with them pause for reflection and cruel loneliness.

While the bells tolled, proclaiming the birth of Christ and then later the start of another year, Dragwlya sat alone, contemplating the number of holidays his father and brother had been robbed of and never celebrated. His emotions were like alternating storms of sorrow and hate. Any thought of weeping for his loss was always suppressed by the need to maintain absolute control.

Simultaneously, in the capital city of Buda, Ladislas sat alone. Unaware of his counterpart's brooding, the young Hungarian king thought about his father as well, a father he had never known. Ladislas' knowledge of his father came from stories told by his mother and others. He had been forced to find father figures, men he trusted to teach him how to fight, to rule, to live. They were his mentors. They gave him life. Count Cilli had been one of those men.

Cilli's death at Hunedoara's command weighed heavily upon Ladislas. His hatred for the Transylvanian governor had festered for almost two months. The time for retaliation was now. László would suffer for the pain he had inflicted upon Cilli, for the pain he had inflicted upon Ladislas.

ANDRINOPLE
January 19, 1457

Belgrade was mine. My plan was flawless; my generals were not. Why?

"Why did Allah show me victory and then desert me when I needed him most?"

Mehmed still tried daily to comprehend how he had lost twenty-four thousand of his best soldiers to a mob of eight thousand farmers and peasants. The battle had been a complete embarrassment to him, to the entire Turkish world, to Allah.

"Perhaps there is no Allah."

Mehmed did not respond to the comment immediately. His thoughts moved from the battle to his retreat toward Sofia.

Retreat.

The word stung like the venomous strike of a viper. Defeat had caused the sultan to lose his temper; his generals were the target of that anger. Mehmed spoke with each of them individually. Those found to be responsible for his loss were punished by his own hands and then executed. Finally, the comment blurted out earlier reached him. The sultan rounded and met the gaze of his favorite minion.

"*No Allah?* Indeed Allah exists."

"Then why has he forsaken you, the man chosen to lead *his* people?"

Mehmed waited a moment before answering, waiting to be enlightened. "I know my god exists. In fact, my faith had been reaffirmed."

"How so?" Radu sounded and appeared intrigued.

"Belgrade was a test."

"A test?"

"Yes, Allah found it necessary to test my faith...He knew I had begun to think I could conquer the world without his guidance...Understand, Allah will give me the world only if I take it for *Him*."

"Will that be enough for you?"

At his epiphany, Mehmed had completely forgotten about Radu's presence. "Every town, every home, every piece of gold and silver... every life, must be taken for *Him*. I see that now. That was my mistake. I will not be so foolish again."

"Does that mean you were premature in executing all those generals?"

Radu's inquiry brought Mehmed out of his trance-like state. He could sense a tone of insolence rarely present in the young man's voice. "Why are you cross with me today? Is there more you desire than what I have already given you?"

"Is there more?" Radu's tone was that of a person knowing what they had been deprived of.

"You have your own court, a wife, and a child. What else must you have to satisfy you?"

"I would have asked by now if I knew." Radu's statement was genuine. Although it appeared he had everything one could possibly want, he often appeared depressed.

"You know what you want. And I have told you once before you shall have it when I am able to give it to you."

"You mean Wallachia." Only by saying it aloud did Radu know it to be exactly what he desired.

"Do not insult my intelligence. You know it to be so...I wonder which you desire more, the throne or the distance it will place you from me?"

TÎRGOVIŞTE
February 3, 1457

A vision had come to Dragwlya in November of last year while thinking of the numerous boyars he had recently disposed of the previous month. Exiting the north wing of his palace, an image appeared before him.

Staring, he marveled at an imaginary watchtower that reached upwards of twenty meters. Its base was square and tapered gradually inward as it rose to a point where all four sides switched to forty-five degree angles for a meter or so. The tower then took on a cylindrical form, aiming skyward. There were eight openings total on the cylindrical part, ascending as they wrapped around the tower. A lower opening on the southern side and one on the northern side were larger than the others, and small balconies jutted out approximately two meters from each of them.

The tower would allow the garrison the advantage of seeing enemies well in advance, keeping the countryside under constant watch. Dragwlya's primary purpose for the tower, however, was what delighted him most. Perched above his courtyard, the prince would have a proper vantage point to view any sentences being carried out. On high, Dragwlya would see proper justice administered.

What was once a dream loomed before Dragwlya now in stone and wood. Built to his specifications, the laborers had made it a reality.

"Sire?"

Dragwlya's stare moved from the tower to the head mason.

"Sire, I have been informed it is safe for you to go to the top if you wish."

A broad, closed-mouth smile crossed Dragwlya's face as he fought to contain his excitement. Moving his attention back to the structure, the prince felt giddy as he moved toward it. His stride was lengthening with each step, and he could feel his heart racing when he reached the door leading inside.

For a few seconds he just stood at the entrance. The mason stared at the prince's back, wondering why he had not entered. It startled him to see Dragwlya execute an about-face and begin walking back. He knew the prince's short temper and the manner in which he dealt with dissatisfaction. A lump formed in his throat as Dragwlya stood next to him, staring at the tower somberly.

"Are you not pleased with my work, sire?"

Dragwlya nodded. "I will wait until it is finished. I am pleased with your work to this point."

Relieved by the response the mason sighed through his nose and felt the tightness in his muscles subside. "As you wish, sire. I estimate it will be finished in one week's time."

"I expect it to be completed in three days."

This sort of statement was what the mason had dreaded since being forced into the project. During his tenure at the palace, he learned the prince must be addressed diplomatically. Doing so was vital to one's existence.

"Sire, I am honored greatly by your confidence. I do not, however, wish you to be disappointed with the final product. For my sake, I implore you. Allow me the entirety of the week to adequately capture in this tower the greatness of your reign." Instinctively, the mason began to pray.

A look of disgust took hold of Dragwlya's face. His response caused a shudder to shoot up the mason's spine. "You *doubt* my judgment?"

"Of course not, sire. I simply do not feel three day's time is enough to adequately honor you."

Dragwlya was hardly unaware of the chess match the mason was trying to win. In fact, he would hold the mason in check regardless of what move he made. "You have hands suitable for labor but possess the mind and tongue of an emissary. Perhaps I shall make you an ambassador."

"As your humble servant, sire, I shall do as you see fit."

Dragwlya chuckled. "You have six days. Surely you can finish in the amount of time it took God to create the entire world." Without another word, Dragwlya turned and disappeared.

Sitting on his throne, Dragwlya debated if the tower would be completed in the time allotted. The mason would have to be killed were he to fail in finishing the task. Even if he did die, Dragwlya could at least rejoice in the knowledge that his tower would soon be finished.

"Your highness?"

With a jerk of his head, the prince gazed with some interest at the entourage now before him and the man who had addressed him; obviously a merchant, obviously Italian.

"Who are you?" Dragwlya asked indifferently.

"Sire, my name is Metha. I have traveled from Florence and am making my way to Constantinople. It is my wish that you provide me with servants to keep watch over my goods while preparing for the next leg of my journey."

"As you prepare for the rest of your journey you will stay here as my guest. Have your carriage taken to the public square and then return here." Dragwlya leaned forward on his seat slightly, eagerly anticipating the reaction of the merchant. Undoubtedly, Metha would find the response absurd. Dragwlya could hear the merchant's protest in his mind as though the merchant was saying it aloud. *Leave my carriage in the public square? Are you mad?*

To his surprise, Dragwlya saw no visible reaction by Metha indicating disapproval.

"Thank you, my lord."

No change verbally either.

"I will escort your servants to the public square where they are to be posted," Metha added.

Perhaps one last nudge was needed.

"Guards will not be necessary... My people shall keep watch over your property."

The next few seconds brought with them the reaction Dragwlya had expected. Panic-stricken, Metha began to feel himself becoming short of breath.

Leave my carriage unattended? He cannot be serious.

"My lord, are you certain my property will be safe?"

Yet another fool questioning his judgment today. "You do not believe what I have told you?" More than just a test for this merchant, this was a plan conceived by Dragwlya to learn how much his peasants feared him.

"Of course I do, sire." *I'll not allow my money to simply be given away by this madman.* "In fact, I shall give your people the added advantage of having my men watch over the carriage with them."

"No."

The single word shot from Dragwlya's mouth and found its target inside the ears of Metha. Sustaining itself there, it reverberated over and over.

What demented sort of game is this?

"Your men will feast alongside you and sleep in the comfort of my home. Now, take your carriage to the square and leave it."

Bowing, Metha answered the prince solemnly and then signaled for his servants to follow.

Mischievously, Dragwlya laughed to himself.

This is intolerable! Metha turned over onto his back for what felt like the hundredth time, blowing the air out of his lungs in a vain effort to relax. Sweat soaked his body as two thoughts occupied his mind. Distraught over the idea of how much money he would lose this night, he vowed to never again pass through Wallachia.

Metha sat up numerous times, wanting desperately to race to his carriage. The temptation was great, but he knew leaving the palace would be viewed as an insult. Possibilities of what may happen if he ventured out were too disturbing to imagine. Sinking back down on his bed, Metha stared up at the ceiling and flung the covers from his saturated body. He hoped the sun would soon rise.

A lone figure traversed the public square, his face hidden by cloth, only his piercing green eyes visible. He stopped and waited across from Metha's carriage, listening to the sounds of the night. Wolves howled in the distance, and the wind rustled everything. From behind, the sound of uneven footsteps rose up. His partner was approaching.

The first figure looked over the pitiful excuse for a man—old, somewhat lame, destitute. In short, unfit for existence. A gravelly voice emitted from the second figure.

"I am here as instructed. What is this all about?"

"For your cooperation you will receive one hundred and sixty gold ducats. No questions."

"What must I do?"

"You must do as I say."

Barely making a sound, the two shadowy forms swiftly proceeded to the carriage. Once there, the first figure took the lead, breaking into the carriage and finding Metha's strongbox. He opened it, revealing a treasury well over one thousand gold ducats. The older man's eyes bulged as he tried to comprehend the sight of so much money. He licked his lips and swallowed so he could speak.

"What are you waiting for?" As the man reached for one of the strongbox handles, an arm abruptly came up and violently ripped his hand away.

"Do not touch this box again!" the first thief hissed.

Recoiling his hand, the older man winced in pain and watched in disbelief as his partner began counting out the ducats.

"What are you doing?" The old man asked in a forceful whisper. "There's no time for this! We can count it later!" He could feel his body tensing, anticipating being caught.

No reply came. The first figure simply continued to count out the ducats. In less than a minute, one hundred and sixty ducats had been counted, slipped into a pouch, and handed to the older man.

"Go."

This simple word's force smashed into the older man like a runaway cart, sending his mind reeling. Everything in his head told him to run away as fast as his legs would allow. His joints had all frozen, however, and moving seemed impossible.

"*I said go!*" Thunder accompanied each syllable from the man's mouth. Someone would be rushing to the square at any moment. That thought was enough to move the older man. He ran, fearing for his life. With a hidden smirk, the younger of the two fled as the voices and footsteps of several soldiers began flooding the square. He felt nothing, no anxiety whatsoever, and gave no thought to being captured. These feelings disgusted him to an extent, but he understood his intelligence and cunning were superior.

After ducking into numerous alleys, the older man found little comfort or relief once he finally stopped and huddled in a corner. Breathing heavily, he tightly clutched the pouch handed to him. His eyes were open, continuously scanning to see if anyone had followed him. Actual sounds mixed with imaginary ones, compelling him to remain ready to run again. Letting down his guard for a moment, he quickly glanced at his hand.

His fingers were clamped around the pouch and, although covered with grime, were white from the pressure. Repeatedly, he cursed himself for agreeing to participate in such a scheme, knowing full well what being caught meant. Money has such an effect on those who have none. Likening himself to Judas Iscariot holding thirty silver pieces, he imagined his lifeless body dangling in mid-air. If he were caught, the punishment would be worse than his relatively painless vision of suicide. There truly was no rhyme or reason to what the prince would do to a thief. The only certainty was death.

Standing alone in his chamber, Dragwlya peeled back the hood hiding his face and shed his black robe like a snake would its skin. There were still a few hours before dawn, ample time to rest before having to listen to the whining voice of Metha sobbing over the ducats stolen while he slept. He expected that reaction. How the city would react to his proclamation over the ordeal and how Metha's integrity would fare in his challenge were Dragwlya's concerns.

Once granted permission, Metha had burst into Dragwlya's hall and reported the details regarding the crime. His tone cried out that he knew this would happen. After listening to the man babble on for a moment or two, Dragwlya simply raised his hand, palm toward Metha, to quiet him.

"I am appalled and outraged that you have been violated in this manner. Obviously, your ability to rejuvenate yourself before the remainder of your journey is hindered... For that I apologize." Dragwlya sounded sincere as he comforted the merchant. "This transgression will not go unpunished."

Dragwlya motioned for the criers to come before him.

"Call together the whole of my capital and announce that if the thief who has stolen this merchant's gold is not made known to me by dusk I shall destroy the city and everyone in it." Dragwlya stared at the criers for a few seconds. "Are my instructions clear?"

The criers answered affirmatively, bowed, and immediately set off. Looks of horror and utter astonishment surrounded Dragwlya as he sat with a stern look upon his face. Everyone present knew the prince's words were no hollow threat. That was what frightened them most. Dragwlya's gaze finally met the open-mouthed stare of Metha. Shaking his head he spoke again.

"My people are honest, but there are always exceptions. By nightfall your money will be returned and the culprit exposed. Now go and eat."

Metha was unsure as to what his response should be. Settling on what seemed appropriate, he spoke. "Thank you, sire." It was all he could think of to say before bowing and turning away.

Grinning wickedly, Dragwlya reached into his robe, produced a pouch, and motioned one of his servants over. It jingled as he presented it to the man.

"Take this and empty its contents into the merchant's strongbox."

With a bow, the servant took the bag and left for the carriage. Unknown to everyone but Dragwlya, the servant would shortly be replacing Metha's lost ducats with ones from the prince's own treasury, with one small difference. Dragwlya's pouch contained one extra ducat, a test for the unassuming merchant.

Had the ability to look down upon Tîrgovişte from hundreds of meters above existed, the scene could have been compared to the sight of an anthill recently agitated by some foreign missile. Franticly, the citizens of the capital city sought the one responsible for incurring the wrath of their prince.

As the hunt continued, Dragwlya's servant made his way to Metha's carriage. With four swift movements, he opened the strongbox, emptied the pouch's contents, closed the strongbox, and slipped back into the crowd undetected. Just as he moved away, Metha approached.

Metha knew it was within his rights to complain about the stolen money, yet felt miserable that this simple loss to him may mean the lives of so many. For his own peace of mind he felt he must be absolutely sure. After allowing himself a moment of hesitation, Metha opened the strongbox and began the unnecessary effort of counting his money. Seconds passed, then minutes, ultimately an hour. Metha had counted the contents of his strongbox three times. Each time ended with the same result and with him shaking and scratching his head in bewilderment and disbelief. There was no mistake. Not only had all of the missing ducats been replaced, but there had even been an extra ducat added.

Perhaps the money had been there the entire time and his original count had been hasty. Surely, the anxiety plaguing him the night before could easily be blamed. *But one hundred and sixty gold ducats?* Such an oversight would have been too great for him to have made. No, the thief had returned the missing money or citizens concerned for their own lives had replaced the lost funds to save themselves. Regardless of which, the merchant knew his next move must be to report this discovery. Giving the prince another gift for his hospitality would be an appropriate gesture as well, he thought.

"I did not believe it myself and counted the contents three times, sire. All of my money has been returned. Only, there is one extra ducat."

Dragwlya studied Metha for a long moment, nodding his head. *His honesty is refreshing.* "Your statements please me, Metha. Had you-"

At that precise moment, a great commotion could be heard just outside of the hall. All eyes turned as the doors opened. Two guards appeared in the doorway followed by a second pair dragging another man who was kicking and screaming continuously. Metha subsided as the man was brought to Dragwlya's feet. Dragwlya's stare rested for a second on the man and then moved to one of the guards.

"What is the meaning of this?"

"Sire, this is the thief who stole from the merchant's carriage last night. We found this, my lord." As he spoke, the guard produced a pouch and handed it to Dragwlya. "It contains one hundred and sixty gold ducats."

Metha's shock at this revelation could be related by hundreds of adjectives, none sufficient enough to describe it properly. The questions he had now were barely contained, and it took all of his willpower to keep quiet.

"Excellent. You have done well." A smirk crossed the prince's face. He began to look down and in doing so was not surprised to hear the thief imploring him for a pardon.

"Please, sire, you must forgive me. I-" Upon looking at the prince, silence grasped the thief's tongue as his mind tried to process the inconceivable reality before him.

Dragwlya continued to smile. Before him stood the thief from the night before, the very man whom Dragwlya himself had handed the pouch containing the gold ducats to. He could see the revelation take hold of the old man. Once more Dragwlya moved his stare to Metha.

"Had you not admitted to the extra ducat, you would have been impaled alongside this wretch. Your honesty is a testament to your moral character."

Giving a slight bow, the merchant watched as the thief was taken hold of by the guards with no sign there would be more protesting. Once the guards had disappeared, Metha again approached the prince and produced a golden chalice.

"Sire, I ask that you accept this humble gift as a token of my appreciation for your overwhelming hospitality."

Reaching out, Dragwlya took the chalice from the merchant. It was decorated elaborately, an exemplary work of art.

"Extraordinary." Metha's gift captivated and nearly mesmerized him. Dragwlya stared at it, wondering how the beautiful piece had been crafted, imagining how long it had taken to create. "Absolutely exquisite. I know exactly where it shall be kept."

Metha could not help but feel pleased that the prince had already found a suitable staging area for the chalice.

"Guard, see to it that this is placed upon the fountain in the center of the city. There it will stay, accessible to any weary traveler who should require a drink."

The statement nearly drove Metha to the point of rushing up and reclaiming the present. He had gasped loudly at the thought of such a valuable piece being left out in the open, an easy target for anyone stopping to quench their thirst. Without question the merchant's reaction was heard.

"As I have shown you once today, you should have no doubt about the honesty of my people. As you give me the chalice, I will share it with everyone, a sign of my faith in them. It will remain at the fountain for all time, a sign of their faith in me."

Not faith ... fear. Metha decided reluctantly to simply bow and forget the chalice ever existed.

PEST
February 18, 1457

Shortly after the incident at Belgrade, Ladislas began formulating his plan of revenge for László and the entire Hunedoara family. A few days ago, the Transylvanian governor and his younger brother, Matthias, had been placed under arrest and brought before the tribunal in Pest. Already both had been tried and were now awaiting their sentences. László had been found guilty of the murder of Count Cilli. Matthias' crime had been that he was a Hunedoara.

Whether the trial was in or out of session, the brothers were kept apart, communication with one another disallowed. They exchanged glances full of doubt and despair often as more evidence mounted against them. After deliberating for more than eight hours, the members of the tribunal emerged.

Ladislas looked on, confident of the sentence. Perhaps Matthias would not receive death, but László's fate was certain. The king of Hungary had attempted to sway as many as possible to give both men the maximum penalty, but the tribunal's opinion diverted when it came to the younger brother. No evidence existed to prove Matthias had knowledge of a plot to kill Count Cilli. No reasonable reason to execute him could be found.

The scene was hardly dramatic. Open support for the Hunedoaras was nonexistent; those loyal to the family buried their feelings deep. For them, the guilty verdict seemed inevitable. Still they prayed for the deliverance of László and Matthias.

With unreadable expressions the tribunal strode before an audience now growing silent at the sight of their return. Each member took his place without betraying his thoughts and stared out into the gathered crowd, focusing on no one. Void of sound, the air grew dense. Everyone searched the eyes of the tribunal for some insight, László and Matthias more so than anyone. There was none. László wondered how much time remained before his life would end. Matthias allowed the uncertainty of the situation to overtake him. Sweat ran down his face, flowing from his pores like a river carving a course.

"László Hunedoara, you have been found guilty of the murder of Count Cilli. The sentence is death."

László would not allow himself to flinch. He looked at Matthias, who stared at him with hate and fear wrenching his mind.

He looks so much like father, László thought.

"Matthias Hunedoara, you will be detained while we continue to investigate your involvement in this matter."

Matthias did not relinquish his stare. He barely heard the tribunal's ruling and had yet to process it. Time was moving forward and standing still simultaneously. Only Ladislas' voice managed to bring back his focus.

"…with the permission of this body take possession of all estates held by the Hune-doara family."

Matthias and László glared at the Hungarian king, ready to pounce, knowing full well what immediate consequence it would produce. Ladislas did not return the stares. He contained the smile ready to burst upon his lips and continued to look at the members of the tribunal, awaiting their answer.

"We will honor your request, sire."

"László Hunedoara, your sentence will be carried out at noon tomorrow...Remove the prisoners."

Ladislas watched with a certain amount of joy as Ioan Hunedoara's sons were taken away. With László no longer a factor, he knew of only two possible candidates for the throne from the Hunedoara family. One, Matthias, was currently being led to a prison cell. Mihály Szilágy, the brother of Ioan Hunedoara's widow, was the second and presented a minor threat. Were he to back Matthias, however, the younger of Hunedoara's sons would become a formidable foe and easily gain the advantage needed to secure the throne.

Ladislas was certain he would have, at the very least, the support of most of Hungary, the German towns of Transylvania, all of Wallachia, and of his former guardian, Holy Roman Emperor Frederick III. Uprisings of any sort would have to be handled quickly and decisively. The feud between he and the Hunedoaras for the crown had escalated once more.

CHAPTER XXX
EASTER SUNDAY
TÎRGOVIŞTE
February 27, 1457

Feeling the parchment already slipping, Dragwlya opened his fingers fully. Slowly, the letter descended to the floor. He stood up and gazed upon the countryside as the evening sun continued to fade. His thoughts regressed from the view back to the correspondence he had just finished reading, yet another from Mihály Szilágy.

László Hunedoara's death surprised no one but sent shock waves throughout Eastern Europe. As word spread of King Ladislas' involvement, every last village swore allegiance to either the Hapsburgs or the Hunedoaras. The German towns and Frederick III openly supported the young Hungarian king. Word had not yet reached Ladislas of Wallachia's formal declaration of support. It wouldn't.

After weeks of contemplation, Dragwlya sided with Mihály. The determining factor proved to be that the Hunedoara family was responsible for his being on the throne. Dragwlya often wrestled with the duality of his relationship with the Hunedoaras. Were it not for them, none of this would have happened.

Without Ioan Hunedoara's aid, the twenty-six year old prince would not likely be sitting on Wallachia's throne. Without the treachery of the Hunedoara family, Vlad Dracul would perhaps still rule. Without the Hunedoara family, Dragwlya would still have a family of his own—a father, a brother.

Mircea.

Images of Dragwlya's murdered brother appeared vividly before his eyes. Was he wrong for supporting those that had taken the lives of his relatives, or was he right in siding with the family who had helped make Wallachia his? There was no right answer, simply questions that once answered generated more questions. For the moment, Dragwlya contented himself with the knowledge that no matter how, he was prince of Wallachia. His accomplishments would be of his own accord.

You have forsaken me. The voice frightened Dragwlya and caused him to cringe. *I trusted you to avenge me... You have betrayed me!*

The prince answered softly. "No."

You stand beside my killer... Beside those who killed our father!... You think because you possess the throne your actions are justified?... Answer me!

"I-" Staring into the anguished eyes of Mircea, Dragwlya became guilt ridden. "Forgive me!... Forgive me!... Forgive..."

Mircea's face dissolved, leaving only emptiness as the prince opened his eyes and breathed heavily. Dragwlya wiped the sweat from his forehead, assuring himself it was all a dream. The echoes of his brother's words convinced him otherwise. Mircea *had* spoken to him from beyond the grave.

Of course... the grave! But where is it?

Dragwlya recalled the images Cazan had painted regarding Mircea's death so long ago. He had to find his brother, had to ensure the body had a proper resting place. He had to find Mircea now.

Less than ten minutes had passed, yet Dragwlya's search team was already assembled; among them was a servant who had been in the service of Vlad Dracul. The young woman had remained loyal to the Drăculeşti and had witnessed the beating and burial of Mircea. Flanked closely by Dragwlya, she led the party with a heavy heart. Flames from the torches flickered, lighting the trees exactly as they had the night she watched helplessly in horror her beloved being broken and discarded into the pit. Hidden safely from view by the trees, she had wept continuously.

Journeying to the gravesite would take only a few moments. She knew the exact location and visited often. It was a holy place, though she had not always thought of it as such. Once everyone had vanished that evening, she sat on the freshly turned earth and placed her ear to the ground, hoping to hear him shout for help. Eventually, she cried herself to sleep.

For seconds at a time Dragwlya would study the face of the woman as they drew closer to their destination. Her eyes were glistening. "Why are you on the verge of tears?"

As she looked at Dragwlya, the woman stopped and raised a hand to wipe the evidence of her pain away. Her voice trembled. "Forgive me, sire." The young woman's crying could no longer be contained.

"Why are you crying?" There existed only sincerity in the prince's voice. He could see her suffering.

With ample hesitation she spoke. "Sire... I cared deeply for your brother. He was kind. He did not deserve the fate he received."

Dragwlya understood now that the woman was feeling loss, not sorrow. She had lost the chance to express her love. Now it could never be realized. "You had strong feelings for my brother." It was as much a question as it was a statement, and she simply nodded. Highlighted by the torchlight, her features were pleasing. She radiated innocence. "Have you loved any other as you did my brother?"

She managed to whisper a response. "No."

"He stares down from Heaven upon you. Your feelings are known to him."

For the first time this night a smile appeared on the woman's face. "Thank you, sire."

"Now, end your torment, and his, by leading me to him."

Her crying ceased. A look of determination replaced the previous one of grief, and the woman began the journey again. Although she did not voice it once they had done so, Dragwlya knew by her sudden deflation when they had reached the end of their trek.

"Where?"

Dragwlya watched as the woman spun around slowly, picked up her head to look at him and then allowed her stare to transfix on the very spot where she stood. His eyes widened and Dragwlya motioned to his men to begin the grisly task of digging. Without resistance the woman floated away from the spot as the first spade broke the earth.

Torches illuminated the site as the prince stared at the ground. Each scoop of dirt reflected the man-made fire as it flew through the air. Dragwlya's heart pounded heavily with anticipation every time one of the spades dug in. After some time and thought, he suddenly halted the progress of his men.

"Stop." All eyes turned to him and the emerald eyes staring into the forming pit. "I do not want my brother to suffer any further indignity... Dig with your hands."

Instantly, all spades were thrown aside and the work continued. Handfuls of dirt were added to the pile that had been built up as the men hurriedly scooped. Suddenly, one of them stopped, immediately drawing the prince's attention.

"Sire." His voice was nearly devoid of sound.

"You've found something?" Dragwlya could not yet admit to what had been uncovered. Doing so would destroy every fantasy he had conjured in his mind of Mircea escaping, waiting for the right moment to make himself known to the world once again.

"Yes, sire." The man's voice was grave as he swept dirt out of what seemed to be hair. The others continued with their work, not daring to stop. Each of them had now uncovered a piece of clothing or something far more telling of Mircea's fate.

Dragwlya, already peering down into the hole, watched as the outline of a dressed body lying on its stomach materialized. The prince took his torch and traced down to the feet of what he knew in his heart to be the body of his brother. He could see the broken bones of Mircea's legs, a femur completely in two, the tibias and fibulas of both legs smashed. Dragwlya closed his eyes, turned his head, and released his breath through his nose. He tried desperately to maintain his composure but instead flung his torch with all his hatred.

"What should we do, sire?"

Dragwlya ignored the question for a moment. Some time passed before he opened his eyes. Again he was compelled to stare down at the remains of his brother.

"Go back and procure a coffin. Bring it here and place my brother in it. Once you have done so, come to me."

Dragwlya walked away, not waiting for an answer, not wanting to hear any more questions. Grabbing another torch, he proceeded home alone.

Thousands of thoughts raced through his mind now, just as they had when he first saw Mircea's body. Rapidly, his thoughts were transforming into doubts and questions.

How can I support the family that did this to my brother?... Perhaps I have rushed into this alliance...No, it was the empire that tried to withhold Wallachia from my family. Hunedoara gave me the chance to retrieve it...The empire is at fault... as is Hungary. They supported my father's enemies and were aided by the boyars. The boyars are the ones who truly killed Mircea. They are responsible for this. It is my brother's will that I exact revenge... It is God's will.

SIGHISOARA
March 8, 1457

Mihály refolded Dragwlya's most recent correspondence after reading it to Erzsébet and looked up at her.

"He cannot be trusted," Erzsébet said.

"He is not our only contingency."

"I will not place my son's future in the hands of that madman... not even partially."

"What do you suggest? Would you rather him fighting *against* us?"

"Of course not." Erzsébet stared at the ground, absorbed with the prospect of never again seeing either of her sons. The void in the conversation that followed was filled with images of László as he was executed and of Matthias wasting away in a cell.

Mihály chose his words carefully, knowing what he said would offer little comfort. "I can control him...He will be subservient. Dragwlya yields to real power. He knows we possess it."

"He serves only himself. He always has!" Erzsébet bit back. "He has just sworn renewed allegiance to Ladislas and the German towns, now he will betray them...What makes you believe his loyalty to us is any greater?"

"You have heard the letters...We have a common crusade. Ioan helped him secure Wallachia and now he will honor that debt."

Erzsébet laughed sarcastically. "Ioan killed his family...Have you paid *any* attention to what he has done, to what he is doing to the nobility? Eventually he will seek *us* out to satisfy his need for revenge. How will you control him then? What of the reports he has sent contingencies to Andrinople?"

Mihály had become visibly frustrated. "I said I can control him, and I will."

"If he succumbs to the Turkish, they will use Wallachia to stage their conquest of Europe."

"I can't predict the future. Neither can you. Either we take risks or we hope and pray events favor our side so that eventually, when the last of the Hapsburgs has died, we might have a chance at the throne! We watch and wait as *nothing* happens! I *will not* do that... I can't. I have too much respect for Ioan, for László, for Matthias, for myself, and my family to simply wait and *allow* things to happen!"

Mihály's agony as he proclaimed the names of everyone Erzsébet loved struck directly at her heart. Two of the three were now gone, and Matthias faced the possibility of assassination every moment he was held captive. She meditated for a moment on everything that had occurred in the past few years—Ioan's involvement in the crusades, his death, László becoming governor, Cilli's death, László's murder. They all seemed to have transpired within a week with each holding a unique moment in time. Erzsébet moved toward Mihály and took his hands.

"I have faith in you, Mihály. I always have." Her tone was benevolent. "If anyone betrays our trust—Surely you do not fault me for my concern?"

"No. You are right to be cautious, but we don't have the luxury of being hesitant. We must act now. We must have as much support as possible."

"I never imagined I would see the day when it would be me fighting battles instead of Ioan."

Mihály kissed her forehead gently. "We will live to see Matthias on the throne…I swear it."

TÎRGOVIŞTE
March 22, 1457

More than a millennium had passed since Christ conquered death. In remembrance and celebration of the holiest of all Christian holy days, the populace of Tîrgovişte turned out to thank the Lord for the gift of his only begotten son. Like Christ, Dragwlya knew he had been chosen by God to lead, to rule. Whereas the Lord forgave the trespasses of his enemies, however, Dragwlya would not.

Many of Wallachia's boyar families had made the pilgrimage to the capital city to pay homage to both of their lords. Most had the good sense to be more fearful of their earthly one. Then there were those who looked upon Dragwlya as they would any prince; ultimately he would be manipulated or killed. Manipulation was a game the boyars played well, siding openly with whomever held power while secretly trying to secure a more favorable candidate to replace the current ruler. Not all of the boyars shared this characteristic, but it was common to most—a trait that must be eradicated.

Music played on the kamayachas of gypsies, filling the midday air. Two elaborate masses, the first a vigil the night before and the second a sunrise service on Easter morning, had been performed at the Paraclete Chapel. A celebration of rejoicing for Christ's sacrifice followed the latter. Almost immediately following the recessional, the boyars' families, the elite of the populace, and well-to-do merchants joined together to make the day a true festival.

Cost had not concerned the prince as he prepared for the festivities to be held in the royal garden surrounding his city. The aromas of roasted lamb, cakes, and fine delicacies provided those in attendance reason to build up an appetite by dancing and playing games. Beginning to long for food, they quenched their thirst with wine.

Motionless, except for his calculating eyes, Dragwlya fought off the urge to unsheathe his blade and lop off the heads of everyone present. Closing his eyes, he focused on the reasons this festival was being held and not solely upon revenge. The task grew nearly impossible but, as time passed, Dragwlya could see all of his careful planning would be rewarded.

Merry and near intoxication, those in attendance failed to notice throughout the day more and more guards and soldiers placing themselves in strategic locations to surround them. A perimeter had been established, ensuring there would be no escape.

"My lord, everything has been prepared in accordance with you instructions."

Dismissing the servant with a wave of his hand, Dragwlya continued to stare. It was quite a spectacle. With twilight descending, several of the boyars and leading citizens were hardly able to stand. A few were unable to stand at all as the children of the elite danced around their fathers and mothers.

Gluttons...Murderers... Two-faced bastards...

"Take them now!" Dragwlya's command silenced the musicians. Most stopped dancing and tried to decipher what he had said, but the sound of metal chains rattling deafened them. All but a few stood, frozen with shock. Some ran, foolishly thinking themselves capable of eluding the trap.

Dragwlya's guards were legion and ready to comply with the order. They focused on the boyars and the boyars' families, easily identified by their elegant and elaborate clothing. Mothers began screaming, screams that were imitated by their children. The boyars shouted, demanding the prince explain himself. Dragwlya's answer outraged and terrified them as they were led to a specially constructed paddock hidden not far away and then manacled to one another. They were then inspected.

Following the prince's instructions, Dragwlya's soldiers carefully examined each man, woman, and child. If it was determined a grown man or woman was of a certain age, or if any man, woman, or child was deemed unfit, they were immediately removed from the compound. Once a few of the prisoners had been beaten brutally for noncompliance, little resistance was met as the inspection continued.

As the sun sank deeper behind the Carpathians, the number of those removed from the paddock increased. There were no more shouts of protest, no more screams; only bewilderment. Slightly more than two hundred men, women, and children watched from within the human sty as nearly another hundred men, women, and children were forcibly led away by Dragwlya's men. Minutes passed and then those being held in the pen heard horrible shrieks and wails of intense pain.

What is he doing to them? was all those in the paddock now wondered. Children began to cry in fear again. Their mothers tried to calm them while suppressing their own need for comfort.

Cries of mercy unanswered were carried to the isolated families by a crisp breeze. The boyar families who had not been separated out contemplated what they had done, or failed to do, to deserve whatever was happening.

"My good friends and loyal nobles!" All heads immediately turned to see who had shouted the salutation and focused on the man standing before them. Other than the occasional shrieks from those who had been led away, the newly born night produced no sound. "Some of you understand why this is happening. You who do not are simply in denial of your crime."

Murky shadows swayed lazily around, set in motion by the light of numerous torches casting their glow on the captives and their captors. Folding his arms, Dragwlya watched the faces of his prisoners. Their looks of confusion and murmurs began to multiply. Some seemed genuinely unaware of their guilt.

They block it out of their memory... Simply dismiss their treachery like it never happened.

"God commanded you, 'Thou shalt not kill.' You have disobeyed and have not begged for His forgiveness. Fear of our Father and His son has not compelled you ... has not been strong enough to dissuade you from the darkness. Satan has possessed your souls since the night you entered the pact with him to kill my father and brother, and God has instructed me to cleanse you of this sin that has until now gone unpunished. I shall drive the Devil from every last one of you!"

Mild protests from those accused quickly transformed into harsh sentiment. "You are possessed!"

"May your souls be reclaimed!"

"He *is* the son of the Devil."

Maneuvering purposely about the pen, Dragwlya gave the appearance of a wild beast stalking, gauging its prey. He traversed halfway around, all the while being verbally assaulted, and stopped to face the northwest where he simply stared. Motioning with his chin toward that general direction, Dragwlya raised his voice so that all would hear him clearly.

"My home here in Tîrgoviște is at a disadvantage. It offers no strategic superiority. I am vulnerable from all sides. That is unacceptable. It is necessary to invest time and resources in a new home. You have graciously volunteered to help me realize this project." With a sudden twist he faced them. "I am giving you your only means to achieve salvation...I am your sovereign and savior!"

Mixed emotions swept over the elite as they were ushered from their pen. Not one of them spoke a word or made a sound of any sort. Even the children understood something bad was happening, something they should be afraid of like their parents were.

"March!" Dragwlya gave the command and rejoiced as the boyar families complied.

God, save us. Leaving the city, this whispered prayer was all most could coherently recite. Looking up on either side, the manacled families were bid farewell by the impaled bodies of those who had been separated from them earlier. This had been the source of the screams they had heard. Two rows of men, women, and children, one on either side of the road, pointed the way to their intended destination.

On horseback, Dragwlya mirthfully led the boyars on a two-day march that spanned nearly fifty miles. There had been few intermissions, only short breaks for the prince, his men, and their horses to properly hydrate. During the trip, twenty-seven of the workforce succumbed to fatigue and heat exhaustion. The remaining captives wondered if surviving the tedious journey was in their best interest.

Morning of the second day had just broken when the peasants of Poenari were awakened by what sounded like an approaching army. Commands were being shouted, and the echo of horses' hooves clapping the ground resonated in their ears. The peasants were not fearful of being attacked though. Everyone in the vicinity had been anticipating this day since the prince had visited and ordered special ovens and kilns be built to produce bricks for the rebuilding of the old castle perched atop the Argeş River.

The peasants gawked upon seeing the parading boyars and their families dressed in their finest Easter attire, what remained of it anyway. During the march, some had ripped away much of their clothing for comfort's sake. Many had not yet accepted that their titles and status meant absolutely nothing; that they were merely slave labor. Holding on to their Easter finery, though torn and filthy, allowed them to retain an air of nobility.

Majestically, the slopes surrounding the Argeş rose in front of the boyars and their journey came to an abrupt end outside of the village at a place known as the "Source of the River." From here the boyars were able to glimpse the ruins of the fortress they were to rebuild.

"It is humid today." Dragwlya was peering over the Poenari bluff to the site of his future retreat while speaking to his commanders and master builders. "Have them form a chain from this bluff to the Argeş fortress to transfer all of the old brick, but make sure there are enough hands to start making new brick to the specifications agreed upon. They can make camp once the sun sets."

"My lord, I suggest the children be brought to the Argeş side to clear it for construction."

"Fine," said Dragwlya after pondering the commander's thought. "Once that is completed, they will spread the mortar for the bricks. We will build the strength of the older ones so that they may handle heavier work also."

Less than an hour passed before the boyars had all of the necessary assembly lines in place. Dragwlya surveyed the progress of his men, now commanding the boyar families with their voices and whips. It would take a few months at the very least to complete the restoration, and he would personally oversee every stage of the building of his retreat, every stage of the breaking of the boyar families.

May your soul finally rest, Mircea.

CHAPTER XXXI
ILLUSION OF CONTROL & CASTLE DRAGWLYA
SIGHIŞOARA
April 12, 1457

"**D**o you still believe you can control him?" Erzsébet stared at Mihály, her voice condescending.

During a recent visit to Matthias, she had overheard several conversations relating the events of the Easter festivities in Wallachia. Hungary was taking particular interest in Dragwlya due to a prescription strictly forbidding a vassal to raise a structure in order to protect himself. Ladislas, understanding the mind of a young prince, allowed the infraction to convince Dragwlya he still considered him loyal.

"At first only the boyars were calling him the son of the Devil. Now the peasants do as well… when they don't call him *The Impaler*. He disregards the nobility entirely. I have no wish to find myself upon a stake in his courtyard. Do you, Mihály? This latest spectacle breaks the treaties he has signed with both Hungary *and* Turkey. Why do you-"

"Enough!" Mihály broke in, causing a chill to run the length of Erzsébet's spine. "If he is against Hungary, if his acts violate provisions with Hungary, then he is our ally! Until he marches against us, he is our ally! What will it take for you to understand that?"

"Until he raises his sword on the battlefield in defiance of the Hapsburgs, I *will* question his loyalty! And if he should ever fight alongside us, I will continue to question his allegiance!"

Storming out of the room, Mihály muttered without stopping. "Impossible woman."

Once Mihály had vanished, Erzsébet turned away from the door. Moving toward the window, she placed her hands upon the sill and peered into the street. It pained her to see mothers with their children, playing, talking with one another, simply walking, taking each other for granted.

I've lost so much already. I will not apologize for my cautiousness.

Erzsébet watched a toddler escape from the grasp of his mother and wander into the middle of the street. The child began to run and, just as quickly, lost his footing. He prevented his face from hitting the ground by stretching out his arms, allowing his hands to take the brunt of the fall. After the initial shock, the child began to wail uncontrollably. Hearing her son cry, the mother instantly turned around and lifted the boy to his feet, all the while futilely brushing the dirt off of his clothes.

The sight reminded Erzsébet of the countless times she had nursed the injuries of her own sons and the lessons she knew they learned with each cut or bruise. For László there would be no more lessons learned, the final one had come at the considerable price of his life.

Erzsébet was not being too protective. Now, whatever the costs, she must ensure the Hunedoaras and the Szilágys learned from László's mistake, even if it meant crossing Mihály.

ANDRINOPLE
April 15, 1457

"Your brother is drawing attention to himself."

Radu looked up from his reading. "Another attack against the boyars," he said dryly.

"Ah, so you have already heard." Mehmed moved close to Radu and sat beside him. "It truly is amazing." A look of awe overtook him as one of ignorance did Radu. "Since we were children, I have known your brother would be a nuisance. His transgressions until now have been negligible. But this latest act, fortifying himself in such a manner, does not sit well with me."

"This act breaks part of his treaty with the Hapsburgs, as it does yours." Radu laid the parchment in his hand on a nearby table.

"It does."

"Let *them* handle this." Mehmed looked at Radu intrigued. "This affects their holdings more so than yours."

"Have you developed sensitivity toward your brother?" asked Mehmed with a smirk.

The expression on Radu's face became one of hatred. "Vlad's interest is Wallachia alone. He has no desire to rule anymore land, but like a mother bird will protect and defend his nest at all costs."

"An interesting analogy." Content, Mehmed rose and began to walk out. Nearing the door he turned to address Radu once more. "If he becomes too unruly, I shall be forced to dispose of him."

"I agree, my liege." As he spoke, Radu disregarded his company and again began his reading.

"You dare disrespect me in my own home?" Mehmed's tone was subdued.

Radu knew well the limits he could go to with Mehmed, knew how much the sultan reveled in flexing his muscle. He looked up from his reading and threw Mehmed a look suggesting to the sultan how unafraid he was of any consequences his actions would have. Laying down the papers, Radu stood and bowed. "A thousand apologies, my liege. I shall never dishonor you in such fashion again."

Racing back to Radu, Mehmed grabbed him by the throat as the stunned young man tried in vain to protect himself. Immediately, he began to gasp, horror filling his eyes. Mehmed stared into Radu's soul, holding on tightly. "Make certain you do not," Mehmed said, his voice still subdued. Then, lightly kissing Radu on the forehead, he threw him down. "It would be a shame if I had to dispose of *you* as well."

Clutching his throat and coughing, Radu watched Mehmed leave. Quickly, he stood, breathing heavily. Mehmed stopped and peered back at him.

"Good."

TÎRGOVIŞTE
May 26, 1457

Of the boyar families who survived the journey to Poenari, almost three-quarters had managed to survive the construction. All were worked from before dawn until well after dark, fed just enough to keep them alive, and eventually had the clothes on their backs fall from their bodies.

The dead had either succumbed to malnutrition, fallen down the slopes while working or trying to escape, or had simply been beaten to death at Dragwlya's command. Nevertheless, Dragwlya's castle now stood complete, two months ahead of schedule. While overseeing the building of his retreat, the prince took measures to guarantee his security on the throne, establishing two forces to protect himself.

For those carrying out the sentences imposed by the prince, his council, and the state since assuming the throne, the position call the armaş was created. While a few members of the armaşi were Romanian, they were far outnumbered by Serbs, Hungarians, Turks, gypsies, and Tartars. Well-paid men with little regard for life kill easily. Secondly, Dragwlya established a military nobility, the viteji, selected from the free peasant landowning class, the moşneni. Dragwlya's honoring them in such a manner was due entirely to their loyalty, integrity, and willingness to fight. The prince's viteji would be separate from the independent military force used during peacetime for repression and policing purposes. Dragwlya's personal guard, the sluji, would be responsible for performing those tasks.

Once the castle had been completed, every last survivor humbly accepted Dragwlya's gracious offer to personally escort them back to Tîrgovişte without manacles. No one would dare defy him now. Unlike the journey north, the journey south would last a day longer on account Dragwlya was not extremely eager to reach his destination. With dusk drawing near, the prince decided to make camp.

Nighttime skies fascinated Dragwlya. "Beauty manifested" was the only term he could think of to describe it, millions of miniscule beacons of light flickering, dancing against a pitch-black backdrop. It amazed him that God had created something so elegant and untainted yet had also giving life to something so impure as the majority of the nobility.

As the hours passed, Dragwlya's boredom grew. In the survivors' camp music was played loudly. Singing and dancing celebrating the return home could be heard. Momentarily, the prince thought to put a stop to the revelry but quickly reconsidered. Taking no action served to show his leniency. After some time, Dragwlya decided to join his subjects.

Inebriated much like they were Easter Sunday, most did not give a second glance to the recent arrival to their party. Why should they? Much like them, he wore filthy tattered clothing. A hooded cloak partially hid his face, and he kept his distance, somewhat hidden in the shadows. He simply observed the sons and daughters of the boyars as they danced around the bonfire, allowing all of their youthful emotions to burst forth. Licking at their bodies, the flames appeared to add even more movement to their gyrations. This night was the first in many months that they had smiled and laughed. Ironically, the atmosphere of the evening eerily mirrored the day they had been led away in chains. A solitary moment passed before Dragwlya's attention was seized. Captivated, the prince stared.

Simply astonishing. In all the months he resided at Poenari, Dragwlya could not recall ever seeing her toiling. Perhaps she had been a brickmaker in one of the nearby villages; perhaps his attention had been too focused on the completion of his retreat. Regardless, he noticed her now.

The way her long dark hair whipped around as she twirled, the brilliant smile her red lips drew back to reveal, the sound of her laughter, the flash of elegance in her eyes; Dragwlya memorized every nuance, every detail. Trailing her with his eyes as she orbited the bonfire, the urge to be closer motivated him to move toward the light. Timing his approach, he filed into the group directly behind her.

Breathtaking.

The view from afar hardly compared. Her dancing was spirited. Her mind and body were possessed it seemed by the music, which told her when and how to react. Entering the circle, the prince had removed the hood from his head and revealed himself to all present. Either no one recognized him or had thought better than to inquire about his likeness to the monster that had forced them into slavery.

Abruptly, the music ended and applause rang out. The musicians had succeeded in making life bearable again for a few moments. They put their instruments down, indicating an intermission had come and there would be a chance for everyone to recuperate.

Sadly, the brilliant smile Dragwlya had been admiring disappeared, and the girl slipped away from the group. Sliding down against a tree, she sat alone. He felt genuine pity for her. No creature so stunning should look so lifeless. It only took a few seconds before the prince reached her and stared down at her. Long seconds passed, yet Dragwlya remained silent, wishing only to observe. He could now close his eyes and describe her features down to the smallest of imperfections, miniscule though they were. The mere thought of her beauty caused him to sigh.

Somewhat startled, the young woman looked up with a gasp. Realizing his error, Dragwlya looked away, cursing himself, and then returned his gaze to her.

"I did not intend to frighten you."

The woman's look of surprise gave way to one of sadness as she lowered her head again. Concluding his identity remained unknown, Dragwlya lowered himself and sat a few feet away, facing her. He waited, wondering if she would speak. When she did not, he tried to engage her.

"Why are you so unhappy? We will soon reach Tîrgovişte. Your family will return home."

She lifted her head quickly and stared with tears in her eyes at the man before her. "I have no family."

"Where are your parents?" He knew the answer but asked anyway.

"My father was killed the night we left for Poenari."

"And your mother?" Tears began to flow as the woman hid her face from view. "Did she suffer that fate as well?"

Again the woman looked up, pain and torment clearly in her eyes. Sniffling, she began to speak.

"Two nights ago, my mother was taken from the camp by the prince's men. She was beaten until she could no longer struggle or scream for help, then they..." Her voice trailed off, knowing she had already properly conveyed what had happened. Stopping made her wonder why she was revealing something so personal to a complete stranger. Still, she felt compelled to continue. "When they were finished, they killed her." Except for quiet sobbing, the woman fell silent.

Dragwlya stared at her, identifying with her, knowing exactly what emotions were controlling her. Mircea and his father had both suffered being helpless victims, too. But they had not been criminals like this woman's family had been. Even though her parents' deaths were untimely in her eyes, they were justifiable. Thinking of his own mother, Dragwlya sympathized with the woman and began to think while justified, the death of the woman's mother had been extreme. Suddenly, he was hit with a shocking realization.

"You saw all of this happen. Didn't you?"

Nodding her head a few times, she shut her eyes tightly, desperately trying to separate herself from the images, knowing it would be impossible to do so.

No matter how many times he recreated the scene in his head, Dragwlya realized he would never truly bear witness to the murders of his father and Mircea. He understood he could never feel the pain this woman harbored.

"I wanted to stop them... She wouldn't let me."

Dragwlya refocused his attention, replaying in his head what she had said. Finally he heard her.

"I awoke and noticed she was gone so I began to look for her. I heard her screaming.

Not calling for help, just … screaming…"

"And then?"

"I began running toward her. Four men surrounded her, each having their turn with her. I saw her face … It was barely recognizable … Then she saw me…She began calling out to me." At this point, the crying woman allowed her voice to gain volume. "No! Get away! Don't! She just kept shouting it over and over. The soldiers thought she was yelling at them." Her voice faded. "They didn't see me, didn't care that someone may be watching them."

"And these men, would you recognize them if you were to see them again?"

"They guarded our camp nightly. I know their faces…I could never forget them."

Extending his arm and thumb, Dragwlya gently wiped the eyes of the woman. "These soldiers should be disciplined for their lack of responsibility. They obviously have no sense of duty to their prince, abandoning their posts in such a manner."

Just as the music began to play again the woman shouted a response. "They should be killed for what they did to my mother! Their prince should be killed for their actions as well as his own! He is entirely responsible for all of this!"

"It is the boyars whom you have to blame for this situation. Because of their treachery, their class had to be purified."

"Have you forgotten? Only a few days ago you were building the prince a private retreat. He forced you to march to Poenari and work as a servant for his benefit? You are defending the Devil himself!" Disgust resonated in her voice.

Dragwlya stood and held out his hands to her. "Come with me."

Although subdued, his voice forced its way into her head, dominating the music and noise from the ongoing celebration. At the suggestion of his command she extended her hand for him to help her, without hesitation. Willingly, she followed him away from camp, through the surrounding forest, finally stopping where a fallen tree provided seating and the moon gave ample light.

Captured by her dark brown eyes, Dragwlya smirked and asked playfully, "Do you really think me a devil?"

Her mind processed what he had said, instantly revealing him. She had guessed some time ago, now it was confirmed. Desperately, her ears searched the night air, hoping to hear someone approaching. Screaming would be a useless gesture, bringing with it certain death. One option remained.

"No, I know you to be *the* Devil."

Dragwlya did not show how impressed he was with her demeanor. She displayed no sign of anger, no sign of fear. She remained calm and composed, the mark of a worthy adversary.

"And why is that exactly?"

"Have you stared into the eyes of your dead father as he hung in mid-air by a stake piercing his stomach, or watched your mother lose her footing and fall from the cliffs of Poenari, screaming all the way down?" Her voice now betrayed her hatred for him. At any moment she would strike.

Dismissing her questions, Dragwlya continued with his own. "What is your name?"

"Demon!" As she lunged for Dragwlya's throat the prince redirected her momentum, sending her crashing to the ground.

"Demon?" Dragwlya shook his head. "What I did was the will of God. I did what I had been commanded to do. All in *His* name. Now once again, what is yours?"

"The will of *God*?" She looked up at him in disbelief. "You are possessed."

With a quick flick of his wrist Dragwlya held a dagger, tensely resting at her throat before she could react. Wildly, her eyes searched for a way to escape.

"Your name... Now!"

"E-Elizabetha."

"Your family name."

"Blasko."

A moment of silence passed before Dragwlya spoke again. "Blasko... I know your father's name well... He helped murder my brother and father, along with all the other traitors. I have been told he was one of those who broke my brother's legs and cast him into a pit to be buried alive. Have you ever dug up the corpse of your murdered brother, only to find him lying face down in the mud?"

Afraid to answer, Elizabetha silently knelt on the ground, waiting to join her mother and father. Her death would extinguish an entire family, a history vanished without record of its ever existing.

"It is shameful that a young woman such as yourself has lost her family. You should, however, view your removal from their influence as a blessing. A miracle really." Slowly, the dagger fell from her neck. "You have been delivered to me to be renewed. From this moment onward you will reside with me and will do as you are told to atone for the sins of your family. Through servitude you may make your family's name pure."

The ideas and thoughts he spewed were so fantastic they could be created only by someone completely unaware or concerned with reality. She could say no, but what then? Would she be killed instantly, left out in the wilderness to fend for herself against nature, or be brought back to Tîrgoviște and made an example of? No, she would not allow any of those things to happen. Elizabetha now understood him, how he rationalized. She thought about it constantly day after day while toiling to build him his castle. Now she knew. Now she understood how to remain alive in his world.

"As you wish, my lord."

A reasonable answer from a rational person. Obviously, she was only telling him what he wanted to hear, but he chose not to punish her for it. He now had what he wanted, a subservient mistress who would do his bidding, regardless of what it was.

"Good. Come with me. There is no need for you to retrieve your belongings. You will be provided for in every way.

CHAPTER XXXII
STRENGTHENING CUSTOMS
TÎRGOVIŞTE
June 22, 1457

Political diplomacy and its intricacies intrigued Dragwlya. Like chess it was a game, but the strategy involved and the satisfaction of victory outweighed those of chess one hundred fold. There were, of course, more pieces to keep track of when it came to diplomacy.

Sinking behind the Carpathians, the sun cast long shadows that rushed away to the opposite horizon, seemingly to pull the sun back from under the earth. Within his palace, Dragwlya was holding an audience with a trio of Turkish ambassadors sent to discuss a treaty. After six hours of negotiating, little had been resolved.

"For eight hours we have sat here, waiting. We should forget about this principality and leave."

Shaking his head, Gustavo countered. "Patience, Benito. Our time will come."

"Let Lorenzo come and wait himself! I fail to understand why we have to be here at all!"

"Benito!" Although not directed toward him, Gustavo felt personally insulted by the comment. "A show of respect from you would be welcomed, even if it were only lip service."

"I agree, Benito. Your lack of appreciation for the Medici is deplorable." Both Benito and Gustavo looked at Sandro, the third member of their party.

Endless bickering had accompanied the three ambassadors along their journey from Florence. At the request of Duke Lorenzo de' Medici, they departed Italy and were venturing east in search of art and knowledge. The duke, himself a poet, insisted on having leading artists and intellectuals at his court.

"We are in the middle of nowhere!" Benito half yelled. "I have never heard of this Prince Vlad, or of any great painters, sculptors, or musicians from this region." Benito had now been in the service of the Medici for more than fifteen years. Although in his early thirties, he had the look of one in his forties and the impatience of a two-year old.

Gustavo's dark brown eyes stared harshly at Benito. He too had served Lorenzo for some time now. With his forty-sixth birthday only months away, this would be the last of such journeys he would make for the duke. Traveling had kept him in the shape of a man in his twenties, and his mind possessed the wisdom of every man he had spoken to, every parchment he had laid hands upon.

"Exactly. It is our duty to find the hidden treasures of the land," chimed in Sandro.

The youngest of the three, Sandro looked and acted his twenty-two years of age, viewing each day as a challenge to overcome. Most days failed to live up to his expectations, and often he turned his focus to women.

"Neither of you realize our importance. New ways of thinking have-" At that moment Gustavo was interrupted by both Benito and Sandro simultaneously.

"...opened up the eyes and minds of those who perceived art as a two dimensional medium, further knowledge as unnecessary, and the world as a static body." Benito and Sandro laughed as they sarcastically finished Gustavo's speech, one they had obviously heard countless times.

Hardly amused, Gustavo responded. "Laugh now, clowns, but I assure you-"

"The prince will grant you an audience now."

The heads of the ambassadors flinched quickly to find the origin of the voice. Almost immediately the figure of a servant came into view. Benito rose first.

"Finally. Perhaps we will dine before midnight after all."

Gustavo followed the servant closely, flanked by his two companions, toward Dragwlya's main audience room. Strangely, no sound emanated from within the chamber. Surely the prince had a full court. What caused such silence?

"My lord, ambassadors representing Duke Lorenzo de' Medici."

Approaching Dragwlya, Gustavo, Benito, and Sandro each looked around the room, determined to learn the reason why the audience chamber lacked activity though at least fifty people were present.

"Gentlemen, I am honored by your presence."

The ambassadors could not help but feel uneasy. A room filled to near capacity, a cordial prince, and yet the court was lifeless.

"As you can see, I am also currently entertaining guests from the Ottoman Empire. I offer you my most sincere apologies for having to wait so long."

Gustavo spoke once they had stopped before the throne.

"Good evening, your highness. Your apology is unnecessary. We are journeying on behalf of Lorenzo de' Medici in search of art and knowledge. My name is Gustavo and these are my companions, Benito and Sandro." Gustavo motioned with his hand respectively to his counterparts.

Silence fell over the room once again as the three men, out of respect, removed their hats and bowed slightly. They stood upright once again, puzzled by the instantaneous murmuring now flowing around them. The three envoys turned their heads from side to side, trying to comprehend the commotion. Ultimately, their ignorant gazes fixed on one another.

His attention drawn, Dragwlya stared at the ambassadors before him, his gaze resting entirely on their heads and the skullcaps they wore.

"My lord, have we done something to offend you?" Gustavo inquired.

Still seated, Dragwlya spoke. "Why do you dishonor me?" The question created quizzical looks upon the faces of the envoys. "Your skullcaps. Why have you not removed them?"

Benito's temper had been simmering for far too long. After waiting for hours to see this man, this prince now claimed *he* was being dishonored? The audacity! They were ambassadors from Florence, and *he* was being dishonored? Before Gustavo had a chance to calm the approaching storm, Benito let loose one of his own.

"This is *our* custom." Benito's tone hinged on the fringes of ridicule. "We are not obliged to take our skullcaps off under *any* circumstances, even during an audience with the sultan or the Holy Roman Emperor himself."

Dragwlya allowed himself to glance at the Turkish envoys still present. *I am not surprised your master allows such lack of respect.*

Gustavo winced internally, wanting with his last ounce of strength to reach into Benito's mouth and rip out his tongue; he doubted even that would be enough to quiet him. He feared what the prince's reaction would be. A rift had been created, one that required mending.

Dragwlya motioned the servant next to him to lean over, allowing him to whisper. Once the servant moved away Gustavo spoke.

"Prince Vlad, forgive our ignorance. This is simply the custom with the rulers of our country. Our skullcaps are never removed unless our rulers ask us to do so." Gustavo clenched his hands and felt the pulsing of blood throughout his body. Hopefully, his statement repaired some of the damage caused. He had now given Dragwlya an opportunity to instruct them to remove their skullcaps.

Dragwlya watched two guards position themselves behind each of the envoys. "In all fairness, I want to recognize and strengthen your custom so that you may adhere to it even more rigidly."

Thank God. Gustavo had found the prince's favor once more. Dragwlya could be reasoned with and respected what he did not necessarily understand. "Thank you, sire." Gustavo bowed and instructed his companions to do so as well. Standing upright, Gustavo continued. "We shall always serve you with your interests if you show us such goodness, and we shall praise your greatness everywhere."

Looking past the ambassadors as though they were not present, Dragwlya nodded to the positioned sluji. Instantly, they grabbed the ambassadors and forced them to their knees.

"What are you doing? What is the meaning of this?" All three of the Florentinians had been yelling these questions repeatedly since they had been grabbed from behind and driven to the floor, none louder than Benito.

"Prince Vlad, release us immediately! I demand to know you inten-" Something felt as if it were penetrating into Benito's head as he barked at Dragwlya. There was a searing pain and repetitive pounding that seemed to be reaching deeper into his skull.

Sandro was the first to scream, followed almost instantly by Benito and Gustavo. The skullcaps they wore were being affixed to their heads with three-inch iron nails. Their cries were agonizing, the sound of the hammering surreal. Every member of Dragwlya's court watched, wanting to look away.

Satisfied with the sight of the ambassadors' blood flowing down their faces, Dragwlya smiled as his attendants continued their work. "Believe me, this is the manner in which I will strengthen your customs."

With the last ping signifying the completion of their task, the sluji let go of the Florentinian ambassadors, allowing them to raise their hands to their heads to try and stop the pain. Torment crashed into them as they lay curled up on the floor, clawing at the metal nails now embedded in their heads.

Dragwlya continued to observe as his floor turned red. The ambassadors' shrieks were in some way soothing. If this was how he would be forced to bring about civility, so be it.

"Now go!" At this command, the sluji dragged the Florentinians to their feet and pushed them toward the doors. "Go and tell your master that *he* may be accustomed to suffer such indignity from his own people. We, however, are not so accustomed. Tell him not to send either to this country or elsewhere ambassadors *flaunting* his customs. They will not be received so kindly!"

Though they vanished from view, the cries of the ambassadors reached the ears of all present at Dragwlya's court. Many were appalled, shocked by the never-ending depths he dove to for his vanity and the ways he justified it. His infliction of pain was for personal gratification only. It served no other purpose. Yet, there would be no outcry. No one desired a harsher punishment for failing to agree with the decision of the prince.

Dragwlya's gaze quickly fell to the leader of the Turkish envoys, whom he had been speaking with prior to the appearance and hasty departure of the Florentinians.

"We may continue our discussion now."

Recalling his own entrance into the audience chamber, the Turkish ambassador breathed hard as he remembered the exact second he and his companions removed the hats from their heads and then the fezzes underneath. Staring at the prince, he managed to muster a smile.

Praise be to Allah.

ANDRINOPLE
July 1, 1457

"He had them nailed to their heads, my liege! Then, as they were lying on the floor, covered in blood, he told them it would be in their best interest never to return and that you should not send ambassadors elsewhere displaying such contempt."

Mehmed glanced at Radu inquisitively and back to the merchant standing before him.

A loyal subject, the merchant felt obliged to report all he had heard. Upon his arrival in Turkey, he was told an astounding, horrific story of how Prince Vlad of Wallachia had nailed the fezzes of three Turkish envoys to their heads for their lack of respect and as a show of defiance against the sultan.

"I thank you for your devotion. You may go now."

After bowing the merchant made a quick exit, prompting Mehmed to again stare at Radu.

"I know your brother derives pleasure from inflicting pain, but would he do such a thing? Would he insult me in such a manner?"

"The practice is uncommon, but not unheard of."

"I know he *would* do it, but would he do so to my envoys? To me?"

"I doubt it. But he is nothing if not unpredictable."

"If the story related by that merchant holds true, your brother's reign will not see summer's end."

"All myths are derived from some factual basis. That he heard this tale only after reaching Turkey indicates my brother did *something*. The truth will be revealed eventually."

By Allah.

The phrase was gasped over and over by thousands throughout the day as the story of the Wallachian's mistreatment of Mehmed's envoys spread through both Andrinople and Constantinople. The tale had been related to merchants and travelers departing for other cities and sailors destined for far-off ports. They would repeat it to others in the East and the South, never knowing their error.

Completing his evening meal, Mehmed rubbed his stomach and belched. Since early this morning he had recounted the merchant's words continuously, wondering if it were all true. With mixed emotions Mehmed got up and moved away from his dinner table.

"My liege, they have returned."

Mehmed twisted around to see one of his servants standing there. Immediately, he began walking toward the man and then quickly past him. At nearly an all out dash, the sultan raced to his main audience room, eager to see.

Rushing in, Mehmed searched with his eyes to locate the ambassadors. Once he had caught sight of them he changed directions, heading directly toward them. Skidding to a stop, the winded sultan commanded them in a sentence broken by sporadic breathing. "Remove…your…fezzes."

Tentatively, the ambassadors looked to each other and then at the sultan, now hunched over, trying to regain his breath. At a loss seeing the sultan in such a state, they failed to comply with his order.

"Now!"

Jolted by his reiteration, Mehmed's envoys started with fright, but recovered immediately and removed the fezzes covering their heads.

"Bend down!" Mehmed had recuperated fully, and his order was promptly obeyed. Laying his hands upon the heads of the envoys and searching through their hair, Mehmed checked each in turn thoroughly to find the marks left by the nails. He found nothing. The ambassadors' heads were completely unscathed. No scars; no indication of the reported traumatic event. "Stand up." The envoys' faces told Mehmed his actions did not baffle them, that he had just cause for them. "This morning a merchant told me a fantastic story about your visit to Wallachia. You stare at me knowing what I seek. Why have I not found it?"

"My liege," the leader of the envoys spoke, "the story you have heard is true. We, however, were not the victims of the prince's cruelty…though we were in attendance when it occurred."

"What *did* occur exactly?"

"As I stated, my liege, you know the basic story, but it was a Genoese delegation sent by Lorenzo de' Medici who suffered Prince Vlad's mercilessness. We watched his men carry out his orders, praising Allah all the while for giving us the insight and wisdom to remove our fezzes in the prince's presence."

Mehmed stroked his short beard as he listened. "You are no doubt aware it is being proclaimed that you three were the recipients of this treatment."

"Yes, my liege…and, we are responsible." The envoy's head drooped in shame, a sharp contrast to Mehmed's verbal reaction of intrigue. Reluctant to continue, the ambassador shook his head before continuing. "After witnessing that inhumane display, we left Price Vlad's castle, declining his offer to stay. We traveled for some time before stopping at a small town where we sought lodging for the evening and were relieved to find some of our countrymen staying in the same inn. We were dining with these men, one of whom was a merchant, and as the night wore on we became intoxicated." The envoy's shame had grown with every word, leading up to this sin. "I believe that in telling the story to these men we may have…embellished it slightly and claimed *we* were the ones who had suffered the horrific fate."

Mehmed simply stared at the three men before him. "Surely these men asked to see the nails embedded in your heads. How did you succeed in honoring their request?"

Overcome with embarrassment, the ambassador deferred to one of his companions. "My liege, we told them once the nails were removed, the wounds were instantly healed by Allah."

Mehmed's laughing was deafening. For nearly a minute he laughed, ultimately crying because of the hilarity he found in the situation. Not wanting to insult him, the ambassadors joined him. Mehmed's chuckling ceased abruptly, ending the laughing of the envoys as well. The sultan merely shook his head, a smile still plastered to his face.

"Merchants, sailors, and beggars are making their way from city to city, port to port, spreading a story of the Wallachia prince who hammered nails into the heads of three Turkish envoys."

"My liege, we had no intention of this lie being told, definitely not of its spreading. We shall proclaim it a falsehood to anyone we speak to until this matter-"

"No." Mehmed broke in before the ambassador finished. "You will do nothing of the kind. In fact, you will recount the story to anyone who asks about it as you did at the inn. Because of your sins, the greatness of Allah will spread."

"My liege, if you had only seen—witnessed what this demon is capable of-"

"I know what he is capable of. You are dismissed."

Mehmed watched as his ambassadors bowed and left uneasily.

Like children. Why do I employ their services?

"Are you certain you know *all* he is capable of, my liege?"

Mehmed immediately sensed Radu's presence as the young man stepped out of the shadows.

"He has not insulted me with this incident. It was not my men who suffered at his hands."

"Ah, but because of your men, the world will think otherwise. The world will know a treaty was being negotiated when Prince Vlad III of Wallachia found the terms of the sultan disagreeable and, to show his dissatisfaction, mutilated his men."

Mehmed sneered. While the name of Allah would be praised for His greatness in healing the envoys, the sultan knew his own would be ridiculed. "Let the masses believe what they will. I will prove my superiority when necessary."

He is overconfident. No one knows the mind of my brother... not even Vlad himself.

SUCEAVA
July 2, 1457

Six years had passed since Bogdan II's assassination. Petru Aaron, his brother, his murderer in many respects, had remained enthroned, doing for the boyars what Bogdan would not. He had succumbed to every whim of the Ottoman Empire. Now his reign was being challenged.

"I want him driven out! Why is that such a difficult task?"

"Stephen is no longer a mere boy, my lord. He is grown, fueled by vengeance, and has the support of rebellious boyars and his cousin."

Petru stared at his advisor. "Do you have any information of which I am not already aware?"

Fearfully, the advisor cowered. "My apologies, my lord."

"This revolution must be stopped before it has any chance of beginning." Turning to his spies and soldiers, Petru gave out his final order before retiring for the evening. "Find him and kill him."

EAST OF FALTICENI
July 4, 1457

"Vlad has assured me when the time is appropriate he will send at least five thousand men."

"And you believe him?" Ridden with disbelief, the boyar's tone conveyed how naïve he thought the young man to be.

Stephen remained calm. "I have no reason to doubt him."

"Forgive me, my lord, but the oath you swore with him was more than six years ago. Is it not possible your cousin's thoughts are concentrated on matters other than assisting you in attaining your throne?"

Stephen retained his composure through his own uncertainty. "No." He stared with confidence at the doubter. "Vlad wishes to be rid of my uncle as much as I do. He will keep his end of the bargain."

Everyone, Stephen included, contemplated this last thought. Loyalty existed as an intangible that held more wealth than any precious metal or gem and served as the main means by which a man could be trusted. Stephen would not take Dragwlya's trust lightly.

CHAPTER XXXIII
PRINCES OF WALLACHIA
BISTRIŢA
July 24, 1457

Finally, the moment had come for Erzsébet to prove to Mihály the prince of Wallachia's true loyalties. She would expose Dragwlya and prove just how poor a judge of character Mihály was.

The revolt of Bistriţa's German population had come as no surprise. Complaints of fiscal abuses by the Szilágy had been lodged for months. All charges had gone ignored. The family's silence was taken as an admission of guilt. Insurrection followed, beginning with the seizing and fortifying of Bistriţa, an act that demanded an immediate response. Mihály viewed this as two opportunities. Of utmost importance, he would be able to eliminate a portion of the Germans opposing him. Secondarily, he could show Erzsébet Dragwlya's devotion. Upon learning of the revolt, Mihály immediately dispatched an appeal to Dragwlya, one that had been answered timely.

The prince of Wallachia sent a messenger to inform Mihály he was en route with a large contingent. To Erzsébet's shock, and Mihály's relief, Dragwlya remained true to his word. He had rendezvoused with Mihály's force earlier this morning near Bistriţa and fell in with the established ranks. Mihály had smiled when the messenger delivered the news of Dragwlya's eminent arrival, but seeing the banners of the Wallachian gave him greater joy. This, he hoped, would prove to Erzsébet Dragwlya's true allegiance once and for all.

Dawn had just broken when the attack began in earnest. A small force that comprised most of the resistance fought Mihály outside the fortified walls of Bistriţa. The city's permanent compliment, a smaller contingent, had barricaded itself inside. Dragwlya knew Bistriţa would fall swiftly, regardless of who led the charge, and could have been overrun by the men he alone provided. This was Mihály's fight though, and Dragwlya would relegate himself to the role of follower.

Effortlessly, Mihály and Dragwlya advanced to the walls of the city. Short moments passed before a juggernaut forced open the gates of the city, allowing Mihály's men to pour in like water rushing through a compromised dam. Soldiers targeted the homes of the most prominent citizens, looting and burning the houses of those suspected of leading the insurrection. Mihály and Dragwlya forced captives to watch the destruction of their homes. The suggestion came from Dragwlya that once flames consumed their world, they too should be eliminated. Though reluctant, the thought of reprisals convinced Mihály of the idea's merit.

Flames reduced the elegant homes of the Germans to smoldering rubble. Billows of smoke still rose from the debris, blanketing Bistriţa. An unusually bright crescent moon allowed everyone to view the plumes being driven across the night sky by a gentle breeze. Little celebration continued while the leaders of the triumphant force remained awake, discussing the quelling of the rebellion and other matters in the comfort of the seized home they would reside in for a few days.

"People continually ignore God's will and the leaders He has installed. The result is the action we were forced to take today. The indignity and weeks of lawlessness suffered by you and your sister were caused by men taking an idea placed in their heads by Lucifer himself and trying to make it a reality." Dragwlya sat back in his chair, replaying the battle mentally. He critiqued his performance, finding too many missteps. There was one second when he had hesitated. It had nearly cost him his life.

Cutting down opponent after opponent, Dragwlya found himself covered in the blood of his enemies. Each time the blood of one of his victims splashed his body he felt stronger, more invincible.

Is it possible to somehow absorb the life of another?

"Have you not heard a single word I've said?" Mihály's question was accompanied by laughter.

Dragwlya shook his head slightly, indicating he had not. "Forgive me, Mihály. My thoughts returned to the battlefield."

"I agree with your statement concerning the lower classes attempting to think for themselves regarding matters they cannot possibly grasp."

"My belief is that they should not be allowed to think at all." Dragwlya's attention had completely refocused. "They simply await a shepherd to follow while grazing mindlessly."

Mihály allowed for a moment of silence before laughing. "Well, you have proven your command over the flock is infallible. In gratitude I would like to offer you a gift."

Dragwlya stared at Mihály, wondering what gift he would bestow. "That is not necessary."

"It is a gift. Its acceptance is not subject to question, and its refusal will not be tolerated." Given an agreeable look, Mihály continued. "Near Rodna at the Borgo Pass there is a castle that once belonged to my family. It now belongs to you."

"Your generosity is too overwhelming, Mihály. Such a gift exceeds the minor task I performed." *A castle on the fringes of Moldavia. It will cost men and money I cannot spare just to maintain it.*

"Nonsense. Do not be modest about your strengths on the battlefield. Embrace them, make them greater. Show others the power you possess."

"I shall take your advice to heart."

"As well you should. In time you will develop the gifts God has bestowed upon you and appease him by using them to their fullest potential."

Dragwlya's tolerance for conversing had been exceeded. Raising his arms above his head with his hands clenched in fists, he forced himself to yawn. Once it had passed, he rubbed the inner corners of his eyes with the thumb and index finger of his left hand and squinted. "Forgive me, I–"

"Not at all. My disregard for your fatigue is unacceptable. I have kept you from well deserved rest for far too long. I wish you had interrupted me long ago."

As do I.

"We will discuss our victory tomorrow."

The prospect of further dialogue in the morning did not thrill him, and Dragwlya was more than willing to snatch the chance of any reprieve he may be granted. Smiling as he stood, the prince bowed slightly. "Until tomorrow."

"Rest well."

Once he was facing away from Mihály, Dragwlya allowed the smile to melt away. *Hopefully the sun will rise later than usual.*

BRAŞOV
August 6, 1457

In the aftermath of the battle at Bistriţa, the surviving rebels fled south. Though few in number, they formed two contingencies. One made its way to Sibiu while the other sought refuge in Braşov. Both were determined to rid Wallachia, and themselves, of the son of the Devil. They made certain to tell all they came in contact with of their persecution at Dragwlya's hands. The German cities now held Dragwlya in contempt.

"He called us his friends ... *brothers* even! I want no part of *this* family! Do you?" The mayor of Braşov addressed the city leaders with the same passion he always did. This time though, the edge of his argument was sharper than usual. His short, portly body shook with frustration. His reddened face looked to individuals for a response to his question. When none came, he continued. "We had a pact. He pledged his loyalty to us and, less than a month afterwards, he sent a contingency to the sultan! We have no choice! Vlad *must* be deposed!"

Emotionless faces stared at the mayor. While everyone agreed with him, no one was brave enough to have their voice heard first. Their silence, their cowardice, did not surprise the mayor.

"Dan Dăneşti has been residing here since Dragwlya killed his brother Vladislav. He must be recognized and accepted as the new prince of Wallachia."

Everyone present realized what this would mean. Dragwlya would not give up his throne simply because the Germans wished it.

"We all share your belief in this matter and wish to see a swift end to Prince Vlad's reign. What exactly are your intentions regarding his ousting?"

A slight grimace adorned the pudgy face of the mayor. "I am not suggesting we assemble an army and march on Tîrgovişte if that is your concern. If we can secure the appropriate support necessary there will be no need to fight. We will take the throne without raising arms."

"Unless, of course, Prince Vlad decides to march against *us*," interjected a boyar.

"If need be, we will fight. With the support of the others, Dan will be prince."

Merely one day passed before part of the Braşovian mayor's vision came to pass. In a ceremony performed by rebel boyars, some of whom had escaped Dragwlya's two mass impalements, Dan was crowned prince and took up residence with his court in Braşov's Romanian district, near Tîmpa Hill.

There were now two princes of Wallachia.

SIBIU
August 7, 1457

"In light of all this, we have no choice but to champion a replacement to the throne of Wallachia."

The mayor of Sibiu was steadfast in his statement; one he presented to the city council after it had convened shortly following the arrival of the refugees from Bistriţa to discuss their options.

"I am certain our brethren in Braşov share our opinion and will fully back Vlad Dăneşti as the prince's successor." The council members agreed in unison with their leader. "The monk is the obvious choice to replace his brother. Braşov will no doubt agree."

SIGHISOARA

Basarab Laiotă, son of Dan II, reviewed the boyars before him. There weren't many, mostly those unwilling to journey as far south as Braşov or Sibiu. Little effort would have to be expended to gain their support.

"It is not only the Germans... Look at how he mistreats his own people. His very actions, the cruelty he inflicts upon Wallachia demands he be ousted. How much will the sultan endure before he tires of Dragwlya and invades our land? Is that what you want? Is Romania to become an Islamic nation, devoted to the ideals of *Allah*?"

Opposition to Dragwlya's leadership quickly became voiced in a near shouting frenzy, culminating in a unified chant.

"Death to Dragwlya! Death to the traitor!"

SUCEAVA
August 20, 1457

Stephen had waited for what seemed like a lifetime.

Six years… Has it really only been six?

Stephen couldn't verbalize how much more time he felt had passed since he and his cousin had fled Moldavia. The event triggering that flight remained fresh in his memory. It was as though only this morning his father had been murdered. Now the mastermind of Bogdan's assassination stood across from him on the battlefield. Every movement had been carefully considered. Stephen's strategy could be likened to a painting started two years ago, simply awaiting the final stroke. The finishing touch of this masterpiece would be Petru Aaron's death.

"My lord, everything is in order per your instructions."

Stephen's attention was so focused on the sight of Aaron that he failed to respond.

"My lord?"

After allowing himself one more second to stare, Stephen acknowledged the boyar next to him. *Vlad's talent for coercion is unparalleled.*

Along with several others, the boyar had been compelled by Dragwlya to back Stephen as his candidate for the Moldavian throne. Playing on their emotions, the Wallachian had managed to convince many that Aaron had reduced their once proud principality to an obedient Turkish vassal state, turning a once proud people into nothing more than minions of the sultan. Dragwlya's gift for manipulation was evident in that every man ordered to fight alongside Stephen now stood on the battlefield, willing to lose his life for someone he barely knew.

Seeing Stephen successfully capture the throne was a secondary desire for Dragwlya. He believed that with his cousin ruling Moldavia his northern border would be less prone to attack. That was his primary motivation.

"Shall we ride out now to hear their terms, my lord?"

Stephen looked to heaven and squinted. It was overcast, with just enough light seeping through the light ash colored clouds to hurt one's eyes if he gazed up long enough. Stephen smiled, again looking back across the battlefield. Three of Aaron's generals were now waiting for him. Stephen stared at them briefly before focusing again on Aaron, wanting him to know he was the hunted.

Look at me!

Stephen knew their eyes were now locked. He didn't dare flinch. Soon the moment would come.

Aaron turned his head away and said something to one of his commanders, but his stare quickly turned back to Stephen. At the precise second Aaron broke eye contact, Stephen had given the order to charge. Without hesitation, Stephen's force blitzed toward its opponent and watched with growing confidence as Aaron's generals retreated toward their own ranks.

Battle cries calling for Aaron's head rang out from Stephen's men. They felt momentum was theirs, felt strength in their leader. They knew God had created them for the sole purpose of delivering Moldavia from the hands of Allah. The cries melded into one unified scream seconds before the swords of Stephen's men met the swords and flesh of Aaron's.

CHAPTER XXXIV
NIGHT EXCURSION
TÎRGOVIŞTE
October 2, 1457

"They mean to replace you, my lord."

Dragwlya eyed the head of his chancellery and smirked, shaking his head negatively. "Priboi, they have three candidates amongst them who share no commonality. They are un-unified. The Saxons were attacked, and those in power have decided to use the event as a mean to achieve their own ends."

"Are you not the least bit concerned?" Priboi was a middle-aged boyar who had been loyal to Dracul and remained devoted to the Drăculeşti. Often he wondered about Dragwlya's seemingly dismissive attitude. His blue-grey eyes remained transfixed upon the prince as he awaited a response.

"They won't invade, and now that Stephen sits on Moldavia's throne, my northern frontier is secured. They must be punished though, with that I do agree."

At this statement, Priboi perked up a bit. *Finally, he is making sense.*

"They have voided the treaty assented to last year. The most favored nation clause once exclusively held by them will be extended to *my* merchants, Caffa, and to the Florentinians." Here Dragwlya's provisions stopped with Priboi anxiously waiting for them to continue. Nearly half a minute passed before the boyar said a word.

"What other conditions do you wish to impose, sire?"

"That is all for now. I believe it will be enough to persuade them to cease this foolishness."

Knowing better than to question Dragwlya's policy, Priboi remained silent even as his reasoning screamed in frustration.

"Leave me now."

Priboi bowed his head. "As you wish, my lord." Departing the throne room, Priboi was joined by another boyar, Mihail. Once they had reached a distance out of earshot, conversation erupted.

"His father would have suspended *all* trade with the Saxons and would be preparing to invade right now," said Priboi.

Slightly younger than Priboi, Mihail had become a boyar only after the beginning of Dragwlya's second reign. He was soft-spoken and shared the wisdom he possessed often. "Yes, and countless Wallachians would have been killed needlessly."

Priboi stopped walking and stared, examining Mihail as the younger boyar passed two steps in front of him and rounded slowly. "For all we know, three separate armies are readying themselves to attack Tîrgovişte."

"For all we know, there are three false princes of Wallachia who have only a court of disgruntled boyars and Saxons supporting their causes."

Priboi's annoyance at Mihail's calmness took over. "What do you think will happen to us if Vlad is overthrown?"

"We will either swear allegiance to his successor or be killed, I suppose."

"You have never been one of the outcasts, Mihail…When Dracul was murdered, I paid the price for my devotion...You have no idea what it is like to be persecuted, to have to hide your loyalties and bury your beliefs. Vlad's actions will cause consequences that may well jeopardize our lives."

"They always will, Priboi… As will our own."

A sharp breeze gave an edge to the crisp autumn night. With the hour nearing eleven, little activity occurred on the streets of Tîrgoviște. Most gatherings were happening in taverns or inns, except for the gypsies who held their own festivities outside of the city.

Donning the dress of a peasant, Dragwlya secretly left the confines of his home to find amusement. Curiosity of what the life of a commoner offered piqued his interest sporadically, leading to such excursions. Their lives appeared to be little more than a dull chore, he thought. There was a well-laid plan for each of them: master an assigned skill, swear allegiance to the prince, obey the prince. More like dogs than people. Every so often one stood out from the rest—the occasional poet, artist, or warrior. But for the most part they were either interchangeable or expendable.

Venturing through the streets gave Dragwlya time to clear his head and speak with his father and brother. Sometimes they answered his questions, but not often. Tonight the only question beckoning was with whom would he share the night?

Five months had passed since Dragwlya had met Elizabetha. Though he was growing tired of her, he still had every intention of keeping his promise to her. There were times when he found her unappealing. He blamed her for his inability to become aroused and, on such nights, would venture out to indulge himself elsewhere.

Recently, the prince had found a woman who met his needs. Few were aware of Dragwlya's affair with this peasant mistress. None who were dared question it, publicly or privately. Reaching the woman's home, Dragwlya knocked and waited for her to answer.

Although she was four years younger than Dragwlya, many considered Smaranda old. No husband, no children; she lived a solitary life earning wages as a seamstress and, when necessary, by prostitution. Little she had dreamt of in her childhood had come to pass, almost nothing in fact other than finding someone she cared about. But how could a common whore declare her undying love for her prince? The absurdity of such a thought repulsed even her, reinforcing the understanding her feelings could never be made known to anyone but him.

Without verbal greetings, Smaranda's door closed almost as quickly as it had opened, locking away from the rest of the world the immediate rapture that followed.

Dragwlya stumbled back to his own bed shortly before dawn. Elizabetha awoke immediately.

"You were with her again." Elizabetha's voice implied some sort of betrayal had taken place.

"Even if you were the princess of Wallachia, your accusation would be irrelevant... Do not force me to rescind my promise to you."

PRAGUE
December 9, 1457

"Try and eat something, sire." A worried, helpless feeling overtook Andras as he attended to his bedridden king. With great discomfort a response slowly slid from Ladislas' colorless lips.

"No... I'll only-"

The reply ended abruptly, cut short by a low, rumbling belch from the king. Knowing what would follow, Andras grabbed a nearby bedpan a second before the deluge of vomit. This was the third consecutive day the thirteen year-old king failed to leave his room for meals or anything else, including the conference he had been invited to Prague to attend. Over the last seventy-two hours, his state had deteriorated rapidly without explanation.

Andras' despair was now on the verge of becoming hopelessness. There was nothing left to do except wait for an improbable miracle. Everything physically possible had already been done.

Holy Roman Emperor Fredrick III had spent much of the past three days waiting, something he was not accustomed to doing. That he did not have complete control of the situation caused him to agonize over the endless possibilities and countless intricacies that could go wrong. For this to work, for him to succeed, would require having to trust others.

Fredrick anticipated the moment someone would inform him of Ladislas' death. The thought of having a thirteen year-old boy killed weighed on him heavily, but Ladislas was the king of Hungary, his enemy. Circumstances did not allow for sympathy simply because of age. Too much power was at stake. The truth surrounding the Hungarian king's death would remain a mystery. Fredrick would ensure it did. Those involved were trustworthy, but expendable.

Time's peculiar way of plodding when someone desires it to rush by began having an effect on the emperor. Dawn crept toward Prague as the sun seemingly held itself below the horizon, unwilling to allow the day to begin. Fredrick stared at the red-orange orb as it laboriously inched upward, willing it to rise with every breath. Hearing the sound of someone entering his chamber, he spun around. Bags under his eyes betrayed to the servant now before him that he had not slept. His stare conveyed desire, however, not exhaustion.

"What?" Fredrick's voice cracked slightly, this being the first time he had spoken since the previous night.

Without hesitation the young man answered. "Sire, King Ladislas is dead."

Fredrick nodded a few times as he solemnly answered, "Very well." With a wave of his hand, he dismissed the servant and stared at the door for a few seconds once it had been closed. Turning back around, he could see the sun had cleared the horizon and was well on its way to showering the city with its light. A faint smile appeared on his lips.

Today will pass quickly.

CHAPTER XXXV
QUESTIONS ANSWERED
SIBIU
February 3, 1458

Oswald glanced up momentarily from the letter in his hand without attempting to mask his contempt. One phrase stood out prominently—the mayor should reconsider his backing of "a Wallachian priest who had established himself in *his* Duchy of Amlaş with the connivance of the authorities."

Pompous fool.

After the actions Dragwlya had taken, after siding with Mihály, he expected loyalty? Intolerable. His request would be ignored. The city's support of Vlad the Monk would continue and the prince would be dealt with accordingly.

Too much was changing for Oswald's comfort. Ioan Hunedoara's son, Matthias, although not officially crowned, had been elected king of Hungary less than a fortnight ago. He was backed by his uncle, Mihály Szilágy. This would cause problems for the German towns. Control had to be regained, and ridding Wallachia of Dragwlya was the logical first step.

Oswald stared at the head of Dragwlya's chancellery, Priboi, and the boyar, Mihail, with a false look of urgency.

"Gentlemen, return to Tîrgovişte and inform Prince Vlad I will respond to his request and inquiries before long. The council must convene to discuss this matter, and it will be some time before I am able to send an appropriate reply. I am certain he will understand."

Mihail and Priboi stared at one another. Before leaving for their journey, Dragwlya had instructed them not to leave Sibiu without the mayor's word that all loyalties to Vlad the Monk would be terminated immediately. Mihail spoke.

"Honorable mayor, the prince wishes for an immediate response and requests assurances that the city of Sibiu will no longer support a campaign for the throne of Wallachia from *any* candidate."

Before Oswald could speak, Priboi interjected.

"Sir, similar correspondence has been sent to Braşov. As you are no doubt aware, they back Dan III as a candidate for Wallachia's throne. I believe it vital for your people's sake that you meet with the council immediately and send word to the prince of your decision."

The unmitigated gall…

"Obtaining any communal answer at this time is impossible… A reply will be sent shortly."

Mihail waited a moment before responding. "If that is your final decision, we will return now and inform the prince."

"Would you not care to stay at least for the night?"

"It would be best if we returned now, sir," said Mihail.

"Very well. I shall have my servants attend to you and help you make ready for your journey. Good night, gentleman."

Mihail and Priboi watched Oswald disappear with despair for Sibiu in their eyes.

"*You* are the head of his chancellery," Mihail said almost breathlessly.

"I am, and as such I have the authority to make *you* inform him of Sibiu's response."

Priboi sighed heavily as he stared at the doorway Oswald had exited through.

CASTLE DRAGWLYA
March 19, 1458

It was now mid-afternoon. For twelve days Dragwlya had been preparing a small cavalry for mobilization at his mountain retreat. He watched the rushing water of the Argeş flowing downstream. Six weeks had passed with no reply from the German towns that they would cease backing their respective claimants to his throne. While there was no consensus among them as to who should be on the throne, there was a consensus to overthrow him. The situation was unacceptable.

Force seems to be the only language they comprehend or respond to. Perhaps when they see their families dying they will answer me.

A glance to the West assured the prince that even if the sun refused to set, its rays would soon be blocked out by a cell of dark clouds lumbering east.

Without any formal declaration, the Saxons would shortly find themselves on the losing end of Dragwlya's personal war. It would be quick, decisive, and negate the incentives anyone saw in vying for the already occupied throne of Wallachia.

The time has come.

Emphasizing Dragwlya's thoughts, a rumble of thunder rolled over the mountains, causing the earth to shake slightly. Dragwlya stared into the heart of the oncoming storm as his body vibrated from the sound waves.

If they cannot reason for themselves... I shall make them understand.

COZIA MONASTERY
March 21, 1458

In the Byzantine-style church of the Cozia Monastery, Dragwlya solemnly knelt before the tomb of his grandfather, Mircea the Old, who had established the monastery seventy years ago. Numerous candelabras illuminated the interior, providing the only light this evening. Seeing the church in such fashion reminded the prince of the Christmas season, even without the traditional adornments.

Dragwlya closed his eyes and shut out the sight of the mausoleum before him. His thoughts turned to his grandfather; how he had united Wallachia, Transylvania, and Moldavia; how he had fought valiantly against the Turkish at the beginning of his reign and defeated them; how his reign ended with Wallachia becoming little more than a vassal state, forced to pay a yearly tribute to retain its autonomy. This sole failure of his grandfather nearly overshadowed all the other accomplishments. Dragwlya's chest expanded as his lungs filled with musty air. He expelled the breath out of his nose and opened his eyes.

"I must succeed." His words, little more than a whisper, were a declaration directed to God as he looked up to Heaven. "I have fought twice already to claim my throne for you…to do *your* work. If the Saxons are allowed to defeat me they will crown an unworthy weakling, one the Turkish will overrun before the year is out. I cannot believe you wish that to happen." Dragwlya stared back at his grandfather's tomb. "I do not wish to fail you, grandfather, or you, father. What can I do that I have not already done?"

After a few minutes, Dragwlya smiled. "Thank you."

CODLEA
March 28, 1458

Dragwlya unleashed his fury on the Saxons and those loyal to the claimants to his throne with ravenous velocity. Leading his men up the Olt River, the prince had them cross the mountains past the valley of the Hîrtibaciu River into Amlas. Here, Vlad the Monk's Saxon supporters in the villages of Hosman, Caşolţs, and Satul Nou were decimated. The grief they felt for the loss of their homes was short-lived, ended by the loss of their lives. Filled with confidence, Dragwlya then moved east to Ţara Bîrsei, to the land controlled by the supporters of Dan III.

Word of Dragwlya's rampage raced ahead of him to Braşov and some of the surrounding regions. Many took the news that entire villages and towns were being destroyed as fantasy. Only the villagers of Codlea gave any credence to the stories being told. Fully aware of Dragwlya's capabilities, preparations were made to fend off any attack from the prince of Wallachia. Firm supporters of Dan III, the inhabitants knew what lie in store if their village fell.

They are the first to have fortified against my arrival, Dragwlya mused to himself as his cavalry approached. Codlea had indeed taken great pains to protect itself, knowing war was eminent. *Nevertheless, I shall be victorious.*

"Captain." Dragwlya waited until the man had flanked him. "Do not be lulled into thinking the traitors of this village will be as easily defeated as the others. The village is ready for battle and has the advantages of rest and strategic placement on their side. They do not have the superior force. Lead the men according to plan and we will succeed."

Heeding the prince's last statement as an order, the captain instantly commanded the cavalry to initiate the attack. Left with a small force, Dragwlya watched horses and men rush by and sensed the adrenaline coursing through their veins as his men yelled for the blood of those loyal to Dan III. Visualizing the carnage to come caused him both joy and trepidation.

They harbor no doubt Codlea will fall.

Dragwlya watched his small cavalry force shrink. For nearly an hour he had witnessed a debacle exceeding that of Ioan Hunedoara's at Varna. The captain charged with leading the attack had made miscalculation after miscalculation, each edging his force closer to defeat.

This cannot continue any longer.

Readying himself to ride into the fight and take command, Dragwlya heard the order to retreat. Humiliation gripped him as he ripped the battle helmet from his head and forcibly threw it to the ground.

"No!"

The tone and volume of Dragwlya's disapproval terrorized those who had remained with him, making them fearful of what would happen to whomever he held responsible for this failure.

Bruised, beaten, and humiliated, the remnants of the once arrogant cavalry limped back toward their prince, hopeful they would receive forgiveness and again find the will to fight. The farther they moved away from Codlea, the louder the cheering of the villagers became. Their relief deafened Dragwlya, further souring the despicable taste of defeat.

Upon his return, the captain dismounted and approached Dragwlya. Once handsomely clad in his battle armor, the captain now looked every bit the defeated soldier. Blood and grime covered him as he nursed several wounds and mild cuts from the arrows and swords of Codlea.

"My lord, I cannot carry out your instructions. The inhabitants are brave and well fortified, and they fight with great courage."

A long moment of silence passed before Dragwlya responded.

"You have failed me, captain," Dragwlya intoned. "You have failed your men and have disgraced the memory of those who died under your command. Even now their souls cry out for justice. Seize him." Two members of the sluji grabbed the captain as Dragwlya continued to speak. "For disobeying my order to capture the village of

Codlea, and for the deaths of my men, you are being placed under arrest."

Certain of his fate, the captain franticly pleaded for his life. "I obeyed your orders to the best of my abilities, my lord! Please…I am loyal to you!"

Dragwlya approached the man and spoke gently. "Loyalty is not enough. I require competence." Turning away, Dragwlya ordered the captain be stripped. An armaş armed with a pale meant for a victim from the village was already moving into position behind him.

"For your crimes, the sentence is death."

Cries of mercy came from the captain as he stood, held fast by the two guards. With a quick, sudden thrust, the cries of mercy became cries of agony; the stake had penetrated deep into the captain's entrails. A second thrust forced it to puncture his stomach. Excruciating pain consumed him. He could now feel his body being elevated. Tearing his arms free from the sluji, the captain grabbed hold of the wooden pale now protruding from his abdomen. The thought of dying overshadowed his desire to scream, but not the pain.

From this moment on, Dragwlya thought, *I shall defer nothing.*

Mobilization of the cavalry commenced shortly after the captain's impalement. Following the defeat at Codlea, responsibility to others was delegated with extreme scarcity and only after severe scrutiny. Dragwlya would not allow himself to be embarrassed again by others' incompetence.

Talmeş would be Dragwlya's next target, and its inhabitants would suffer the brunt of the prince's frustration. Following a short decisive battle, Dragwlya had the city burned. Survivors were either impaled or suffered being hacked to pieces by the armaşi while Dragwlya took pleasure in watching their executions.

Talmeş' destruction, though decisive, was not enough to satisfy Dragwlya fully. Before returning to Tîrgovişte, one final statement was required.

BOD
March 30, 1458

Dragwlya's campaign would soon end just north of Braşov. To prevent a second Codlea, the prince gave his cavalry plans exceeding even his usual overbearing detail. The importance of this last attack had been explained clearly to everyone involved. Losing the last battle would make Dragwlya appear vulnerable, unable to finish what he started. No order of retreat would be given. Anyone surviving defeat would be put to death for not giving his life for the prince.

They are so unassuming.

Prepared to give the command to attack, Dragwlya watched peasant lives play themselves out in the village of Bod. His cavalry had obviously arrived before word of its previous actions had. Closing his eyes and exhaling, Dragwlya concentrated on quelling the feelings of overconfidence responsible for his failure at Codlea. It proved difficult.

Why should he not be confident in himself, in his God given ability? Perhaps it was not confidence but pride that tainted everything. Emotions such as this made men vulnerable. After all, how could a feeling, an adversary that could not be seen, heard, or touched ever be defeated?

They are weapons as well. I have the ability to take a man's fear and make him succumb to it… and me. Emotion is the most powerful weapon in my arsenal. Fear, hate, anger, aggression… they are all my allies. Each dutifully serves my cause. Each conquers hope. Each suppresses rebellion.

Only now did Dragwlya come to the realization his thoughts had carried him into the thick of battle. The vast amount of preparations, combined with the pathetic resistance from Bod, made fighting secondary. His inner monologue was hardly distracted.

I have used such tactics since beginning my first reign. An image of Radu and him fighting while prisoners of the sultan flashed somewhere in his memory. *My God… Have I used this weapon for so long? Now that I understand I—*

A wave of warmth spattered Dragwlya's face, breaking his concentration. Drops joined and flowed to his mouth. Instinctively, he allowed his bottom lip and tongue to clean his moustache.

Salty…

With a quick jerk, Dragwlya removed the Toledo blade from the chest of his opponent. The man's throat had been slit, an act Dragwlya did not recall performing. Steadily, life flowed from the dying Saxon. The prince now felt something running down his cheek. With little regard he dismissed it as perspiration and wiped it away. A flash of crimson struck him as he lowered his hand and, looking down, Dragwlya' realized what he had perceived to be perspiration wasn't.

Blood…

Familiar sensations screamed out, compelling Dragwlya to remember when he had felt this way previously. The correlation was instantaneous, and he recalled this feeling of power from before.

Why does it seem so much greater this time? Dragwlya passed his tongue over his top lip and moustache, again savoring it as he realized. *I have consumed it. It is nourishing me, giving me the life it once gave him. The blood is the life!*

Enlightened, Dragwlya stared at the continuous flow, resisting the urge to fall to his knees and drink. He could not place himself in such a defenseless position. His craving must be denied for now.

Bod had been completely overrun. The village itself sustained little damage; the only real sign of fighting was the bodies of most of its former inhabitants. Those managing to survive the onslaught were bound and grouped together, their fate not yet decided by Dragwlya.

With more awareness than he dreamt possible, Dragwlya absorbed everything. Constantly, his senses were bombarded by every sight, every sound, every touch, every smell, every taste. Ignoring anything was as impossible as he had once felt knowing everything would be. Never experiencing anything like this before, it took some time to identify the feeling.

Omnipotence...

Why God had illuminated him to this extent Dragwlya was uncertain, but God's message to him was clear: By consuming the lives of others, you will grow stronger.

BUDA
April 4, 1458

"And you condone this action?" Matthias stared at his uncle with severe scrutiny. "How do you know *we* won't end up impaled in his courtyard?"

"Because I know... He is rash... and unorthodox, but his loyalty is unwavering...The Saxons have every intention of overthrowing him, going so far as to crown *three* separate candidates to his throne. His first course of action was a request they refused. Would you have acted any differently?"

Matthias contemplated the question. *You know him better than I do, but if I detect any sign of perfidy, our alliance will end, with or without your consent.*

"I trust your judgment. Our alliance with Prince Vlad will continue, at least until the Saxons have been defeated. The eastern border must be secured."

Mihály could visualize the man Matthias would eventually become. For a brief moment his mind deceived him into believing he was speaking to Ioan. "Your appraisal is wise. I suggest we offer our assistance to gain control over the Saxons."

You rule, even though I am king. I am ready to make my own decisions about our destiny. "They will not be ruled willingly."

"No one ever is, Matthias." The young king's eyes revealed his ambition. *Just like his father, he hides his true desires and intentions well. Before long he will rule of his own accord. I do not have to control him forever though, only until I am satisfied both our positions are secured.*

CHAPTER XXXVI
A SUITABLE WIFE & RELIEF FOR THE POOR
TÎRGOVIŞTE
June 13, 1458

*M*y best endeavors to rid Wallachia of all crime have failed.

Dragwlya's body recoiled, repulsed while stalking through the marketplace in disguise. No transgression remained hidden in the midday sun.

Can there be any question why my land is mocked? My very capital is a congregation center for beggars, the lame, and thieves committing their crimes for all to see.

Dragwlya took a moment to consume every last sin.

The majority are not even Wallachian. Vagabonds, interested only in taking as much as they can from wherever they happen to be. Even if they do leave, their filth and disease remain. I must stop this. But how can I –

Disgusted, Dragwlya broke off in mid-thought and pivoted. For an instant he thought his eyes were deceiving him, but there was no denying what he saw. This had been one of the instances in which armaşi had been allowed to follow him as he braved the city incognito. With a quick hand signal, Dragwlya motioned his men to apprehend the peasant who had just walked by him. Not stopping to witness the commotion this caused, Dragwlya quickened his step, heading homeward.

Now in his throne room, Dragwlya stared in what amounted to horror at the man his guards had brought before him. This pitiable creature's appearance was the sight powerful enough to shatter Dragwlya's concentration in the marketplace. It was intolerable. The peasant's ragged shirt hung down only to the middle of his knees, exposing homespun trousers that were exceedingly tight.

"Do you have a wife?"

The response, although shaky, was immediate. "I do, sire." This was the man's first audience with any noble and, to this point, he remained unaware of why he had been summoned.

"What is your name?"

Once again an immediate response came. Now in possession of a name, Dragwlya motioned, causing two armaşi to leave the room.

"How do you earn a living?"

"I am a mason, sire."

For nearly half an hour, Dragwlya piqued the man's interest with his inquiry. It puzzled the peasant that the prince would be so interested in his life. Never having received such attention before genuinely embarrassed and frightened him. The return of the two armaşi dispatched earlier prompted an abrupt change in the tone of Dragwlya's questions.

"Your wife is assuredly of the kind who remains idle. How is it possible that your shirt does not cover the calf of your leg? She is not worthy of living in my realm or any other!" Dragwlya's voice, laced with ferocity, made those assembled imagine what spectacle they would be forced to witness today.

The peasant was well aware of the prince's reputation for irrational behavior. If Dragwlya wished someone to perish, it usually meant it was to be so. It dawned on him that he had been in the prince's presence for quite some time, long enough for the armaşi to hunt down and return to the castle with his wife. Perhaps they had killed her already. Nonetheless, his plea on her behalf was calm.

"Beg forgiveness, my lord, but I am satisfied with her. She never leaves home and she is honest."

Dragwlya harbored no doubt of the appeal's legitimacy. Still he knew it his duty to save this simple, honest man from the Devil, who had obviously blinded him to his wife's laziness.

"You will be more satisfied with another since you are a decent and hardworking man." Instantly, the peasant's wife was brought in screaming, demanding to know why she had been arrested. Seeing her husband, the woman directed her shouting toward him.

"Enough!" Dragwlya stifled the woman, his order caused her to become quiet and stare at him all at once. "Your *own* actions have brought you here today! Through the fault of no one else you appear before me with overwhelming evidence of your sloth!"

Bewildered, the woman again turned her gaze to her husband. Their marriage had lasted long enough that they could read one another's expressions and had witnessed enough of the prince's reign to realize what would happen. The only suitable punishment for a deadly sin was death. Tears welled up in her eyes, making it difficult to keep the room in focus. Surely, something could be said to save her life, but what? Before she formed another thought, Dragwlya barked out another order to his men. Within seconds the wife of the peasant stood naked. She struggled to comprehend what was happening. It took all of her faculties just to remain standing. Crying out for mercy or in fear would have completely drained her.

Is cruelty all you are capable of? Elizabetha had witnessed Dragwlya's justice before. Thus far, this was meager in comparison to other scenes. She stared at the peasant woman striped of her clothing and dignity, imagining why anyone felt the need to cause such torment, knowing he was driven by madness. She wondered how long it might be before she befell a similar fate, knowing it could be at any moment and without rational reasoning.

Most winced or looked away as two armaşi spread the peasant woman's legs while a third inserted the stake into her. Driving it deeper inside generated cries of agony that ricocheted off the walls. Once lifted upright, her blood oozed down the pike toward the floor. Elizabetha closed her eyes tightly and delayed for only a second before exiting.

Dragwlya relished in the knowledge that justice had been served. His attention was momentarily diverted from the scene before him, drawn away by a feeling he had only experienced sporadically as of late. He was aroused. Watching the woman's suspended body writhe in self-induced pain, Dragwlya commanded an armaș to bring forth a young woman he felt worthy to marry the peasant. She was ushered hastily to the foot of his throne.

Every bit of the woman's willpower labored to keep her attention fixed on the prince, not the woman suspended six feet in the air. Minutes labored on with Dragwlya studying the younger woman's face, its reactions to the sounds made by the woman he intended for her to replace. Fear was all he saw. She appeared to be wondering how she too had insulted the prince, asking herself how long it would be before she met her own end.

"Step forward." Dragwlya motioned for the peasant man to move next to the younger woman. "She is your new wife." He proclaimed this with a nod and next addressed the young bride. "The woman behind you saw fit to embarrass her husband and brought shame to his household by her laziness. Her actions have condemned her in this life and in the next." He motioned to the peasant with his hand. "This man is now your husband. Do not disgrace him as your predecessor did. Otherwise her fate will be yours...Watch as she dies. It will serve to remind you of what awaits should you commit the same sins."

With the newly united couple staring at his victim, Dragwlya rose and left the throne room, headed for the Chindia Tower.

Unhindered, the light of the sun blazed across Tîrgoviște, revealing it as a ravaged city. Casting a glare of repugnance down from the top of the tower, Dragwlya's thoughts dwelled once again on the state his land had fallen into.

Their numbers continue to increase. Vagrants from who knows where, the lame, the old, the poor. They flock here like vultures, picking at a decaying carcass. I cannot allow them to devour what remains any longer. They burden others... play on their emotions. I must show them the error of their ways. They must be made to suffer. Those like them elsewhere must be made aware there is no room in my land for anyone who would remain idle or would not put forth the effort to contribute to society.

Dragwlya knew for certain the manner he chose to handle this situation would require a dramatic visual display to ensure as many as possible learned. The lesson taught would make it absolutely clear there would be zero tolerance for anyone who chose to prey on Tîrgoviște. The weak would no longer be given a chance to destroy what so many had given their lives to build.

His father, his grandfather, Mircea; all had sacrificed to make Wallachia better. Their voices filled his head, pleading for him to restore order and respect to the land they had preserved for him, but not telling him how to do so.

Help me…

Nothing. No one answered him; nothing revealed itself as the answer he sought. In frustration he shut his eyes.

There must be an answer… There must…

Minutes passed with Dragwlya waiting to no avail. He opened his eyes once again and adjusted as they were flooded with light.

What is it they want? The question seemed to enter Dragwlya's mind of someone else's accord. Before beginning to formulate an answer, the prince allowed the query to repeat itself in his head. *What is it they want?*

They want what they do not have, what they will never achieve because they choose not to work for it. They are beggars and want what they are given… The less they must do to get it the better. They steal, and it is called charity.

Dragwlya's gaze settled abruptly on the estate of one of Tîrgovişte's richest boyars, a home encompassing an unusually large dining hall. Thoughts and images of righteousness flowed through Dragwlya's conscious. A grin of relief, of thankfulness, enveloped him.

Praise be to you, Lord, for answering me.

June 20, 1458

Tîrgovişte's citizenry considered the past six days among the darkest they had ever known. Today was indeed the darkest. They fought desperately to understand not only why this atrocity was occurring but being welcomed. Throughout the previous week, the city had been saturated with the old, the ill, the lame, the poor, and the blind. The prince requested their presence with the promise of making their lives better. Dragwlya's radical change in attitude toward such vagrants convinced Tîrgovişte of his madness.

Using treasury funds, Dragwlya ordered thousands of baskets to be filled with new clothing and made arrangements for a massive feast to be prepared. To many it appeared a royal wedding may be in the works, but disdain grew rapidly when all learned of Dragwlya's intentions to feed and clothe as many vagabonds as possible.

Converging like moths to the flame, Dragwlya thought as he watched from atop the Chindia Tower. Disgust intensified within as he forced himself to watch countless degenerates enter a once handsome estate. Quickly, it had been transformed into a holding pen for filthy, unkept animals. Dragwlya's own servants stood vigil at the estate, witnessing it being marred with the ugliness of sin and sickness. Diligently, they handed each attendee a basket of clothing and ushered Dragwlya's guests into the dining hall. *They will be rewarded for their service today. I have asked nearly too much of them. They will come to understand their effort was a necessity.*

After nearly an hour, the final animal received its basket and entered. Watching her eagerly step through the doors gave Dragwlya satisfaction that soon his principality would be rid of so many useless individuals. Taking little time to savor the emotion, he set out for the estate.

By the time Dragwlya reached the home of the boyar, the atmosphere within was nearing festival-like proportions. For the first few moments all had stared in silence, gawking at the feast laid out for them. It did not take long before their hunger and thirst overcame them, however, revealing them for the gluttons they truly were. Stuffing themselves, the vagabonds sang the praises of the prince's grace, many wishing to thank him personally. The sight served as testimony to Dragwlya's belief that the occupants of the estate were little more than parasites, feeding off of the deeds of others.

Staring at this wretched hive, Dragwlya listened as joyful songs and cheers for him emitted from the dining hall and watched as the last of his servants exited the estate. Their expressions conveyed how thankful they were to be away from the stench and sight of so many diseased and unscrupulous degenerates. Those inside not currently intoxicated would soon reach the point where they would have to rely on the support of others to remain upright. The time had come to relieve Wallachia and the world of the burden of this filth.

Dragwlya's order to bolt all the doors was carried out nearly before he gave it. Though not obvious before, all outside were now aware that every window had been sealed as well. The once noble home of the boyar resembled a condemned structure, destined to be demolished to make way for something new.

Although few had been made privy to the prince's entire plan, a sizable crowd of curious onlookers had gathered. One in particular voiced his concern regarding this day's events directly to Dragwlya himself, and with good reason. To his credit, he did so calmly and diplomatically, but as time pushed onward his composure began to fade.

"My lord, I would do anything for you, anything for Wallachia, but are you quite certain my home is the proper venue for such an event?" The boyar was slightly older than Dragwlya and his insides churned at the thought of the infestation that his estate now endured. Dragwlya's charity affair would taint his home forever. Seeing his once stately manor boarded up, knowing what lurked within, depressed and disheartened him. Why would the prince reward laziness in such fashion? It sickened him.

"I am certain. After today an even greater estate will be built for you here."

"Thank you, my lord." Only as he finished responding did Dragwlya's words register with the man. "My lord, what do you mean *built* here?"

Dragwlya motioned to the armași with a simple nod. "I doubt you'll wish to live in ashes amongst the charred remains of so many sinners."

Seeing the armaşi moving toward his estate with torches revealed Dragwlya's plan to the boyar. He stared, horrified. The thought of all he would lose enraged him. "Your assumption is correct, my lord. Sighing inaudibly, the boyar swore mentally. *Could you not have burned your own castle?*

Dragwlya's anticipation rose with the flames. He had managed to shut out the distraction of the boyar. No longer were there any questions as to why the vagabonds had been invited to Tîrgovişte. The rising flames grew, as did the number of onlookers. Increasingly, black smoke began to pour through the boarded up doors and windows of the estate. He was consumed by relief. The responsibility for those inside was now to be shouldered by Satan. Dragwlya's burden of freeing the world from so much disgrace had ceased.

Screams and cries for help pierced the crowd. Hacking coughs and shrieks filled with excruciating pain stung their ears. Everyone understood. Dragwlya would help save the wretches of his land by baptizing them with fire.

Those brought out by curiosity were even more shocked now than when they had first heard the proclamation for all in need to travel to Tîrgovişte to partake in the generosity of the prince. Hearing the voices from within the estate solidified the reality of what they were witnessing. No one could argue that the prince failed to rid Wallachia of its ever-increasing population of vagabonds. No one would openly question him about his method of doing so, save one.

Although these people were not his equals, the master of the burning estate still felt some degree of compassion for them. A second of weakness allowed his thoughts to slip out for Dragwlya to hear.

"Surely these people do not deserve so cruel a fate."

Dragwlya's first impulse was to immediately terminate the boyar's life for daring to speak out against his judgment. Figuring the man to be suffering great grief at losing so many cherished possessions, however, he made an allowance. Though he needed to give justification to no one but God, Dragwlya chose to explain to the boyar.

"These men live off the sweat of others. They are useless to humanity. It is a form of thievery." Dragwlya paused momentarily. "In fact, the masked robber in the forest demands your purse, but if you are quicker with your hand and more vigorous than he you can escape from him. These vagabonds, however, take your belongings gradually, by begging. But they still take them. They are worse than robbers. They must be eradicated from my land."

Realizing his folly, the boyar tried quickly to redeem himself. "Forgive me, my lord. Your punishment is a fair and just decision."

"It is God's decision. Not mine."

Thankful that it appeared he would not suffer for his outburst, the boyar resolved himself to quietly observe the inferno that was once his home.

As the voices from within dwindled, the sight and sounds offered by the fiery spectacle continued to mesmerize Dragwlya. No one inside remained alive to apply what they had learned from the experience, but the prince was certain, judging by the looks on numerous faces, that all in the crowd understood what had been taught to them today. Everyone would be required to perform their fair share of the work. Everyone would receive that which they rightfully earned. No more, no less.

CHAPTER XXXVII
MIHÁLY RETREATS & MATTHIAS TAKES CONTROL
SIBIU
October 9, 1458

Mihály swore loudly upon learning more of his men had chosen to desert rather than die fighting. Over the last few months, Hungary's push to dominate the Saxon towns had intensified. Confident he could sack Sibiu, Mihály had informed Matthias he would indeed do so. The fulfillment of that promise now seemed bleak.

"Governor, we must fall back. They are too well fortified!" Mihály's general continued with his report, shouting it over the city's cannon fire. "What few supplies we have left should be conserved! Our best course of action is retreat, sir! Otherwise we risk losing all we have gained!"

Mihály despised both the thought of retreating and that the general's appraisal was irrefutable. If he continued to fight, all would be lost. Defeat existed in whichever action he took, but dying valiantly for the crown hardly seemed sensible.

"Order the retreat!"

Without hesitation, the general rode away, determined to flee Sibiu with as many men as possible.

Mihály blamed his self-assuredness. Until now, battling the Saxon cities had been laughable. Each fell easily, strengthening Mihály's belief he had assembled an unbeatable force. Sibiu proved how wrong that assumption was. The minute flaws of Hungary's force were exposed and exploited to the fullest with devastating results.

Jubilation and cannon fire exploded from the city once its enemy's retreat became apparent. Mihály's men rode and ran away, frustrated and confused by their sudden inability to outmaneuver an adversary. Disappointment and anger manifested with no one knowing where blame for this horrid disaster should be placed. Responsibility would ultimately be assigned.

TÎRGOVIŞTE
October 12, 1458

"It was then that the order to retreat was given, my lord."

Dragwlya listened with keen interest as the messenger relayed the events surrounding Mihály's failed attempt to sack Sibiu. He questioned whether he should have done more to ensure victory. Eventually, the Saxons would fall, but the idea that a setback occurred was somewhat alarming.

Matthias was already itching to rule without the interference of his guardian, and

Mihály's defeat would only further his need to scratch that itch. Sibiu's victory would allow Matthias the opportunity to fill the heads of many with doubt as to what Hungary's
future actions should be. It would give him more independence, more power. Dragwlya
was certain of Mihaly's abilities and certain Matthias must be controlled more now than
before.

"Where is the governor now?"

"He has regrouped in Sighisoara, my lord."

"Sighisoara…" Dragwlya repeated the city's name quietly, permitting random images of his first home to flash through his mind. He remembered little of it but imagined
how different life would have been had his father not chosen to leave for the promise of
Wallachia's throne. "And what of Braşov?"

"Negotiations are continuing with Braşov, but in light of the failed attack at Sibiu
their leaders have become more unwilling to compromise, more defiant."

This situation teems with uncertainty. Something must be done to regain the advantage.

"They have made a gesture of goodwill to you, my lord."

The messenger's statement sparked Dragwlya's curiosity. "Oh?"

Motioning to the guards, the messenger had the Saxons' act of faith escorted in.
The prince watched as a single line of youths ranging from age seven to twelve filed into
his throne room. Subconsciously, he began to count them until finally the precession
ceased.

Forty-one.

"What is this supposed to be?" Dragwlya asked.

"My lord," a smile beamed on the face of the messenger as he spoke, "these children
have been sent by the Saxons so that they might learn Romanian."

Suspicion held Dragwlya captive as he looked over his court's new arrivals. Some of
them had blue eyes and blonde hair and reminded him of Radu. The mere sight of them
made Dragwlya nauseous. Each was a demon, biding its time before wreaking utter
havoc.

Forty-one spies.

"Impale them all … Immediately." Dragwlya's order was cold and prompted the
armaşi present to spring quickly to grab the children. Many of the youths understood
and were sobbing uncontrollably for either their home or their parents, neither of which
they would ever see again.

They are only children, Priboi thought. The heinous nature of this act compelled
him to speak "Forgive my ignorance, sire, but why do these children need to be put to
death?"

Dragwlya stared at the boyar as though the man had no head. "Your ignorance is
forgiven. The people of Transylvania speak Romanian as fluently as the people of Wallachia, do they not?"

"Yes, my lord."

"Why then should I allow these spies in my land and give them the opportunity to gain knowledge of our secrets?" Dragwlya continued to stare at the man, waiting for some sign of understanding. "Propagandists for my would-be successors shall not be permitted to create subversion.

"These Saxons, they are indeed a cold people. The mere fact that they sacrifice their own children confirms they are unrefined, power-hungry madmen and have no respect for their fellow countrymen. It is yet another lesson they will have to be taught."

Without another word, Dragwlya walked out of the throne room to view the impalements. Striding toward the Chindia Tower, he reflected on his childhood, how his father had nearly sacrificed both he and Radu. Dragwlya would not allow these children to suffer as hostages the way he had. They would never learn the hurtful truth that their parents willingly traded their young lives in order to preserve their own unfulfilled ones.

The Saxons have no wish to end this. They would be content with this war raging on until no one was left standing. My nation's welfare must be ensured. The duty to stop this needless killing is mine now.

Dragwlya knew any action he undertook would affect Wallachians currently in Saxon-controlled lands, including his principality's merchants.

Ignorant fools. I have no choice but to call them home. For their own protection their profits will have to be diminished.

Dragwlya mulled over the fact that there was presently a large population of Saxon merchants in Tîrgovişte. Some were all but permanent fixtures, but most were simply resting before continuing their journey to Brăila. Beginning now, the rules that had been established, which required traveling merchants to unload their wares and pay any necessary fees, would be enforced to the fullest extent. Compliance was mandatory under penalty of death. If his people were going to be put in harm's way, the enemy's most certainly should be.

BUDA
October 13, 1458

"Uncle's failure strengthens what I have known to be true all along. Our alliance should be with the Saxons, not the fools he has entrusted the security of my kingdom to... Certainly not the Wallachian."

Erzsébet would have sworn that Matthias was mouthing her own thoughts regarding Mihály. "What do you suggest?" In her mind, she had already fixed a charted course of action but wished to see just how synchronized in thought she and her son were.

"I want the Saxons to feel secure, as though I would turn to them for support. An envoy should be sent to Braşov without uncle's knowledge with the purpose of reaching an accord."

His mind is my own. "I agree. Your appraisal is the correct action to take."

Matthias' face beamed, knowing that his first real action as king was being met with approval.

My uncle will be shown the error of his ways.

TÎRGOVIŞTE
December 1, 1458

Dragwlya's plan for overcoming the plight his merchants would endure had succeeded. In addition to confiscating the goods of some six hundred Saxon merchants he had impaled for not assenting fully with the trade laws, he placed nearly five hundred Saxon representatives sent to Tîrgovişte under house arrest toward the end of October. During the past month, Matthias' plan began to take shape also.

The young king had opened secret negotiations with Braşov, which served to bring about official talks with Mihály Szilágy. An accord was reached toward the latter part of November. Terms agreed to by the Braşovians stipulated that Dan III would be surrendered, and he and his boyar supporters extradited. Ten thousand florins would be paid to Mihály for war damages and, in exchange, Wallachia would grant Braşov and Sibiu commercial privileges once more.

As it was written, Dragwlya was agreeable to the accord and retained complete faith in Mihály. He sincerely hoped the Saxons would be true to their word. Though he remained skeptical, Dragwlya's intent was to be honorable in giving them a chance to redeem their past treachery as he extended to the Saxons the opportunity to secure peace.

> Know that I shall keep the word ordered by my brother and Lord Mihály
> Szilágy. Your men can travel in our land freely to buy and sell without worry
> and without prejudice as if they were in their own country.

Dragwlya placed the quill down, mentally convincing himself.

They will not keep their end of the bargain. Mihály knows this. The Saxons have given up too much in their minds already to simply hand over their claimant. Even if they do, another will take his place shortly. I will be true to my word, but only until I feel it necessary.

SIGHISOARA
December 23, 1458

Exactly one month had passed since the accord with the Saxons was reached. Mihály laughed at his own naivety, for believing he still had control. Through interrogation, he had learned his nephew had orchestrated the accord with the Saxons. He knew nothing of it until weeks afterwards. Mihály drew two conclusions: Matthias was capable of carrying out his personal agenda without revealing it, and it would not be long before the young king assumed total control. He realized the implications.

Effectively, his role as guardian was ended. Matthias, unchecked, would now pilot Hungary into its future alone. The Saxons had agreed to the accord only because they were certain the king's intent was not to enforce its sanctions. With Mihály's power diminished, the Saxons would become allies instead of adversaries. Mihály was not prepared for any of this, and that his nephew had solidified his own alliance with the Saxons made him realize he would be unable to stop the changes.

Mihály's thoughts suddenly focused on Erzsébet.

Conniving bitch… She couldn't have her will carried out through me, so she gained the advantage through Matthias. I always knew I would have to relinquish my hold on Hungary at some point. I presumed it would be on my own terms. I am still governor of Hungary… Will that change as well? Vlad must be warned… He should not have to suffer because of my carelessness.

BUDA
January 4, 1459

Each new day afforded Matthias opportunities to further separate from the ideas and politics of his uncle. To many it appeared the young king was determined to assert himself by acting opposite in every way Mihály would. There had been no recklessness on Matthias's part thus far, but it seemed without the governor as guardian anything might happen.

Benedict de Boithor regarded Matthias warily. Less than ten seconds had passed since the king had informed him he would soon be traveling to Tîrgovişte to meet with Prince Vlad. He was not inclined to make the journey, even for a good reason. To this point, none had been presented.

"Beg your pardon, my lord, but what purpose is this visit to serve?" *He has no purpose other than to show his might.*

"I am sending you to Tîrgovişte because it is necessary to make certain my accord with the Saxons is upheld by Prince Vlad. My eastern border is secure only if they know I will not betray them. I am leaving the duty of solidifying the agreement with the Wallachian to you."

Every fantastic story Benedict could remember hearing relating Prince Vlad's means of ruling flooded his head. One involving three Genoese ambassadors stuck out prominently. Envisioning giant iron nails piercing his skull, Benedict struggled to hide his fright at the prospect of having to negotiate anything with a man willing to inflict such torment.

"My lord, I do not see how a diplomatic visit to Tîrgovişte can accomplish much of anything. Perhaps it would be better if visits were made to Sibiu and Braşov to give the Saxons reassurances of our alliance." Benedict doubted his plea would be successful, but taking a meaningless risk to avoid an audience with Vlad seemed prudent.

"This is exactly why it must be you, Benedict." Matthias nearly laughed aloud, deflecting the monk's verbal thrust. "You are the best envoy in my service, the only one I feel possesses the ability to convince Vlad his faith and trust are misplaced."

Benedict easily sensed Matthias's unwavering attitude regarding this. Nothing could be said now to deter the young king. The nobleman knew better than to try.

"When do you wish me to make this visit, my lord?"

"You will leave tomorrow." Matthias expected a reaction, and Benedict's expression of shock betrayed that there would be one.

"Tomorrow, my lord?" Concern engulfed the envoy's response.

"Yes." Matthias shot the word out quickly, without hesitation.

"With all due respect, I feel more time should be invested to make certain I fully understand what you wish to accomplish. Even if a messenger were dispatched today, he would arrive in time to give Prince Vlad little notice before my appearance in his court. Surely we-"

"A messenger was dispatched three days ago."

Benedict's training as a diplomat allowed him to quell his desire to throttle Matthias. *This is madness. It is as if he is trying to kill me.* "My lord, I suggest this visit be postponed for at least a month. Its purpose is not crucial to your overall objective."

Benedict prayed for deliverance. Hopefully, the trip would be delayed. Hopefully, after some time, Matthias would reconsider its necessity all together.

Fighting off impatience to steady his voice, Matthias spoke. "You should have more faith in your abilities. After an audience with Prince Vlad, I have no doubt you will agree with my decision."

Even if I survive that is unlikely, Benedict retorted mentally. *Erzsébet has taught him how to play this game well. I doubt he is even aware of her influence. He has managed to find a no-lose situation… If I survive the Saxons will view Matthias as a capable leader, one able to sway their greatest enemies. If I die, he will use the event to fuel the notion that Vlad is not to be trusted, that he himself is their only means to survive. He will also use such an incident to link Mihály to Dragwlya. There is no telling where that could lead. Milhály's assassination would hardly surprise me...Not that I would ever know.*

"I do not doubt your judgment, my lord. As a diplomat it is in my nature to question and view all sides of a situation. Forgive me if I have insulted you."

You have every right to be afraid, Benedict. Your sacrifice will serve to further my cause. "That is why you must not refuse me, Benedict. No one else shares your ability to digest so many points of view. This meeting is too important. I can not send an apprentice to do work only a master is capable of completing."

I should have returned to Krakow when the opportunity arose.

"Your compliment is gracious, my lord. As always, I shall do my best to serve you."

"There is no doubt in my mind of that, Benedict."

TÎRGOVIŞTE
January 26, 1459

Dragwlya anxiously awaited the arrival of Benedict de Boithor. He had prepared extensively and was now atop the Chindia Tower, idly watching criminals having their sentences being carried out in the courtyard. His thoughts had been focused on the upcoming audience since the arrival of the messenger sent to prepare him, meticulously picking apart the purpose Matthias had for it.

Dragwlya concluded this was no diplomatic visit but in actuality a test, a means by which Matthias could gauge him. It would not behoove Dragwlya to kill any diplomat sent by Matthias unless absolutely necessary, and yet there existed a need to inform Hungary that Wallachia demanded respect.

"Sire, my name is Benedict de Boithor. I have been sent by King Matthias of Hungary to-"

"You do not look or sound Hungarian. Your accent is ... flawed."

On more than one occasion, Dragwlya had proven himself an impatient and impulsive man. The wrong look, the wrong statement and the prince's victim would find himself or herself on a fashioned stake. Every situation was life threatening. Benedict disguised suppressing the lump in his throat by pretending to clear it and buried the image of the three Genoese ambassadors deep within himself.

"You are extremely perceptive, my lord. I am Polish by birth."

Dragwlya's emerald green eyes studied the man, wordlessly attempting to evoke some sort of reaction. There was none.

"As you are undoubtedly aware, sire, I have been sent-"

"Join me in my dining hall. We will talk there."

"As you wish, my lord."

Thus far the prince had barely allowed Benedict to finish more than a few sentences concurrently. Not only did he believe God had placed him in this position, he felt in some way he was a god. *He plays with the lives of others as though he were responsible for creating them,* Benedict thought.

A slight smirk drenched Dragwlya's lips as he silently led the procession. Diplomacy was indeed second only to battle.

Approaching the room, Benedict swore he heard what sounded like the moaning of wounded animals coming from inside. The nobleman had prepared himself for anything that might transpire during this mission as best he could. Still, his curiosity caused his mind to imagine what lay in waiting on the other side of the doors. No one could totally prepare for an audience with Dragwlya. His irrationality hardly afforded one the ability to make even an educated guess of what to expect.

The inside of Benedict's nose burned with an odor he had never known. Its repugnance was so foreign to his system that the diplomat had no idea how to react to it. Nearing the doors the smell intensified. For each step they took forward, he wanted to run back ten. Finally, they entered.

Vehemently, Benedict resisted the impulse to vomit. Continuous waves of rotten air permeated his body, rushing through him like an incinerating wind. Tears formed as he blinked profusely, an effort to rid himself of the stinging sensation he now felt in his eyes. Struggling to breathe, the diplomat gasped for fresh oxygen like a fish removed from water.

Throwing a glance over his shoulder, Dragwlya eyed the nobleman for a second before turning back around. He found it difficult to stifle a chuckle after seeing the shade of green his guest had turned.

Stepping through the archway of the room, Benedict fought every instinct to simply run away. Unbearable as the sight was, the diplomat forced himself to stare. Regardless of where he looked, his vision was filled with a panorama of stakes occupied by a corpse or of a body on the verge of becoming one. This was the smell in the corridor—the stench of death.

The moans of the dying grew louder once the doors had been opened. Continuous feeble pleas of mercy simply went unanswered. Apprehension overloading him, Benedict followed the prince through a labyrinth of impaled bodies toward his main dining table. On more than one occasion an ailing victim grabbed the diplomat. With a flurry of swats, he warded off the unwelcome advances, all the while searching for a space where he would be untouchable. There was none.

Resting comfortably in his seat, Dragwlya stared at the diplomat, trying to sense what he was feeling. No readable emotion appeared on the man's face. *He hides his feelings well.*

"Please," Dragwlya said motioning with his hand to a chair across from him, "sit."

Making every effort not to collapse into the offered chair, Benedict focused his eyes on the prince. He had seen enough of Wallachia and Prince Vlad to last many lifetimes. Though he was doing his best to ignore them, Benedict could not escape the sight of limbs flailing in the background. Even worse, he was unable to turn a deaf ear to those surrounding him. Their tortured cries persisted.

"Tell me, why did I place this stake here?"

Focusing all he could on the image of Dragwlya, Benedict failed to hear the prince's question, though he was certain he saw his mouth move. Eventually, the question reached him, but the diplomat had difficulty understanding at first.

Which stake? We are engulfed by them. Suddenly, Benedict understood.

If not for the impaled bodies encircling him, Benedict would have noticed that directly in front of Dragwlya's table there was a stake more than two meters tall, gilded in gold. Rays of sunlight filtering into the hall danced on it and emphasized that it had been right in front of him the entire time. Everything else in the room seemingly disappeared. Only Benedict's feelings of dread remained.

My life depends upon my response. At least he thought enough of me to fashion my stake out of gold.

Retaining his composure, the diplomat responded. "My lord, it would appear that some great man committed some crime at your expense and that you wish to reserve for him a more honorable death than that meted out to humbler men."

Dragwlya nodded his head, continuing to envelope the diplomat with his stare. "You spoke well. For you are the representative of the great King Matthias...I have reserved this stake for you."

Without breaking away from Dragwlya's stare, without hesitation, Benedict answered. "My lord, if I have committed some crime that deserves the death penalty, do what you think is just, for you are an impartial judge, and it would not be you responsible for my death, but I alone."

Dragwlya smiled and followed closely with laughter. "Had you not answered me properly, you would be on that stake now."

Benedict disguised his sigh of relief by joining in the laughing. *He is truly possessed.*

"You will be welcome in my home for as long as you wish and may have anything you desire so long as I have the means of providing it."

"Thank you, my lord. I am appreciative of your generous hospitality. King Matthias has no desire other than to maintain a healthy, friendly relationship with his neighbors."

"As do I."

Benedict's sense of smell had been decimated to the point the stench no longer nauseated him. Whether that was due to his fear of being killed he was uncertain. It gladdened him that the odor was no longer detectable but frightened him that one could overcome the stench so quickly if forced to focus on something else.

Although the smell no longer bothered him, the sounds and view remained horrific. Would he be able to look at all of this and not see it for what it was, too, or listen to the moaning without hearing it? Is this the type of apathy the man sitting before him felt? Benedict quickly looked around.

This is not apathy. It is the work of a demon.

"I am optimistic the agreed upon accord can be solidified," Benedict offered.

"You are fully worthy of being an ambassador of a great ruler, since you have mastered the art of speaking to another great sovereign. But do not send any ambassadors to me who have not been properly educated in the art of diplomacy."

CHAPTER XXXVIII
DRAGWLYA'S DEFIANCE
BUDA
February 9, 1459

Dumbfounded by the story Benedict de Boithor told him, King Matthias struggled to imagine being as close to death as the diplomat had been. Benedict had stared down fate and had changed it. Few possess the skill to do so. Most in that situation would have lost their lives. Benedict's survival proved Vlad could be reasoned with if properly approached and appeased. But Matthias doubted he would be sending envoys to Wallachia again anytime soon.

He has agreed to adhere to the terms of the accord, Matthias reasoned. *For now that is enough.* Mentally, the young king set a level of tolerance Dragwlya would not be allowed to cross. *If he doesn't adhere to his word, I will make certain he understands just how much I value commitment.*

ANDRINOPLE
March 22, 1459

"What?" Mehmed sounded amused at the report just given to him by one of his envoys. Obviously, the man was unaware of what he had said.

"My liege, Prince Vlad has refused to pay the yearly tribute, citing financial burdens that do not allow him to honor the agreement. He stated this is by no means a refusal to meet the annual amount, merely an inability to do so at this time."

Mehmed dismissed the envoy with a wave of his hand, without another word, and looked at Radu. Vlad's younger brother had become accustomed to this particular gaze and understood it to be a request for an opinion. Pausing to give the appearance of gathering his thoughts, Radu stroked his chin for added contemplative effect.

"This perplexes me just as it does you, my liege. My brother has always paid the annual tribute before. He knows the penalty for refusing to pay and nothing has happened between the two of you to warrant such behavior."

Mehmed sensed a counterpoint loomed closely.

"If Vlad *has* formed an alliance with someone powerful enough to provide him adequate protection from invasion, this course of action would indeed coincide with his methods."

Asking for his opinion is pointless, Mehmed mused. *He simply presents both sides of the situation without providing a definitive suggestion or course of action to take. If he looked like his brother, I never would have bothered with him.*

"I am certain your input will prove invaluable." Allowing Radu a moment to thank him and bow his head in appreciation, Mehmed continued. "Your observation that this is the first occurrence of your brother not paying the tribute is correct. I find the concept of Vlad allying himself with someone else to defend against me farfetched. He is experiencing turmoil from Hungary and the Saxons. The last thing he would do now would be to infuriate me, making himself vulnerable to an enemy attack from yet another front. I shall send word to Wallachia, extending the deadline for payment. That should ensure our relationship is maintained."

Radu returned Mehmed's gaze, masking his skepticism. He found it difficult to accept his brother's explanation of non-payment. In fact, he was certain that Wallachia, if anything, had a surplus.

"Are you certain there is no better course of action, my liege?" asked a present vizier.

"What precisely would you suggest?" While answering the man, Mehmed gave Radu a knowing look, one assuring the young man the sultan knew he wasn't being completely forthcoming.

"I believe Wallachia should be made to pay the tribute *now*. It has never failed to do so before."

"Continue."

"My liege, even if the proper amount of ducats cannot be obtained by Prince Vlad to make the full payment, which I sincerely doubt, surely there are items of equal value that can be substituted to offset the shortage. By allowing an extension, the world is shown they do not have to comply immediately with your orders. What will stop others from adopting the same attitude?"

Mehmed answered directly, not allowing for any question of his superiority. "*I* will stop them. When I refuse an extension to anyone requesting it and then proceed to conquer their land for being unable to pay, they will understand their mistake in attempting something as foolhardy as crossing me."

Wary of falling further from the sultan's grace, the vizier apologized and bowed his head.

"The Wallachian will have more time to pay the full tribute. Should he fail to do so, I will make the world understand my generosity is not something to be taken advantage of."

TÎRGOVIŞTE
April 3, 1459

I have adhered fully to all regulations, yet the Braşovians have failed to extradite Dan and his supporters. Matthias does nothing to make them comply, and they will never do so willingly. Their treachery is not surprising. Were I to attack them, Matthias would surely denounce

*me for betraying the accord and support an effort to remove me. Ultimately he, Dan, and the
Turkish must be crippled permanently. That will be difficult should this crusade remain mine
alone.*

"Do I no longer satisfy you?"

A dejected expression stared at Dragwlya in the darkened room, waiting for an answer. Unable to completely discern whom he would be addressing, the prince gave the only answer he felt he could.

"What?"

Rejection devoured Smaranda as she dishearteningly asked again. "Do I no longer satisfy you?"

Still at a loss, Dragwlya waited until the dark cavern of his mind found sudden illumination. Within that second, everything revealed itself and his consciousness ignited once more. He now recalled venturing out in the dead of night, away from his castle, away from Elizabetha, to find some peace, some hint of joy. His flight had ended at Smaranda's home. The sensation of her hair lightly brushing his hand immediately jarred him. They were in bed together. That his black locks hung down on her as they did suggested to him they had, or were, engaged in sexual intercourse at some point. Her face conveyed she had gone unsatisfied. Obviously distracted, Dragwlya answered.

"My thoughts are elsewhere."

Tears welled in Smaranda's eyes. "I used to make you forget everything else."

This was not the first time this had occurred with Smaranda or other women. Dragwlya's silence gave Smaranda the opportunity to continue.

"What must I do to make you forget again?"

A strenuous moment of quiet uneasiness passed as Dragwlya averted his eyes from those of his mistress. An audible sigh accompanied his action of letting go of her, all the while frustration sent his mind in search of the reason he could not perform. Without another word from either of them, Dragwlya donned his garb of a simple peasant. Refusing to even glance at Smaranda, he dressed hastily and left her bedchamber and her home.

While crying in her bed, Smaranda's mind raced. She searched inwardly for the reason why she failed to satisfy her beloved. Smaranda understood the pressures he currently faced weighed upon him heavily. Eventually, she would have to find some way to restore their passion. If such a way existed, she would make certain to discover it.

SOFIA
April 9, 1459

"Europe does not appear overly concerned with you," Radu stately boldly.

Mehmed had just concluded an audience with his advisory council, the main topic of which surrounded the upcoming congress called by Pius II.

"Why do you think that is?" Mehmed looked at Radu, truly wanting an answer to the query. The possible postponement of the Pope's congress to call a crusade against the Ottoman Empire did nothing but strengthen Mehmed's belief the time to engage his enemy was eminent.

"You are like a ghost to them. They think you exist but because they have not seen or touched you they do not believe you can affect them."

Confidence welled within Mehmed. For so long he believed the war with Europe would be a hard fought one. He had expected a united front, individual nations eager to put aside their minor quarreling for the common good. Was it possible he had overestimated their humanity? If they could not come together to fight for their god, what *would* unite them?

"They appear more concerned with their personal treasuries than their religion," Mehmed offered. He continued to look at Radu, wondering how much he still thought as they did.

"As you say, they are more willing to fight for personal glory, for self-preservation. If God is saved as well, so be it."

"Patience has allowed me to achieve much. If I chose to organize a campaign now, it may cause them to embrace Pius' plan. They may actually band together in an attempt to stop me."

"Pius is fearful of you, my liege, and worried about what will or will not occur at Mantua…and rightfully so. Once he reconvenes his congress, he will realize he should have combined what little support he received from the beginning, instead of allowing three months to pass while hoping others would change their minds. That will be the time to attack—once he sees how apathetic the heads of Europe are. Once he knows this fight is his alone, he will simply attempt to save what is his from falling into your hands."

Mehmed smiled. "Each day you convince me more Europe will be conquered."

With a voice and eyes that seemed to lose life for an instant, Radu answered. "Each day, Europe gives me more reasons to believe it will be."

Mehmed sensed what he felt to be sorrow from Radu but ignored it. "Preparations will be made now for Smederevo's capture. If Pius' congress fails to produce a significant union, I shall move swiftly to take the advantage."

TÎRGOVIŞTE
May 16, 1459

Dragwlya impatiently awaited what he anticipated to be the justification of a strong suspicion. For two days now, a rumor circulated throughout Tîrgovişte that a peasant carried his unborn child. Little credence had been given to the claim and little attention paid to it until the woman confessed to the prince himself she had become pregnant as a result of their affair.

Smaranda choked back tears as the examiner prodded and poked her, searching for an indication she was with child. Over the past few months nearly all her encounters with the prince ended with little fanfare. His thoughts were always occupied with the Turkish, or the Saxons, or Matthias, or something else. Depression would besiege him from the moment he arrived until he left, making it difficult for either of them to become aroused or experience any sort of satisfaction. Smaranda sought and eventually uncovered what she believed to be a solution guaranteed to lift his spirits.

Following the latest rendezvous with her lover, Smaranda had proclaimed to several individuals the offspring of the prince now grew inside of her. For what could bring a man more joy than the knowledge that a child will be born to bear his name? Dragwlya himself learned the news from sources other than Smaranda initially. Once confronted, she had confirmed the reports.

How can this be? Eternal moments of silence lagged on as Dragwlya observed Smaranda's appearance. Nothing indicated she carried a child in her womb. Her figure remained the same as Dragwlya last recalled it. What caused much of the prince's apprehension to the claim, however, centered on his knowledge of the nature of their relationship as of late.

It hardly seemed possible that their unions could have produced anything beyond frustration, and yet Smaranda now proclaimed conception had occurred. Aware of his inabilities, Dragwlya convinced himself the likelihood of Smaranda's pregnancy teetered on a high wall of improbability, one that appeared destined to crumble. His certainty prompted the examination now taking place.

Futilely, the examiner prodded in one last attempt to discover the alleged seed eluding him. A sense of frustration gripped him as he stopped. He turned to face the prince, revealing a look of negativity, signaling the woman was no more pregnant than he. Bowing his head, the man snaked away from the examination table and its occupant as the prince approached.

Now standing at her right side, Dragwlya looked down upon his mistress. Smaranda had been relieved of her clothing and bound to the table. Feelings of betrayal riddled the prince, now fighting to comprehend her rationale, her motive for lying to everyone, to him. What had she hoped to gain from this charade? Notoriety?

Being the mother of the prince's child could possibly provide one with a secure living. The temptation to make such a claim obviously proved too great for Smaranda. Her falsehood indicated she had never really cared for him, that their relationship had been cultivated in a garden of deceit. Once again the axiom that those without will do whatever necessary to achieve their ends proved legitimate.

Loss, sorrow, shame, and regret reserved positions in Smaranda's head and heart. She understood the man she had grown to love to be harsh, one who refused to allow injustices to occur when possible; one who punished injustice always. Yet she had committed no crime.

Sharing a stare with Smaranda momentarily allowed Dragwlya to forget everyone else in the room. Seeing her, lying there naked, evoked no thoughts of passion, no desire, no wont for the love or peace he had once found through her. Hatred was all he felt, all he would feel for her ever again.

With the room silent, Smaranda only mouthed her question to him. "Why are you doing this?"

Without hesitation the prince answered in slightly above a whisper. "You are a thief and will be treated as such." Before she had a chance to refute his charge, Dragwlya continued. "You stole from me joy, the promise of the birth of a child...of *my* child."

All in close proximity heard what the prince had said. If he did indeed consider this woman to be a thief in any capacity, she would soon be impaled, just as all the others.

Grabbing hold of one of the examiner's blades, Dragwlya swiftly inserted its tip into the woman and violently slashed upward until reaching her breasts. Blood splattered many as Smaranda writhed and screamed in torment. In disbelief, witnesses to the scene continued to stare.

I will not be made a mockery of by some whore. Throwing the blade down, Dragwlya turned and stormed out of the room, exclaiming coldly as he did so, "Let the world see where I have been."

CHAPTER XXXIX
DEAF EARS
MANTUA
June 1, 1459

An imminent threat to the very existence of Christianity is no longer reason enough to take part in a crusade. If incentives of wealth and power are not present, no one is interested.

"Unsettling" was one of the infinite adjectives Pope Pius II found to describe today's debacle. He had once harbored hope the groundwork for a common crusade against the Turks would be laid here. Hope no longer existed, only greed among the crowned heads of Europe and others.

Pius fought but could not contain a quick spurt of laughter from slipping out. As absurd as it sounded, today proved that Muslims were more willing to fight the Turks than were the Europeans. How else could it be explained that Uzun Hazan, the brother-in-law of the sultan, appeared at the congress, yet many of the Mediterranean merchant cities, France, England, and Hungary were not represented? Why did no one understand the threat Mehmed posed? Perhaps when they found themselves battling the Turks on their own soil it would register how expensive the price of avarice could be. Admittedly, Pius knew what caused such strong feelings of self-indulgence.

Though he hated his insight passionately, it took only a slight nudge for Pius to rec-ollect days when no one mattered but himself. Memories he wished to bury where no one could find them resurfaced with buoyancy, eager to remind him he had not always been so righteous. Indulging in life's most putrid and indecent behaviors had once *been* his life. Nothing could change the fact that he had fathered children, two that he knew of, and that those children were raised without knowing a father's love. He thanked God they never knew the man he was. He cursed himself because they would never know the man he had struggled to become.

Then, Pius had been Enea Silvio de' Piccolomini. Only the memory of that youth existed, but it pained him to know how much suffering he had caused others in the past. He hoped he had been successful in repairing some of the damage. In large part, Pius' prior selfishness allowed him to understand the prevailing attitude of not fighting with-out immediate reward. Conversely, he knew this crusade was necessary, more so than any other preceding it.

Officially, Pius delayed the opening of the congress, rescheduling it for a date to be named shortly to give everyone more time to prepare and attend. Unofficially, Pius wondered if there existed a time when the Christian leaders of Europe would willingly journey to a meeting regarding anything. Without greater participation, there would be no need for a congress.

TÎRGOVIŞTE
June 9, 1459

"Aside from Pius and yourself, no one fears Mehmed." Though not a question, the statement begged for a response, and Elizabetha awaited one. Tonight had been one of the few times when Dragwlya conversed with her about world events. He honestly held genuine interest in her commentary. The paradox that he could be such a diplomat and gentleman and then without warning morph into the unholy terror many perceived him to be, the unholy terror she knew he was, perplexed Elizabetha. Reverent fear constantly reminded her to remember with whom she frequently shared a bed.

"They are all fools; more concerned with fighting one another than combining forces to face the greater foe, the true enemy...My cousin has chosen to fight Hungary instead of Turkey, yet his lands are as threatened as my own."

"Stephen chooses to fight Matthias because the king provides sanctuary to the man responsible for his father's assassination. I doubt your fight would be with anyone other than Ioan Hunedoara were he still alive."

Impressive, Dragwlya thought. Her comment dredged up memories from the night his uncle was assassinated, forcing him to align with his own father's murderer to capture his throne.

"At times you have remarkable insight for a woman, flawed as it may be. The fault with Stephen's war does not lie with the opponent; it is the timing of the fight. Should Mehmed succeed, there will *be* no Moldavia."

"Why are *you* ready to fight the Turkish? The Saxons still oppose you, and while you may be willing to forego the fight, they do not appear to be so inclined."

"You're right about the Saxons." *Very astute.* "I am concerned about Dan, about what he would try should I put all focus on Mehmed. The Saxons have reneged on their promise to give him up. He will have to be dealt with before I can fully commit to anything else."

"Like everyone else, you are more concerned with your own needs."

Hesitation from Dragwlya suggested to Elizabetha she had overstepped an undefined boundary.

"The difference is that while everyone else is trying to amass *more* power, instead of joining together, I simply wish to retain what is already mine. I *am* concerned with my own *needs*. Everyone else is concerned with their own desires. Europe's indifference toward the Turkish will be its undoing."

Hesitant to answer, Elizabetha allowed herself a moment to reflect. Finally, she offered a response fueled by dread. "If what you say is true, than the response to the Pope's congress will demonstrate there is no unified front against the Turkish."

"Yes." Without another word Dragwlya pushed her to finish her thought.

"Mehmed will be encouraged to attack." The realization frightened her, especially the knowledge that Wallachia would be the inroad.

"Albania will sign a truce with Mehmed, the Golden Horde will prevent the Russians from caring about what is occurring so far away from their home, and everyone else is concerned with civil war or conquering more of Europe for themselves. Mehmed wants this continent, and the continent appears willing to allow him to overrun it at his leisure."

"And what will you do?"

"I will make certain there is no worry of attack from Dan. Then my efforts can be turned southward."

"And what then?"

"By that time, hopefully, the Pope and I will not be the only ones fighting."

CHAPTER XL
ELIZABETHA'S FEARS
SMEDEREVO
June 20, 1459

Mehmed swept across Bulgaria and into Serbia with no resistance. Like Constantinople once had, Smederevo now represented the last bastion of Christianity on the fringes of the empire. Like Constantinople, Smederevo would fall.

The doomed city would soon be in sight. Obviously, the infidel forces were amassed there, indicating they felt their best chances lie in defending the city from within and near its vicinity. No other explanation sufficed as to why the Ottoman army was being allowed unhindered passage to Smederevo's gates. Refreshing coolness washed over Mehmed from the front, a cleansing breeze explained by the fact that the city rested right on the banks of the Danube.

So close now...

Gradually, the immense fortifications built by George Branković were emerging, seemingly pushing up through the earth in response to Mehmed's approach. This would be a hard fought battle, one the sultan surmised could last a month. He did not, however, doubt what the outcome would be.

Smederevo could now be seen in full by the entirety of Mehmed's force. *Surely the city is aware of my arrival.* As if answering, one of his scouts alerted him the gates were opening. Before long the defenders of this already lost fortress would make their way out to fight a lost cause.

Certainty exuded from Mehmed. "Allah will lead us to victory in battle."

"I do not believe so, my liege." Stunned by the comment, Mehmed prompted the scout to explain. Knowing he had been misunderstood, the scout swiftly retorted. "My faith has never been stronger, my liege. I only meant to convey there will be no need for fighting today. Those emerging from the city are led by banners of truce. It appears they will make no attempt to oppose you."

Straining his eyes, Mehmed could see the scout's observation was correct. The party now riding toward him appeared to be doing so with the intent of surrendering the city without conflict.

They change their minds from minute to minute like children. One day they wish to risk their very lives to deny Europe the true faith; the next they are ready to give in to my every demand no matter what the monetary cost, wanting only to retain what they already possess. They are unworthy of Allah, yet all must be brought the true faith.

A collection of twenty or so of the most notable citizens from the city were trooping out toward him, looking not only as though they expected him, but as though they had invited him. Dressed in its finest attire, Smederevo was welcoming the sultan with open arms. Converging less than a mile away from the city itself, the entourage of Mehmed and that of the fortress came together with little fanfare. Tension rested solely on the side of the representatives of Smederevo.

"Good afternoon, my liege. We welcome you and present you the keys to Smederevo."

Mehmed beheld the finely dressed man addressing him with little regard.

Weaklings. They know I will overrun them so they chose to simply give themselves up, praying I will allow them to live. Their fear is too strong to even try and negotiate… As it should be.

"Your surrender is accepted. You will be advised of the terms shortly." Without another word, Mehmed turned away from them with revulsion.

Why do they even bother worshiping a god they feel will not deliver them? They waste their time and mine. Hunedoara would not have allowed this. He would have fought my army alone if it came to it. Perhaps the time has come to give my concentration to the East, instead of the West. I have no great enemy here now. The time for putting an end to the unrest in Trebizond has come.

TÎRGOVIŞTE
July 8, 1459

In less than two weeks the Ottoman army could be standing at the doors of Dragwlya's castle, a notion Elizabetha had not been able to cope with since it was learned days ago. How could she? Despite his madness, life with Dragwlya held higher promise than becoming one of the sultan's concubines did. That would never happen. She would never allow it to, regardless of the consequences or sacrifice.

Elizabetha knew Dragwlya had prepared extensively for the possibility of a Turkish onslaught. She knew no one would come to his aid. If Mehmed wished to march into Wallachia and claim it for the vassal state it was there was little hope of stopping him from doing so. Additionally, Dragwlya had failed to pay the principality's annual tribute, giving the sultan more than ample justification.

She watched Dragwlya. Not once did he let down the mask to show his fear of losing the throne to anyone. Elizabetha knew it existed. She had heard him speak of it while he slept. Nothing prevented him from expelling all his thoughts during slumber, and never would Elizabetha make him aware of what he had unwittingly told her.

"He has already suffered defeat at Belgrade. He is not willing to take the risk of doing so once more. Mehmed believes he has conquered Europe already. The war is over in his mind, and all that remains is to simply tour the continent. He has convinced himself all will gladly hand over their cities as Smederevo did. Mehmed will turn his attention elsewhere. He will not waste his time and energy marching his army into lands he feels he already controls, regardless of their proximity."

Priboi continued to stare at Dragwlya once the prince finished addressing the council. Dragwlya was being cautious but showed no real concern despite the Ottoman army being approximately three hundred kilometers away. This sort of recklessness on his master's part kept the nerves of Dragwlya's chancellor on edge, constantly questioning if supporting the Drăculeşti had been in his best interest.

"Sire, is there no more we can do? No one else we can call on for assistance?"

"No, there isn't. If I called upon the whole of Europe, Asia, and Africa, no one would respond. Still, I will do whatever is necessary to protect Wallachia from the sultan. Hopefully, that will only require paying the tribute I have already refused and reaffirming my loyalty. If my throne is threatened in any manner, however, I will not hesitate to fight to retain what is mine."

MANTUA
September 26, 1459

"A gateway to Serbia" was one of the terms Pius had bestowed upon Smederevo since its fall in June. Much the same as Constantinople, the loss of the city to the Turkish evoked hopelessness, disheartenment, and disgust in the Pope. His disgust stemmed not from Smederevo's capture but the manner of its occurrence. While Constantinople had been lost after a valiant attempt to save it, Smederevo was handed over without remorse. The Bosnians had willingly betrayed Christianity.

For the second time in the Cathedral of Mantua, Pius was opening a congress whose aim was to wage war against the Ottoman Empire. For the second time, his plea filled only apathetic ears. While more leaders were in attendance, the same attitude of serving whomever paid the most still prevailed. Still, for nearly two hours, Pius attempted to change their minds.

"We ourselves allowed Constantinople, the capital of the East, to be conquered by the Turks. And while we sit at home idle, the arms of these barbarians are advancing to the Danube and the Sava. In the Eastern imperial city they have massacred the successor of Constantine along with his people, desecrated the temples of the Lord, sullied the noble edifice of Justinian with the hideous cult of Mohammed; they have destroyed the images of the Mother of God and other saints, overturned the altars, cast the relics of the martyrs to the swine, killed the priests, dishonored women and young girls, even the virgins dedicated to the Lord, slaughtered the nobles of the city at the sultan's banquet, carried off the image of our crucified savior to their camp with scorn and mockery amid cries of 'That is the god of the Christians!' and befouled it with mud and spittle. All this happened beneath our very eyes, but we lie in a deep sleep.

"We are able to fight among ourselves, but let the Turks do as they please. For trifling provocations the Christians take up arms and fight bloody battles; but against the Turks, who blaspheme our god, destroy our churches and seek to extirpate the very name of Christianity, no one is willing to raise a hand. Verily, all have withdrawn, all have become useless; there is none to do good…none.

"It is thought perhaps that these things are already done and can no longer be altered, and that from now on we shall have peace. As though peace might be expected from a nation which thirsts for our blood, which after subjugating Greece has already thrust its sword into the flank of Hungary. Peace, from an enemy such as Sultan Mehmed! Abandon this belief, for Mehmed will never lay down arms except in victory or total defeat. Every victory will be for him a stepping-stone to another, until, after subjugating all the princes of the West, he has destroyed the Gospel of Christ and imposed the law of his false prophet upon the whole world."

Shifting in his seat, Pius embraced as best he could the pain in his knees and ankles. His joints were inflamed and reddening. Some days he thought he would be unable to move. On others he couldn't.

Gout was gradually taking hold of his body, but he refused to allow it to dominate his thoughts. He couldn't. Christianity's fate mattered too much for him to cower to this simple affliction. As the Devil once ruled his life with ecstasy, now he was attempting to do so with agony. This time would be different. Pius no longer desired to give in. Now God's mouthpiece, and the rock upon which his church rested, he couldn't. Enea Silvio de' Piccolomini no longer existed.

CONSTANTINOPLE
October 12, 1459

"Nothing has changed since last month's congress, according to the Italians." Mehmed's voice was almost careless. "No one is willing to fight for Pius. Some promise him thousands of men while remaining home. I find it difficult to believe such lofty commitments will be kept."

"As do I, my liege."

Mehmed studied Mahmud Pasha, trying to determine if the man possessed the ability to betray him as Halil Pasha had. Anything was possible under the wrong set of circumstances. Continuing the discussion, he would be certain not to reveal anything that could hinder him from achieving his future goals. His plans would be kept safe from potential saboteurs.

"Europe is being served to you, my liege. Now is the time to feast."

Mehmed continued to stare at Mahmud.

"Perhaps. But I will not make the mistake of rushing into such a decision. The Christians' unwillingness to fight has unlocked more passages than just those leading into Europe. When the time is appropriate, I will know."

CHAPTER XLI
TÎMPA HILL
BRAȘOV
December 26, 1459

Informants from Constantinople, and Mehmed's actions, confirmed for Dragwlya that the sultan would occupy himself with matters in the East for the time being. He was now provided the impetus for a winter raid, one designed to capture Dan III and his supporters.

Traversing the Prahova River Valley, Dragwlya's army reached Brașov in three days. Once in close proximity, he ordered the villages, forts, and towns they passed through to be burned, along with their crops. All captives were ordered to be immediately killed until Brașov had been reached.

Two hours had passed since sunset, leaving the city and its suburbs in virtual darkness. The meager light of torches was not enough to expose the predators lurking just outside of the wooden palisade surrounding the areas of Spenghi and Prund. Here, in the Romanian section of town where Dan III and his boyars held residence, Dragwlya had decided to concentrate his attack once one vital piece of information was obtained.

"Which one?" The intensity in Dragwlya's voice and eyes demanded an immediate response.

"My lord, though I have learned the location of the false prince's home, I regret to inform you I have also discovered he and his court have fled the city and have gone into hiding. A servant remained behind. I was forced to dispose of him when he threatened to compromise the secrecy of our raid."

Dragwlya's nostrils flared at the scout's report. *Somehow the bastard was warned. He knew of my plans and chose not to warn the city. He felt no need to save those who have crowned him. I shall show Brașov's leaders how devastating his disregard for their welfare has been.*

"Proceed as planned. Burn everything. By noon tomorrow, nothing of the Romanian sector is to be left standing."

"And what of the inhabitants, sire? Does the standing order to kill on sight still remain?"

Dragwlya stared at his captain and the boyars surrounding him. "No…That order is repealed, captain…I want them taken alive." *They must be shown.*

Erected in 1342, the old chapel of Saint Jacob had survived for one hundred seventeen years. Princes and governors had come and gone, territorial boundaries were drawn and redrawn, but this monument remained. At the foot of Tîmpa Hill, the edifice withstood natural and worldly onslaughts without yielding, failing to collapse for anything or anyone, until this day.

Ravaged by flames, the chapel's roof caved in approximately an hour after midnight. Its destruction assured Dragwlya no help was being sent from within Braşov to assist the relatively unprotected regions outside of it. Without remorse, the Romanians were being sacrificed by the Saxons. By early morning, Dragwlya's orders had been carried out, and the captives had been brought to the summit of the hill above the gutted chapel.

The sun will begin to rise in two hours. Braşov's treachery is responsible for this. My example to them will be completed before sun up… They must be made to see.

Distrusting one's senses ultimately leads to madness. Those who observed what Dragwlya intended to be their lesson could not believe their eyes. They wouldn't believe because doing so was impossible. Either Satan himself had presented them all with a true vision of Hell or, more frightening, what they observed was no imaginary creation and indeed the manifestation of man's most maniacal capabilities. The apparition's refusal to vanish made its appearance all the more vivid when they closed their eyes in an attempt to will it away.

Little more than a smoldering pile of ash, the chapel of Saint Jacob represented the mildest of atrocities. Above its ruins, through a smoky haze, there was something far worse to be seen.

In a formation of perfectly straight lines of small interval, lengthwise and crosswise adorning Tîmpa Hill, the impaled bodies of nearly all the Romanian captives were arranged for the populace of Braşov to bear witness to, to learn from. Most of the victims ceased breathing long ago. Loss of blood, not impalement, had been the actual cause of their deaths. To attain so precise a pattern as had been achieved, Dragwlya found it necessary for the armaşi to amputate many limbs. Like discarded trash, the once obtrusive body parts littered the ground in small piles. No more than ten meters from the first column of bodies on the western side, a table was neatly set for Dragwlya's dinner.

Wishing to dine alone, Dragwlya proceeded to the table without inviting anyone to join him. He did, however, force the boyars and priests accompanying him to remain close to the rancid orchard he had ordered planted. None complained about not being asked to accompany him.

"Am I to eat my meal from off of the table?" Dragwlya's query, directed toward his servants, was made after he noticed his setting did not include a plate.

Immediately, someone rushed up to answer his question. "Forgive me, sire, but every plate has been broken. I have been unable to locate any suitable replacements."

I am made to take care of even the minutest of details.

Reacting to the first agreeable object he saw, Dragwlya motioned one the priests over. Once the clergyman arrived, the prince pulled from his hands what had attracted his attention.

"You may return now." Dragwlya said this, ignoring the presence of the man. He was already studying what would soon become the platter for his dinner. His fingers traced over ornamental work adorning the outer coverings of the priest's icon. The panel, split in two down the center, was hinged on either side. Pulling up on the shutter-like doors, Dragwlya opened the relic. Divinely, the face of Christ stared at him. "Serve me with this."

Refusing to show his reluctance and disgust, the servant took the opened icon and answered as evenly as he could. "Yes, sire."

A flood of scents contaminated Braşov's atmosphere, including Dragwlya's food and the smell of the smoke from the burning of the Romanian sectors. Both were overpowered by the odor of coagulating blood and human excrement. The stench reached the surviving captives being held not far from Dragwlya's table and the boyars accompanying the prince on the raid.

"My lord? Perhaps it would be best if you were to allow the remaining prisoners to be set free." Unannounced, one of the boyars, Bolintineanu, had approached Dragwlya.

With frustration, the prince detached attention from his example to the city for this distraction. "For what purpose? To allow potential uprisings from them in the future? I have destroyed their homes and their possessions. They have no place to go... Braşov would not help them defend what was theirs. Do you expect the Saxons to show compassion now? No. Before nightfall, no prisoners will remain."

Dragwlya's full attention was drawn to the boyar as the man produced a handkerchief, which he placed over his nose while turning his head away.

"Is something the matter, Bolintineanu?" *Thus far he has dared to interrupt my meal and has offered inane advice.*

"The stench, sire, I do not think I can bear it much longer."

"Leave me now to dine. I will attend to you and the others later."

Thankful to be dismissed, Bolintineanu hurriedly left the prince's table. Dragwlya contemplated the boyar's fate for a moment as the servant returned with the icon, now holding his food. With a quick gesture, the prince summoned the head captain of the armaşi.

"Yes, sire?"

"Fashion a stake, twice the length of any now before me, and bring the remaining captives forward. I wish to waste no more time with them. Order your men to behead each of them in turn but only after removing at the very least the hands and feet of every individual."

"Yes, sire."

While some verbally damned Dragwlya, the majority of the captives remained silent, choosing instead to pray for the welfare of their souls. One by one they were brought before the prince's table and slaughtered in the manner he had specified.

"Hellspawn! You will burn for all eternity and never know peace!"

Unceremoniously, Dragwlya continued to dine, paying little mind to any of the words the Romanians wasted on him. He sensed the ever-growing rage of the captives. Those being brought before him now engaged in more unruly behavior than when his meal had begun.

"Do not ignore me, son of the Devil!" Emphasizing he wanted the prince's undivided attention, the man spat. Although he missed, the desired affect was achieved.

This one's will is superb. Dragwlya centered his focus on the man as armaşi began beating him, ending his outburst. *It is unfortunate he is my enemy.* Joyfully, he watched an axe land on one of the captive's ankles, severing it immediately. The distressed sound of his screaming and the sight of the man's blood flowing from the wound awakened something within Dragwlya. It enhanced his senses, resurrected something else. Something instinctive.

"Stop. Do not remove any other limb or appendage from his body."

The armaşi stared at the prince as the Romanian continued to cry out.

Dragwlya grabbed his cup and, emptying the wine, presented it to the man closest to him. "Take this cup. Slice his throat and fill it with his blood." Because of the large amount of blood already lost, the captive perished soon after Dragwlya's cup had been filled and returned.

The pool of thick, red liquid mesmerized the prince, much like staring into the heart of a flame for too long would. Exactly as fire would, the blood beckoned to Dragwlya to be touched, to have its warmth felt. His finger barely broke the surface and drew back quickly. For a few seconds he let the blood run down before bringing his thumb to it and rubbing in a circular motion. He glanced just far off enough to see a piece of bread he had cut for himself laying on the table.

Grabbing the bread, Dragwlya stained the dough with crimson fingerprints and held the slice just above the cup, letting it hover for a moment. Gently, he lowered his hand until the crust was dipped. Full of life, the blood raced up toward his fingers as it was absorbed. Unwavering, Dragwlya lifted the dripping piece of bread to his mouth and bit into it heartily.

Without chewing, Dragwlya swallowed the soaked dough. As before, instantaneous sensations of rejuvenation and invigoration exploded within him. The evidence was undeniable. When consumed, the blood of strong-willed enemies would provide renewed strength and heighten one's senses.

"Sire, the stake you requested is completed."

The armaş seemed to be shouting at him. He wondered instantly if his senses could be controlled when under the influence of so potent an elixir. The pale held by the man stood almost four meters tall, well above the height of any other implanted on the hillside.

"Excellent." Placing the remainder of his piece of bread down, Dragwlya turned his head slightly over his shoulder. "Bolintineanu, come forward."

Prolonging another appearance before the prince as long as possible, the boyar shuffled toward the table. Immediately, his attention was drawn to the partially devoured piece of bread stained red and imprinted with Dragwlya's bite marks. The realization of the contents of the prince's cup proved too much for Bolintineanu. Combined with the scents, the sight forced him to hold up his nose in revulsion.

"Does the stench continue to trouble you, Bolintineanu?"

Close to gasping, desperately trying to find some hidden pocket of fresh air, the boyar answered. "It is unbearable, sire."

"You can see I have taken measures to help alleviate your suffering."

The pale, and the armaş brandishing it, immediately stood out from their surroundings. Words failed Bolintineanu. His body froze.

"You shall live up there, where the stench cannot reach you." Instantly, Dragwlya had the boyar seized and impaled. While watching the armaşi attending to Bolintineanu, the prince once more picked up his bread and resumed eating.

CHAPTER XLII
KAZÎGLU BEY
BRAŞOV
January 19, 1460

Five days ago, a bull issued by Pius proclaimed a three-year crusade and formally closed the Congress of Mantua. In recognition a new religious association, the Order of Saint Mary of Bethlehem, was created and the delegates in attendance feasted on the stout oxen donated by the Duke of Milan. Shortly afterwards the attendees abandoned the city, leaving the ailing Pope with empty promises. He would soon begin the journey home with no illusions the efforts he made to fight the Turks would succeed.

Before returning to Tîrgovişte, Dragwlya led an attack against the church of Saint Bartholomew, setting it ablaze without removing any of its treasures, chalices, or priestly vestments. To the shock and dismay of many, he succeeded also in breaking into Braşov itself and had attempted to burn its Black Church. Thankful for having been able to repel the berserker, the citizens still had yet to cope with what had transpired and with all they had seen on Tîmpa Hill. Upon his return from hiding, Dan III beseeched the city and surrounding areas to support him in ousting Dragwlya.

"He has sold himself to the Turks." Dan addressed the council of Braşov, knowing the Saxons' hunger for revenge. "I entreat you, the honest and good citizens of this city and those of Ţara Bîrsei, to all their brethren, their friends, their relatives, and sons who have lost a dear one because of the actions of this lawless, cruel, and faithless tyrant responsible for torturing and killing people aimlessly and devastating whole areas to fight with me. Take action against the beast who has taken so much from you."

It took little more than this for Dan to convince the council. Planning for the ensuing campaign began immediately.

NEAR RUCĂR
March 27, 1460

After two weeks, Dan's campaign for Dragwlya's throne would end. Since the middle of the month, he had taken possession of Amlaş and Făgăraş, arresting and killing Dragwlya's supporters whenever possible. With Braşov's support, Dan had marched into Wallachia along the commercial road that paralleled the Dîmboviţa River from Braşov to the northeastern frontier outpost of Rucăr. Here, Dragwlya had in reserve a sizable force to protect the principality from attack. Until now, the fighting between the two armies were minor skirmishes. This would be the defining engagement.

The fight was decidedly Saxon versus Wallachian. Witnessing Dragwlya's madness first-hand, the surviving Romanians surrounding the areas around Braşov chose not to join Dan, fearful of what would happen should they fail to overthrow the prince. They hoped this would be enough to curtail further incursions.

"We must retreat, sire! The men we have remaining will soon begin to desert if we don't!"

"There will be no withdrawal! I refuse to give up my throne to *him*!"

"Withdraw now, or you will die!"

"No! If you want to abandon me do so!"

"Your pride will destroy you!" These were the last words spoken by the boyar before he turned to flee. He was the third to do so.

I will fight alone if I have to! Taking this silent vow, Dan charged into the marrow of the melee.

Unwilling to sacrifice their lives, the Braşovians began surrendering individually and in small groups to Dragwlya's men. Laying their weapons down on the battlefield showed the claimant the extent of their commitment. No one truly believed in him. They did not fight with abandon as did Dragwlya's men. Knowing this destroyed his desire. He could not win and was no longer entirely certain he wanted to. Virtually surrounded, he surrendered, offering no resistance.

Of the numerous boyars accompanying Dan, only seven eluded being captured or killed. Those remaining had been gathered together by Dragwlya. Guarded by several soldiers and armaşi they knelt down, hardly comprehending what they saw. Before them Dragwlya stood alongside his priest, who was dressed in the formal liturgical funeral vestments for reading the mass for the dead. Also before them lay Dan, his arms crossed, his eyes closed, very much alive and conscious.

"Your prince is dead." Dragwlya addressed the boyars. This one last torture remained before he would end their lives. "You will serve as the choir of his mass and sing for the forgiveness of his sins, as well as your own… I urge you, sing loudly." With that, Dragwlya had his priest begin the service.

"Blessed is he whom Thou hast chosen and taken, O Lord."

The choir answered the cantor with cracking, nervous voices. "Alleluia… Alleluia… Alleluia."

"His memory is from generation to generation."

"Alleluia."

"His soul will dwell amid good things."

"Alleluia."

The priest continued through the litany. "… For Thou art the resurrection, the life, and the repose of Thy departed servant Prince Dan III, O Christ our God, and unto

Thee do we send up glory, together with Thine unoriginate Father, and Thy most holy, and good, and life-giving Spirit, now and ever, and unto the ages of ages."

"Amen."

Outwardly, Dragwlya was solemn, displaying little emotion for what was taking place. Internally, he laughed at the spectacle. While brassy and horrid, the sounds produced by the boyar choir were comical; the sight of Dan III shaking as he lay on the ground nothing less than hysterical. The prince himself served as reader for the service.

"Our Father, Who art in heaven, hallowed be Thy name. Thy Kingdom come. Thy will be done, on earth as it is in heaven. Give us this day our daily bread. And forgive us our debts as we forgive our debtors. And lead us not into temptation, but deliver us from the evil one."

Here the priest resumed. "For Thine is the kingdom and the power and the glory, of the Father, and of the Son, and of the Holy Spirit, now and ever, and unto the ages of ages."

Dragwlya and the choir answered him. "Amen."

"O God of spirits and of all flesh, who hast trampled down death and deposed the Devil and given lift to Thy world; do Thou, O Lord, give rest to the soul of Thy departed servant Prince Dan III, in a place of light, a place of green pasture, a place of rest, whence all sickness, sorrow, and sighing are fled away. Pardon every sin committed by him in word, deed, and thought, inasmuch as Thou art a good God and lovest man. For there is no man that hath lived and not sinned against Thee; Thou alone art without sin; Thy righteousness is an everlasting righteousness, and Thy word is truth."

Hearing his name again being used in a manner indicating he were deceased caused Dan to flinch. Everything had deteriorated so quickly, so fast, that he couldn't mentally reconstruct all the events that had led to such failure. Before long Dragwlya's priest would give the dismissal. Would he still be alive? What if he were? What then?

"May He who hath dominion over the living and the dead, who Himself rose again from the dead, Christ our true God, through the prayers of His most pure mother; of the holy, glorious, and all-praised apostles; of our holy and God-bearing fathers; and of all the Saints; commit the soul of His departed servant Prince Dan III to the abodes of the righteous; give him rest in Abraham's bosom, and number him among the just, and have mercy on us; for He is good and loveth mankind."

"Amen."

"Give rest eternal, O Lord, in blessed repose, to the soul of Thy departed servant Prince Dan III, and make his memory eternal."

Dan stared at the blackness of his eyelids, waiting. The priest was silent, the boyars no longer sung. Perhaps he was already dead. If that were the case, the blow had been painless. Indeed he felt numb.

My spirit is leaving my body.

A sharp tingle began in Dan's fingers and gradually ascended his arms. They lacked blood and his limbs were making his brain aware of it. Such information mattered only to someone still alive, and the fact compelled Dan to open his eyes. Satisfied, horrible emerald eyes stared down at him, accompanied by a sadistic smile. Dan was still alive and knew his true death would not be as painless.

"Get up!" Dragwlya commanded Dan as he would any servant.

Still wearing his crown, Dan stood and faced the true prince.

"Dig."

Dragwlya forcefully threw down a spade and then unsheathed his own sword to deter Dan from attempting anything foolish.

After twenty minutes, Dan found himself standing in a pit that would soon be his grave.

"It is deep enough." Dragwlya's words stung Dan as he drove the spade into the earth again. "Place the spade on the ground."

With his boyars still on their knees watching, Dan pulled the spade out and gently set it next to the hole. Exhausted, he stared blankly as Dragwlya kicked the tool away.

"You have chosen to live your life as a false prince. I will honor you by allowing you to retain your false crown in death." Dragwlya drew back his blade and began a swing meant to decapitate Dan.

Dan slammed his eyes shut, and his body tensed to absorb the blow. He felt nothing.

"I have reserved for you a death worthy of a prince. Open your eyes and die as one."

Hearing the agitation in Dragwlya's voice, Dan did as he was told and found the prince's blade only inches from his neck. He was astounded. He had seen the swing meant to kill him begin its descent. How powerful was Dragwlya that he could stop such tremendous momentum?

Cocking his arms back, Dragwlya swung once more. This time he did not stop. The blade passed through, cleanly separating Dan's head from his body. Two loud thuds were heard as first Dan's head slammed against the wall of his self-dug grave, followed closely by his collapsing body.

Dragwlya remained motionless, simply breathing with his blade resting on the shoulder opposite of where it had been only seconds earlier. He smiled and held on to the tension that coursed through his muscles. Finally releasing the tightness in his body, Dragwlya ceased smiling and chose two of Dan's boyars to bury their prince. When they had finished, he addressed the entire group.

"You were near to him in life; you will remain so, forever."

The dissident boyars were impaled and placed in a circle surrounding the grave. Relieved, Dragwlya stared at the dead and dying supporters of his former enemy. By no means did this completely secure his northern border, but hopefully it would stifle the thoughts of any other claimant preparing plans of invasion. Dragwlya could not yet afford to simply ignore pretenders to his throne and concentrate on Mehmed. Much work still remained.

CONSTANTINOPLE
April 16, 1460

"In Bulgaria they now refer to him as Kazîglu Bey, a reference to his favorite means of punishment." Mahmud Pasha contributed this final bit of information to Mehmed after summarizing the events that had taken place between Dragwlya and Dan III.

"A suitable title. I remember vividly his infatuation with impalement when we were but children, when he and his brother were detained by my father as hostages. He has explored every means by which it can be done...Refined it. I have heard he managed to keep one victim alive for two weeks."

Mahmud's shoulders lifted and locked while processing the thought. "He is ridding Transylvania of all who would defy him. Once he feels secure, he may attempt to extend his border south."

Mehmed dismissed the notion. "Vlad is an oppressor, not a crusader like Hunedoara was."

"He has yet to pay last year's tribute and has not made payment for this year."

"When the time comes, I will handle him properly."

With hesitation in his voice, Mahmud asked, "Why is that time not now, my liege? Why will you tell no one of your plans?"

The pasha was right to feel trepidation. Mehmed answered in a tone letting the grand vizier know he was being accused of impudence.

"Do not assume as grand vizier you are entitled to know my thoughts. Before Europe is conquered, I must have control of all Anatolia. That is all you need know for now."

CHAPTER XLIII
FALTERING WORDS
TÎRGOVIŞTE
June 8, 1460

"**Y**ou are appointed by God to punish evildoers."

An espousal? Dragwlya scarcely expected either of these monks to understand.

Much like Islam from the South, the Roman Catholic faith had for years invaded Wallachia from the West and North, leaving visual evidence in the form of monasteries as it conquered. Dragwlya had always been wary of the monasteries—independent papal states, free to do as they pleased. Free of him.

Sometimes he wondered if he were saving his principality from the sultan's direct attacks so that it could be discreetly swallowed up by the Vatican.

Less than a month ago, Dragwlya refused to sign a truce with Braşov after intense negotiations. The city sent its leading citizen, Johann Gereb, on its behalf. He was, of course, reluctant to go and was persuaded only after much difficulty to attempt preventing anything like what had occurred upon Tîmpa Hill from ever happening again. Throughout their conversations, Dragwlya became impressed with his wit and allowed him to return with the understanding he would not agree to peace with anyone while formidable claimants to his throne remained. Even now preparations were being made to resolve the issue. Soon he would move against Amlaş with his primary objective being the death of Vlad the Monk.

"This is not the punishment of evil. It *is* evil! No man has the right to subject anyone to such pain!" The second monk could not abstain from admonishing the prince as his colleague had.

It would be too great a feat for both of them to comprehend.

Dragwlya overlooked the courtyard from the Chindia Tower, just as the monks had been doing, without saying a word. He saw the common scene of impaled criminals, thinking only of justice's triumph over the wretched filth below. How the second monk's view could be so skewed eluded him.

"You do not feel it is my right to administer justice?"

"As prince you are *obligated* to administer justice, sire. There are, however, means other than simple butchery by which justice should operate." The monk's tone was unwavering, almost defiant.

The man is wrong, but those are his true feelings. Dragwlya turned back to the first monk. "Do you not object as your counterpart does?"

Sweating, the monk wondered how the air surrounding him had become stifling so quickly. His eyes shifted from the prince to the courtyard and to his fellow monk as he answered. "There are alternatives to capital punishment-"

Dragwlya interrupted the man. "Then you *do* agree with him."

"Well, yes my lord, but I-"

Receiving a knowing nod, the armaşi atop the tower moved toward their prince as he again broke off the monk's statement.

"I do not wish to speak with you any longer as I cannot discern what is truth and what is not." Dragwlya's men took hold of the monk. "Like so many of those in my courtyard, you have tried to deceive me. You will suffer as they have. Perhaps then you will *truly* believe God has appointed me to punish men such as yourself." Another nod and the monk was lead away, screaming and fighting.

Dragwlya turned to the remaining monk. "Though you disagree with my methodology, you have the courage to state your true position. For that, I would be honored if you would join me for dinner."

Not wishing to insult the prince, the monk agreed. Knowing the rashness and unpredictability of his host, he would make certain not to contradict anything he said for the duration of his visit.

BUDA
August 20, 1460

Over the last few months King Matthias and Mihály Szilágy had gained some measure of trust for one another. Gradually, the governor of Transylvania let subside his feelings of dejection in an attempt at reconciliation. Though the boy wearing the crown did not bear his name, he did at least share his blood. "We will do nothing to assist them." Matthias' statement shocked most of his advisory council. "I have also ordered my uncle to abstain from interceding on behalf of the Saxons." *Not that he would ever raise arms against Vlad.*

"But sire, what if Prince Vlad does not stop? He has destroyed numerous villages in the Făgăraş district, killing everyone he has come into contact with, and continues to move toward Amlaş."

"Your information is incorrect." Well aware Dragwlya had already killed nearly fifteen thousand Saxons in hunting down Vlad the Monk, Matthias felt no pressing need to stop the prince. He had not yet satisfied himself that his power and command were widely recognized. Making another potential enemy, one with the ability to motivate men the way Dragwlya did, was not an option at the moment. "He has not killed everyone. My sources inform me he has made every effort, and has succeeded, in steering his attacks away from my garrisons.

"His raid is not intended as an assault on Hungary. Still, I do agree peace between Wallachia and the Saxons is in everyone's best interest."

UNTERWALD
August 24, 1460

Moisture clung to every leaf of the forest in millions of miniscule drops. Every so often some moisture would gather together and roll off, causing leaves to bob down and up slightly. Morning light began piercing open spaces between the leaves and branches, bouncing around and reflecting off the already drawn swords of Dragwlya's cavalry. His offensive against Amlaş would commence shortly.

The feast day of Saint Bartholomew swiftly transformed from a time of jubilation to one of abject despair for Amlaş. Within two hours, every citizen was led to a great field, their homes set aflame. A massacre followed. Members of Dragwlya's cavalry and the armaşi, per his order, mutilated the captives without discrimination. The bodies were placed upon pitchforks and other makeshift pales.

Vlad the Monk escaped, but a captured boyar was brought before the prince by two armaşi who were certain their prince would want the pleasure of killing the traitor himself. Displeased his men had failed to follow his precise order, Dragwlya scolded them and then had them put to death. He stared at his half-brother's bruised and bleeding follower for some time before returning his attention to the carnage.

"The bastard's lackey is not worthy of my attention. Dispose of him immediately."

Dragwlya continued to watch the slaughter, damning himself for not coordinating the attack so that it would have coincided with dinner. The sight of blood gave him strength, yet he was angered he could not consume it as he had done on previous occasions. It hardly mattered.

He had not needed much strength to defeat them, meaning they were weak. Infusing their blood with his own might make him weak as well.

How will Mehmed's blood affect me?

CHAPTER XLIV
MORE FEZZES, THE POPE APPROVES, SKIN
TÎRGOVIŞTE
September 10, 1460

A second raid into Transylvania failed to meet its objective. As Dan had before him, Vlad the Monk managed to survive unscathed initially. Unlike Dan, however, Dragwlya's half-brother lacked the resources to mount a sizable offensive in retaliation. Despite his minor failure, Dragwlya had succeeded in guaranteeing the security of his northern border. Still, a permanent peace treaty would have to be signed, and an arrangement was already being drafted by Matthias. Before long, Dragwlya would be able to renew his oath and defend Christianity against Islam.

Mehmed relayed word to Constantinople that envoys were to be sent to Wallachia. Officially, their purpose would be to demand all past-due tribute be paid and for the principality to allow the Turkish access to Transylvania. The visit would serve the dual purpose of uncovering Vlad's true loyalties. As he continued his march across Anatolia, Mehmed grew increasingly displeased with the Wallachia's lack of commitment. This visit would serve to establish the benchmark by which Mehmed would approach his relationship with Vlad in the future.

From the moment they were recruited for the journey to Wallachia, the emissaries—Gürani, Hocazade, and Hatipzade—felt they had little chance of survival. Mehmed gave them specific instructions for negotiating and a sealed letter they were not to open until the morning they reached Tîrgovişte. Upon reading its contents, their worst fears were confirmed. Mehmed's edict ordered that under no circumstances were they to remove the turbans from their heads in the presence of the prince.

"He is sacrificing us." Hocazade had read Mehmed's note to the others and was the first to react.

"This is no diplomatic visit. It is a challenge. We are knowingly insulting Dragwlya." Hatipzade waited for a response from the others but did not immediately receive one.

None of them were fighters in any sense of the word. Each had lived a privileged life and did little more than enjoy the fruits of the empire. What they were being asked to do meant almost certain death, excruciating torture at the very least. Average height and build graced them all. Above average intelligence and wealth separated them from most but not enough so that they could disobey Mehmed's commands. Masking as best they could their fear and expectations of a cruel reception, the trio advanced.

Nearly half an hour passed as the Turks discussed with Dragwlya the demands of their sultan. At no time did the emissaries make an attempt to remove their turbans, a lack of respect noticed by the prince's entire court. Everyone, the envoys included, anticipated the moment when Dragwlya would order the armași present into action.

This is overt. They are aware of the punishment and have the appearance of three chickens cornered by a hungry fox. What compels them to act in such fashion? They defy etiquette but do not possess the ability to be defiant. It is a test. Mehmed wants to know my allegiance. Even if these men are acting on orders, they must be punished. They must learn the price of blind loyalty to the wrong person.

Just as he had with the Genoese delegation, Dragwlya ordered the armași to nail the turbans and fezzes of Gürani, Hocazade, and Hatipzade to their heads. The Turks were then taken into custody for an undetermined amount of time while the prince retired to prepare a letter to be sent to Brașov, warning them of the potential of imminent danger.

> … An embassy from Turkey had now come to us. Bear in mind that I have previously spoken to you about brotherhood and peace. The time and the hour have now come, where the Turks wish to place upon our shoulders unbearable difficulties and compel us not to live peacefully with you. They are seeking ways to loot your country passing through ours. In addition, they force us to work against your Catholic faith. Our wish is to commit no evil against you, not to abandon you, as I have sworn. I trust that I shall remain your brother and faithful friend. This is why I have retained the Turkish envoys here, so that I have time to send you the news.

Dragwlya knew he had risked his principality by showing his contempt. The brazenness with which Mehmed had insulted him could not be ignored, however, and in asserting his own power Dragwlya understood he was diminishing Mehmed's.

Information and misinformation abounded, but Dragwlya was willing to believe the spies whose reports indicated the likelihood Mehmed would pursue matters in Anatolia instead of trying to conquer the West in the near future. It seemed logical. Like Dragwlya, the sultan could not rest or advance without safeguarding himself from those around him. Mehmed would not be able to defeat Christianity while having to defend his own land in a civil war. At least this was the gamble Dragwlya was willing to take.

While Mehmed had his back turned to Europe, now would be the time to consolidate the leaders of the continent into a united front. Dragwlya would begin with the one man he knew to be open to defending his land from the onslaught of the Turkish.

ROME
October 23, 1460

Desperate for an end to the conflict, the city council of Brașov had met with Dragwlya's representatives. Peace could not come soon enough for the Saxons and, now that the fighting had ended, Matthias finally asserted his authority by claiming he would act as necessary in maintaining whatever accord was reached. After strenuous negotiations, a treaty was signed on the first of the month.

Primarily, the agreement called for the mutual extradition of Romanian boyars and political enemies of the city, the restoration of commercial privileges promised to the German cities in 1456, maintenance money to be paid to Dragwlya for a mercenary army of 4,000 to defend the townships from Turkish invasion, and restitution by Dragwlya to the German merchants of Sibiu and Braşov for losses suffered during his raids.

Upon learning of this last stipulation, Dragwlya had his lead representative impaled. Assent to such an outrageous demand made the prince think he would be viewed as remorseful for his actions, somehow wishing for forgiveness for a committed wrong. It undermined much of the progress he felt had been made. Nothing could be done to rectify it though. With Matthias backing the accord, Dragwlya would do nothing to encourage the king to march against him. Not when it meant jeopardizing the promise of an unthreatened border. Not when he understood where the true threat to his principality lie.

"Like his father, Vlad remains loyal to his faith, to his oath," Pius looked from cardinal to cardinal as he addressed them, gauging their expressions. "His land rests on the fringes of the Ottoman Empire. Is it any wonder he has such great interest in the organization of a crusade? I am told he was at one point in his childhood a hostage of the previous sultan. He knows firsthand what they are capable of, knows their methods, their tactics. He will prove invaluable as a defender of Christendom."

Unable to respond verbally to Pius' affirmation of Dragwlya as a potential Christian crusader, the cardinals shared knowing looks. Their inability to speak stemmed from their astonishment.

Had Pius not heard the actions this berserker had taken in Transylvania and his own principality? Embellished or not, the stories from German Catholic monks who had fled Transylvania, barely escaping with their lives, painted a picture of a bloodthirsty, tyrannical madman interested only in self-preservation and cruel punishment or death for those who violate the most insignificant laws and etiquette.

"Excellency, are you certain the fight to preserve Christ should involve men such as Prince Vlad? His reasoning for responding to your appeal would appear more self-serving than God-serving. He is not even Catholic. The stories of his atrocities involving the killing of monks, women, and children-"

"Yes, I have heard many of the stories of which you speak. From what I gather, Prince Vlad's methods of ruling have been utilized with the intent of maintaining his own principality." Pius had difficulty believing he was finding ways to justify his acceptance of the Wallachian's response to the call to arms. But the prince had been the first and only leader of Europe to show true indication he would willingly take up the sword against the Turks. Pius' desperation was beginning to overshadow his judgment. He wondered how much he could overlook, even in God's name. "Fighting is not for the faint of heart. Wars are fought and won by men such as him. If the prince wishes to charge in the name of God, I will allow him to do so. For the sake of Christendom, some of his eccentricities must be overlooked."

TÎRGOVIŞTE
November 19, 1460

"They were together in my own bed, sire! He bettered me and escaped before I was able to grab him. She won't tell me who he was!"

Dragwlya listened as the peasant before him explained details concerning his wife's adulterous relationship with an unidentified man. Her swollen eyes and face convinced the prince the peasant attempted to beat the answers he sought out of her. She was simply another tight-lipped whore, undeserving of a husband or of life.

"You could not recall your lover's name for your husband. You *will* do so for me." Dragwlya waited for a response. Understanding he would not receive one, the prince continued. "It appears you lack the willpower to abstain from desires of the flesh."

Because of the beating she had sustained, the woman would have barely been able to see him through her nearly closed eyes were she bothering to look at him.

"You show no respect for me. I can only conclude you lack respect for and obedience to your husband. Because you are unable to control your lust for skin, I will remove your burden."

Onlookers continued to fill every last space of Tîrgovişte's public square, drawn by the presence of the prince and the promise of an execution. Dragwlya stood alongside the husband of the accused woman, listening attentively as an armaş shouted out her crime and the sentence to be imposed.

Crippling shrieks of torment from the peasant woman blasted everyone's ears as Dragwlya's men carried out their orders. Bound, she lay naked upon a table, stretched out to capacity. Her cries and writhing had started as her sexual organs were cut. Like a thief losing his hands in the Arab world for stealing, Dragwlya first punished her by destroying the part of the body made offensive and unclean.

Uncertain what to think or feel, the woman's husband remained silent alongside the prince. He wanted desperately to turn away, knowing he could not. To do so would be seen as a sign of weakness by everyone, as though he were admitting his wife did not deserve such treatment. It would also be an insult to the prince's judgment and authority. Turning away might result in his death as well. Unwavering, he continued to watch the armași administer Dragwlya's justice.

Why is sin so irresistible? Is it an act of free will or Satan forcing his will to be done? If it is free will, it can be deterred by the punishment of those who engage in deeds such as this woman. But what if they cannot control themselves? What if they are possessed, carrying out, unbeknownst to even themselves, the commands of the Devil?

Dragwlya tried, to little avail, not to allow the questions to interfere with the scene before him. The armași were now beginning to relieve the woman of that which had caused so much temptation for her. As promised by the prince, the peasant was being relieved of her skin. With precision the armași skillfully began the task of flaying the woman alive. Her screams and the pain she felt were excruciating. Nerve endings sent impulse after impulse of agony to her brain from the tearing away of her skin. A gentle breeze that once would have passed over her body and cooled her engulfed her like flames. The pain would not last long.

If they are the ignorant servants of the Devil what, if anything, can be done to prevent such behavior? Dragwlya began to salivate at the sight of the woman's blood as it engulfed the table to which she has been bound. He could feel sweat accumulating in his fists. *Nothing… Nothing can be done to prevent it. It is the will of God, and my duty, to end the treachery and stop debasement when I am able to by ensuring it shall never again spring from the same poisoned source.*

Unceremoniously, the flesh once covering the peasant woman was put on a pole placed near the table. It would hang there until it fell, until the birds and other creatures picked at it and her corpse, until everyone in Tîrgoviște had the opportunity to see and learn. Some would heed the example set for them. Those who did not would ultimately suffer a similar fate.

CHAPTER XLV
MEHMED IGNORES THE INSULT
CONSTANTINOPLE
December 19, 1460

"**M**ore important matters require my attention."

"More *important* matters?" Radu was quick to question the sultan. "When this cruelty was inflicted upon the Genoese delegation and you believed it to be your own, you vowed his reign would not see the end of summer. Now he *has* insulted you. It *was* your emissaries, and you will do nothing?"

Mehmed saw the scars this time. It wasn't some wild tale told by a Turkish merchant. He had challenged Dragwlya and received a defiant response. He was satisfied the prince would never pay tribute, would never be loyal, and could no longer be trusted. But Dragwlya was not an immediate threat.

"Your brother is insignificant. His defiance is unfortunate but not unforeseen. Before long, when I am prepared to do so, I will remove him and place you on Wallachia's throne."

And when will that be, Radu wondered.

"In the eyes of your court, your people, and Europe, my brother defies you without suffering any consequences. Your lack of action makes you appear hesitant, as if you fear him in some way."

Mehmed laughed and shook his head as he responded. "You know well what fear looks like, don't you? You wear it well... In time everyone will see why I choose not to attack immediately. Your brother will come to know he has been defeated for quite some time."

WEST OF NICOPOLIS
February 12, 1461

Under the cover of darkness twenty-eight men led by Mihály Szilágy crossed the Danube from Wallachia into Turkish Bulgaria. Since Smederevo's fall, Mihaloğlu Ali Bey had been responsible for multiple raids on the Hungarian Danubian border territories. Mihály had led several reconnaissance missions into the occupied land in an attempt to better prepare those most susceptible to attack.

Silently, Mihály's party ventured along the river's bank and allowed it to determine their path. They would delve deeper into the forest and virtually disappear but only after coming much closer to Nicopolis than the ninety kilometers now separating them.

"You will proceed no further!"

Hearing the order, Mihály's men crouched immediately. It had come from their right, hidden among the trees. Mihály's eyes shifted from right to left, peering into opaque air, searching for the Turk who had given the order. Uncertainty gave way to anxiety as he imagined how many more Turks were ready to pounce upon them.

"Your position is surrounded. Any attempt to escape will result in your immediate death."

Not one man in Mihály's group dared move since stooping down. For all intents and purposes they were naked. Nothing hid them.

I have to assume we are outnumbered.

"Governor Szilágy, surrender peacefully and you and your men will not be harmed. If there is any delay on your part, I will not hesitate to execute your entire party."

How do they know I am here? How could they-

"I have followed your excursions for some time now, governor. This will be your last."

There is no other choice… It's an ambush.

Though he was compelled to resist, to fight until the last man in his party was dead, Mihály stood. Stunned adequately described his men's feelings. Never did they think he would give them up to the Turkish, yet one by one each of the twenty-eight rose, assenting with the course of action taken by him.

From the shadows more than fifty men appeared, including their leader. Mihály instantly recognized Mihaloğlu Ali Bey and wished he had ordered an attack. The bey's death would have possibly stopped the frequency of the raids taking place on Hungarian soil.

"Lay down your weapons."

Mihaloğlu Ali's words were ignored until Mihály nodded, a silent order for his men to comply. Once the last sword hit the ground, the bey commanded his soldiers to move forward and manacle the Hungarians. Mihaloğlu Ali personally chained Mihály.

"By order of the sultan, you and your men are charged with treason. Offer any resistance and you will be executed."

Mihály remained silent, arguing with himself instead of giving the bey an excuse to kill him.

February 27, 1461

"Impale them all, except for the governor."

Mihály cursed himself, his nephew, and sister for all of this. He and his men had marched for two weeks to Constantinople and were brought before Mehmed immediately upon arrival. The first words from the sultan's lips formed the death sentences of the twenty-eight men who had followed Mihály's every command. He had led them to the slaughter.

"Spare my men. They have done nothing but follow my orders."

Mihály found himself on his knees shortly after the plea, driven to them by a sharp pain resulting from a fierce blow to his calves at the hands of Mihaloğlu Ali.

"Do not dare speak to my master again, unless his commands you to do so."

Mehmed gave neither a response favoring nor disapproving the action, an indication to Mihály his men would indeed be executed, regardless of what he said. Remaining silent appeared more beneficial. From this point onward he resolved himself to do so completely, no matter the punishment.

March 1, 1461

Mihály stared at Mehmed through swollen eyes.

Nearly three days of torture and interrogation had yielded nothing. Mihály maintained his silence. Now, strapped to a table in the sultan's throne room, he continued to ignore the questions posed to him.

"What preparations have been made at Belgrade and Chilia since Smederevo's fall?"

Silence.

Razor sharp teeth from the saw's blade raked into the right side of Mihály's midsection. Before long he could feel them moving back, against the grain of the first cut, digging deeper into flesh and muscle. His body begged for him to cry out, to answer and relieve it of the pain.

Silence.

"What commitment has Prince Vlad given to Hungary?"

Silence.

Clenching his hands into fists, Mihály bit into his tongue. His fingers and toes were cold. His body, in an attempt of self-preservation, was moving blood from his extremities to where it perceived it was needed more. Nothing prevented its exit though, and the gash would do nothing but grow larger.

Finally, Mehmed gave up trying to obtain any information from the man. With a nod, he bade his men to mercilessly cut through the abdomen and spine of Mihály Szilágy.

Silence.

Nerves tingled, desperately searching for the rest of their own fibers as Mihály's exposed entrails began to slide out onto the table and to the floor. The two halves of his body writhed, squirming with determination to reconnect. In a flash his thoughts became jumbled. There was no focus, no organization. Nothing made sense. Quickly, he would succumb to the blackness clouding his mind.

For a nanosecond, he regained his faculties and an image flashed before him.

Damn you, Erzsébet.

Silence.

Hours after Mihály Szilágy's execution, Mehmed sat in council with his viziers and others to lay out his plans for the Ottoman Empire's immediate future.

"My liege, we agree with this course of action." Mahmud Pasha voiced the opinion of the majority of the viziers. "The leaders of Europe promise Pius much but bend to the will of those who fill their treasuries. The Italians have proven they do not care for this proposed crusade."

"Because of neglect, and my desire to control the West, the princes of the East have gone unchallenged. They are fully united against me and have grown strong. Their commitment is real, unlike Europe's. My brother-in-law's presence at Pius' congress proves that. They will do whatever necessary to take control of my empire. It is time to attend to the problem the East has become."

Nods of agreement for Mehmed's intentions abounded. Only those confident they could argue well their opposition voiced it.

"My liege, what of Hungary? Certainly they will retaliate."

All heads turned to stare at Radu, whose eyes failed to waver from those of Mehmed.

"They will do nothing. They will do nothing because they are alone. Europe will not fight for their god. Europe will certainly not go to war for Szilágy. Like they did when Smederevo and the city we inhabit now fell, they will squabble, place blame as to who is responsible until they can no longer remember the cause of their fighting. This Hunedoara does not worry me."

"And what about Vlad? He considered Szilágy a brother."

"My only regret is that Szilágy died without revealing any information about your brother's commitments to Hungary or about Belgrade itself…Wallachia is mine…A simple vassal state is not going to attempt an offensive against an entire empire. Your brother is mine."

Just as Mehmed had foreseen, Szilágy's death was viewed as an atrocity and incited outcries from even the Pope. As Mehmed had predicted, no one showed real signs of seeking vindication for the fallen governor, and plans continued for the sultan's campaign against David Comnenus. Unable to act against Mehmed for the murder of Mihály, Dragwlya felt some of the same helplessness he had upon learning of the deaths of Mircea and his father.

To Dragwlya, Mihály had become the brother he had lost in Mircea. Now twenty-nine years old, it had been more than seventeen years since Dragwlya had even seen Mircea alive. Mihály's face was vivid, as were his voice and mannerisms. Dragwlya and Mihály had fought side-by-side, and the former governor, on more than one occasion, had secured with Hungary Dragwlya's position as prince of Wallachia. The similarities Mihály shared with Mircea helped to spur their cultivated kinship as well.

Like Mircea, Mihály had been struck down in his prime, mercilessly tortured, and executed inhumanely. Mihály was older than Dragwlya. He shared with the prince knowledge and wisdom no one else had. As with the killers of Mircea, Dragwlya now yearned to bring the killer of Mihály to justice. Unlike exacting revenge against the boyars though, he understood Mehmed's sentence would not be carried out so quickly. With Europe's prevailing apathetic attitude, it would likely never occur.

CHAPTER XLVI
ȚEPEȘ
THE MONASTERY OF SAINT GALL
April 6, 1461

Nestled close to the Jura Mountains, the Monastery of Saint Gall's serenity could almost make a man forget Transylvania's recently changed landscape; its burned-out villages and fortresses and row upon row of impaled bodies. Almost, but not completely.

The monastery had become a host for refugee monks fortunate enough to survive the torching of their monasteries at the hands of Dragwlya. For many the only remaining possessions they owned were the horrific stories of how they came to find themselves so far from their homes.

"His own people call him Țepeș... *The Impaler.* It is far and away the method by which he delights most in killing." Tonight was the first time since his arrival to the monastery that Brother Michael found himself able to disclose all he knew and had heard about the Wallachian. Initially, not discussing the actions of this monster was easier. He now realized he would find relief only by informing as many as possible of the demon lurking near the Carpathian Mountains. "It is not the only method."

Spellbound by what they were hearing, the monks and scribes listening to Michael sat speechless, wanting him to continue with his tales but unable to ask him to do so.

"Some he has had crushed beneath the wheels of carts; others have been bound naked and skinned up to their waists while still alive."

Only one or two of the dozen or so in attendance even blinked. What he was telling them was implausible and incomparable to anything they had ever heard.

"He has roasted people on red-hot coals." Michael's voice cracked more as he continued. "But no other man living has explored impalement to its fullest like he has. Through people's heads, navels, buttocks, and their entrails until the stake emerges from their mouths. I have seen women with pales through both breasts with their babes attached to them." Some of the monks could not help gasping. The cruelty of this man was boundless. They wondered how much more Michael had to reveal. His demeanor changed abruptly from somber to disgusted.

"He enjoys eating amongst his victims and sometimes places a table in the middle or at the head of the pattern he has them arranged in to watch them suffer as he dines. I have personally witnessed him demand bowls of blood from these victims, which he then dipped his bread into and ate."

Revolted, a few of the monks stood and removed themselves from the conversation while the scribes worked furiously to record everything Brother Michael said.

"Many of his own people think him to be a *strigoi.*" Michael could see by the looks on some of the monks' faces they were unfamiliar with the Romanian term, and so he offered the German translation. "They believe him to be…*nosferatu*." Michael continued on as the others crossed themselves. "I assure you he is not. He is mad to an extent the world has never before known.

"He once asked me if God has a place reserved for him in paradise, if in fact he could be considered a saint, seeing as he had shortened the heavy burdens of so many unfortunates. Knowing what fate awaited me should I answer negatively, I told him he *could* obtain salvation; that God has saved many a tortured soul, even when His divine mercy was belatedly revealed at the moment of death. But that was not enough reassurance for him. He consulted another—Hans— and asked specifically what his fate would be in the afterlife.

"'Great pain and suffering and pitiful tears will never end for you,' he was told, 'since you, demented tyrant, have spilled and spread so much innocent blood. It is even conceivable that the Devil himself would not want you. But if he should, you will be confined to Hell for eternity.'

"Knowing his death was certain, Hans paused and asked that he might finish his sermon before having his life ended…Dragwlya consented.

"'You are a wicked, shrewd, merciless killer, an oppressor, always eager for more crime, a spiller of blood, a tyrant, and a torturer of poor people!' he continued. 'What are the crimes that justify the killing of the pregnant women you have impaled? What have their little children done, some of them three years old, others barely born whose lives you have snuffed out? You have impaled those who never did any harm to you. Now you bathe in the blood of the innocent babes who do not even know the meaning of evil! You wicked, sly, implacable killer! How dare you accuse those whose delicate and pure blood you have mercilessly spilled. I am amazed at your murderous hatred! What impels you to seek revenge upon them? Give me an immediate answer to these charges.'

"Dragwlya responded calmly, 'I will reply willingly and make my answer known to you now…When a farmer wishes to clear the land he must not only cut the weeds that have grown but also the roots that lie deep underneath the soil. For should he omit cutting the roots, after one year he has to start anew, in order that the obnoxious plant not grow again. In the same manner, the babes in arm who are here will someday grow up into powerful enemies, should I allow them to grow into manhood. I wish to destroy and uproot them. Should I do nothing, the young heirs will otherwise easily avenge their fathers on this earth.'

"Hans did not accept that as reason enough for his actions and again scolded him. 'You mad tyrant, do you really think you will be able to live eternally? Because of the blood you have spilled on this earth, all will rise before God and His kingdom demanding vengeance. You foolish madman and senseless unhearing tyrant, your whole being belongs to Hell!'"

Michael's voice had begun to tremble as its volume increased. Hoarsely he concluded the story.

"Dragwlya had him lie on the floor and, taking hold of a pale, repeatedly forced it into his head until the friar's screams and writhing subsided." Michael's mimicking of the prince stabbing the monk through the head visibly disturbed all around him. "He then had him strung up by his feet and hung outside his own monastery on the tallest of stakes…That was when the rest of us fled."

Michael's eyelids dropped, and there was silence for a moment.

"He treats his people like animals."

Methodically, Michael opened his eyes and stared for a few long seconds at the young man who had spoken before offering his response. "Exactly as he does animals… To make certain every bit of Hans was extinguished, Dragwlya ordered his donkey impaled as well."

BURSA
April 7, 1461

Alone inside the domed mausoleum of his father, Mehmed passed most of the last evening and night praying to Allah, asking his ancestors to watch over him in his conquest of Trebizond. He had yet to tell anyone of his exact plans and decided the success of his campaign hinged on not divulging any of his strategy until the moment the tactic should occur, a proposition that sat well with no one.

Mobilization began this morning with the simple order that the army was to move east. Comprised of three hundred vessels the fleet, under Admiral Kasĭm Pasha's command, was ordered to sail for the Black Sea. Mehmed revealed nothing more. An hour into the trek, the army judge approached.

"My liege, a vast fleet and more than one hundred and forty thousand follow you on foot, on horseback, and with artillery. Where are you leading them?"

Irritated, Mehmed stared at the man. "Do not ask me again… If the hair of my beard knew my plans, I would pull it out and burn it!"

TÎRGOVIŞTE
April 18, 1461

Dragwlya learned of Mehmed's campaign to recapture Trebizond. It was welcomed news. With the sultan otherwise occupied Dragwlya could focus on gathering support from those willing to crusade as the Pope had asked at Mantua more than a year ago. Even though he marched east, Mehmed's orders to those left behind in Serbia and Bulgaria continued to be followed, much to Dragwlya's chagrin.

"Again, my lord, I must report Turkish recruiting officers have crossed into Oltenia."
Dragwlya stared at the messenger. "How many this time?"

"Thirty-two, sire."

In addition to the ten thousand-ducat annuity, Mehmed had decreed that five hundred Wallachian boys would be delivered annually for service in the Janissary corps. Both conditions had gone unfulfilled by Dragwlya for three years now.

"Bring this message to those along the Danube from Oltenia to the Black Sea. Any Turkish commander caught stealing Wallachia's children is to be immediately impaled."

Certainly not unaccustomed to his master's impulsive edicts, the thought of providing the sultan with even more impetus to march against Wallachia still did not sit well with Priboi.

"Sire, I must advise against any policy that will assuredly widen the already formed rift in our relationship with the Turkish. We are lagging in our annual tribute to the sultan by thirty thousand ducats and have not met the request for five hundred boys annually during that time."

Dragwlya answered, unnerved by the facts. "I am aware of all of this, Priboi. I am also aware that in the view of the Ottoman Empire, Wallachia is a vassal state, not a Turkish territory. They violate their own provisions by venturing across the Danube and stealing our children. You said yourself we have not met their *requests*. Requests are not guarantees. Requests are not necessarily granted."

Priboi would not dare push Dragwlya any farther than he already had. "No, sire, they are not."

ROME
April 27, 1461

Just as I saved Paul from a life filled with sin, I have done so with you. Only through your guidance, your instruction, can Mehmed and his people be saved.

But how, father? How am I to accomplish this?

No answer came.

Father? How am I to accomplish this?

Again nothing.

Father?

"Father!"

Pius awoke suddenly and found himself alone.

ORSOVA
May 11, 1461

Lazily, the Danube flowed past the township of Orsova. With little humidity to

weigh it down, the breeze sweeping over the river was cool, giving relief from a week
of muggy nights. It would have been the perfect time to enjoy the change in weather,
but the entire populace had instead turned out to watch Dragwlya's men carry out their
orders.

Dragwlya's troops had captured six Turkish officers crossing into the principality on
a recruitment mission nearby. In accordance with the prince's decree, the men would be
impaled and put on display for those watching from the Danubian bank of Bulgaria to
see. It would be a sight the peasants had witnessed before, and the tenacity of the Turkish led few to believe this would be the last of such scenes.

TÎRGOVIŞTE
May 25, 1461

Before the end of June, the Church of Saint Nicolae at Tîrgsor would be erected. In
Dragwlya's mind, its completion would atone for the death of Vladislav II. Delighted
with his act and generosity, several priests from the city were dining with the prince,
updating him on the progress being made.

"It will indeed be a marvelous achievement, sire." The city's spiritual leader, Father
Jacob sat next to Dragwlya at the table. In his early forties, the priest was well respected
for being a true man of God and an authority on the subject of the Old Testament's
teachings. Everyone else present voiced their agreement. "Truly another example of the
numerous good works you have done."

"Thank you, Father Jacob."

"I would also like to commend you on the near extinction of crime in Wallachia."
More attuned to the Bible's 'an eye for an eye' teaching than its notion of 'turn the other
cheek,' Jacob truly meant what he had said. Though he felt the prince's methods in some
cases were severe.

"The safety of my people and respect for what belongs to them will forever remain
high priorities." Continuing with his meal, Dragwlya sliced a piece of bread from the
loaf in front of him and placed it beside his plate while Jacob expounded on the prince's
thought.

"Both worthy ideals, sire. The mark of a true leader is that he can protect those he
has been chosen by God to rule. After protecting them he must help ensure their possessions remain items whose personal value and integrity are respected by others. A
civilized society does not exist if people are allowed to lay hands upon the property of
others and take what does not belong to them."

More statements of agreement arose from the other priests. Concluding his re-
marks, Jacob picked up the slice of bread next to his plate and bit into it.

The priest's hypocrisy startled Dragwlya. After lecturing at length how sinful it was to lay hands on the possessions of another, the priest did not hesitate in taking Drag-wlya's bread.

"Why are you above such laws, Father Jacob? Or could it be you simply aren't civil?"

Somewhat unnerved by Dragwlya's question, those at the table all stopped what they were doing to stare at the prince, including Father Jacob who swallowed a mouthful of bread to answer.

"Forgive me, sire, but I am ignorant as to what you mean."

"You profess civilized society cannot exist when people take what does not belong to them, yet you indulge in the practice yourself."

Confused, Jacob sought clarification. "What have I done to make you think such a thing, sire?"

Matter-of-factly, Dragwlya answered both Father Jacob and the inquisitive faces of the others present. "Here, at my dinner table, you have stolen the bread I cut for myself to eat. How are you to be trusted with the spiritual leadership of my people when I cannot trust you while sitting by my side?"

Stunned by the prince's condemnation, Father Jacob stared at the hand that held the remnants of the slice he had picked up from off of the table. "Sire, the bread was by my plate. Naturally, I thought it had been given to me by you for my own consumption."

"Because something is within your reach you simply assume it is yours?"

Unsure of what to say, Jacob made the mistake of stating the first thing that came to mind. "Forgive me, sire, but how could I have possibly known?"

This was all Dragwlya needed to hear. Obviously, the man should in no way be responsible for the well-being of anyone's soul and could hardly be trusted with any monetary funding he would be provided as head priest of a newly constructed church.

"Like any man who is uncertain, or who harbors a bit of courtesy, it would have been wise to have inquired. Surely you have read the verse, 'ask and you shall receive'?"

Signaling to the armași in the dining hall, Dragwlya gave them the order to immediately have Father Jacob impaled. Utterly dumbfounded, the priest continued to argue his innocence over the simple misunderstanding to no avail. Dragwlya resumed his meal with the others as his men carried Jacob away.

The places where I find corruption no longer amaze me.

CHAPTER XLVII
MEHMED CONTINUES EAST & PIUS DREAMS AGAIN
ERZURUM
July 2, 1461

Mehmed's campaign took an abrupt turn northeast after reaching Ankara, aiming for Sinop on the Black Sea. Word had already been sent to Ismail Bey of his brother-in-law's imminent arrival and demand for surrender. Ismail Bey understood any attempt at resistance would simply prolong the inevitable. Sinop was handed over without any bloodshed, and the sultan gave Ismail Bey the city of Philippopolis and its vicinity as compensation.

Still cloaking his true intentions, Mehmed, instead of marching directly toward Trebizond, led his forces southeast along the military highway passing through Amasya and Sivas. He then headed due east, giving many the false impression he was moving against Uzun Hasan. Along the way, Sara Hatun, Hasan's mother, met with Mehmed and negotiated a peace for her son, promising he would no longer give aid to Trebizond. All efforts she made to include the Emperor of Trebizond in the negotiations failed dismally, however, as did her efforts to persuade the sultan from his plan to capture the city.

By tomorrow the fleet would arrive and begin the siege of Trebizond. From Erzurum, Mehmed would lead the army north and cross the coastal mountains to reach the doomed city. Finally, he revealed to his grand vizier his intentions.

"Once I have united Anatolia and shown I am deserving of the name *Warrior of the Faith*, I will take the West."

"My liege, while you seek supremacy in the East, the West continues to become more unruly," Mahmud Pasha said. "Nine more recruitment officers have been captured and impaled by Kazîglu Bey's men...His continues to insult you. Before long, he will march against you."

"March against me? You make me wonder if you are competent to serve as my grand vizier."

"I am in complete control of my faculties, my liege, and I promise Kazîglu Bey will take advantage of you if allowed to do so."

"Like too many others, you elevate him to an unworthy standing. I cannot fathom why. After Comneni is overthrown, I will show everyone how harmless Vlad truly is."

TÎRGOVIŞTE
August 3, 1461

For the fifth consecutive day, Elizabetha awoke nauseous. She had known since May that she was pregnant. That only one man could possibly be the father repulsed her initially, inspiring her to imagine ways to lose the baby. She wanted no part of bringing into the world the offspring of a man capable of all she had seen Dragwlya do. As the days passed though, she realized the child belonged to her, was a part of her, could be taught how vile and disgusting its father was, could work to restore her family's name.

"I am with child." Elizabetha stared at the beast before her, wondering if there had ever been anything good inside him.

Dragwlya returned her stare. Elizabetha was indeed inviting to look at, but there was never anything more than occasional physical attraction now. News of a bastard child did not upset or elate him. He was completely indifferent.

"You are certain it is mine?"

"I have never known anyone else, my lord."

Dragwlya detected the resentment in her voice but did not care enough to pursue the matter. He knew she was not lying as Smaranda had. There was nothing for Elizabetha to gain. She already lived like the princess she wasn't. He wondered how happy she was to be the mother of a future prince.

"You needn't worry. I shall care for the child greater than I have done so for you… The child will bear my name. It cannot be held accountable or responsible for its mother's lineage, that blame lies squarely upon my shoulders… Is there anything else you wish to discuss with me?"

Or that of its father! Elizabetha shouted internally as she answered she had no more to say.

"Very well." Upset God chose Elizabetha to be the mother of his child, Dragwlya watched in near revulsion as she walked away. *My compassion will be my undoing.*

TREBIZOND
August 16, 1461

David Comneni was hardly concerned with the assault his city had to defend against from Mehmed's fleet. Trebizond could not be taken by sea alone. Believing his closest ally, Uzun Hasan, was engaged in battle with the sultan's land forces, the emperor was confident in the knowledge the city had vast supplies of food and ammunition. Then came the report Hasan had made peace with Mehmed. Sightings of the sultan's army closing in on Trebizond confirmed this, compelling Comneni to negotiate a treaty. He would attempt to save whatever he could.

Less than a week had passed since Mahmud Pasha found himself fighting for his life after a Turkish assassin slashed his face just below his left eye. He was saved by the sultan's personal physician and two days ago delivered, in an unmistakable tone, Mehmed's demand for surrender to Comneni.

"To the Emperor of Trebizond of the imperial family of the Hellenes, Mehmed the Great King declares: You see how great a distance I have traveled after deciding to invade your territory. If you now surrender your capital without delay, I shall make over lands to you, as I did to Demetrius, the Greek prince of Morea, on whom I bestowed riches, islands, and the beautiful city of Aenos. He is now living at peace and is happy. But if you do not give ear to these proposals, know that annihilation awaits your city. For I will not leave this spot until I have leveled the walls and ignominiously killed all the inhabitants."

Comneni failed to call Mehmed's bluff. It could not be considered anything else. Had Comneni not lacked the spirit to withstand the sultan's onslaught, he would have succeeded by virtue of attrition.

In choosing the most roundabout route possible to reach Trebizond, Mehmed had crossed over the craggy, near barren mountains of Zigana, a trek lasting eighteen days. Passing over the range required leaving behind all siege guns and nearly all cavalry. Supplies were running low and had been for much of the latter part of the campaign, forcing Mehmed to simply bypass fortresses and castles against his will.

Upon hearing the emperor's terms for surrender, specifically that the city be turned over without anymore violence, Mehmed decided to take the city by force. Dissuaded from his rashness by his viziers, however, Mehmed took control after granting all of the emperor's terms.

"Breathtaking, my liege." Mahmud Pasha stood with Mehmed on one of the terraces of the golden palace that formerly belonged to the Comneni. The view was filled with lush gardens and valleys, vineyards and olive groves, flowing rivulets, convents and hospices. "The winter here will be pleasant."

Taking note of the many fountains below, Mehmed replied. "When Iacopo saved your life, did he remove your reason?"

Irked by the response, Mahmud suddenly felt the wound on his face begin to throb under the bandage, though nothing irritated it other than the sultan's question. "My liege?"

"Breathtaking as it may be, we will start for Constantinople before summer's end. I will spend the remainder of the year and the winter in Andrinople. The East is now attended to. The West beckons."

ROME
September 17, 1461

Save him, Pius… Save his people.
For the first time since the dreams had begun, Pius understood what God asked of

him.

He is Islam's defender, Father. How can such a man be converted?

You must show him, Pius... You must.

Pius awoke, void of drowsiness, as if he had not been asleep at all. The Pope left his bed, settled at a nearby table, and began to write. His hand scribbled furiously.

For my part there is no hatred toward you, for my Lord, *the* Lord, bids me to love my enemies and to pray for those who would persecute me. You are wrong to assume your weapons can conquer the Latin world as they have the Asiatics, Greeks, Serbs, and Wallachians. They are all infidels, heretics, and must be saved as well. You can rule among the Christians if you wish, and raise your name to great glory. To do so requires no money, no weapons, no armies, and no navies.

An insignificant trifle can make you the greatest, the most powerful, the most famous of living mortals. You ask what it is? It is not hard to find; there is no need to go far in search of it. It can be found everywhere: a little water with which to be baptized, to be converted to Christianity, and to accept the faith of the Gospel. Once you have done this there will be no prince on the whole earth to outdo you in fame or equal you in power. We shall appoint you emperor of the Greeks and the Orient, and what you have now obtained by violence, and hold unjustly, will be your possession by right. All Christians will honor you and make you arbiter of their quarrels. All the oppressed will take refuge in you as in their common protector; men will turn to you from nearly all the countries on earth. Many will submit to you voluntarily, appear before your judgment seat, and pay taxes to you. It will be given you to quell tyrants, to support the good and combat the wicked. And the Roman Church will not oppose you if you walk in the right path. The first spiritual chair will embrace you in the same love as other kings, and all the more so accordingly as your position is higher. Under these conditions you can easily, without war or bloodshed, acquire many kingdoms...We should never lend aid to your enemies, but on the contrary call on your arm against those who sometimes usurp the rights of the Roman Church and raise their horns against their own mother.

Just as abruptly as he had begun writing, Pius put the quill back in its resting place and returned to his bed. Relief took hold of him, enabling him to lay his head down and relax for the first time in what felt like years. Though the writing was not his own, he knew it would serve as the basis for ending the Islamic threat. God finally saw fit to show him the way.

CHAPTER XLVIII
MEHMED TURNS WEST
CONSTANTINOPLE
September 25, 1461

"No less than one hundred recruitment officers have been impaled, my liege."

"And the payment of this year's tribute?"

"Payment has yet to be made for this year...or the previous two. The request to provide five hundred males for the Janissaries has also not been met."

"You may leave."

Mehmed ran his fingers through his beard, allowing them to sporadically capture a few strands of hair between them.

"You have conquered the East and have every intention of taking the West. Why do you allow the leader of a vassal state to openly defy and insult you as much as this one, my liege?" Mahmud's frustration with the situation could be heard in his voice. Of course some of his anger derived from his wont to still be lounging on balconies overlooking the sea and countryside of Trebizond.

Mehmed's tone cautioned he felt no need to answer. "I have watched Kaziglu Bey for nearly all my life. If I can unlock the mystery of controlling him, he will cease being a liability. I will learn the secret and use him to push my authority deeper into Europe."

"Are you certain you have been watching?" Radu decided he wanted to rule Wallachia and could contain his desire no longer. At every opportunity, he urged Mehmed to eliminate Dragwlya. "My brother is irrational. Controlling him is equivalent to handling a flaming powder keg. Eventually, there will be an explosion."

"I agree, my liege." Mahmud did not concur with Mehmed's minion often. "Your interests would be best served by removing him." Mahmud's scarred face lent intensity to every word spoken.

"Wallachia is thriving. The economy is rich. Crime is virtually non-existent. Destroying that would be foolish...I will grant you he is wild."

Mahmud disliked the prospect. "Not wild, my liege. Rabid. Foaming at the mouth in anticipation of his next victim. Do not risk being bitten."

"You two would have me just put him down, whereas I will nurse him back to health."

Putting him down is the only cure, Mahmud thought.

TÎRGOVIŞTE
November 26, 1461

When word arrived that Matthias would agree to a strategic alliance, Dragwlya's confidence increased dramatically. Supported by Hungry, Wallachia would be able to withstand a Turkish attack and may even be able to crusade in an attempt to regain Serbia and Bulgaria.

Dragwlya needed time to secure ample support from wherever else he could. Any offensive against the Turkish could not be rushed. Unfortunately, Dragwlya began to believe he may have no other choice. Only yesterday a message arrived from Constantinople inviting him to come and meet with Mehmed to settle all differences. If not at Constantinople, the meeting could take place at any agreed upon city located within the Ottoman Empire. Instantly, Dragwlya's thoughts had turned to when he was a boy, when a similar message lulled his father into a trap.

He would not be so foolish. Immediately, the prince prepared a missive to deny the sultan's request, one that would have the added effect of making Mehmed believe Wallachia was in no way prepared or even capable of causing harm.

> ...because of the treacherous nature of the Saxons and the boyars of my own land, the past three years have forced me into relentless defense of my country. The almost constant struggle has exhausted my treasury and I regret I could not possibly pay the outstanding debt I am aware I owe...
>
> ... It is they who prevent me from paying you homage in person, for if I should leave my country my political opponents would invite the Hungarian king to rule over my domains. Should you send one of your trusted pashas to watch over the country, I could journey to Constantinople...
>
> ... I do wish for us to remain allied, and as a gesture of my loyalty will provide many children and horses, so that the sultan may not reproach me for not having served him well, and I will count the amount of the tribute and add gifts of my own...
>
> Wladislaus Dragwlya

Nearly every sentence he wrote was a lie. Dragwlya had no wish of finding mutual solutions regarding any matter with Mehmed. He simply had to prolong the calm before the storm.

CONSTANTINOPLE
December 10, 1461

Convinced of Dragwlya's willingness to serve him, Mehmed accepted his proposal and readied a diplomatic mission to be sent to Tîrgovişte led by the Bey of Nicopolis,

Hamza Pasha. The mission was designed to map out plans for repayment and to settle all territorial disputes along the Danube. Less than twenty-four hours after dispatching them, Mehmed had the party halted to await further instructions.

Earlier this morning a messenger arrived at the sultan's court and presented him with letters intercepted in Serbia. After examining them, Mehmed immediately ordered that Hamza Pasha should not be allowed to proceed, and a messenger was sent to stop him. The letters, en route to Buda from Wallachia, contained evidence of an established military alliance between Dragwlya and King Matthias, proving to Mehmed the Wallachian's treachery.

Mehmed exalted Mahmud Pasha's wisdom, vowing never again to disregard it and convened a council comprised of himself, Mahmud, Radu, and an envoy named Thomas Catavolinos. A Greek, Catavolinos understood power and knew Mehmed possessed it. Typically cocky, his words alluded to the fact his actions were backed by the approval of an empire.

"I have been naïve about Kazîglu Bey and will not allow him to dishonor me any longer." There was no anger in Mehmed's voice, but the others detected agitation. "Hamza Pasha will continue on to Giurgiu and wait there." The sultan looked directly at Catavolinos. "You will go to the Wallachian capital and escort the prince to the vicinity of the fortress where he is to meet with Hamza. You will inform Hamza of your progress so that he might know your exact time of arrival. There Hamza's force will ambush Kazîglu Bey and bring him to me."

"And what of Wallachia, my liege?" Mahmud asked the question Radu wanted the answer to.

Mehmed looked at his grand vizier. "Once Kazîglu Bey is in my custody, a contingent led by Radu will proceed to Wallachia. He will be invested as prince."

Radu's pessimistic nature caused him some discomfort. "Who else knows of this plan, my liege?"

"No one."

"My brother is famous for recognizing traps such as the one you are setting. The fewer sources he can learn of this from, the better its chances of success."

"There will be no failure." Mehmed's voice was stern. His words disallowed any further possibility of such thoughts. "You will be on the throne before the end of this year."

"Forgive me, my liege," said Catavolinos, "but why not simply march on Wallachia and take the throne by force? Why go through this charade to take what rightfully belongs to you?"

"I have asked much of my men this past year. The Trebizond campaign has taken a great toll on them. My preference is to handle this diplomatically."

TÎRGOVIŞTE
December 22, 1461

Dragwlya's suspicions were aroused after being told Hamza Pasha would not be making the journey to Tîrgovişte and that an envoy was being sent to escort him to Giurgiu. After the missive Dragwlya had sent, it made little sense for Mehmed to force him to leave Wallachia. The abrupt location change of the meeting had been equally perplexing.

"I am concerned, sire." Priboi verbalized both his and Dragwlya's thoughts. "The sultan has specific motivation for moving this meeting into his own territory...You *must* refuse to go."

"I no longer have that option, Priboi." Dragwlya's frustration made the head of his chancellery uncomfortable. "Mehmed has lost confidence in my loyalty. Disobeying him now would strengthen whatever feelings he has. I must agree to meet with Hamza Pasha on the sultan's terms, unless it is proven he wishes only to remove me from my throne."

December 23, 1461

"Catavolinos sends messengers, constantly updating Hamza Pasha of his location and his estimated time of arrival here in Tîrgovişte. When you arrive in Giurgiu, you are to be captured and brought directly to Constantinople."

With his small council in attendance, Dragwlya conversed with the spy who warned of the planned ambush prepared by Mehmed. In less than twenty-four hours, the prince had gone from the decision of appeasing the sultan to doing more than simply defying him.

"No one outside this room can know any of this." For a long moment Dragwlya was silent, quietly staring at the spy, then at the council, then at Priboi. "There is no alternative, I must strike first. I must do so now." The council became restless at the notion of Wallachia launching an offensive against the Ottoman Empire. Dragwlya quickly quieted them. "I have no other choice! He will kill me and take my throne if I do nothing! I cannot wait any longer for Rome or Hungry. This crusade is mine alone."

"Sire, how can you possibly hope to win?"

"I do not intend to retake Constantinople, just the Danube along Serbia. From there I will fortify my position and wait until help arrives from Matthias."

"And if assistance does not arrive, sire?" asked Priboi.

"It will. Matthias will honor the alliance. Once I prove to him the Turkish can be repulsed, he will aid in the fight. The Catholics will then join in the crusade proclaimed at Mantua."

NEAR GIURGIU
December 30, 1461

Thomas Catavolinos arrived, surprised to find Dragwlya ready to make the journey to Giurgiu. Based on the prince's reputation the envoy expected he would have to spend one night in the capital city for Dragwlya to make final preparations. Catavolinos found his eagerness to leave disturbing.

Hamza Pasha had the meeting site moved away from the sight line of the island citadel and surrounding area of Giurgiu, hoping to avoid attention. If any of Dragwlya's supporters were there, they would not learn of the prince's capture until it was far too late to do anything about it. He remained composed while watching Catavolinos lead the condemned prince to him. Kazîglu Bey's entourage consisted only of a small bodyguard. There would be little resistance met when the ambush was sprung. To maintain the appearance that this was a diplomatic mission, Hamza wore his finest ceremonial dress. Nothing about the trap looked or felt suspicious. His arrangements were perfect.

Hamza could see Catavolinos and Kazîglu Bey now discussing something that appeared to be upsetting the envoy. Suddenly, Catavolinos halted his steed. His facial expression was one of shock and despair. What happened next caused Hamza to feel the same. He was certain now of what the envoy had been told. Kazîglu Bey began shouting to his entourage, who in turn began shouting. The prince ripped Catavolinos from his saddle with a quick blow, sending the envoy sprawling to the ground. Kazîglu Bey then stared at Hamza as thunder shook the ground.

Hamza realized the rumbling was not coming from the cloudless sky. Emerging from behind the prince and his small bodyguard was a sizable cavalry, charging to attack. In informing only the necessary amount of men to stage an ambush, Hamza Pasha and his men were grossly outnumbered.

How could he know? Regaining his senses, Hamza began giving his men orders to arm themselves and attack. He would die giving his life for Islam and for Mehmed.

Before leaving for Giurgiu, Dragwlya gave the strict order that Hamza Pasha and Catavolinos were not to be killed, only captured, and that as many Turks as possible should be taken alive. To be certain no harm came to Catavolinos, Dragwlya stood watch over the body of the unconscious envoy as his men flew past. The skirmish would not last long.

"What do you intend to do to us?" Hamza Pasha's pathetically weak words were as much a plea to be killed mercifully as they were a question.

Within thirty minutes, every last soldier of the failed Turkish ambush was captured or killed. Dragwlya stared at the bey and the envoy.

"Your master was foolish to believe I would be duped so easily by such simpletons."

His gaze elicited no response. "For this feeble plan you were willing to sacrifice your lives?"

"So, you will have us put to death," said Hamza. "My master will have your head for it!"

Unaffected, Dragwlya coldly responded. "If your master cared for you at all, he would have taken greater pains to assure your survival."

"What is it?"

Shortly after nightfall, the sentries had summoned the Turkish garrison commander at Giurgiu.

"Sir, a small cavalry is approaching."

"Whose cavalry?"

"Ours sir, although there has been nothing to indicate such a force would be arriving."

Straining to see through the haze of twilight, the garrison commander identified the men as wearing the uniforms of Turkish soldiers, though some appeared badly tattered and stained.

Dragwlya led the procession of his men, all disguised as Turks, to the gates of the citadel. They had taken the uniforms of those captured and of those who had fallen during their short battle.

In flawless Turkish, Dragwlya began shouting. "Let us in immediately!"

"Identify yourself!" The garrison commander squinted, trying futilely to recognize the leader.

"We are returning from a secret mission ordered by the sultan himself, led by Hamza Pasha!"

Recognizing the name of Hamza Pasha, the commander immediately inquired to his whereabouts.

"The Bey of Nicopolis has been slain! Our mission was to capture Kaziglu Bey and bring him to Constantinople! We were defeated and forced to retreat here! I fear the prince of Wallachia is not far behind and will attempt an attack! We must be allowed to enter before he arrives!"

Hearing the name of *The Impaler* prompted the garrison commander to order the opening of the gates. Eagerly, he raced down to speak further with the man now leading the cavalry.

With much of his force now inside of the fortress, Dragwlya waited for the commander to approach. Repressing the urge to charge toward him, he allowed his men to disperse themselves deeper among the Turkish soldiers of the garrison. Eventually, the commander arrived and stood beside him.

"You may be in command of this contingent, but I am commander of this garrison and Giurgiu. Dismount and show proper respect."

Smiling cruelly, Dragwlya destroyed the man's hard glare with a glance. In one fluid movement he drew his sword and killed the commander with a devastating thrust. The sound of the man's body hitting the ground was accompanied by Dragwlya's order to attack.

Seeing their commander die so unexpectedly sent the garrison into utter chaos. No one was prepared to assume control quickly enough to disseminate orders and, even if they had done so, Giurgiu was a free-for-all in which only commands given beforehand could be followed.

Dragwlya had the citadel set aflame, plunging the Turkish into further disarray. Not knowing whether to fight the fires or Dragwlya's men, the confused Turkish garrison segmented into smaller fragments that were easily captured. Before long, Dragwlya and his men were looting Giurgiu. Entering the home of one of the prominent citizens, Dragwlya found two slaves bound, kneeling on the floor. Immediately recognizing him, the slaves began to chastise the prince.

"Our master will avenge us for your crimes!" Dragwlya watched the elder slave's mouth open and close, spitting out the bold proclamation. "After this, the sultan will no longer listen to your lies!"

The second slave was just as brazen as the first. "Wallachian swine! Your stench and your treachery will be known throughout the Islamic world!"

Calmly, the prince walked over to the younger of the two slaves. Emotionless, Dragwlya produced a knife and grabbed the right ear of the man. Instantly, the slave began thrashing around to avoid the blade. Tightening his fist around the handle of the knife, Dragwlya pulled it back and threw a punch that landed squarely between the eyes of the slave, effectively stunning him. Again the prince grabbed the right ear of the man and sliced through it, cutting it off. He repeated the process with the slave's left ear and then, pulling his head back by his hair, Dragwlya placed the blade at the base of the man's nose and began sawing upward.

Certain of his fate, the older slave began struggling to escape by inching away. Ultimately, he lost his balance and, after falling over, squirmed along the floor on his side. Managing to move only a few feet, he started screaming when he felt a hand take hold of his ear and warm metal piercing it. Dragwlya then grabbed the other ear and, after using it to turn the slave's head, repeated the action. The slave continued to scream as the prince proceeded to cut off his nose.

Flinging the useless piece of skin and cartilage across the room, Dragwlya quietly exclaimed to both of them, "Now neither of you will have to listen with your ears to my deceit or smell with your noses my stench."

CHAPTER XLIX
DRAGWLYA ATTACKS
CONSTANTINOPLE
January 21, 1462

"He controls every major port along the Danube on both the Wallachian and Bulgarian banks, from Vidin to Brăila." Pausing, Mehmed stared at his grand vizier to allow him time to comprehend how fantastic the statement sounded. "How, in only two week's time, did he manage to accomplish this?"

Mahmud Pasha wondered why he had chosen to personally deliver the news to Mehmed. "The winter has been harsh, my liege. The Danube is frozen in some areas, expediting crossing from one side to the other. Kazîglu Bey divided his army into smaller forces and sent them in opposite directions to accelerate his attack. He continues to stay at Giurgiu."

"Where are Hamza Pasha and Thomas Catavolinos?"

Mahmud's head sank before he could prevent it from happening. His response was unnecessary. "Hamza Pasha and Thomas Catavolinos were led toward Tîrgovişte, along with more than one thousand others. Kazîglu Bey had them impaled... after nailing their fezzes and turbans to their heads." Mahmud's eyes sprung up immediately at the sound of his master's cursing.

Mehmed had stood up and was charging toward the grand vizier, propelled by anger. In an instant Mahmud found himself on the receiving end of a thrashing he dare not defend against. Blow after blow struck his head and body until Mehmed felt enough blood had spilled onto his floor.

Radu stared at Mehmed, now pacing around Mahmud like a caged tiger, wondering if the sultan would continue his barrage. None of Dragwlya's previous actions had caused such furor. Seeing Mehmed pummel his own grand vizier in this manner convinced Radu his brother had finally exceeded the sultan's limit. A full-scale invasion would no doubt be ordered. Tîrgovişte would be the primary target.

Mehmed shouted at Mahmud like a parent reprimanding a disobedient child. "Your failure to anticipate his reaction to the ambush has led to the deaths of two high ranking officials and thousands of my best men!" Mehmed could not hold himself accountable for this failure.

He is lecturing himself, Radu thought. This was not the first time he had witnessed the sultan transfer his own faults onto someone else.

"You will repair the damage you have done... Get up."

Mahmud's voice faltered in no way as he answered. "What is your command, my liege?"

"Wallachia *will* become my territory, and I will place in command someone who will have no difficulty obeying any of my provisions." Mehmed glanced at Radu. Just as quickly his gaze returned to Mahmud. "You will sail to Brăila and raze it. Once you have done so, I will arrive with reinforcements.

"Before summer, Kazîglu Bey will suffer the fate he has inflicted upon so many."

GIURGIU
February 2, 1462

> By the grace of God, as I was journeying to the frontier, I found out about
> their trickery and slyness, and I was the one who captured Hamza Bey in the
> Turkish district and land, close to the fortress called Giurgiu.

What more can I write to convince Matthias he must send troops to aid me?
Dragwlya continued to hold his quill slightly above the parchment, hoping the necessary dialogue would either enter his head or appear before him. When neither instance occurred, he raised his eyes and rested his gaze upon the decapitated bodies of three of the more unruly villagers he had executed recently.

How many must I purge before others are convinced they must join me? After a moment, Dragwlya realized how to gain Matthias' immediate support. *My success can be quantified. Sheer numbers will persuade him.*

BRĂILA
February 8, 1462

Mahmud Pasha surveyed the devastation and contemplated the future. Accompanied by more than twenty thousand men, the grand vizier reached the port of Brăila and did exactly as commanded by Mehmed. In many places structures continued to burn. In most areas the city had been reduced to rubble.

The force I command nearly doubles that of Kazîglu Bey's entire army.

Mahmud had never perceived them as an insult, but the blows he received by Mehmed's hand for the deaths of Thomas Catavolinos and Hamza Pasha now weighed heavily on his mind. Even though he understood their murders were not his fault, there still existed in him the desire to return fully to his master's good graces. The ease with which Brăila had fallen convinced him more could be done, that the answer to pleasing Mehmed involved exceeding expectations dramatically.

I must regain that which Kazîglu Bey has stolen, without Mehmed's assistance. Once he sees I have restored the Danube and knows it is within my reach to hand him the entirety of Wallachia, my rightful stature will be reclaimed.

TÎRGOVIŞTE
February 9, 1462

"You will be nothing like him." In less than a whisper, Elizabetha addressed her newborn son. Dragwlya's son. The boy bore the almond shaped eyes of his father and the same nose, lips, and chin. There was no doubt of his lineage. "Nothing like him at all, Mihnea." Her voice trembled and nearly failed as she said this.

Elizabetha reasoned that if Mihnea looked exactly like his father, perhaps he would think and act the same way. It was tortuous for her to even conceive such a thing to the point she prayed she had not brought into the world another sadistic madman.

"You'll be nothing like him because I won't let you ... I won't. I will save you from him, regardless of the consequences ... No matter what."

Throughout her pregnancy, Elizabetha had questioned how far she would go to make certain her pledge was carried out. Only now did she realize the sole way to save Mihnea's life may be to take it from him. The thought horrified her. She could hardly fathom taking her own life. How could she possibly end the life she held most valuable?

Were she to commit suicide, Elizabetha knew her soul would burn for taking what belonged to God. If she killed her child, again she would be consumed by hellfire, but Mihnea would be saved and would remain in Heaven forever. His eternal salvation far outweighed her soul's eternal damnation.

"No matter what," she whispered once more.

BRĂILA
February 16, 1462

A second missive sent by Dragwlya yesterday again implored Matthias for reinforcements. While word from Hungary was sporadic, scouting reports from the East were plentiful, though disturbing. Mahmud Pasha had organized a party of eighteen thousand for the purpose of raiding deep into Wallachia. Villages were being burned and pillaged. Their inhabitants were being captured when convenient and led away, never to return.

Dragwlya wasted no time preparing to retaliate. Mahmud Pasha's attacks against innocent peasants were irritating. That the areas he attacked were so near the heart of Wallachia was unsettling. Assembling his army without delay, Dragwlya marched toward Mahmud's staging point. Now, undetected by the Turkish, Dragwlya's army stood ready to charge.

Because of their leader's self-assuredness, his overconfidence, Mahmud's rear guard was about to be overrun while attempting to cross the Danube into Dobruja. The number of Turkish soldiers remaining on the west bank was considerable, and the loss of life would be great. Conservatively, Dragwlya estimated five thousand of their ranks would be killed.

BUDA
February 18, 1462

Matthias could not place the odd odor in his throne room. It had arrived with the envoy of Prince Vlad and, as best he could determine, was emerging from the large sacks before him. The Hungarian king chose to read Vlad's correspondence before inquiring as to the contents of the sacks, but increasingly his attention was distracted by what had become a sickening smell.

> I have killed men and women, old and young, who lived at Oblucitza and Novoselo, where the Danube flows into the sea, up to Rahova, which is located near Chilia, from the lower Danube up to such places as Samovit and Ghighen. We killed 23,884 Turks and Bulgars without counting those whom we burned in homes or whose heads were not cut by our soldiers.

The date of Vlad's letter flashed again in Matthias' eyes. *Seven days ago.* He continued to read. Like an accountant would money, Vlad had counted his victims. Their numbers were documented for each township attacked, giving Matthias an idea of the prince's path.

> At Giurgiu there were 6,414; at Eni Sala, 1,350; at Durostor, 6,840; at Orsova, 343; at Hirsova, 840; at Marotin, 210; at Turtucaia, 630; at Turnu, Batin, and Novogra, 384; at Sistov, 410; at Nicopolis and Ghighen, 1,138; and at Rahova, 1,460.

Matthias grew queasy, though not because of the statistics. The odor was intensifying every second to the point of being unbearable, and the Wallachian's envoy, Farma, looked every bit as disgusted as the king.

"What have you brought into my home?"

The envoy had to force the answer from his lungs, wishing to take as few breaths as possible.

"Your highness, my master offers you proof he has broken the peace with Sultan Mehmed." Farma's words were strained as he resisted the impulse to breathe deeply. "He felt it necessary to-"

"Tell me what it is now." Matthias' voice did not raise to the point of yelling, but the tone effectively communicated he refused to wait for a direct answer any longer.

Since starting on his mission to Buda, the envoy had rehearsed this moment, repeatedly editing his phrasing to explain the contents of these two giant sacks. Even with all of the rehearsals, his response was repulsive and hearing himself say it aloud nearly drove him to vomit.

"Your highness, these bags contain body parts from those killed."

In not saying anything and only offering a questioning look, the king expressed he wanted the envoy to continue.

"They contain the ears, noses, and heads of those overrun by the army of my master."

Matthias remained still. There existed in him no desire to peer into what he could only imagine to be the most gruesome of sights. It surprised him little though that Dragwlya thought to go to such lengths to gain favor and support. Matthias found that the most frightening of all.

Suppressing his disgust, the king stated softly, "Remove them from my home immediately." With the order being carried out, Matthias' eyes fell back to the correspondence he still held.

Thus Your Highness must know that I have broken the peace with him.

Processing the line, Matthias realized the scope of what Vlad had accomplished.

He controls the Danube to the Black Sea. Mehmed has no means of getting his ships up the river unless he battles through the Wallachian's defenses … Uncle was right. His strategic abilities are unparalleled, despite his madness…But his actions are rash. This will incur Mehmed's full wrath. Nothing will stop the Turkish from launching a full invasion aimed right at Wallachia and then Hungary.

We will all suffer because of this.

CHAPTER L
THE FIGHT CONTINUES & ELIZABETHA'S DECISION
CONSTANTINOPLE
February 21, 1462

Mehmed wanted to disbelieve the reports, was certain each account he had heard could not be factual. But now Mahmud Pasha, his grand vizier, knelt before him in utter humiliation after recounting the events at Brăila. There was no denying the truth.

"Do you recall the blows you received before embarking on your mission to capture Brăila?" The question, confusing to Mahmud Pasha at the moment, left him silent far too long. "Obviously, they did little to enhance your ability to follow my orders." Mehmed remained seated. Were he to stand, he would either collapse or within seconds end the vizier's life with his bare hands. "The army of twenty thousand I placed under your command now numbers only eight thousand."

"My pride is to blame, my liege," Mahmud responded without daring to glance upward.

"Your *pride*?" Mehmed considered rising to deliver a death strike. "You believe your *pride* to be worth more than ten thousand of my men?"

Mahmud gathered enough courage to stare into Mehmed's eyes. "Of course not, my liege. My intentions were honorable. I only wished to regain your favor."

"Do you believe you have?"

Steadily, the weight of Mahmud's disgrace forced his eyes and head down.

"Get out of my sight…Do not return unless you are commanded to do so."

Without breaking visual contact with his feet, without answering, Mahmud Pasha rose to slink away from the sultan.

"He has brought the fight to me. He desires war. I will no longer deny him his wish."

ROME
March 1, 1462

News of Dragwlya's exploits spread from Wallachia to the West, where word reached Pius' ears.

"Truly remarkable…remarkable," the Pope commented to one of the more aged cardinals. "How is it possible for a man to succeed facing the odds he does? Where does he get the drive?"

"He fights like Hunedoara did."

Immediately, the name conjured up images of the crusader in the mind of the Pope. Memories were quickly recalled of a time when everyone answered the call to crusade.

Pius wondered if Dragwlya could inspire such unity. "Yes, very much so."

"I believe because he is forced to."

"Oh?" Intrigued, Pius allowed the man to continue.

"The Wallachian is much like Hunedoara in that his spirit will not enable him to be ruled. Just as his father and his grandfather before him, he must rule. Wallachia belongs to him, to those of his blood. He will see no other control it."

"And why is that?"

"Because he would rather die."

TÎRGOVIŞTE
March 20, 1462

> You also may have heard that the sultan has set up a huge army against us. If this land of ours is subjugated, please realize that they will not stay content with our land but will immediately make war on you, and the inhabitants of your land will suffer great misfortunes at their hands.
>
> So now is the time: by helping us, you really help yourself by stopping their army far from your own land and by not allowing them to destroy our land and harm and oppress us.

Dragwlya could not recall the amount of times he had written down such sentiments in the past few weeks in letters intended to reach far west and east. Not one request for aid had been answered. Desperate for an assured alliance with the Hungarians, Dragwlya even proclaimed his desire to marry into the royal family. Knowing he was preparing for all out invasion, he was willing to do anything.

There would be no yearly tribute, concessions, or mere subjugation. Instead, a force the likes of which Europe could hardly imagine would sweep into Wallachia, intent on complete domination.

BUDA
March 28, 1462

> If, God forbid, we should fail, the consequences of such a Turkish victory would be severe for all Christianity.

Dragwlya's latest correspondence was proving to be the most compelling to Matthias.

That the Wallachian's words showed he firmly believed his land would soon be invaded, and by such a sizable force, piqued Matthias. Not of the mind-set to panic or be swayed by words alone, however, the king of Hungary paid little attention to the Wallachian's argument that any support would have to arrive before April 23rd. The prince's willingness to marry into his family compelled him somewhat, but not enough for Matthias to change his focus or curb his own desires.

"Until the crown is mine, I will not give Frederick the opportunity to rid himself of me by committing the bulk of my army for the purpose of saving Wallachia." Matthias had already told his chancellery his intentions. Merely to satisfy their curiosity, he explained himself.

The Holy Roman Emperor possessed the one thing that would give Matthias' rule legal sanction—the Crown of St. Stephen. Until he held it in his own hands, Hunedoara would refuse to leave himself vulnerable for any easy attack the lack of an army would invite.

"Word will be sent to Chilia for my garrison there to aid the Wallachian, should the Turkish move on the fortress. That is all I will commit."

TÎRGOVIŞTE
April 7, 1462

Silence returned to the early morning once Mihnea began feeding. Elizabetha looked down to watch her infant son suckle, absentmindedly estimating how long it would be before the sun began to rise, wondering if a day would soon come when it failed to do so.

Rumors circulated that before long the banners of the Turkish would appear in Tîrgovişte, signaling the absolute domination of Wallachia. Reports of a massive force being gathered by the sultan struck fear in the boyars, some of whom were foolish enough to suggest to Dragwlya that he succumb to every last demand and request of Mehmed.

Made privy both directly and indirectly to much of the information gathered, Elizabetha's fears were growing with each account of more divisions being added to an army whose only purpose was to completely wipe out every last facet of Dragwlya's reign.

"You are worried."

Startled by the voice, Elizabetha nearly jumped from her seat. The jolt inconvenienced Mihnea for a few seconds before he again found her nipple. Settling back once more, Elizabetha searched through the dim light and could see Dragwlya's eyes fixated on her from the bed. Choosing to ignore him, she let her gaze fall back to her son, their son.

"You should be." Dragwlya's eyelids closed, "Mehmed will find every last man he can, every last cannon, ship, arrow...Whatever it takes, he will succeed in taking Wallachia from me. I assure you."

"What makes you think I am worried?"

Dragwlya opened his eyes again. He expected her to remain silent for much longer than she had. For some time now, he could see her weakening, her spirit diminishing. "The way you look at him."

Elizabetha's head rose, allowing her to meet Dragwlya's stare. He had meant Mihnea.

"I look at him with the love and concern every mother has for her child."

"No. You look at him with fear, as though you are imagining him as a prisoner...as though you are imagining yourself as a courtesan."

"Neither will ever happen." Elizabetha's words were hushed, but the emotion was unmistakable.

Dragwlya knew were she not currently holding Mihnea she probably would have attacked him for even suggesting such a thing. He stirred and leaned toward her while supporting the weight of his torso on one arm. "And how will you prevent it?"

Her answer was not instantaneous. "It will never happen."

Elizabetha had reached a conclusion she had not thought possible. She now knew, truly knew, that if it came to answering the ultimate question of life or death she would willingly answer death for both herself and Mihnea.

Dragwlya let his body slump back down and shut his eyes. "Don't do anything extreme." Failing to receive any sort of response after a few minutes, Dragwlya addressed Elizabetha once more before falling back asleep. "They will attack, and we will be overrun. We will flee to the North. Hopefully reinforcements will arrive with at least enough men to rescue us."

Elizabetha retorted silently. *And if they don't, I will do everything to ensure my child will be free forever.*

CHAPTER LI
MEHMED MAKES LANDFALL
CONSTANTINOPLE
April 15, 1462

"**H**e is unlike any man I have ever faced."

Mihaloğlu Ali Bey felt the heavy weight Mahmud Pasha's words carried. Filled with fear, they came from the lips of a defeated soldier, one futilely fighting the reality that he had been beaten.

"You speak as though you have already conceded."

Mahmud Pasha raised his head to face the bey, confident it was the first time during this entire conversation he had done so. "Perhaps I have."

The response did not shock Mihaloğlu Ali in the least.

"I am ashamed to admit that I have given serious thought to fleeing...I am not the only one."

The bey feigned surprise. "Oh?" Mihaloğlu Ali was not hearing this sentiment for the first time. Still, it intrigued him that yet another trusted in him enough to confide such treachery.

"There are others who feel the way I do."

"And what will you and those like you do when Mehmed hunts you down for this betrayal?"

"He will not be alive to do so."

Certainty dominated Mahmud Pasha's voice, and Mihaloğlu Ali finally heard what all had been trying to express. They feared not only for their own lives but for the life of the empire.

"If you and those who think as you do choose to flee, Mehmed will indeed die," Mihaloğlu Ali lightly laid his hand on Mahmud Pasha's wrist. "Mehmed will fight, with or without you. He will march regardless of whether you and those who think like you are there at his side. Without you he will lose and will be at the head of a shapeless, directionless mob when he does so." Mihaloğlu Ali withdrew slightly. "You must decide how you are going to portray the Ottoman Empire for those yet to come. Will they see a weak people, fearful of a single man who kept them from conquering the world for Allah? Or will they recognize those who stood together in adversity in all its forms for *His* greater glory?"

TÎRGOVIŞTE
May 4, 1462

True to his word, Matthias sent no additional aid, and the day by which Dragwlya had hoped assistance would arrive came and went without anyone answering his pleas. His force would number less than thirty-thousand, including cavalry, and would be attempting to hold off another that by all accounts was already well over twice that size.

Nine days ago a supply fleet of one hundred seventy-five vessels had sailed. By way of the Black Sea, it would enter the mouth of the Danube and venture inland as far as possible.

"He remains in Constantinople, but will not do so for much longer. From what intelligence we have managed to gather, I am confident he will march within two weeks."

Little changed in the reports Dragwlya's spies had brought him over the past week. They continued to tell him Mehmed was coming but not when. He was beginning to grow impatient with their lack of information and considered impaling a few to have the others reassert themselves in their effort to discover the exact date the sultan would embark on his campaign.

"Is there any word from the envoys?" Dragwlya asked.

The prince's question was fielded by another member of the chancellery, but the response was just as useless.

"The ambassadors have yet to return, my lord, and no correspondence has been sent."

Though the responses were all dismal, Dragwlya had expected every last one of them. He now saw how ignorant and uninformed the leaders of Europe were in their understanding of the Turkish, of exactly what was going to happen.

TURNU
June 5, 1462

Furiously, Dragwlya rode along with his cavalry and entire force. Mere miles away from his main camp at Turnu, the Turkish had begun to disembark last evening.

After having two spies executed for their failure to learn Mehmed's plans, Dragwlya quickly mobilized. Dawn had arrived, and he was certain the sultan's forces had made landfall. Little question remained in his head as to whether Mehmed was already marching to meet him. Upon his arrival, Dragwlya found the whole of the Janissary corps and Mehmed's infantry deeply entrenched to ward off any major attack by cavalry. Surprisingly, the sultan had yet to cross the river.

Mehmed watched from the opposite bank as some three hundred Janissaries were killed before the firepower of his cannons managed to force Dragwlya back. Despite the loss of men, Mehmed had gained a firm foothold. Dragwlya's withdrawal signaled to the sultan it was time for he and the rest of his retinue to cross into the land he would soon control.

Retreating into the marsh and dense forest nearby, Dragwlya knew there would be no more battles for his army, not in the traditional sense at least. Fighting for the Wallachians would now consist of a systematic retreat, one insuring the least amount of resources would be left behind for Mehmed to utilize. Assessing what remained of his forces would be Dragwlya's first priority.

Passing through squad after squad, Dragwlya examined the wounds of his men. While he did so to make certain the bulk of his army was still in fighting condition, the main intent of this action was to sort out those who were not in optimal condition, specifically those who would betray him should the opportunity arise. Stripped to their waists, the men waited, arms extended, palms down. Though the grime was caked on in layers, the red of blood was easily identified. In some cases it continued to flow.

Stopping only briefly in front of each individual, Dragwlya searched their bodies in one glance down the front and then up again for their backs. Those that had sustained any injury to the front of their bodies were given a few gold ducats. Those suffering any significant damage to their backs were treated much differently. Dragwlya could only conclude that if a man's back had received any major trauma, it was because he was running away from the battle, fleeing when he should have been fighting.

"You are not a man; you are a woman."

Wounds obviously made by the piercing of arrows marked the left shoulder and lower left back of the peasant soldier Dragwlya stood before. Upon being called a woman, his eyes shut tighter. A second later he began to turn around to face his prince.

"Do not face me." Dragwlya's tone remained civil. "The evidence before me proves your complete lack of respect. Do not force yourself to look at me. It is obvious you would rather not."

CHAPTER LII
NIGHT ATTACK
NEAR BUCHAREST
June 11, 1462

Wallachia is not worthy of the effort I am exerting, Mehmed thought.

Over the past six days the Turkish had marched north until reaching the monastery of Glavacioc and then moved west. The bulk of Mehmed's force now lie in wait near the banks of the Dîmbovița River and Bucharest. Until now, Mehmed's men had done little to diminish Dragwlya's contingency.

Retreating north toward Tîrgoviște, the prince moved methodically, ordering the abandonment of villages as he went. The Turkish found only deserted hamlets and went days without seeing a soul or finding anything of value. Crops, and most homes, were burned. Pastures were devoid of herds, which had either been led away or slaughtered. Dragwlya had also ordered dams be built to reroute rivers to create more marshy conditions, more havoc for the sultan's beleaguered army. All wells were poisoned, making it nearly impossible for the Turkish to find fresh water. Thirst was compounded by the inescapable sun, relentlessly beating down. Mehmed's men were beginning to doubt his strategy and were growing more fearful of their enemy.

Disease riddled the Turkish camp. Some suffered from plague, but leprosy and tuberculosis were the main worries. Unbeknownst to the Turkish, the rash of illnesses was somewhat unnatural in origin. Disguised as Turks, Romanians hopeful of a reward should they survive both the sultan's soldiers and their own illnesses, agreed to infiltrate and spread their sickness.

Mehmed's experience taught him his enemies were more willing to cooperate if they were rewarded for betrayal instead of threatened with torture. Regardless what he offered though, the sultan found his gifts refused by the peasant soldier of Dragwlya's army standing before him. Captured in battle, the man had done all he could to die fighting. Ultimately, he was overcome and brought before the sultan to provide any information he might possess. Hardly a minute passed between the moment the interrogation began and the moment the soldier interrupted his interrogator.

"I realize that my life is in your hands and you will order me to be killed, but you will find out nothing from me about my master. I want to die for my country and not betray him."

Everything about this campaign has been difficult, thought Mehmed.

Mobilization was difficult, planning for the unorthodox methods Dragwlya was using was nearly impossible, infiltrating the Wallachian's camp *was* impossible, and now this. Even under the certainty of torture, Dragwlya's men were unwilling to give up the slightest bit of knowledge. The soldier's silence enraged the sultan, but his anger was, in actuality, a reaction to the fear he felt. Dragwlya's peasants were more afraid of their prince than they were of their enemies and captors.

"If your master had many soldiers like yourself, in a short time he could conquer the world."

Those surrounding the Wallachian soldier were surprised at Mehmed's unexpected reaction.

Silently, the soldier responded. *They are all like me.*

Radu studied the soldier. Though the man knew his life may come to an abrupt end at any moment, he still was not compelled to provide Mehmed with any information. *He has no designs for the world. My brother wants only what he believes to be his. Nothing more.*

A tickling sensation irritating the back of Radu's throat began to grow, letting him know it would not be suppressed much longer. His only means to relieve himself of it was to cough, and the hacking caused everyone to turn their attention to him. It was the same cough being heard throughout the camp by many of those infected. While Radu eased his own concern with the explanation he was falling victim to a summer cold, no one else imagined it to be anything short of plague.

June 17, 1462

For nearly a week Mehmed's forces had marched toward Tîrgovişte. Bucharest remained in the hands of the Romanians, as did the island monastery of Snagov, which the Turkish had passed in reaching this point. Some thirty miles away from their final destination, the army of the sultan made camp as the end of another day fell heavily upon them.

The sun had set more than two hours ago, handing the earth over to the night. Once it had done so, Mehmed isolated himself, attempting to discover some refuge where he would endeavor to understand all the hardships he had been made to endure since leaving Constantinople for this undertaking.

This is my campaign, yet I have dictated no part of it.

Lying down, staring at the ceiling of his tent, Mehmed wondered how much more he could ask of his men without them abandoning him. Their spirits were low. The fight became more meaningless to them every day. The point at which they would break was drawing near, and Mehmed now doubted he would be able to prevent the ranks from disbanding should another catastrophe befall them.

Only a few more days, Mehmed assured himself. *A few days more and this entire ordeal will end.*

He has become careless, Dragwlya thought. *His entire force has become careless.*

Dragwlya analyzed Mehmed and the Turkish army, sensing just how close he was to vanquishing the invaders from his land. His spies were correct in their assessment of the sultan's camp. Fortifications were minimal, and the trenches encircling them hardly resembled those encountered previously. Everything Dragwlya wanted to know about their mental state he learned from their lack of preparedness.

Three hours into the night, Dragwlya was about to launch an attack he knew would end both Mehmed's campaign and Mehmed himself. Joined by half his men, Dragwlya would rush one flank of the camp. The other half of his army, led by a boyar named Galeş, would charge from the opposite side. They were to meet in the center and then together achieve ultimate victory with the death of Mehmed.

Cloaked in darkness, Dragwlya's men would have only the light of the camp and the stars to guide them. He hoped to maintain the surprise of the assault for as long as possible, but knew it would not be long before a general alarm would be given. By that time it would be too late for the Turkish to organize and Galeş would already be moving in with the rest of his army, closing in on the confused mob.

Without further reflection, a silent signal was made, and Dragwlya's night attack began.

"Kazîglu Bey is here!"

For nearly twenty minutes Dragwlya's men remained undetected while wading through Mehmed's camp and butchering anyone and anything they encountered. Dragwlya knew such secrecy would end and was proven right. In the dead of night, the screaming of the Turkish would signal to Galeş the time to charge had arrived.

Mehmed awoke to screams, to chaos.

While Dragwlya was leading a confident contingent toward the sultan's red tent, the Turkish were in complete disarray, somewhere between the instincts of finding their commanders and of abandoning their camp. Three hours had passed since the initial cries of infiltration and, only recently, had the Janissaries and cavalry posted themselves as a formidable front surrounding Mehmed's tent.

Thirty minutes ago, Dragwlya's force had arrived at what he believed to be Mehmed's tent. A miscalculation had led them instead to the quarters of the viziers Mahmud Pasha and Isaac Pasha. It was precious time wasted for Dragwlya, precious time Mehmed needed.

Realizing his mistake, Dragwlya redirected his force, hoping his men led by Galeş had found the correct target. Again he was to be disappointed. Not only had Galeş not arrived at Mehmed's tent, he had failed to charge.

The concentration of cavalry and Janissaries convinced Dragwlya he had reached his intended destination. With approximately five thousand men, he had successfully reached the heart of the Turkish camp. He could not complete his objective, however, without the men under Galeş' command. Though he understood this, every instinct urged him to continue. Knowing how close to achieving total victory he was would not allow him to order a retreat.

Mehmed remained sheltered in his tent like a pearl in an oyster that refused to be shucked. Much like a pearl being formed, layer by layer, the once disjointed Turkish forces were amassing to create an ever-growing impenetrable barrier around the sultan's quarters in the absence of Dragwlya's combined forces. As the barrier grew so did Dragwlya's realization that Mehmed would survive this night. He also understood if he did not withdraw soon, there would be no opportunity to do so. Cursing himself for his misjudgment in selected both the wrong target and the wrong man to lead, Dragwlya begrudgingly gave the order to retreat.

Escaping from the Turkish camp proved an arduous process with Mehmed's men in full pursuit. Dragwlya escaped unscathed. Nearly one thousand of his men had not been so fortunate. They were captured and, upon being brought back to Mehmed, disposed of brutally.

"Your cowardice has caused the deaths of many of my men." Dragwlya's voice was subdued, not much more than a whisper as he spoke to the nearly lifeless body of Galeş that drooped as it rested on its pale. There was no sign Galeş was still fighting to live.

In a show of his ferocity, Dragwlya had Galeş held in place while he himself rammed the pale through the stomach of the boyar. He wanted to see the face of the coward as he waited for him to expire. He wanted Galeş to be able to understand him for as long as possible as he suffered. That meant being able to read the prince's lips should his sense of hearing fail.

"My blade was at his jugular and you pulled it away...Traitor."

Though not completely certain, Dragwlya thought Galeş was attempting to say something after the accusation of treason. The boyar's right arm did flinch, but Galeş' blood loss was too great to allow him to speak. It hardly mattered.

I will be forced to fight again. Next time, without the advantage of attacking at my discretion.

CHAPTER LIII
FOREST OF THE IMPALED
NORTH OF TÎRGOVIŞTE
June 19, 1462

Continuing the campaign had not been Mehmed's first inclination. Dragwlya's night raid had mentally broken many, but the losses suffered were not as great as the sultan had initially feared. More livestock had been killed than soldiers. That Dragwlya had penetrated so deeply into his camp and remained undetected for so long caused Mehmed to wonder if his men truly understood the enemy they were facing though.

Once his forces had been reassembled, Mehmed detailed to his beys the exact plan of attack he would unleash against Kazîglu Bey. He anticipated the siege would be lengthy, but there would be no stopping him from gaining a foothold from which he could launch himself deeper into Europe.

An advance party was sent and saw exactly what it expected, a barricaded city. Cannons were in place; the residents of the outlying townships had been called to take up residence within the city walls. Everything was as Mehmed knew the scouts would find it. They traveled around the city, heading north in their search for suitable encampment areas for what was sure to be an undertaking to rival that of Constantinople. What they found, none could even begin to comprehend.

Though faint, the air reeked unmistakably of death, of decay. What surprised Mehmed most was learning he was still some ten miles away from his intended destination. Those who had returned to describe to the sultan what they had discovered sounded so fantastic, Mehmed thought them mad.

Even as the stench of rotting flesh grew so dense that it seemed traveling a few meters forward would make it tangible, Mehmed denied the plausibility of the accounts of his men. A congregation of circling birds was the second indicator that the soldiers' stories were true. They, too, were dismissed by Mehmed. Obviously, they were hovering over a fresh kill or some dying animal, waiting to swoop down and eat. Nothing would make the sultan believe, nothing except seeing for himself.

From a distance they looked like trees—thousands of twisted, gnarled offenses, standing out dramatically from those surrounding them. Unable to distinguish their species, the sultan watched as birds flew in and out of the grove before him. A slight breeze began to blow, eliminating the odor somewhat, but not nearly enough for Mehmed to think he was breathing clean air. The limbs of the taller, lusher looking trees swayed slightly. Their movement was not graceful. Now the birds were more identifiable, ravens mostly. Mehmed could see them nestled on branches.

For twenty minutes the sultan had not said a word, and no one dared to say anything to him. It was all true. Mehmed was approaching something so incredible he still discounted its existence. But it was real. From more than twenty thousand stakes it stared back at him.

"An entire forest…"

Soon after the words were whispered by Mehmed, the breeze shifted, redirecting a warm current of decay directly into his face, choking him. Arranged in a semicircle pattern spanning a mile, the bodies of Turkish soldiers and others adorned the roadsides. Cries from the birds sounded like horrific laughing as the sultan watched them resting, not in the branches of trees, but in the rib cages of what once were men, women, and children. What he had mistaken for leaves earlier proved to be tattered garments.

Every one of them appeared to have been impaled differently—through the chest, through the back, bent in half, through the entrails. Regardless of where Mehmed looked, there was something different about the next body. Two in particular drew his attention. Unidentifiable by their mercilessly pecked faces, Thomas Catavolinos and Hamza Pasha resided near the center of the formation on stakes taller than any others. Their clothing allowed Mehmed to identify them.

Mehmed simply stared. Gradually, his gaze was drawn to Hamza Pasha. Movement in the eye sockets caused the sultan to flinch, and the sudden appearance of a bird exiting Hamza's skull forced Mehmed to close his eyes and shudder.

He cannot be beaten.

Still peering into the darkness of his eyelids, Mehmed assured himself victory could not be obtained. He thought he had done so silently.

"You sound certain."

Mehmed was shocked that someone had answered him. Drawing in a quick breath, he opened his eyes and, directing his head to the right, found Radu waiting for him to comment further. Even Radu's green-blue orbs were not enough of a distraction to pull Mehmed away from what was around him. He hoped his young minion did not realize that his initial words were not intended to be spoken.

Looking up at Catavolinos' skeleton, Mehmed tried to imagine the bones covered with the muscle and skin that once made up the Greek's features. His memories of the once fiery gaze of the envoy had been replaced and consumed by the empty, hollow stare now looking back at him. Mehmed felt defeat emanating from his entire body.

"Are you willing to give up Europe simply because of *this*?" Radu, his hand palm up, indicated the nearest victim as he spoke. "This would stop you?"

Somehow Mehmed had been blind. At some point, Radu, like Dragwlya, had lost his humanity.

"Your heartlessness is equaled only by your naivety," Mehmed said somewhat forcefully. "You have seen the faces of my men…*This*," Mehmed mimicked Radu's gesture, "has paralyzed my men with fear. This…is only a slight indication of all your brother could achieve."

Radu heard a mixture of admiration, resentment, and resignation in Mehmed's statement; enough so that he wondered if the sultan was going to order a full retreat immediately. He hoped so. Opposition to Dragwlya was on the rise in Wallachia and, while most of it was due to the prince's own actions, some of it was spurred on by his brother. Whenever possible Radu would speak with any boyars wishing to meet with him. War, he had determined, was not the only way in which he could obtain what he wanted.

"We will begin the retreat tomorrow."

Without another word Mehmed turned his charger around and began leading the animal away from a sight he knew would never be purged from his mind.

You believe him to be unbeatable, Radu thought to himself. *I will change your opinion.*

BUZĂU
June 26, 1462

What remained of Evrenos Pasha's army limped away from the battlefield. Mehmed and the rest of the Turkish forces were well on their way to Brăila, and Dragwlya knew this would be the last time he would encounter the sultan's soldiers during this campaign. It would have to be.

The Turkish had attacked the fortress of Chilia four days ago. Along with Dragwlya's garrison stationed there, one sent by Matthias was involved in the defense. Mehmed's soldiers were only a complimentary unit. The actual enemy was Moldavia... Stephen.

Surprising as it was, Dragwlya reasoned his cousin's treachery and betrayal were logical. Were Mehmed to capture Chilia without assistance, it could lead to the end of Stephen's reign. Stephen was fighting to preserve what belonged to him. While Dragwlya appreciated that, the fact his cousin had chosen to align with the Turkish disheartened him. Stephen, however, was the least of his concerns. Though he was successful in pushing the Turkish back, Dragwlya's army was shrinking with each passing day. The number of boyars supporting him was dwindling as well.

Somewhere in the Bărăgan, Dragwlya's former supporters were being consolidated and prepared for their new prince. Dragwlya wondered how long it had taken Mehmed to convince Radu to remain and attempt to take peacefully what he himself had not been able to wrestle away forcibly.

For a brief moment, Dragwlya contemplated the ridiculous notion Radu had masterminded this, using his heritage to convince others of his ability to rule. Dismissing the idea, he still grasped that even under the control of his incompetent brother an army knowledgeable of his tactics, and of the countryside's landscape, would be far more formidable than any force Mehmed could assemble.

While he remained hopeful he would receive reinforcements from Matthias, Drag-wlya was not factoring in the additional forces into any of his immediate plans. Like he had for much of his fight with the Turkish, he realized it would be necessary for him to retreat north once more.

CHAPTER LIV
ELIZABETHA'S CHOICE
POENARI
September 19, 1462

Clouds hid the stars, making the night sky an unlighted abyss. For one individual, the lack of illumination afforded the perfect, and only, opportunity for success.

Managing to scale Poenari Hill undetected, the Janissary examined with his fingers the message affixed to the end of the arrow, making certain it was secure. There would be only one shot. Should he fail, there would be no chance of saving Wallachia. Without hesitation, he drew back the arrow and waited. He watched in the upper battlements of Dragwlya's mountain retreat as a candle's flame shimmered. Every so often a shape would pass, eclipsing it momentarily. There was no knowing when it would pass again, and he hoped no injury would come to whomever it was. He exhaled and let go.

After burning Brăila, Mehmed returned home. In Adrianople, festivities were held to commemorate the victory over Kazîglu Bey. The soldiers' faces told a story different from those the court historians would soon be writing, however, as did the news that no further incursion into Europe was imminent.

With the threat of the Turkish forces abated, the boyars answered the appeals of Radu. They knew life would be considerably easier if the sultan were paid a yearly tribute. It was a satisfactory alternative to fearing for their lives on a daily basis because of Dragwlya's unpredictability and irrationality.

Weary of war and conscious of the depleted state their principality's army was in, Wallachia's peasantry was easily swayed by the promise of peace with the Turkish as well. Added to this mounting pressure for Dragwlya was the simple fact that if Matthias was going to send reinforcements, they would not arrive soon enough. Combined, the factors necessitated the prince's flight to Poenari. For more than a month now Radu and his supporters had been in control of nearly every town and main road of Wallachia, forcing Dragwlya to retreat to his mountain fortress.

Reaching the zenith of its arc, the arrow began to curve downward, racing toward one of the windows overlooking the Argeş River. Traveling on what appeared to be a predetermined path, it disappeared from sight as it entered the opening.

Momentarily reveling in his skill, the Janissary smiled. He was a Muslim but not Turkish. Wallachian by birth, and a distant relative of Dragwlya, the man felt compelled to warn his brethren of the unrestricted assault soon to be unleashed upon the mountain fortress. His message warned the prince to escape while the possibility remained. Seeing the shadow of a woman holding the arrow, the Janissary's smile crept away. The rest of him followed as he began the task of returning undetected.

Absorbing the message rapidly, Elizabetha's eyes widened with each line. She pulled the paper away from her face and dashed to the window. The darkness offered no revelations as to where the shot came from. Instinctively, her arm rose again as she backed away. The words, still fresh in her mind, beckoned to be read once more.

> …in the gravest of danger…full assault…must leave now…any resistance is doomed to fail…

While watching her mother being brutally raped and tortured not far away from the very spot she was now standing in, Elizabetha had been devastated. Learning to survive in the midst of Dragwlya's unpredictability frightened her at times. Being captured by the Turkish would be different.

Potentially, it meant Elizabetha would become a concubine for the sultan, for one of his numerous beys, or someone else she would be sold to. Though it was true she was little more than that now, Elizabetha knew it would be much worse were she a captive of the Turkish. While the memory of seeing her mother being abused did not terrify her, the thought of becoming her mother, suffering in the same manner, did.

Thinking about her mother brought to the forefront of Elizabetha's consciousness her own child. She realized she had been terrified one other time in her life. She recalled the terms and price at which peace had come at in the past—an annual tribute and the annual loss of five hundred Wallachian boys.

Sacrifices.

Imagining Mihnea as one of the sultan's minions, picturing him being molded into a Janissary, had terrified her. What she felt now wasn't terror. It was hopelessness. It gripped at her unlike anything else ever had. Her stomach felt empty; her heart sank. Summoning every last bit of determination she had, Elizabetha stormed out of the room in search of Dragwlya. She found him alone, just having ended a meeting with seven local peasants and a few of his most trusted boyars.

Her pallor was deathly white, and Dragwlya regarded her entrance as he would that of a dog. A glance was given to acknowledge her presence, nothing more.

"You must read this."

Dragwlya stared at her incredulously as the parchment was thrust into his face. His motion in taking the paper from her showed that he was doing so not because of her words but because he chose to do so. Dragwlya scanned the note. When his eyes stopped moving, he balled it up and let the crumpled piece of paper fall to the floor.

"There is no need for concern. Go and rest."

Dragwlya's nonchalant attitude made her want to lash out at him, beat him senseless, or beat him until she believed he had gained some measure of sense.

"Rest? How do you suggest I rest with the knowledge that at any moment the army surrounding us will close in, make us their prisoners, and take us to the sultan? How does that not concern you? Does it also not concern you that your son will become a minion of your enemy?"

"Nothing of the kind will happen," Dragwlya said while retaining a calm tone.

"Only because I will not allow it to," Elizabetha snarled. "You would prefer to have Mihnea raised by those *animals* instead of claiming him as your own! You would prefer to see me taken away in chains and carted off to the ends of their empire just to be rid of me!" Dragwlya was beginning to speak over her now, attempting to quiet her after a rant that had gone on for far too long. In the short period of time it had taken for the conversation to devolve, Elizabetha had decided what course of action needed to be taken. "I would rather have my body rot and be eaten by the fish of the Argeş than be led away in captivity by them!"

Not a word of what Dragwlya had said was processed by Elizabetha. Her own thoughts had drowned out everything else and already she was retreating through the entrance from which she had come. She was not running away. She was running with purpose.

Cradling Mihnea in her arms, Elizabetha continued to stare straight ahead. Everything was saturated by darkness. There was no breeze. Nothing moved, and the night's stillness made the air feel unnatural, stale, dead. She realized she, too, was already dead. Her next act would do nothing but solidify that to the rest of the world. Soon after Mihnea's birth she had thought about this moment, how nothing could ever drive her to do something so drastic. She had been wrong.

Elizabetha's bare toes grasped the edge of the battlement, literally the precipice of life itself and, for the first time, she dared to look down. Nothing was there. Nothing existed except the all-encompassing maw waiting to swallow her whole.

But there *was* something there. She could hear it.

Current after current crashed on the rocks below, giving some shape to the unseen mass lying in wait to grab hold of her. The moment when she promised herself she would not falter had arrived—the moment when she would protect her child from all the world's evil and, for the remainder of eternity, suffer because of her love for him. All that was required now was to fall.

Warm tears streamed down Elizabetha's face as she squinted, burning tracks along her cheeks. She began to shudder and felt her toes clinch and push off of the stone. Her arms tightened around Mihnea simultaneously. Elizabetha then felt nothing. Her heart raced as the wind did its best to stop her and Mihnea from falling. Unaware of what was transpiring, the infant continued to sleep, safe in the comfort of his mother's arms. Elizabetha thought she was experiencing the sensations a bird must have the first time it spreads its wings and soars away from the nest. Complete release, absolute freedom. But then Mihnea began to cry.

Beginning with a faint whimper, Mihnea's voice grew louder, forcing Elizabetha to open her eyes. In doing so, the cold stinging of the stone beneath her feet brought her back to reality, to the harsh truth that she still remained stationary, high above the Argeş.

Every instinct begged her not to, but it was useless. Elizabetha's head fell and her eyes fixated on the tightly clenched hands and face of her son. It was a sight she could not withstand. Her pulse elevated. Sweat beaded upon her brow, and she screamed. A primal wail of pain tore through the air in every direction. Fiercely, the sound ripped across the river into the Turkish camp then bounced back across the bluff until finally dissipating.

Unable to control her own sobbing, Elizabetha tried vehemently to stop Mihnea's as she stepped back from the edge of the abyss before her, squatted, and laid him down. Her tone was hushed, but through her tears it sounded disjointed and was in no way soothing.

"Don't … cry … Mihnea … Don't cry. I … will always … be with you … Will always … be here."

Still bending down, Elizabetha tried her best to regain some composure, to tell herself what she was about to do made no sense, that there had to be some way other than killing herself to avoid this looming disaster. But she had thought about this very situation for some time now, had pondered every possible contingency. Elizabetha was attempting to be rational when she couldn't possibly be rational. Nothing could be done to counter a thought process in place for years.

Kissing the forehead of her baby, Elizabetha quietly proclaimed her love and again stood upright. With Mihnea's cries filling her head, she stepped forward once more to the edge and attempted to stand still. It proved impossible. Her body shook uncontrollably from an imperceptible chill, one known only to a mother who is about to die believing that her child's life will in some way be better for it.

Closing her eyes, Elizabetha took a shallow breath, exhaled, and fell.

The servant described for Dragwlya how she had reached the battlement just in time to see Elizabetha falling from the precipice. She had found his son crying quite close to the point from which Elizabetha had leapt.

Genuinely shocked, Dragwlya sat quietly. The action being related to him was that of a desperate person, of one with no ability to reason. Although he did not care for Elizabetha, neither of those attributes described her. She had never been one to respond rashly. Her timing was beneficial, however. It would be much easier to escape without a woman slowing his party down. When Elizabetha had interrupted him earlier, he was finalizing the preparations for their escape. A secret passage would lead his party to the banks of the river. From there they would have to endure trekking across the Făgăraş slopes. The local peasants Dragwlya had been meeting with were a clan whose assistance and expertise would be needed to navigate them successfully.

"I believed she was stronger."

Dragwlya's comment came in a tone suggesting the prince was now doubting himself. Nothing could be further from the truth. Elizabetha's decision to end her own life was something Dragwlya would not do, something he could never do.

Unsure if she was supposed to respond, the servant girl said nothing, waiting to see if the prince would push her for some sort of reaction. He didn't and simply dismissed her.

Dragwlya knew he had been defeated for some time. That still did not make the flight away from his castle any easier. Knowing who would sit upon his throne infuriated him. Along with the local clan accompanying him in his escape, a small mercenary force joined the party that would travel north to Königstein. There they would wait until it was determined Matthias had arrived in Braşov. Then the group would travel to meet the Hungarian king. Dragwlya expected the king's arrival to be eminent.

With their shoes shod backwards, the trail left by the escape party's horses led toward the bluffs. Dragwlya hoped that once they entered the forest most signs of their flight would disappear. Speed was of the essence now; it mattered little to him the amount of noise being made. By any measure the noise was minimal and, other than the galloping and snorting of the horses, there was nothing to be heard. Even Mihnea, tied to the back of his father's steed and sleeping, remained silent.

For the duration of the ride, Dragwlya tried to discover the reason for his failure. Obviously, it was the treachery of the boyars. They had willingly sacrificed his land, their freedom and, in all likelihood, the whole of Europe just to secure their own holdings. Their selfishness had been his undoing, and he knew there was little he could have done to prevent such an inevitable fall from happening.

No other rational answer readily presented itself because there was none. Dragwlya believed he had taken enough precautions, made enough concessions, and purged the nobility enough that something like this would not and could not occur. He had been mistaken. He realized his measures had not been severe or widespread enough to fully eliminate those who would cause turmoil. Once he returned, he would be careful not to make the same errors again.

His mind continuing to wander, Dragwlya was not aware they had reached the foothills until those before him had begun to dismount. When he got off of his horse, a disturbing discovery was made. The soldier who was taking care to remove Mihnea from the prince's charger found the infant missing.

"Sire?" The man's voice was nothing but a timid whisper.

"Yes?"

"Your son, sire."

"What about him?" Both men's voices sounded equally confused as they tried fruit-lessly to extract information from the other.

"Where is he, sire?"

Casually, Dragwlya walked to the rear of his horse where his son had been secured at the start of the journey. Just like the soldier, he found nothing there and surmised what happened.

"He must have fallen out along the way." Dragwlya's voice was indifferent, as if he were talking about the loss of some cheap bauble.

With a stupefied look, the soldier reacted. "Do you wish for us to search for him, my lord?"

The reply came instantly. "No." *I have taken great pains to escape with the best of my remaining men. I will not have them lost in a vain effort to find an infant somewhere in the dark. It is likely he is already dead; either consumed by some animal or trampled.* "We shall continue on."

SCHEII DISTRICT, OUTSIDE OF BRAŞOV
November 4, 1462

For the entire month of October, Matthias and his court had remained in Sibiu. Months before learning Dragwlya was deposed and replaced by Radu, the king realized it would be necessary to rethink his attitude toward assisting the prince and his feelings about the crusade in general.

Prior to arriving in Sibiu, Matthias began hearing rumblings that the German town-ships were giving their support to the Turkish. Now that he knew who truly controlled the region, it took little time for the king to align with Radu. Furthering Hungary's cause, Matthias agreed to sign a five-year armistice with Mehmed. He had decided upon this last point only yesterday.

Despite these concessions, Matthias had proceeded to Braşov with everyone still under the assumption he had done so to aid Dragwlya in the fight against the Turkish. Popular belief still held he would allow the Wallachian to marry into his family, solidi-fying an alliance. No attempt was made on the Hungarian's part to make people think otherwise. In fact, such thoughts were encouraged.

While preparing for his first face-to-face meeting with Dragwlya in some time, Matthias was interrupted by a group of patriots from Vienna who had orchestrated and participated in an assassination attempt of Holy Roman Emperor Fredrick III. Their assault on the emperor's royal palace occurred October 15th and was the direct result of the monarch's attempt to force new taxes upon the capital's citizenry. The group was willing to reward Matthias for his support, should he agree to back them.

While their offer was solely for the Hapsburg estates, Matthias understood the connotations. He was being given an inroad to the ultimate prize—the imperial crown. Such an enticing offer proved too much to resist and the king, whose family had once restored Dragwlya to his throne, would now be responsible for the prince's arrest to make certain the suddenly developed peace in the region held.

Like his father, Matthias possessed the ability to see past people's exteriors and tell what they were truly thinking. He hardly needed that gift now. Across from him, Dragwlya looked every bit the confident warrior. His unyielding eyes did not appear to be those of a prince who had lost his throne. Matthias knew better, understood all that the prince had lost and no longer held.

Power was all that mattered, and Dragwlya was no longer in possession of that valuable commodity. While Matthias was already aware of this, he wondered if the former prince was. He wondered what Dragwlya would say to try and convince him otherwise.

Dragwlya understood his situation to be grave. He considered himself a refugee at best, nothing more than a freedom fighter with very little in the way of support for his cause. He had nothing but empty promises to offer and seriously doubted there existed a chance for him to convince Matthias, or anyone else, that they should rush to fight by his side.

It was nauseating. Dragwlya had succeeded more than anyone ever had in repelling the Turkish. The threat to the whole of Europe now appeared extinguished. Peace was all but assured on the borders. Christianity and the crowned heads were safe from outside invasion, free to continue and pursue the infighting they obviously preferred. In essence, all of Dragwlya's victories, all of his successes and advancements had doomed him. Everyone else had found security at his expense and would do nothing except watch him flounder about, desperately seeking nonexistent support to retake his throne.

He had made himself expendable.

December 2, 1462

For four weeks Dragwlya met with Matthias daily in the hopes of changing the king's mind. His efforts were more futile than he could possibly know. As he continued to try and convince Matthias his throne must be reclaimed, the king was taking every precaution to guarantee Dragwlya's arrest would transpire seamlessly.

Still vivid in the minds of the leaders of Europe was the Wallachian's success against the Turkish. Some would require justification from Matthias for taking a man considered one of Christianity's greatest heroes as a prisoner. Only one reason presented itself as justifiable.

Matthias had three letters drafted. One was addressed to Mehmed, one to Mahmud

Pasha, and the third to Dragwlya's cousin Stephen. All three proclaimed unreservedly Dragwlya's desire to atone for his crimes against the Ottoman Empire and his wish to aid the sultan in any manner, including campaigning alongside him to seize Matthias himself. Should the necessity arise, the Hungarian king would show that these letters fell into the possession of his spies, validating the arrest of the former prince.

Never one to show discomfort during negotiations, Dragwlya knew the amount of his fidgeting had increased over the last few days to the extent he was sometimes forced to concentrate in order to sit still. Nearly a month's time wasted. Meanwhile, Radu was fortifying himself. The longer Matthias hesitated, the more difficult it would be to recapture Wallachia.

"I fear if we do not act immediately the chance to regain control of Wallachia will disappear." Dragwlya's voice was steady, but deep in his eyes hopelessness threatened to sabotage his front. "Every day we talk my brother becomes more entrenched. I am not certain the gravity of this situation can be made any clearer, my lord. I must have your help to liberate Wallachia. I must have it now."

In what almost amounted to a demand, Dragwlya had forced the king's hand. Though the question was not phrased in such a manner, the response could simply be given with a yes or no response. Of course it would not be, and the former prince wondered how long the 'no' response would be.

"I agree."

Unbelievably, even to himself, Dragwlya's face remained expressionless. Though his face gave no indication of his disbelief, that he remained silent for a slightly uncomfortable period was telling. Once he regained the ability to speak, Dragwlya's response sounded even.

"This is a decision you will not regret, my lord."

CHAPTER LV
DRAGWLYA IMPRISONED
KÖNIGSTEIN
December 6, 1462

Dragwlya felt like a prince once more. From just outside Königstein Castle in the Făgăraş Mountains he watched as his men were lowered down a precipice to the valley and to the village of Dîmbovița, the next point along the journey to recapturing his throne.

Four days had elapsed since Matthias agreed to join the fight to rid Wallachia of the Turkish, hardly enough time for Dragwlya to fully accept the surprising change of attitude. He expected to wake from this dream at any moment and find himself still in Braşov. Jan Jiškra's presence let him know this was no dream. Once a Slovak Hussite leader, Jiškra was currently in Matthias' retinue. The king had granted him a contingent with which he was to help Dragwlya.

Soon, Dragwlya would be reunited with the contingency that had remained loyal to him through the severest of tribulations. He would not question the intentions of any of its members. They had thrived through trials that would have broken most. Each had earned Dragwlya's respect. Those below in the valley now would attain a similar standing, he hoped.

"They are all safe. No harm can come to them now."

Dragwlya felt, then saw the Slovak creeping to stand next to him as the words were spoken. "They are good men, Jiškra. They will continue to serve me well."

Something that sounded half like a chuckle and half like a sigh escaped from Jiškra's mouth, giving Dragwlya enough reason to face him.

"You find amusement in their devotion?"

"No, in your gullibility." Jiškra's words were punctuated with a gesture that caused two soldiers to approach Dragwlya and take hold of him. Taken completely off-guard by the sudden seizure, Dragwlya was unable to contain himself, or to break free of the grip the soldiers held him in. "Do not struggle. My men will gladly subdue you by force."

Perspiration dripped down Dragwlya's cheeks and wisps of hair clung to his face as he stared up from under his scrunched brow at the Slovak. "What do you think you are doing?"

"You are under arrest." The shouts of Dragwlya's men from below mixed with Jiškra's response. The Slovak stared down at them and smiled. "The belief of your great cunning seems unwarranted. I thought it would have been much more difficult to separate you from all of your men."

Dragwlya cursed himself silently and assessed the situation. It was difficult for him to believe how careless he had become. "You have harbored ill-will toward me ever since I aligned myself with the Hunedoara family. Have you given any thought to what Matthias will do to you when he learns of this betrayal?"

Jiškra's laughing would have overpowered the rising voices of Dragwlya's soldiers had he allowed it to. Instead, he leaned down until his nose nearly touched that of his prisoner. "Surely, you are not that naïve."

Tension began to melt away in Dragwlya's face. Once taut muscles relaxed with understanding. "Matthias." The Hungarian king's name slid out of Dragwlya's mouth, acting as a cue for Jiškra to back away from a man who appeared lost in his own thoughts of the betrayal he had just suffered. "Why? Why did he not just arrest me in Braşov?"

"The Saxons want you executed for what you have done to them. Had you been arrested in Braşov they would have claimed jurisdiction over you and taken you for their own purposes. Matthias wanted you taken prisoner on his own land so he would be free to decide your fate."

"What does he have to gain from this?"

Jiškra turned back to face Dragwlya. "With the Turkish controlling Wallachia, there is no war...Apparently, Matthias feels safer upon his throne with you off of yours."

Matthias wants me alive, otherwise he would have given me to the Saxons or had this fool kill me here. But for what?

"Where am I to be taken now?"

"Back to Braşov. That is all I have been made privy to." Jiškra walked past him and made an unseen motion to the men restraining Dragwlya to follow.

BUDA
March 12, 1463

Before Christmas, Dragwlya had been delivered back to Matthias' capital. By February the king was being forced to account for his actions by several concerned governments and was doing his utmost to preserve the truth for as long as possible. He tasked his spies with intercepting letters destined for the various heads of state, including the doge of Venice, Christoforo Moro.

Moro's spokesman, Pietro Tommasi, had tendered his resignation to the Venetian Senate once he learned of Dragwlya's arrest and Matthias' scheme to keep it secret. The doge and senate were aware of Tommasi's misgivings from his correspondence, which included questions of the validity of three fantastic letters that had miraculously appeared and revealed the Wallachian's treachery.

Tommasi's resignation was refused, but the action served as a prelude to his expulsion by Matthias once his spies and advisors deemed the man understood far too much of the actual nature of the Dragwlya affair. A replacement was sent, and Rome dispatched Papal Legate Niccolò Modrussa to ascertain the truth regarding the diplomatic mess Dragwlya's arrest had created for the king.

"You are more valuable to me away from the throne." Matthias stared into the hard-set emerald eyes of his prisoner. "What role you play in the future largely depends on you."

For the second time in his life Dragwlya was at the mercy of the Hunedoaras. The cyclical nature of it all was not lost on him. They had taken his father out of power and then dangled the crown in front of him like a treat before a child. It appeared that scenario would be played out once again.

"I did your father's bidding to gain back my throne. My loyalty was proven before he allowed me to take my rightful place. What must I do to regain my family's land now?" Dragwlya's voice hardly matched the intensity of his eyes as he pushed Matthias for some hint as to what was expected of him.

"I have not yet decided if there is anything you can do," Matthias retorted stoically. "Besides, your family still controls Wallachia...Your brother sits upon the throne."

The very idea made Dragwlya nauseous. Before answering, he reflected for a moment on whether Matthias was attempting to provoke him. "That fool is no more my family than you are."

"And yet that *fool* is on the throne, and you are my prisoner."

Matthias' grin of self-satisfaction convinced Dragwlya he was now being baited. "Life is seldom fair...The wheel will make its revolution once again."

"So, you are certain you will again rule Wallachia?"

"Much like you hope to someday acquire the crown of St. Stephen to legitimize your rule, I retain the belief I will have what is rightfully mine. I have been given no reason to believe otherwise...Unless of course you wish to do so now...*your highness.*"

Squinting and opening his eyes almost fast enough that the action was not perceivable, Matthias braced against the impact of Dragwlya's thinly veiled insult and took on its full brunt without allowing it to humiliate him completely.

"I have no such reason to give." Content this session with Dragwlya had lasted long enough, Matthias rose and began to leave. He attempted to regain the upper hand before doing so. "For the time being, you will remain here, while your brother wears the crown of Wallachia and resides in your castle along with his wife and children."

My brother died long ago, murdered by your father and his followers. The abomination on my throne may share my name and my blood. But he is not, and never will be, my brother.

TÎRGOVIŞTE
March 29, 1463

Radu awakened with a smile pulling hard at the corners of his mouth. His dreams, dreams of the life he had wanted, were the cause. It wasn't just a dream though. His improbable life was a reality. He was married, had a beautiful daughter, and was the ruler of his homeland. There was no threat of attack from the Turkish, none from the Holy Roman Empire, none from any of the heads of Europe and, most importantly, no chance of reprisal from his brother.

More than five months ago, Matthias had recognized Radu's claim as prince. For the first two months he sat upon the throne, Radu awaited daily news of an offensive being led by his brother. With reassurances and the passage of time, Vlad's shadow shrank and faded, though not entirely. Only one event would give Radu complete assurance and absolute comfort—his brother's death. Only death could stop his brother from regaining the throne.

Attempting to purge the all-too-familiar topic from his mind, Radu closed his eyes and shook his head before jumping out of bed to govern his principality. Those duties were secondary at the moment though. Radu's first course of action this morning would be to relieve himself.

Something felt different, wrong somehow.

Continuing to urinate, Radu moved his index finger back and forth slightly against his penis. Something was there, though he could hardly venture a guess as to what. Touching it did not result in any pain, but that did not quell Radu's curiosity. Shaking the last few lingering drops free, Radu turned the shaft counterclockwise to see the cause of his concern. Doing so revealed a small, firm, white bump.

The placement of the nodule made it appear like a gigantic boil to Radu, ready to burst at any moment. Taking a deep breath, he let go and allowed his hand to drop to his side. The smile he had awakened with returned as his mental image of the chancre became more aligned with reality. He would not allow his fear of what could happen with his brother to manifest itself elsewhere. No reason existed for him to worry about the nodule. In time it would disappear, just as Vlad would.

CHAPTER LVI
RADU FALLS ILL & DRAGWLYA'S MENAGERIE
VISEGRÁD
June 26, 1463

The world was beginning to take shape in Matthias' favor.

Some six months ago the Hungarian king's father-in-law, King George Poděbradý of Bohemia, had come to the aid of Frederick III in putting down the Viennese uprising. Combined with this event, Matthias' decision to forego his designs for the ancestral Hapsburg estates held by the Holy Roman Emperor moved Frederick to fulfill a promise he had made to Matthias years earlier. Pressure from the papacy and eighty thousand gold crowns from the Hungarian king helped persuade him as well.

After five years, Matthias would finally receive the Crown of St. Stephen, legitimizing his title.

Three thousand knights from the finest Hungarian families, dressed in full formal regalia, made the journey to Weiner Neustadt to secure the crown. They had returned with it just days earlier, and plans were already in motion for the first formal coronation since that of Ladislas V. Dragwlya felt every bit the display Matthias endeavored to make of him. Instead of rejecting the role, however, he embraced it, knowing it may benefit him in the future.

The Hungarian king's court had recently taken up residence in the summer palace at Visegrád. Where a Roman fort had once stood, now rose a stunning achievement constructed by the Slovaks after the Mongol invasion more than two hundred years ago. Bela IV, Charles Robert, and others had continued the development of the residence, but it was Matthias who transformed the brick and mortar structure into the renaissance center it was becoming.

Set high on a hill overlooking the Danube's bend where it turns nearly due south through Hungary, the citadel appeared as if it could be swallowed whole by the emerald flora surrounding it at any moment. Heron, egrets, cormorants, and various ducks ruled the nearby marshes, while falcons and other birds of prey patrolled the skies. Dragwlya had been brought to this lush prison to serve Matthias' needs. The Hungarian king knew how useful the very presence of his captive could be when entertaining certain guests, especially those Dragwlya had personally terrorized, especially the Turkish.

Throughout most of their meeting with the king, Mehmed's envoys found themselves missing parts of the conversation. Their attention was monopolized by Kazîglu Bey, who sat quietly near Matthias. Images of fellow delegates, turbans nailed to their heads as they lie on the floor writhing in expanding pools of blood, would not allow them to focus. They understood his presence was a message, a warning that the great

Impaler was under the command of Matthias. Should the armistice be betrayed, the king would release the Wallachian to unleash abject fury upon them.

In his own mind, Dragwlya pictured the same images as the envoys, along with many more they had not been privy to. He imagined their impaled bodies rotting in the midday sun, being pecked at by ravens. The visual brought a wicked smile to his face that the envoys noticed almost immediately.

Pretending to be oblivious to the exchange occurring between Dragwlya and his guests, Matthias carried on as though full attention was being paid to his every word. He was astonished by the envoys' fear and by Dragwlya's ability to instill such terror. More than astonished, he was envious. While he personally would not slaughter his own people or those of another nation the way Dragwlya had, Matthias would not give a second thought to releasing his pet scourge on someone if he felt it would further his own agenda.

Matthias wished simply to hold the Wallachian in check, to use him as a showpiece, and never allow him command of so much as a single soldier. If the situation required it, however, Matthias knew there was no one else he would rather have leading men into the thick of battle. His father had proven Dragwlya could be restrained after being allowed to roam free, but Matthias questioned whether he could make the Wallachian respond to him the same way. With any luck, he would never have to find out.

TÎRGOVIŞTE
June 27, 1463

Holding a small clump of his hair, Radu struggled to swallow the infinitesimal amount of saliva gathered in his mouth. For a third consecutive morning he had awaken to find patches of his hair on his pillow and his throat swollen to the extent that breathing was laborious. Staring at his locks, Radu could see the rashes on his palms were beginning to fade. They had developed, as had those on the bottom of his feet, shortly after the chancre disappeared. None that he chose to share his symptoms with could say with certainty that they were related. Some had heard of similar cases in Italy and France, but there appeared to be no lasting or life-threatening consequences.

For a week, Radu had suffered daily headaches. He was thankful this morning was free of that annoyance at least. They had drained him completely, making him unable to do much of anything, including eat. Over the last three weeks, Radu noted how sullen his expression was, how sunken his eyes appeared, and the bags that were forming below them. He knew he was sick and wondered how long it would be before this illness left his body. A few minutes of just sitting up in bed depleted him. The strain on his muscles made his entire body quiver with pain as he fought off the urge to simply fall back down. Ultimately, Radu found himself on his back, looking up at the ceiling once more.

Radu did not dare stand, fearful his body would collapse and he would end up on the floor. Releasing the hair from his clinched fingers, he closed his eyes and cursed silently as the onset of a headache began to bore its way into his skull.

What's wrong with me?

VISEGRÁD
June 28, 1463

Two days into their visit, Dragwlya's desire to see the recently arrived Turkish envoys suffer at his hands had not subsided. Accompanying those two long days were eternal nights of endless dreams.

Repeatedly, images of the ambassadors he had tortured fused with those of impaled peasants and the deaths of such notables as Thomas Catavolinos and Hamza Pasha. Combined, they created what would be a horrific scene for most. For Dragwlya, hearing the inhuman cries of pain and pleas for mercy emanating from the mass of souls was pleasing. Anyone watching him as he slept would have thought he was experiencing something beautiful, enjoying one of life's greatest pleasures. In his own mind, he was. Now that he was awake, living without such pleasure proved too difficult.

Dragwlya's menagerie was not extensive. It contained an assortment of egret chicks he requested be purchased from merchants at the marketplace and mice he managed to trap himself. As he held them, or studied them in their cages, they quickly took on the shapes of those he had vanquished or wished to harm. In his eyes, they were now animals of another sort.

Taking one of the mice first, Dragwlya cut the rodent to pieces. After sticking each bit on the end of one of the small sticks he had fashioned into stakes, he methodically arranged them in a semicircle. No longer a mouse, the mutilated mess before him was now the bodies of the treacherous Saxons. Unceremoniously, Dragwlya added an additional two semicircles to the pattern. He imagined each piece to be the body of a boyar, a peasant, a Turk, an Italian, or those of Thomas Catavolinos and Hamza Pasha. He continued on until there were no stakes left.

His hands stained red, Dragwlya enjoyed every second of inflicting his will. Momentarily pausing to watch the reactions of those yet to be punished, he realized there were no stakes remaining to enforce their sentences. Still, they must suffer.

Grabbing one of the egrets, Dragwlya struggled with the bird as he choked off its air supply. He watched the animal writhe as it gasped for breath. Unconsciously, Dragwlya's other hand moved to the tail of the egret and, with short, decisive tugs, the feathers of the bird began coming out. Once he recognized fully what he was doing, Dragwlya began ripping out of the feathers, despite frantic squirming and squawking. Only a few tufts of feathers remained on the head of the bird when he finally stopped and released it. Dragwlya's only reaction as he watched the obviously frightened and shocked egret was to smile.

Naked, the bird floundered around, unsure of what to do. It had ceased making any noise and moved its head about frantically, as if attempting to somehow reacquire its lost feathers. Dragwlya studied the animal for a few moments, thinking how much it resembled every enemy he had known. Like the Turkish, the Saxons, and the boyars, the bird had been protected by a layer of insulation. Like those same foes, the egret was now without that layer, vulnerable, and had nothing to protect itself from him.

But not any longer, Dragwlya thought. *Now they have regained some of their protection. Matthias. As long as he keeps me here, they will grow formidable. Even as his captive they fear me. But ultimately they know I am under his control; that they only need comply with his desires in order to escape me. They may still cower in my presence, but it is not enough. They may be afraid Matthias will release me to do his bidding, but they have no fear of me acting on my own.*

The conclusion he was the puppet of the Hunedoara family once more taunted him. Ioan's spirit laughed at him, chastising him for believing he could escape the grasp of a family far superior to his own. Every muscle in Dragwlya's body grew taut, and he shook slightly as the thought attempted to consume him. He would not allow it. He couldn't. His hands shaking nearly uncontrollably, Dragwlya picked up a knife and grabbed hold of the naked egret. Quickly decapitating the bird, he flung its head away and regarded its body with contempt.

"You will fear me," he scolded the foul, which assumed the form of Mehmed. He turned to the full cage of egrets and screamed. "You will all fear me again!"

CHAPTER LVII
THE CRUSADE DIES
ANCONA
August 15, 1464

Pius closed his eyes, confident he was doing so for the final time of his life. Nothing short of a miracle would ensure any other outcome. Recounting the course Europe had forged over the past few years, he hardly expected any miracles now.

Matthias' coronation ceremony this past March at the cathedral of Esztergom had legitimized his throne. Pius viewed the event as the ultimate insult to everything he was attempting to accomplish. His call for the crowned heads to crusade had gone unanswered for five years. Matthias was one of those who had been mute, yet he still had the audacity to accept money intended for fighting the Turkish.

A combined forty thousand ducats from the papal curia and Venice had found its way into Matthias' purse, and there was no doubt in Pius' mind that sum had gone to help offset the cost of the Crown of St. Stephen. All of the pomp associated with Matthias' coronation and the apathy of those who simply watched as the whole of the continent was devoured by the Turkish sickened Pius to the point he could no longer remain inactive. He decided to lead the crusade from the front line.

When he addressed the College of Cardinals, Pius had in no way been disillusioned as to what the near future would likely bring.

"We know it is a serious matter for a man of our age and that we shall go to certain death in one way or another," the aging Pope had intoned. "We must die one day and we do not mind where, provided we die well."

With a force of two thousand ill-equipped, inexperienced men gathered from across Europe, Pius had traveled to Ancona and the shore of the Adriatic. There he and his men awaited the arrival of the Venetian transport ships that would carry them across the sea. Yesterday morning Pius saw the sails of the vessels appear on the horizon. Shortly afterwards, the illness already ravaging his body was compounded with a fever that refused to break.

While his men celebrated the Feast of the Assumption, Pius passed away. Confidence had been renewed within him, confidence bred by his own self-assurances the group he had assembled would bring about change in the minds of men. Someone would pick up the torch where he was leaving it. Whether it would be one of those now awaiting passage over the Adriatic or one of the leaders of Europe he was uncertain. But someone would, someone must. Christianity's existence depended entirely upon it.

Pius had changed his life. Delirium convinced him he had changed the views of others. With that false assertion consoling him, he took his final breath.

VISEGRÁD
February 4, 1465

By the beginning of the year, Matthias' prosperity was beginning to diminish. Shortly after Pietro Barbo succeeded Pius and became Pope Paul II, he voiced his displeasure with the Hungarian king often. Unlike his predecessor, the new pontificate made no attempt to avoid publicly chastising Matthias for purchasing his crown with the Vatican's money. He also called into question the Catholic king's inaction against the Turkish.

Matters deteriorated further last month when Stephen attacked and captured Chilia from Radu. The Moldavian's victory weakened the bond Matthias held with Wallachia. Stephen's control of the strategic fortress meant the Hungarian's relationship with Dragwlya's brother was in jeopardy.

When Matthias had officially recognized Radu as prince of Wallachia nearly three years ago, he did so with the caveat that he would leave the principality alone so long as Radu made no real attempt assisting Mehmed in moving against Hungary. Stephen's victory altered the nature of that agreement. If the sultan felt it necessary, he would attack not only the Moldavian but anyone else he saw as a threat to his vassal state. Unintentionally upsetting the established harmony, Stephen had unwittingly raised the ire of Matthias, causing damage that could not be repaired easily.

Pius' passing meant the death of crusading to many. While Stephen's success against Radu afforded Dragwlya the opportunity to convince Matthias he was needed back on the throne to regain and maintain peace, there had been little consideration to do so immediately by the king. What Matthias had considered, however, was that such a day may eventually come. Over the past two years, Dragwlya had again proven his worth to the Hunedoara family. Matthias decided in December of last year to reward him by officially making him part of the family.

"You will need to convert to Catholicism, of course," Matthias had told him.

Dragwlya appeared as if he were deep in thought. His answer was obvious. This offer was a chance to one day reclaim the throne of Wallachia, his status, and his honor. The value all that entailed surpassed the cost of a meaningless mass.

"I am willing."

"You will wed my cousin, Ilona, and will be given a house in Pest."

Ilona… Szilágy.

The name immediately conjured up images of Mihály, the girl's father, who had at one time been the closest of allies Dragwlya had ever known. Though posthumously, he could think of no one better to serve as his father-in-law.

"Thank you, sire."

Over the past two years, much like the soldiers left stranded on the shores of the Adriatic Sea without Pius to lead them, Dragwlya's faith had quickly deserted him, giving his nightmares free rein. Mircea's spirit, and that of his father, visited him in his dreams nightly, begging him to remain resolute, scolding him when he wavered in the least. Their words were beginning to ring hollow, and Dragwlya continuously questioned them as to how he could do anything more than he had already. They implored him to remain patient, that his chance to once again rule would somehow arise.

Regardless of how much Dragwlya begged and pleaded, however, his father and brother never told him when his opportunity would come. He was certain they were as ignorant of it as he was. They were simply placating him with empty reassurances. Dragwlya had done the same to others during his lifetime and knew well what they sounded like.

After nearly two months of marriage, Dragwlya at least felt his opportunity was being forged. The nightmares had subsided. He and Ilona had been given a house in Pest, and they were already expecting their first child.

CHAPTER LVIII
RADU FACES DRAGWLYA
BUCHAREST
November 22, 1473

There was now only imbalance.

Matthias' talks with Moldavia had deteriorated and declarations of war interceded. The king's fall campaign against Stephen had begun in 1467. When rescued from the battlefield of Baia-Mare in December of that year, Matthias lay bleeding from various wounds suffered at the hands of Stephen's army. One, the result of a blade being thrust into his left flank, was nearly fatal. The Moldavian's victory was decisive and fueled the start of yet another campaign, this one begun by Radu.

For three years, Radu led a war of attrition against Stephen, an effort not only to aid Hungary but to retake the positions Moldavia had previously captured. As his own ranks were depleted, Radu turned to Mehmed for reinforcements that eventually would place the advantage firmly with Wallachia. With the Turkish commitment growing stronger, Stephen set out to replace Radu with Basarab III Laiotă earlier in the fall. Whether he would succeed would be decided today.

Along with a small contingent, Radu had arrived at the fortress of Bucharest. When the outcome of the battle had become evident, he had abandoned his men and fled to ensure his own safety. His army would be defeated and, by as early as tonight, Stephen would be at the gates Radu himself had recently passed through. Considering his next course of action, the prince of Wallachia sat alone in a room of what had become his temporary headquarters.

Radu found it difficult to breathe. His entire body ached, and his heart beat wildly. His hand shook uncontrollably as he reached out to grab a cup. The room was darker than it should be this early in the afternoon. Wanting desperately to attribute all of this to fear, Radu knew it was not the case. Over the past few months he had experienced these effects in even the most serene of surroundings. Cases with similar symptoms were reported elsewhere, and no one could offer an explanation as to what was causing them. Closing his eyes as his head tilted back to drink the cup's contents, Radu felt the liquid spill into his mouth and down the sides of his face.

"Radu!"

With a gasp that brought his head back down and forced his eyes open, Radu visually searched the room. He was shocked to find no one there. The voice had come from right next to him.

"Radu!"

This time there was no mistaking. The voice *had* come from inside the room. More importantly, Radu recognized whose voice it was. Unmistakably, it was that of his brother, Dragwlya.

Impossible. He is Matthias' prisoner, locked away far from here. "Come out where I can see you!"

"Coward! You call me out to face you openly, yet you refuse to openly face *your* enemies."

"Show yourself, damn you!" Rising to his feet, Radu looked around the room frantically. When he failed to see Dragwlya, he began searching around and under the furniture. "Reveal yourself!" Radu's prompt was answered only with laughter. "God damn you!" Standing up again, Radu spun around and found himself inches away from Dragwlya's face.

"You have always been weak," the slightly distorted image of Dragwlya sneered. Unprepared for the sight, Radu stumbled backwards and fell. From the floor he continued to stare into the emerald green eyes that had haunted him most of his life. "Unfit to lead; unworthy of your name. You have sided with the greatest enemy our family has ever known. For that you must atone. You will do so in the next life. I will no longer allow you to dishonor yourself, or me."

Radu's heart raced as Dragwlya drew the Toledo blade and raised it above his head. Years of adulthood melted away. Once more Radu was a scared little boy, praying his mother would rescue him. He closed his eyes as moisture began welling up in them. A single tear fell as he quietly sobbed, waiting for the blow that would end all of this. He was tired of avoiding this fight, knowing all too well he fared no chance of winning. He had avoided this fight since the moment he had taken control of Wallachia. Now he could no longer run. He no longer wanted to.

The deathblow never came. After a few silent minutes, Radu mustered his resolve and opened his eyes to find himself alone. Softly, he called out.

"Vlad?" There was no response. "Vlad?" The call was shouted, but again no answer came.

Placing his face in his hands, Radu started sobbing once more. His crying was joined by the faint sound of Dragwlya's laughter.

PEST
February 10, 1475

Stephen marched into Bucharest triumphantly. Radu had fled and taken up refuge in Giurgiu. In doing so he left behind all of his treasures, including his wife and daughter, to the prince of Moldavia. That very day, Laiotă was proclaimed prince.

For the whole of 1474, Radu fought to regain his throne. Without Matthias' support, however, his forces dwindled and were soundly defeated time and again by

Stephen and Laiotă. Additionally, the new prince of Wallachia had made peace with Mehmed, adding further to the impossibility of Radu's plight.

In January, Radu's condition worsened. His body weakened rapidly, and he became incapacitated. Along with Dragwlya's voice, he began hearing those of his father and Mehmed, saw them all standing around his deathbed. He followed them and others as he was led into tunnels of light and dark repeatedly. Ultimately, he failed to return.

News of Radu's death reached Dragwlya quickly and was followed by a visit from an emissary sent by Matthias.

"I am to inform you that King Matthias has decided you are to rule Wallachia once again."

For twelve years, Dragwlya had lingered, knowing he was expendable. He retained value only as a psychological weapon Matthias could use at his whim. Despite being married into the king's family and having a home with a wife and two sons, he had remained a prisoner. Ten years after agreeing to become a member of the Hunedoara family, Dragwlya would finally get the chance to reclaim what was rightfully his.

"Return to the king, and tell him I am grateful for his faith in me."

"Your message will be delivered immediately." As though his statement served as a proper dismissal, the emissary turned and exited.

Although irked by the man's rudeness, Dragwlya recognized he held no formal title. His reputation, obviously diminished, fell short of inspiring fear in at least this one man. After more than a decade away from the throne, he wondered how much more disrespect he would encounter and to what lengths he would be forced to go to in remedying the issue.

CHAPTER LIX
REUNITED
PEST
April 12, 1475

Unbelievable was the only word Dragwlya could think to use in describing the story being told to him by the peasant now before him. What he was being told bordered on incredible, if not miraculous.

"Originally, I saw fit to look after the child, thinking he had been abandoned. As time went on though, and as the boy grew, there was little doubt in my mind as to who he belonged to. From an early age he bore a strong resemblance to you, sire."

Standing alongside the peasant was a twelve-year old boy he claimed to be Dragwlya's lost son, Mihnea. Dragwlya had no reason to doubt the tale's validity. Almond shaped eyes, his build, and a slight resemblance to Elizabetha confirmed the story for him. The day after Dragwlya's escape, the peasant had found the infant in the forest, had taken him home, and had raised him.

"You have earned my undying gratitude, sir," Dragwlya said. "You have returned to me a son I thought I had lost and will be well rewarded for both your charity and your loyalty."

"Thank you, sire."

The title sounded empty to Dragwlya. Like Ioan Hunedoara had initially, Matthias had yet to inform Dragwlya when his campaign for the throne could begin. Restlessly, Dragwlya was wasting his days in Pest while the rest of humanity dictated its will to him. He could only guess how soon that would change.

With dusk approaching, Dragwlya ventured out into his courtyard. It was a ritual he found himself partaking of on a daily basis. He took walks to remind himself of the opportunity presented to him and to remember what being caged like an animal had felt like in Visegrád.

Dragwlya's attention was suddenly drawn as three of Matthias' officials raced through his gates. He simply stared as the men began looking around, searching for something. They had yet to announce their presence and continued their search even though Dragwlya was obviously standing no more than twenty meters away.

Complete impudence.

A flash from the corner of Dragwlya's eye quickly became the silhouette of a man running. It proved to be the quarry the officials were hunting. In his attempt to escape them a second time, the criminal was blocked by two of Matthias' men, caught sight of just as he had broken out from behind some protective brush. Once more he was in the custody of the king's men.

Dragwlya drew his sword and approached the chief officer holding the criminal as the other two officials stood nearby, ready should there be another attempt at flight. As they began berating the man and beating him down, Dragwlya reared back. With a strong, decisive thrust, the Toledo blade penetrated the chief officer's chest.

Stunned by the scene, the other two officers stood with mouths agape as the criminal they had captured looked up to learn why he was no longer receiving their blows or insults. The officer's body collapsed right beside him, spilling life to be absorbed by the earth.

"Leave immediately," Dragwlya said.

Not needing a reason, the criminal jumped up swiftly and dashed out of the courtyard in which he had sought refuge. He left behind the two remaining officials, both of whom failed to flinch as he passed. Instead they continued to look with puzzled faces at the corpse of their fellow officer.

"That order was meant for you as well."

Not wishing to suffer the fate the chief officer had, the two frightened officers turned and fled. Neither dared look back, fearful there would be a maniac there, ready to wield his sword once more.

BUDA
April 13, 1475

It had not taken Matthias' officers long to reach Buda. Once in the presence of the king, the two men related to him what had taken place in Dragwlya's courtyard and asked that an inquiry be made. Agreeing their request was warranted, Matthias sent a messenger to Pest to ask Dragwlya why he had committed such a crime. He was now receiving the reply.

"I did not commit any crime. It is the political officer who committed suicide. Anyone will perish in this way, should he, like a thief, invade the house of a great ruler such as myself. If this man had come to me first and had explained the situation to me, and if the criminal had then been found in my own home, I myself would have delivered the criminal over to him and would have pardoned him."

Unable to control his reaction, Matthias began to laugh at the response as his messenger read. The stories of Dragwlya's strict adherence to protocol were not exaggerated. Fully aware his action was driven by that policy, and not by any wish to show a lack of respect or defiance, the Hungarian king could do nothing but laugh at the extremity of Dragwlya's nature.

ADRINOPLE
May 4, 1475

Since returning from eastern Anatolia, Mehmed's health had been in decline because of gout. The illness had forced him to remain in his palace through both the past winter and spring and recently had confined him for an entire year.

With an outbreak of the plague reported, the sultan sought refuge in the mountains and had then moved to Andrinople. Again his gout had flared up. Only yesterday he had decided against personally leading a campaign to exact some measure of revenge for the humiliation his army had suffered at the hands of Stephen near Vaslui this past January.

Led by Süleyman Pasha the sultan's men, along with Laiotă, had crossed the Danube into Wallachia. At the confluence of the Barlad and Racova rivers, they were met by the whole of Stephen's army. Combined with Polish auxiliary and contingents of Szeklers, the defenders attacked at dawn on the morning of January 10th.

Arrows rained down upon the Turkish from an enemy so well entrenched they were impossible to detect. The results were disastrous for Mehmed's men. Most fell victim on the field or in the Danube. By Stephen's order, the bodies of the dead were burned and many of the captured soldiers impaled. An even greater loss than the death toll had occurred though. Turkish strongpoints between Moldavia and Bessarabia were all deserted by the sultan's men, and Stephen took each of them without the loss of a single life.

Word had spread through Andrinople of Mehmed's illness and that the sultan was close to dying. Enough of a stir had been caused that even now the populace was marching toward the sultan's palace with the intent of looting it. With the mob close, Mehmed remained in bed.

Let them come. Let them come and kill me.

The pain was nearly unbearable. At this moment Mehmed, who had done his utmost to secure and expand the holdings of his empire, was completely willing to let it all disintegrate and be destroyed by a populace ready to strike at him and all he had created now that he was too weak to fend for himself. Mehmed's viziers urgently begged him to get out of bed, to go to the window and show his people he was still alive. He refused.

"They wish me dead. They think me dead. Why should I not remain so?" he asked. Grumbling to himself, Mehmed closed his eyes as he awaited their arrival. "It would be better if I *were* dead."

Only the voice of Allah changed his mind.

You would dishonor me in this manner? You are not worthy of the gifts I have bestowed upon you, or the gifts I have yet to bear. Fail me now and the death you die will be insignificant to the suffering you will experience for all eternity.

Stirred by the voice of Allah, Mehmed sat up to the astonishment of his viziers and headed immediately to his window. As he approached, the sultan could hear the rising shouts of the gathering mob growing more unruly by the second. Throwing back the curtains, he revealed himself to the crowd below. It took only seconds for the first ones who recognized him to point out his appearance to those who had not yet seen. Within minutes, those who had been ready to storm the palace and make off with whatever they could melted away in shame and fear.

Without a word, Mehmed stepped back from the window and once more crawled into bed, cursing to himself with every movement. Soon he would go on the offensive against Moldavia, even if he could not do so personally.

CHILIA
June 3, 1475

Following the death of Pope Paul II in 1471, Sixtus IV resumed the fight where Pius had left off. With the Turkish threat looming, the Pope had made a plea for the Christians of Europe to unite against Ottoman expansion. Immediate threats were identified, and it appeared as though states were willing to send soldiers, instead of empty promises.

Being one of the principalities specifically called upon by the Pope, and knowing he would soon need aid if he were to continue his fight to stop Mehmed, Stephen embraced the call to arms. That Laiotă was under the complete control of the Turkish simplified his decision. Even now Ion Ţamblac, Stephen's personal envoy, was en route to Buda with the explicit purpose of mending the rift Stephen's earlier betrayal had caused. Uncertain of the consequences, he planned to ask Matthias to reestablished Dragwlya officially as the prince of Wallachia.

MERGHINDEL
November 28, 1475

"Our master once again offers to cede Bosnia in exchange for free passage to Germany and your word you will not interfere in his affairs."

Two years ago, Mehmed had approached Matthias with the same offer. Again the Hungarian king was forced to pose the same question.

"And what if your master's affairs should come into conflict with my own?"

As in 1473, the Turkish envoys were unable to give a forthright answer. They knew Mehmed would be willing to rescind any promises made should they later interfere with his overall designs.

"We can offer you only what our master allows us to, sire."

Matthias understood exactly what Mehmed desired. A secure alliance with Hungary meant protection on the sultan's left flank for any future campaign against Moldavia.

"Inform your master that I am not inclined to enter into such an agreement. Perhaps when the situation in Bosnia has been resolved the timing will be beneficial for both sides to conduct such a treaty."

Flatly rejected, the sultan's envoys exited, leaving the king alone with his advisors.

"He means to attack Stephen soon."

Matthias knew what his advisor had just said to be true. "Yes. Hopefully, Stephen will begin hostilities at his earliest convenience."

"Isn't it likely that Mehmed will attack you first now?"

"He will attempt to rectify his defeat by Stephen first. I have not wronged him. Other than refusing his terms, I have done nothing to warrant a war. He will continue to harass from Bosnia and likely try to secure the Crimea to give himself another route into Moldavia."

"If he does so, the Polish will likely get involved."

Matthias nodded as his other advisor spoke.

"Such a foothold would potentially arouse the interest of the Moscovites."

"Should we send word of this to the Moldavian?"

Matthias remained collected as his advisors made statements and followed with questions. "He is already aware of Mehmed's plans."

"What makes you so certain?"

"Because I know Stephen." Though receptive to Stephen's offer made months ago, Matthias remained diligent as ever in ascertaining the true feelings of Moldavia. Only after meeting with the Hungarian nobles to gain their support; receiving assurances of money and arms from Braşov, Sibiu, and Bistriţa; and imposing a tax of a gold florin per household from each family in Hungary did the king fully begin to put his plan in motion.

Dragwlya was not aware of it yet, but Matthias intended to make him captain to lead his campaign in Bosnia against the Turkish. Even with everything that already had been promised, however, Matthias still hesitated in making Dragwlya his official candidate to Wallachia's throne.

Matthias had reached Merghindel with five thousand troops in October and, along with him, had brought Dragwlya and the exiled Serbian despot Gregorević. Already the king had decided where he wished to strike first in the Bosnian campaign. It would be Šabac. Located to the west of Belgrade on the Sava River, the outpost had been the recipient of strengthened fortifications and of arms and ammunition. Šabac was the ideal target; important enough to be noticed but not the Turkish's main bastion in the region.

CHAPTER LX
THE CYCLE
SREBRENIČA
February 15, 1476

Disguising himself as a common soldier, Matthias had personally traversed the moat surrounding Šabac to identify the weak points of the fortress. He had arrived in Belgrade along with his army in the last week of December and, after scouting, mobilized in early January. The citadel's garrison of one thousand two hundred was well equipped to withstand any barrage. Confident in his abilities, Matthias led his ships into the castle moat and struck anyway.

Reports of a Turkish battalion arriving to provide reinforcements near the end of the month proved accurate. After its leaders witnessed the progress of the Hungarians, however, they hesitated to attack and soon retreated, believing the fortress lost. A week ago, the gates were opened in surrender after a month-long siege. Seeing what remained of Šabac's stock, Matthias chose to repair and improve its defenses, instead of burning the site to the ground.

Knowing his army was in capable hands, Matthias had informed Dragwlya and Gregorević he was returning to Buda. At the moment, he felt the most important thing for him to do was to let the world know of Šabac's fall. Dragwlya and Gregorević would continue on toward Smederevo and were charged with building three forts at Kovin.

While camped outside of the silver-mining center of Srebreniča last night, Dragwlya had ordered one hundred fifty Hungarian cavalrymen, disguised at Turkish soldiers, to ride into town. They were given orders to create as much chaos and confusion as possible the next morning at the town's monthly market. The intention was to cripple the already meager defenses. Led by Dragwlya, an ensuing attack succeeded. Without Matthias present, however, the aftermath resembled nothing like a Hungarian victory.

"Matthias would not have approved of this!" Gregorević did not mind that Dragwlya had led the men in looting the homes of the wealthy merchants. The fact that fire had been set to Srebreniča hardly affected him either, but seeing the Turkish garrison members who had survived now being impaled made Gregorević uncomfortable.

"Do you wish to one day have Serbia back under your control?" Continuing to watch the men carry out his orders, Dragwlya did his best not to be irritated by the interruption. Gregorević seemed squeamish for a despot.

It was a question no exiled leader wants to hear, yet the Serbian could not answer it directly. "This is unnecessary." The volume of his voice lowered considerably.

"Perhaps if you had instilled such punishment when you were in command, you would not be fighting to regain control of it now."

The second jab put Gregorević on the defensive. "Did you not employ such tactics when you sat upon Wallachia's throne?" He made certain to emphasize *when*.

Dragwlya laughed the verbal parry away. "Even the best plans are sometimes thwarted."

TURDA
June 10, 1476

Dragwlya and Gregorević accomplished their mission with ease and, in March, the Wallachian returned to Transylvania and made camp in Turda. From there he began petitioning Matthias to allow him to begin a campaign for his throne.

Still in Buda, Matthias had ordered a small fleet of twenty-four ships to be built that he intended to use in the siege of Smederevo. The vessels were being paid for with a gift of ninety-three thousand gold ducats given to the king by the Signoria of Florence and Sixtus IV. They were to be outfitted with siege machines from Germany, most prominently bombards. Problems arose though when Matthias had asked Frederick III for duty-free passage for his ships and arms. The Holy Roman Emperor refused, and there was no questioning the reasoning or its pettiness—Matthias' impending marriage to Beatrice of Aragon in October. Frederick's delay in allowing the ships to pass proved costly, as they would not arrive in time to continue the push to drive the Turkish out of Serbia.

His attention absorbed by Frederick, Matthias concentrated on gaining the Pope as an ally in his fight against the emperor, neglecting the Turkish front. Distracted, the king allowed the Turkish to carry out raids in Serbia without interference. Likewise, the frontier lands of the empire were being pillaged without resistance from Vienna.

As though it were a fleeting thought, Matthias, at the end of last month, sent to Dragwlya an army of eight thousand infantry and thirteen thousand cavalry under the command of Stephen Báthory with the sole purpose of securing the Wallachian throne. Along with the Serbian despot Vuk Branković, plans were now being drawn for a combined effort between Hungary, Transylvania, Moldavia, Wallachia, and Serbia to restore Dragwlya.

"Here, in this pass, we will unite with the Moldavians," said Báthory.

Those surrounding the war map, except for Dragwlya, each looked at one another in turn as Báthory pointed to an impassable ridge. It was not the first error the man had made in constructing the course the campaign would take. Closing his eyes, Dragwlya debated if he should allow the man to continue bumbling.

He'll kill us all by the end of the summer. While he had not expected Matthias to give him supreme command over twenty-one thousand troops, Dragwlya had believed the king would at least put someone in charge of the campaign that could correctly read a map.

Soon realizing he had made yet another mistake, Báthory turned to Dragwlya for assistance. "You have a better understanding than anyone of this terrain. Perhaps you could suggest an alternative route."

Báthory may have been commander in name, but there was no doubt in the minds of those present who the true leader of this campaign would be.

VALEA ALBA
July 26, 1476

Gout no longer affected Mehmed.

As the Janissaries cowered down and refused to advance into the forest toward their unseen enemy and their cannons, the sultan cursed them all. Shield in hand, he aimed his charger into the perceived heart of his enemy.

Led by Hadim Süleyman Pasha, the Turkish advance guard had suffered defeat at the hands of the Moldavians. Mehmed would not allow the disgrace to repeat itself. Approximately two hundred Janissaries had fled Šabac and had attempted to join the forces at Andrinople. They were promptly disposed off. The sultan had them bound. Stones were tied to their necks, and they were thrown into the river.

Reaching the Danube via the Black Sea, Mehmed marched through Dobruja, forced to do so at night as his men suffered from both a shortage of water and what amounted to a plague of grasshoppers that kept them confined to their tents during the day.

Stephen had hoped to avoid this. He was to join Dragwlya's force in Wallachia before proceeding with any sort of attack. Unexpectedly, however, the Turkish had managed to track and catch up to the traveling force. Now Stephen was trapped on all sides in a valley not far from Cetatea Neamtzului.

Seeing their master spur his horse into the fray, the Janissaries recovered and followed him into the dense forests of this foreign land. In time, Stephen would retreat and would do so with a loss of only two hundred men. He was secure in the fact that he would not be pursued. Supplies would soon run out for the Turkish. The small transport fleet carrying both food and supplies had largely been lost to a storm, and Mehmed would have to retreat to Andrinople.

BRAŞOV
September 25, 1476

Upon learning of the battle at Valea Alba, Dragwlya's forces immediately mounted to rush to Stephen's aid. Once united at the Transylvanian border, the combined army wasted little time in attacking the beleaguered Turkish and defeating them at the Siret

River. With Moldavia secured, the crusaders then advanced to Braşov to plan the final push of their campaign—the ousting of Laiotă.

Each of the chief officers would be in command of his own contingent with the overall battle plan being drawn up and instituted by Dragwlya. Before the campaign began, he wished to make certain none of his political enemies would receive a warm reception in Transylvania should they chose to flee there. Ion Polivar and Mihai Log would serve as Dragwlya's envoys in attempting to win over those he had terrorized more than a decade earlier. In order to succeed, Dragwlya would make concessions the likes of which Braşov had never known under any ruler.

It was decided Stephen, along with his contingent of fifteen thousand men, would be responsible for attacking Wallachia's eastern front. The combined forces of Dragwlya, Báthory, and Branković, totaling some thirty-five thousand, would pour across the principality's northern border from Transylvania. Once peace had been achieved with Braşov and Dragwlya was certain the area was secured, the campaign would begin.

"I've waited a long time for this." Though he was sitting alone with Stephen, Dragwlya was addressing himself more than he was his cousin. "For twelve years I watched as both Radu and Laiotă did their utmost to ruin my land. They nearly succeeded."

Stephen was not under the impression the conversation was rhetorical.

"But they haven't. And now you will have the chance to restore Wallachia to the prominence it held under your father and your grandfather."

Momentarily surprised by the sound of another voice, Dragwlya looked to its source. He laughed to himself at the absurdity of politics. Again Stephen was his ally.

"They were both great men. Mircea may have surpassed them. I doubt I will do so."

Stephen thought such an admission odd. "Why do you say that?"

Dragwlya spoke matter-of-factly. "Too much of my time has been lost, Stephen. I am already old beyond my years."

"You seem fit enough."

"Perhaps... The world has changed little since the last time I sat upon my throne. The Turkish still threaten to overrun us, the leaders of Europe bicker amongst themselves and, while the thought of crusade is talked about greatly, such talk will soon fade. This cycle has no end."

"Then why bother with this campaign? Why risk your life for something you believe does not matter?" Stephen's voice was almost condemning.

Dragwlya offered a half smile. "Because I am part of the cycle as well. It is what I am meant to do." A lengthy pause followed as neither man spoke. Finally, Dragwlya interjected. "And because somewhere inside of me, I hope I am meant to break the cycle."

Silently, Stephen wondered if Dragwlya's assertions were correct and if he, too, served no other purpose than to be part of some cycle. He hoped not.

CHAPTER LXI
DEATH OF THE DRAGON
TÎRGOVIŞTE
November 7, 1476

At the beginning of the month, Dragwlya led his force into the Prahova River Valley. Near Rucǎr, he defeated Laiotǎ's army, killing ten thousand of his enemy's men. He suffered equal losses but, along with Báthory, pushed farther south as Stephen began his attack from the West.

Dragwlya's main focus was Bucharest, but symbolically he wanted Tîrgovişte as well. Because his former capital was on the Dîmboviţa River, he was provided ample opportunity to take the city without having to drastically alter his plans. It was captured easily and offered Dragwlya a chance to see the home he had been forced to abandon so many years ago. Everything felt alien to him, like he was a stranger traversing its streets for the first time. He attempted to pick out sights familiar to him and was completely astounded by one.

While passing through the city's main square, a glimmer caught Dragwlya's eye. There, upon the fountain in the center, was a golden cup. Immediately, he recognized it as the chalice he had ordered placed there so that all could drink from it, much to the dismay of the merchant who had given it to him. The cup's presence amazed him because of what it represented.

For the twelve years he had been locked away, no one had stolen it. After all the time that had passed without him physically being there, despite not having the constant threat of him being in Wallachia, the peasants continued to fear him. They feared what he would do if the cup disappeared. The significance of this could not be overstated.

They continued to obey me. Even in my absence they followed my laws. Perhaps the cycle will be broken.

ADRINOPLE
December 3, 1476

By mid-November, Wallachia was under Dragwlya's control. Bucharest was captured on November 16th by Báthory's army and, just ten days later, Dragwlya was established as prince of Wallachia and now held court there. The very thought of it unnerved Mehmed.

Báthory and Stephen had already returned to their own lands, taking their forces with them. Other than a cursory bodyguard of two hundred left by the Moldavian, Dragwlya was virtually alone. He was in no position to repel a major offensive. Now was the ideal time to strike.

Laiotă had escaped across the Danube into Bulgaria and was awaiting orders from Mehmed and much needed reinforcements for a counterattack. Unlike the two previous times he had taken Wallachia's throne by force, this time Dragwlya had failed to kill his predecessor. Mehmed intended to use that to his advantage. Deposed leaders already had established allies and, even with assurances given and treaties signed, the sultan knew it would take little to sway key elements to his side if the choices were limited to Laiotă and the monster that not long ago had caused enough suffering that his own people welcomed his ousting with jubilation.

Mehmed had decided that the task of ridding himself of Kazîglu Bey once and for all would not be entrusted to a foreigner. One of his own would be needed. Kazîglu Bey would die at the hands of the Turkish, final punishment for the years of humiliation and annoyance he had caused the Ottoman Empire.

"Do you have any questions?" Mehmed looked into the eyes of the assassin.

They were cold, two dark brown orbs that conveyed nothing. "No, my liege. My only concern is that he has thwarted every attempt ever made on his life. He has always uncovered plans such as this."

Mehmed nodded. "This time there are two important differences…He has not been invited to journey anywhere. There is no inkling of an ambush. Secondly, there are only two people who have knowledge of this plan. If it does not succeed, I will have you hunted down and brought back to me. I assure you…you do not want that to happen."

Mehmed's pause conjured all sorts of possible scenarios of torture in the man's head. "I understand, my liege."

"Good," Mehmed's voice grew grave instantly. "You will bring his head to me. Only then will you receive payment. Understood?"

"Yes, my liege."

SNAGOV
December 23, 1476

Dragwlya knew the circumstances were grim at best. Abandoned by Báthory and Stephen, he was unable to create the stability he knew was needed merely to survive, much less rule. Faced with such a dangerous reality, he had chosen not to send for his wife and three sons. He was thankful he hadn't.

While Dragwlya was still attempting to consolidate power, Laiotă was poised for revenge. Along with the resources Laiotă had managed to secure himself, a small contingent had arrived from Mehmed to assist in the retaking of Wallachia. Laiotă had decided the attack would be at night.

Well inside the perimeter of the Wallachian's camp, Mehmed's assassin lay in wait.

He would have to complete his objective before the battle began and, in order to do so, had set out from the Turkish camp some time ago. Not more than ten meters away, Dragwlya sat inside of his tent, awaiting supper. There was little activity—only two of the Wallachian's servants were going about their duties, preparing to feed him. As one of them disappeared inside, the assassin moved. Disguised as a Moldavian, he rose when the second servant turned his back and stealthily strode toward him. He moved purposefully as the crackling of a nearby fire filled the air.

Blade already drawn, the assassin approached the servant, who was now turning to face him. Seeing the dress of one of the Moldavians, he hardly paid the man any attention and was ready to greet him. It was then he noticed the weapon. With two quick movements, the assassin silenced the servant forever and gently eased his corpse to the ground. Seconds later, the other servant emerged from the tent and saw his counterpart lying face down. As he bent over to check on him, a shapeless mass materialized from the nearby shadows. The blade worked swiftly as the assassin killed again. Allowing the second body to fall next to the first, the assassin wiped his blade on the Wallachian's back before standing. He could afford to waste no more time. Laiotă would attack soon, and the entire camp would be in motion. He must be finished prior to that.

Standing at the opening of the tent, the assassin realized his heart had begun to beat faster. This had never happened before, but he reminded himself he had never killed someone of Kazîglu Bey's stature before either. Parting the material the way he had witnessed the servant do so, the assassin peered inside of the poorly lit tent. Before him sat the Wallachian, his back turned to him, dressed in the garb of an ordinary Turkish soldier. The irony that they were each wearing the clothing of their enemy was not lost on the assassin, and he would have laughed if it would not have meant his own death.

Dragwlya flinched slightly at the sound of the cloth being drawn back, but did not look away from the dinner he had already been served. He could not turn around; his mind was too preoccupied to do so. In solitude, Dragwlya sat wondering if he shouldn't leave now. His spies had relayed to him the size of Laiotă's force and, compared to his own, the difference was considerable. It amused him that his third reign mirrored his first in that there was no way he could think of logically to retain the throne. Either he would have to flee as he had done all those years ago, or he would be killed on the field of battle trying to defend his land from a far larger foe. Both options frustrated him. The entire situation frustrated him.

Everything was following the path it had in the past. Nothing was different. He had been foolish to think things would somehow be different this time. The enemies were the same, the circumstances were the same. Yet again he would lose to the Turkish. Yet again he would be reduced to being a weapon for someone else to wield. Yet again he would have to rely on the whims of someone else before being allowed to take control of the land that rightly belonged to him. Once he took hold of it, it would be ripped from him again.

The cycle never changed.

Lost in his thoughts, Dragwlya didn't react to the blur that suddenly streaked in front of him. The sensation of having his hair pulled back and the blade sinking into his throat failed to register until it was far too late for retaliation capable of altering the outcome.

Little time remained before the assassin would completely decapitate him. Slipping into unconsciousness, Dragwlya's final thoughts turned to memories of Mircea and of his father. Like them, he was falling victim before he was supposed to. Like them, he was not going to die in battle, but at the hands of an assassin.

The cycle never changes.

EPILOGUE
TÎRGOVIŞTE
February 19, 1477

There was no moon. Cloud cover cancelled out the stars, leaving Wallachia's capital shrouded in complete darkness.

In late January, confirmation of Dragwlya's death reached Stephen in the most credible of ways. Of the two hundred men he had left behind to serve as bodyguards to his cousin, only ten had survived the attack of Basarab Laiotă to return to Suceava. Shortly after the fighting had begun, the headless body of the prince had been found in his tent. Because of the ensuing confusion, no one remained to claim it.

Rumors abounded. Some said monks from the nearby monastery had retrieved the body. Others pointed to the disappearance of Dragwlya as a sign he was not dead. Some even proposed the prince had passed on from this world and, as punishment for his crimes, would spend all of eternity as a strigoi.

Proof of Dragwlya's death, however, did exist. In Constantinople, Mehmed had received the head of his longtime nemesis. To show the world Kazîglu Bey was no more, he had posted it on an elongated pale for all to behold—a fitting end, Mehmed thought, for *The Impaler.*

Some who had not seen the head of Dragwlya on display firsthand would never believe him to be dead. Others would be convinced once morning broke.

A form darker than the midnight sky emerged into the main square of Tîrgovişte and glided toward the fountain at its center. Grey-blue eyes peered out from under a ragged hood and searched the surroundings. No sign of life existed, human or otherwise, and the absence of any soul only increased the temptation. One final glance over his shoulders compelled him enough and, as he turned back around, a pair of grimy hands shot out from the folds of his cloak and snatched the golden cup resting on the lip of the fountain. Instantly, it disappeared into the cloth. Within seconds the thief vanished, leaving behind the only proof of Dragwlya's death any Wallachian would ever require.

ABOUT THE AUTHOR

Timothy E. Rodrigue is a native of New Orleans and a graduate of Louisiana State University. He has earned his living as a writer and editor for more than a decade now. This is his first published novel. He lives in Denham Springs, Louisiana with his wife and son.

www.ingramcontent.com/pod-product-compliance
Lightning Source LLC
Chambersburg PA
CBHW031436240626
47154CB00001B/287